The Fatal Path

This is an IndieMosh book

brought to you by MoshPit Publishing
an imprint of Mosher's Business Support Pty Ltd

PO Box 4363
Penrith NSW 2750

indiemosh.com.au

Cataloguing-in-Publication entry is available from the National Library
of Australia: http://catalogue.nla.gov.au/

Title:	The Fatal Path
Author:	LaPlanche, S A
ISBNs:	9781922628442 (paperback)
	9781922628459 (ebook – epub)
	9781922628466 (ebook – mobi)
Subjects:	Fiction: Thrillers – Psychological / Suspense / Crime;
	Family Life / Siblings

Cover design and layout by Luke Harris at workingtype.com.au

Cover image by Alessio Cesario and used under license from pexels.com

The Fatal Path

S A LaPlanche

Also by S A LaPlanche

*Stepping Lightly on Australia – A Traveller's Guide to
    Ecotourism*
(Writer and Photographer)

World Travel – A Guide to International Ecojourneys
(Contributing Editor)

Travel Unlimited
(Contributing Editor)

Kevin

You live forever in my heart

PART ONE

THE KILLING

The young woman on the deck of the house raised the rifle, laid it carefully across her upturned hand on the balcony rail, took aim and squeezed the trigger. The man who had been walking along the narrow path around the steep coastal cliff faltered. For a heartbeat his silhouette prevailed dark against the first pink strands of sunrise. The woman allowed herself a mocking smile. Her bullet had found its mark.

She followed the flapping straps as his camera dropped like a bird killed in flight. His strong tanned fingers would grasp at the clumps of grass protruding from the shaly cliff and his feet would thrash frantically, seeking leverage. In his final moments of lucidity, he would try to concentrate but his handsome body would fail him. Death would ooze like mud through his brain. If he cried out it would go unheard, drowned by the savagery of the waves crashing against the sharp black rocks at the base of the cliff. His body would be broken, smashed, lacerated and shredded to a pulp that would be sucked out by the tide and investigated by ocean predators.

She lowered the rifle and let it rest in the crook of her arm as she turned to enter the house, her bare feet silent on the bleached wood deck. With meticulous care she cleaned the rifle, taking pleasure in the smell of solvent, the efficient hardness of the grey barrel and the beautifully crafted handle. When all was done to her satisfaction, she dropped the cleaning rags into the kitchen bin where they sank into the remains of last night's dinner with a soft slurp.

L U C Y

I cross the room to look out the window. There are no bars because I am not considered a danger to myself ... not anymore.

It's spring. The trees planted more than a hundred years ago by the patients when this place was a hospital for the insane spread dappled shade across the lawns and gardens that spill down to the banks of the Parramatta River. Rozelle Hospital is set in one of the most peaceful estates on earth and, as my mind finds peace, I once again appreciate the healing powers in nature. When permitted to walk out into the gardens, I find a big tree that I can sit under and lean against. Its age and quiet strength comfort me.

Then I remember – Sarah is coming today.

Ever since the day I entered the hospital I have refused to see her.

Sarah. I speak her name softly, letting my breath float over my lips. How long is it since I have spoken her name? There are no photos of my family in my room. It's not that I don't love them. It's that I have needed to be alone ... completely alone. I had put their photos away like winter clothes waiting for spring; a spring that has failed to come.

Is this note from Sarah a sign that my spring has finally come? It makes me think about my family and my hands go damp with sweat. Daddy, in whose arms I always felt safe. Mummy, who was beautiful but always so busy. Sarah, my twin, born after me, smaller and a bit nervy. It was me who decided what we would wear and what we liked to eat. I led her safely across the road and watched over her when we went swimming. I was the big sister who protected her until that day in July 1996 when our lives changed forever.

'Tell me about your relationship with Sarah.' Dr Singh, my psychiatrist, would ask and I would answer. 'We are fraternal twins and we love each other very deeply.'

I knew this didn't help him, but I was past caring. A melancholy had taken possession of me as my unshared thoughts tormented me.

When I came into this hospital I was twenty-five ... Dr Singh was a new psychiatrist in my life and although I knew I needed him, I also resented him. However, as the days went by, I started a little game that both frightened and energised me. I'd tell him little things and watch his reaction. Like the time I told him that Sarah liked to hide and listen to adults talking.

'Why did she do this?' he asked.

'She wanted to know what they were saying about her.'

'Where did she hide?'

'You know ... behind couches, drapes, sometimes in wardrobes.'

'Did she ever tell you what she heard?'

'Of course.'

'Everything?'

'Of course. We shared everything. When we were little, we could have had separate rooms but we chose to be together. Some nights she would creep into my bed and we would put a hand on the other's heart to feel it beating. As we got older we shared friends, hobbies, everything. She's been my rock through all my pain.'

'What about that time at Thredbo? You told me you felt she turned against you after that skiing trip. Why do you think she turned against you?'

Now she is coming.

I watch a bird staring at the grass where there is a worm only it can see. Its chick is stalking back and forth screeching *for food, but the mother will wait until the worm is far enough out, then she will lunge, pull it out and quickly give it to her chick.*

Should I have done what that bird did – and waited?

Should I have shown Sarah's note to Dr Singh? I would have if she hadn't sealed the envelope with FWTW, the secret code of our childhood: From Womb to Worms – born together, live together, leave together.

I wipe the sweat from my palms and read the note again: 'Dearest Lucy. Please let me visit. Have awful secret to tell you. It will explain everything and you will love me again. I weep alone. Sarah.'

CHAPTER 1

Lucy and Sarah were eleven years old when their mother announced they were all going to Thredbo to ski because her boss, Liam Marshall, wanted to hold the company's 1996 AGM in Australia. 'I've booked a conference room in Sydney for two days and rooms at Thredbo for a post-conference ski trip.'

'What! All of us?' Mario asked with a sidelong wink at the twins.

'Yes,' Jill said, raising an eyebrow as she looked across at her husband. 'You, me and the twins are going to take my New York boss to the snow and see just how well he really skis. He's always bragging about how good he is. And he's asked me to include Dwight and Charlie, the Sales Managers from the US and Europe.'

'But why Sarah and me?' Lucy asked.

'Because Americans believe in happy families, apple pie and God. I intend to show Liam that my family will support me all the way to the top of his magazine pile.'

'And where do apple pie and God fit in?' Even at eleven, Sarah picked up irregularities in conversation and actions.

Jill smiled. She loved it when her daughters showed how observant they were.

'They're little extras in the American psyche.'

Mario handed Jill a Scotch and soda in a fine crystal glass. They clinked. Jill listened to the ring sing around the kitchen where Mario was cooking up a spicy puttanesca sauce for dinner.

They had met in the early 1980s when they were both cadets at *The Australian* newspaper. He, Mario Borgetti, a cartoonist, the son of an Italian immigrant couple who had separated after a few years in Sydney. She, Jill Pederson, the daughter of a successful Danish immigrant. Her father had started with a small furniture store in Sydney which was now in all major cities and towns across the country.

At first it was just sex. Mario's muscular brown body wrapped around her pale limbs. Jill's blond hair spreading like a veil over the sheets. They were both social beings who partied hard and worked hard. Within six months Mario had left home to rent a terrace house in trendy Paddington and Jill had moved in.

'But Dwight hasn't got a family.' Lucy's voice snapped Jill back to present time.

She smiled at Lucy and took a sip of Scotch before replying. 'True, he's not married but he's New York-smart; belongs to the right clubs; drives a Ferrari; sails and is in a relationship with a very rich girl. Also, he pays a lot of attention to Nuala, Liam's wife. He takes her to shows none of his associates would be seen dead at, and plays second father to the children.' Jill did not add that this put her main rival in a cosy position. If Liam saw through Dwight, he said nothing. Ambition produced loyalty and this semblance of loyalty gave Liam space for his many dalliances.

Mario loved it when Jill was stirred up. 'Tell me dear wife, why does the Irish boy-made-good still have such a plain wife?'

'By plain you mean unsophisticated.' Jill arched her right eyebrow, a sign she was angry or about to give a lecture. 'Liam married Nuala in Ireland when he was just a boy working in the local printer's office. She was the prettiest girl in the village, and they had two boys before he moved them all to New York. His boast is that he went to New York "to pursue his destiny". Sadly for him, Nuala didn't change. She had two more children, girls, after they moved to New York and dinner ready for him every evening when – if – he came home. She was happy with her life. She didn't want anything to do with society ladies and pampering beauty parlours.'

'Does Liam have a lover?' Lucy giggled. At eleven she wasn't quite sure what a lover was, but she knew it was naughty.

Mario frowned at Lucy. 'Why does he want to have the AGM here rather than at his ranch in Wyoming as usual?'

'He has plans to trial a new magazine for teenagers in Australia. Having the conference here gives him a chance to get a feel for our teenagers.'

Jill was the Editor of *Opulence*, his leading lifestyle magazine in Australia. By rights she should be asked to run the new teen magazine, however her spies in New York had warned her she might not. The rumour around head office was that Liam was thinking of sending Dwight to Australia to become his Asia/Pacific manager.

Jill kept her silence in order to protect her spy ring. Liam must never know the extent of the loyalties she had built up during her many visits to head office. She rewarded them well and they proved their worth again and again.

'Is Dwight a good skier?' Mario asked to ease the tension he could see was building in Jill.

'Moderate. He and Charlie will stay on for the skiing. The rest will fly out immediately after the AGM.'

'Hmmm. Is that a good sign?'

'Liam's hard to predict. He needs to be convinced that I'm better than Dwight for the Asia/Pacific region and that I have the perfect loyal family, which every cheating Irish father believes in – the bastard!'

She slammed down her drink and the girls giggled.

L U C Y

Try as I might, I can't free my mind from the way that weekend at Thredbo started with high hopes and ended in tragedy. It started the downward spiral that took control of my life and dumped me here, in this hospital.

How different all our lives would have turned out if Daddy had been stronger. He hadn't wanted us to take the Friday off school, but he let Mummy talk him into it. It wasn't that he was weak, just that he could never deny her anything.

Mummy was in full battle mode as Daddy liked to say, and we tagged along, the perfect children of perfect parents. Not that we minded. We loved skiing and Sarah used the occasion to bargain for new ski suits for both of us.

Sarah's like Mummy. She knows what she wants and can identify her opponent's weaknesses, which she exploits without mercy when it suits her. She has Mummy's green eyes too, whereas mine are brown like Daddy's.

Mummy needed us in good humour and if new ski suits would ensure that, then so be it. I bought an orange jacket with a raised collar that made me feel trendy. Sarah bought a black suit with gold stars on the sleeves and across the hips. Daddy thought hers was too grown up for an eleven-year-old, but Sarah knew how to handle him.

When I want to remember how happy we once were, I get out the photo album Daddy made. It has photos of Sarah and me in the school basketball team, swimming together in the harbour outside our home, me pushing her high on the swing, and the two of us on our ninth birthday with our arms around each other waving madly at the camera. We loved being twins and this photo always makes my eyes sting. We grew our hair long so we could pull it back into a ponytail or curl it and let it cascade like a frothy waterfall.

The album also has photos of our lovely two-storey house at Birchgrove with Yama, my Burmese cat, stalking down the lawn towards the harbour where we have a little sandy beach and a boat house he often sleeps in; and Daddy waving tongs over the barbecue under our big trees; and Mummy at the Louis XVI mahogany antique writing bureau Daddy gave her for her birthday. It's a total contrast to the rest of our furniture which is sleek and modern. I don't know whether she liked it, but she used it all the time.

Sarah would have sat at that bureau to write her note to me. I close my eyes so I can visualise her leaning forward to take a page of bonded writing paper from one of the horizontal slots, an envelope from another slot and the gold fountain pen from its velvet-lined grove. Her legs would be elegantly crossed, and she would have thought long and hard before she eased the pen down onto the paper and started writing. Once started, she would have written without hesitation until the note was finished. Then she would have folded the page precisely before slipping it into the envelope and sealing the flap with the initials FWTW.

Thinking of the bureau reminds me that she will be here soon. I suddenly feel very cold. Her note is in my top drawer, but I don't get it out. Its words are imprinted on my mind.

By now she will have driven out of the garage onto Wharf Road. Birchgrove and Balmain are inner west suburbs located on a peninsula that is just a short ferry ride across the harbour to the city. This made them popular with the ambitious young executive class of the 1990s who worked in the city. She'll have wound her way through the narrow streets that criss-cross Birchgrove into Balmain then she'll follow Darling Street into Rozelle where this hospital was established a bit further up the harbour a century ago. Depending on traffic, it will take her fifteen minutes to drive here.

CHAPTER 2

The AGM in Sydney finished at midday on Friday. Immediately after a sandwich lunch Jill, Mario, the twins, Liam, Dwight and Charlie set off in two cars for the six-hour drive south to the Thredbo ski village. Jill had organised it perfectly. 'Liam, you sit up here in front with me and we'll have Lucy and Sarah in the back. Mario, you take Dwight and Charlie.'

They stopped on the way for dinner at Jindabyne and arrived at their hotel well-fed, tired and ready for bed. Jill always slept well but her antennae were on high alert and she woke early the next morning willing the day to be fine and the snow perfect. She pulled the drapes open and nodded with satisfaction at the crisp cloudless dawn. Brittle light pierced the thin air that tipped the snow-covered tops of the Crackenback Range with a frosty glow. Jill's gaze swept across the parked cars buried under mounds of new snow and the slender icicles that hung like shards of crystal from the eaves above the hotel windows.

'Thank you,' she said aloud. 'You must have snowed all night.'

After a hearty skiers' breakfast Jill led them outside to join the parade of people clattering over the little footbridge to the chairlift. Young and old chattered and jostled in the excitement of a fine day for skiing and snowboarding.

'You can follow me all day if you like,' Sarah said, smiling up at Liam. 'I know the best runs.'

'Now there's an offer I can't resist,' Liam laughed. The crisp air filled him with a sense of wellbeing and he enjoyed this young girl with her good looks and sharp mind. 'She's made for New York,' he thought. 'Like her mother.'

Sarah was intrigued by Liam and pleased she'd chosen the suit with gold stars on it.

'His shape changes to suit his environment,' she whispered to Lucy as they waited for their lift tickets. 'As the boss in Sydney his shape was square and dark. Last night beside the fire it was soft like a fluffy dog. Now he's a clown with a happy face.'

Dwight and Charlie admitted to being just moderate skiers, so Mario took them to the easier slopes while Jill and the twins led Liam to their favourite runs. It was soon obvious he was experienced and fearless on skis and the twins, a little dizzy with their new-found power over their mother's boss, led him down all the most difficult tree and black runs they knew. Jill followed, content to stay in the background where she could watch the rapport between her girls and her boss. Liam's two sons born in Ireland were a bit older than the twins, but his two girls born in New York were about the same age and quiet like their mother. Lucy and Sarah were skiing with confidence and calling out directions to Liam as though he was a long-time friend of the family. Jill watched Liam watching them. She knew he was assessing their potential to be featured as positive examples of Australian teens in his new teenage magazine.

Jill had booked a table at Kareela Hut for lunch at one o'clock and her group were just taking off their skis when Mario arrived with Dwight and Charlie flushed with the success of their morning.

'Kareela can only be reached on skis so you won't find any beginners here,' Mario said as he led them through the crowded tables to the bar. Jill had given him a quick nod and a wink to indicate her plan was working perfectly and he was pleased for her. 'It's tradition to start lunch with a round of schnapps. Everyone okay with that?' Mario shouted above the noise and they all nodded

After lunch, Charlie announced that a morning of hard

skiing, three schnapps, two beers and a huge lunch had done him in. He was going back to his room.

'I'll go with Charlie,' Dwight said. He would have skied on, but he could see that Jill's family had impressed Liam and he was too wise to follow them in a contest he couldn't win. Also, he had arranged to meet a pretty Aussie girl who he had nearly skied into on the slopes for a gluhwein in the hotel bar at four.

Mario decided he'd stay around to show Liam the whole happy family unit Jill had so carefully planned. 'What about you Liam? Another schnapps or out onto the slopes?'

'Onto the slopes,' Sarah said as she strode out the door without even a glance at Mario.

'Looks like it's the slopes,' Liam said with a knowing grin as he grabbed his jacket from the back of his chair. Yes, he liked this family and he had heard that Mario's cartoons were being syndicated very successfully overseas. He had been very impressed by one he had seen in a New York newspaper just before he left for the AGM in Sydney. As he followed Sarah outside he taped his sticks against his leg, trying to remember the details of the cartoon. Yes, that was it … Dolly the sheep had just been born at the Roslin Institute in Scotland. It was 1996 and the birth of Dolly the world's first cloned animal had made headlines around the world. One of the scientists had said the little lamb had been named Dolly because the cell used as the donor was taken from a mammary gland and the most impressive pair of glands they knew of belonged to the renowned country singer Dolly Parton. Mario's cartoon showed a caricature of Dolly Parton nursing a little lamb and singing a lullaby. Liam knew readers appreciated clever cartoons and decided he would look into commissioning Mario for his magazines.

Liam was exhausted an hour later. Even though he had a private gym instructor and kept himself very fit, he was feeling the effects of the altitude and heavy lunch. He slid to a stop, pretending fascination in a cluster of gnarled trees.

'I want to take a few photos of these trees to show them at home,' he said when the twins pulled up beside him. 'We have aspens in our mountains and Europe has pines, but you have these low twisted trees. What are they?'

'They're eucalypts.' Lucy proclaimed, taking the opportunity to show Liam she was a big sister with knowledge. 'They grow all over Australia but they can't grow very tall up here because of the cold and the altitude. We call them snow gums.'

'Aye, a worthy name,' he replied, hunching over like an old crone and making his voice crackle so the girls would stay a bit longer. 'We Irish are superstitious people. I believe such distorted trees must be cursed, to be sure.'

'Cursed?' Lucy had a friend whose older sister had a Ouija board but she had never met an adult who believed in such things.

'Aye, those silver trunks and misshapen branches are enchanting in the sunlight, but I wouldn't want to be here in the moonlight when the leprechauns are about castin' spells and makin' predictions, for sure.'

'Leprechauns?' the girls screeched.

'Aye, the little people. They'd be dancin' round and round up here during the full moon.'

'Are they the same as fairies?' Lucy knew she was too old to believe in fairies, but she still liked to think there might be some, somewhere in the world.

'Could they cast a spell on me?' Sarah looked at life with a more pragmatic eye than Lucy.

'Got ya.' Liam laughed heartily as he raised his hands to do high-fives. 'No, Lucy. Leprechauns aren't real, but I had to get back at you two for taking me down the hardest runs you could find. Now you can be kind to me and lead me down easy slopes to Thredbo village, because you've worn me out.'

When Liam and the twins had stopped at the snow gums, Jill and Mario had skied on down to the village guessing it was time to go in. When they reached the bottom she had slid alongside Mario. 'I've never seen Liam so happy.'

'So, the twins earned their new ski suits eh!'

They locked eyes and smiled knowingly.

Jill had planned a big dinner in the hotel dining room for their last night. Everyone arrived dressed up and ready to party, but by the time they had finished their main course the mood at the table had changed. Charlie complained of a sore leg and went to bed. Jill had followed Dwight out into the lounge off the dining room and returned silent and angry.

Nothing between those two surprised Mario. What did surprise him, however, was that Sarah had disappeared before dessert without saying goodnight to anyone. When it suited her, Sarah could charm a whole room, but when it didn't suit her, she treated people with an indifference that bordered on rudeness.

'Did you see Sarah?' he asked Jill. 'She hasn't had her dessert.'

'No,' she snapped. 'She's probably tired. We all are.'

The dinner dragged on with Liam apparently oblivious to the change of mood around him. After dessert, Lucy and Jill pleaded tiredness and went to bed. Dwight excused himself and went outside to clear his head.

With a rueful smile, Mario looked across at Liam. 'Just you and me, mate. How about a nightcap in the bar?'

CHAPTER 3

The next morning, Lucy woke with a start. She could hear
the clatter of skis coming up from the skiers below the
window making their way to the lifts, but that wasn't what
had woken her. The slither of light between the drapes made
her squint. She closed her eyes to concentrate but what she
so badly wanted to remember stayed annoyingly out of
reach.

It will come to me later, she thought, as she untangled
herself from the bedclothes and looked across at Sarah.
Lucy frowned.

Sarah's shoes were on the floor, but the blankets were
piled up around her shoulders. Lucy could see Sarah's legs
sticking out with her glittery socks and last night's red
pants still on. How strange to see fastidious Sarah buried in
a mess of blankets. It was a standing joke in the family that
you could always tell which bed each twin had slept in.

'Are you awake?' she asked, gently shaking Sarah by the
shoulder.

'Get away from me.'

Lucy jumped back in shock. 'We have to go down for
breakfast and to say goodbye to Liam and the others.'

No reply.

'They're catching the nine o'clock bus to the airport.' Lucy
stood, unsure about what to do. 'Are you all right, Sarah?
Are you sick?'

'Just leave me.' Sarah didn't move as she snapped out
each word making them a separate identity.

Alarmed by Sarah's sharp tone Lucy moved away and
thought back to the night before. Sarah had left the dining
room without a word and when Lucy came up to the room

she was hunched up in bed facing the wall. Lucy was sure she was pretending to be asleep.

Lucy would have liked to stay until Sarah sat up but she knew Jill would be furious if one of them didn't go down to see off Liam. So she went down alone. Jill accepted Lucy's explanation that Sarah was still asleep, although she had some difficulty convincing Liam he shouldn't take up a coffee and croissant. He sensed there was more to it than Lucy was letting on but left with a good-natured smile.

Meanwhile Sarah was sitting on the toilet staring at her hands. She had worked out there are only winners and losers in this world. Last night confirmed in her young mind that her mother was a winner and she would be a winner too.

It was a dull grey day with fat snow clouds hanging low and a forecast of worsening conditions. Mario declared they would ski until lunchtime, which would get them off the slopes in good time to do the six-hour drive back to Sydney by early evening.

With calm indifference, Sarah packed and joined Jill, Mario and Lucy as they walked over to the chairlift. She didn't speak and there was a rigidity in the angle of her chin that screamed 'do not approach'.

Jill ignored her, Lucy kept her distance and Mario worried. Sarah's eyes had an icy glitter about them that made him uneasy.

As the morning wore on, the winds increased and blew squalls of sleet over the ridges and down the slopes. Everything was obliterated except for the occasional skier who disappeared and reappeared like a pale ghost.

Lucy hunched against the sleet that stung her face and clogged her goggles and was relieved when Mario called 'time to go'.

'I'm not giving up yet,' Sarah snapped. They all looked at her in surprise.

'But darling it's no fun in these conditions,' Mario said, banging his hands together to warm his fingers.

'Jill will ski with me,' Sarah retorted, her slim body rigid with resolve. They stared in shock and disbelief at her calling Jill by name.

'No more than a couple of runs,' Jill acquiesced. She was puzzled by Sarah's manner but presumed it would pass. 'Want to join us?' she asked Lucy.

'No.' Sarah snapped as she pushed off towards the lifts. 'Just you and me.'

Lucy looked at her twin. Something in Sarah's manner warned her to keep quiet, but as she watched the chairlift take the two into the swirling gloom, her thoughts went back to the previous night. The only time Sarah had left the dining room was when she went to the toilet but something made her angry because she had stormed back, grabbed her bag and left the dining room without another word.

And she's still angry, thought Lucy. And she just called Mummy Jill?

As she stood peering into the swirling snow, Lucy felt Mario move behind her and wrap his arms around her. She let her mind relax and take pleasure from knowing that while Sarah was freezing on the slopes, she was snug in their father's arms secure in the love flowing from him to her.

But Mario didn't find peace so easily. Sometimes Sarah was an enigma to him. Her bad manners last night, her bad temper today and now calling Jill by her name, disturbed him. He thought back to the day the twins were born. Lucy came out screaming and demanding her mother's milk, but Sarah came out silent and refused to suckle. Jill wanted to breastfeed both of her babies. She tried again and again to bring Sarah's tiny mouth up against her nipple, but every time Sarah would turn away. So, on the doctor's recommendation, they gave in and made baby formula for her.

But Lucy also had her annoying quirks he thought. No sooner had she started to walk than she refused to wear shoes. This lasted nearly two years and people used to stare with disapproval at this toddler with bare feet.

My two self-sufficient little girls he pondered as he swayed Lucy's body lightly from side to side.

CHAPTER 4

On the drive home to Sydney sleet and rain reduced visibility, making it a slower drive than usual. Sarah chose to go with Mario. Jill and Lucy followed in silence, reliving the dramatic change in the mood of the weekend. Jill did not see his car again until she pulled into Wharf Road in Birchgrove. Most of the houses in Birchgrove were built as cottages for the workers when the coal mine and the boat building yards were active during the late 1880s. Theirs was one of the large houses the owners and managers of these businesses built along the harbour so they could have a jetty and a little beach. Mario had opened the double garage doors and turned on the outside lights so they could see Yama, tail up, stalking around looking for Lucy.

Like all Burmese cats Yama was independent and dog-like in his devotion to Lucy. 'Oh, Yama.' Lucy murmured as she cuddled him under her chin. Jill hadn't wanted a cat in the house, but she recognised that Lucy had a lot of love to give. She needed something more than her fairy dolls to smother with affection.

'Come on, Lucy. Help Mum carry everything in while I get the fire going.' Mario always believed lighting the lounge room fire was one of his masterly accomplishments. He would scrunch the newspaper, place it strategically into the grate, then stack kindling carefully over the paper to create a tepee so the flames would flare upwards. Once it was well alight, he would add bigger pieces of chopped wood. Finally, he would add his Triple M – Mario's Magic Mixture – a combination of coal and coke that he claimed made the hottest longest-burning home fire in the country.

'Smell that tang. Home sweet home,' he called out,

although no one was listening. 'I'll leave the Triple 'til you all get here.'

With a sigh of contented weariness, he sat back until Jill and the twins arrived with plates of steaming lasagne.

They all ate in grateful silence. The flicker of the flames and the soft light cast by reading lamps made them drowsy. After eating, Mario skimmed through the weekend newspapers. Jill curled up with a book. Sarah stretched out on the couch flicking through the TV channels.

Only Lucy was restless. She jabbed at the fire with the poker, making it flare and Yama curled into a ball on the mat beside her.

'Don't do that,' Mario grumbled. 'I'll add the Triple M soon.'

'No, Daddy. Let's have wood and big flames like at the ski lodge.'

'It doesn't give out the same heat.'

'But it looks better and makes better patterns. Play images with me. Please?' Images involved identifying scenes in the sparks that glowed in the soot along the back of the chimney. The best image won.

'I can see a skier skimming down the slopes. Sarah, it's you. Look … you're passing a snow gum. Daddy, look …'

Mario wanted to play with Lucy but the warmth from the fire blurred his concentration and he was struggling to keep his eyes open. With a grunt he gave up and the paper fell onto his face where it lay, a corner fluttering with each breathy snore.

Annoyed, Lucy piled on more wood, making the tower higher and higher. With horror, she watched ants flee from the cracks in the logs and scurry to the end where they either dropped into the flames or swirled in panic until the heat shrivelled them into specks of black dust.

'Doomed if they do, doomed if they don't.' Sarah sneered from the couch.

Outside, the storm grew wilder and more sinister. A piece of loose tin on a neighbour's shed rattled and banged. Twigs scratched and leaves slapped wetly against the windows while tall trees bent and snapped like angry dogs.

None of this intruded into the softly lit lounge where the fire was growing hotter, insidiously sucking oxygen from the air.

Jill dropped her book into her lap as she drifted off to sleep. Lucy curled around Yama and rested her head in the crook of her arm. Her long blond hair cascading over the mat glowed in the firelight with the richness of melted honey. The tower of logs burned on. Mario's soft snores blended with the shifting crackle of logs burning to a powdery ash.

Slowly, imperceptibly, the tower started to move. Each little jerk and twist shifted the fragile balance of the top logs until, without warning, they toppled forward, tumbled over the grate, onto the hearth and rolled across the mat towards Lucy. She was in a deep sleep when the first flaming log reached her hair.

LUCY

I take Sarah's note out of the top drawer of my bedside table and read it again. I look at the little alarm clock; twelve more minutes if the traffic is light.

The words in this note have kept me awake night after night. I can't think of when there might have been an "awful secret" she didn't tell me about. Did something happen at university that she kept from me? Or at work? Or a boyfriend cheated on her, although I can't believe this because she's always in control of her relationships and she does the cheating. She can make people believe she thinks highly of them when, really, I know she holds most people in contempt.

Dr Singh is always asking for more details about our ski trip to Thredbo but that's about fourteen years ago when we were only eleven. I can't imagine anything that happened then would matter now, although Sarah was certainly brooding over something. A smouldering anger oozed out of her like lava from a volcano. I remember thinking her anger was directed at Mummy ... and me a bit ... I think. Maybe also Daddy, because that's when she started calling them by their first names and even though I asked and asked, she would never tell me why. I don't think Mummy cared what we called her, but Daddy was very hurt.

I did mention this to Dr Singh once and he said he would be very interested to know what had made her so angry that she would change what she called them.

I return Sarah's note to its envelope and slip it back into the drawer. I'm not sure I want to hear what she has to say. I have a feeling it's not something I will be pleased to hear.

CHAPTER 5

The flames sizzled loudly. Had Lucy not been in such a heavy sleep the sizzling might have woken her, but she didn't wake and more logs fell, tumbling over each other and onto her hair. When one of the logs reached her bare neck, she felt the first stab of searing pain and leapt up screaming. As she rose, most of the logs fell from her, spraying sparks, but the log against her neck caught on the fabric of her T-shirt and dropped down onto her chest.

Confused and panicked, she charged across the room instinctively heading for the door to the hallway that led to the front door and the cold air outside. She could smell hair burning but didn't yet connect that to the searing pain around her neck and head. She grabbed at the door handle. It swung open easily, assisted by a blast of cold air that swept into the hot airless room. The fresh air fuelled the flames along the strands of her hair and the fabric of her clothes flared with renewed energy. Lucy screamed.

This woke Mario who leapt up but as he spun around towards her he tripped over Yama, who was also running for the door. Mario crashed to the floor.

'Lucy, stop,' Mario bellowed as he desperately crawled towards her. 'Stop.' His voice was a command.

'Daddy,' she screamed.

'Don't move. I'm coming.'

Totally disorientated, she clung to the doorknob to gather her thoughts. An instinct for survival told her she had to work out what was happening and do something about it, but she couldn't hold onto a single thought. Should I run outside, or not? What is this pain? What's happening? She squeezed her eyes closed.

'Daddy.' She clamped her lips closed as she felt flames lick into her mouth. She could feel herself losing consciousness. She had to stop the pain, somehow. In a panic she let go of the doorhandle and staggered into the hall.

'No!' Mario bellowed as he lunged toward her.

'No.' He howled as he pulled her down grabbing wildly at her flailing arms and kicking legs. Hysteria had given her astonishing strength and it was precious seconds before he could get her small body enveloped under his.

He didn't see the log under her T-shirt, which was burning deep into her nipple and the tender flesh over her ribs.

By now Jill was also bending over Lucy. She had woken at Lucy's first scream and quickly taking in the situation had shouted to Sarah to call triple O as she grabbed a cotton rug from the couch to smother the flames. Together they held Lucy down, oblivious to the singeing hair along their arms and the burning pain in their hands. It seemed to take an age, but eventually the flames were quashed. They lifted the rug and looked down in horror at their daughter's red raw body. Blisters were already forming.

It was then that Jill saw the log under Lucy's T-shirt. She yanked it out, insensible to the pain as it burnt her fingers. In anger she flung it away, unaware of the spectacle of fine shreds of skin dropping from it.

'Should we wrap something warmer around her?' Jill asked through the tightness in her throat that was threatening to choke her.

Now that the flames had stopped, Mario was overcome with indecision.

'The weight might hurt her. I think I read somewhere that burns should be put under cold water. But it's so cold out here. Maybe another cover for her legs?' He hunched over Lucy's shivering body trying to shelter her from the draught entering the hall through the gap under the front door.

'She's freezing. What about pneumonia? Oh God help us!' Jill dragged off her big loose jumper and tried to tuck it around Lucy's legs, but they were shaking so violently she couldn't get it to stay in place.

'You hold it,' she snapped at Mario as she rushed over to where Sarah was standing beside the phone.

'Did you ring triple O? Is the ambulance coming?'

Sarah didn't answer. The phone was dangling in her hand by her side. Jill grabbed it and listened. She could hear a voice saying 'Is anyone there? Hello, can I help you?'

'It's my daughter. We need an ambulance. Now. Urgently. No, we don't need the fire brigade, we need an ambulance. She's eleven. Yes, she's very badly burnt. Hurry, hurry, please hurry.'

Forcing herself to calm down, Jill gave the operator their address and phone number. Then there was nothing to do but wait. She pulled Sarah into her arms and clung to her as Lucy's screams filled the room, but Jill was too agitated to stay still.

'Wait here,' she said as she released Sarah. 'I'll put on the outside lights so they can find us.'

Sarah watched Jill leave the room. She would never have believed a person could burn so quickly. Lucy had looked like a torch running across the room and her screams had ripped the air with the clatter of a thousand knife blades. Sarah walked over to the log her mother had thrown and, using the fire-tongs, carefully picked it up and placed it back into the grate. For a few seconds she watched the other logs still smouldering on the mat. Then she bent down and replaced them in the grate with the other log.

The paramedics took in the situation at a glance: mother and father in shock but okay except for burns to the arms and hands; young girl near the telephone in shock but not obviously hurt. They set to work on Lucy, checking her airways, breathing and circulation as they discussed in hushed voices their options. They threw a shiny space blanket over Lucy to prevent hypothermia and started an intravenous injection of compound sodium lactate to replace lost plasma. They put on an oxygen mask and injected morphine to ease the pain.

'We'll take her to Concord Hospital,' one said as they lifted her onto the trolley and wheeled her down the hall to the ambulance. 'One of you can travel with her,' he said looking from Mario to Jill. 'Let's go.'

Next door, Mary Clarke had fallen asleep in front of the television. Her daughter Kylie was asleep upstairs and her husband James, a captain in the navy, was away on manoeuvres. It took her a few seconds to realise that the scream of sirens was outside in the street, not on the television. She hurried to the window and, seeing the lights and an ambulance in the Borgetti's driveway, she dragged on a coat and hurried across to them.

Mary liked her neighbours although she was rather in awe of their glamorous lifestyle. She had never expected to see Jill so distraught. Being a former nurse, Mary assessed the situation quickly.

'Hang on a minute, I'll get your jackets,' she said as she ran into the house. Mary quickly found the pile of ski jackets and raced back in time to place one around Jill's shoulders as she climbed into the ambulance.

'Just go,' she handed a jacket to Mario and helped Sarah into another. 'I'll look after everything here.'

The ambulance had disappeared by the time Mario had his car out of the garage, but he knew the way to Concord Hospital and drove fast. Sarah sat silently beside him. He reached over to pat her knee.

'She's going to be fine,' he said, fooling neither of them.

At Concord Hospital they had to wait in a room with rows of plastic seats and a television that hung down from the ceiling. The only other people there were a man with a bandaged head and a woman who appeared to be drunk. Mario paced the room reading the printed signs: "Do not eat or drink until seen by a doctor", "Two visitors per patient only". He was thinking a bit clearer now and wondered if

Lucy was going to live. He didn't think of the disfigurement she might suffer; he just wanted his little girl to live.

After a long wait, Jill appeared glassy-eyed and pale.

'What do they say?' He took her into his arms and she let her head fall against his chest.

'They're still checking her but they won't treat her here. She has to go to that new hospital away out at Westmead.'

'Why?'

'Her skin's coming off in huge pieces.' The thought of what she had just seen set Jill sobbing uncontrollably. 'They've called a helicopter.'

'Then why bring her here if it's the wrong hospital?' Mario growled as he looked around for someone in authority.

'Mr Borgetti?' Mario snapped around at the soft voice.

'I'm Doctor Charleston,' said a tall young man with a warm smile. 'I understand your concern, but we need to send her to the kids' hospital at Westmead,' he said, using the doctors' name for the New Children's Hospital that had opened the year before. 'It's the referral centre now for all children with burns. It has the newest facilities and treatment in the country. We've made her as comfortable as we can. You're welcome to sit and wait with her.'

'Wait?'

'Yes. We've ordered the chopper but you can never tell how long it will take. It depends on how busy it is.'

'Why didn't that ambulance take her straight there?' Mario jabbed his thumb towards the ambulance still standing outside.

'Because this hospital is closer. Westmead is a good forty minutes further west from here and the paramedics knew how important it was for her condition to be stabilised as quickly as possible.'

'How is she?' Mario demanded.

'She's severely burnt, I estimate fifteen to twenty per cent of her body but they'll do more tests at Westmead. Please follow me.' Dr Charleston led the way in his rubber-soled shoes, which sucked softly on the polished floor.

Silently Mario, Jill and Sarah followed him to the emergency room where Lucy lay on a high hard bed. Tubes ran into her arm. An oxygen mask covered her face. She rolled her eyes in their direction but didn't seem to register their presence.

CHAPTER 6

Brightly coloured sculptures hung from the ceilings of the New Children's Hospital. Tuscany-coloured walls were decorated with paintings and photographs of Australian scenes and animals. The carpets were bright and friendly and light flooded through huge windows.

Jill led Mario and Sarah, who noticed none of this as they rushed across the foyer to the reception desk.

'Our daughter, Lucy Borgetti, where is she?' Jill puffed as they descended on the emergency counter. 'She came by helicopter.'

At this late hour the entrance hall was empty. A stormy glow shining through the glass ceiling cast an eerie light over the sparse furnishing. The muffled sound of a child screaming filtered from a closed door somewhere nearby. Mario reached out to Jill and Sarah, putting his arms around their shoulders and with his burnt hands hanging free, he drew them in close.

They waited. After a few minutes Sarah pulled away to unzip her ski jacket and wander around the foyer. Mario and Jill stood sweltering in their jackets but too numb to notice until a nurse came up to them and asked them to follow her into a room where she could tend to their burns. Sarah stayed in the foyer while they went into the room, took off their jackets and grimaced in silence as the nurse cleaned their burns and bandaged them.

Not long after they had returned to the foyer a slightly overweight doctor in a white jacket with a stethoscope hanging around her neck approached them. 'You can see your daughter now,' she said with quiet authority. 'She's sedated but conscious.'

Lucy sensed her family enter the room but struggled to hold onto consciousness. Everything was happening in slow motion. She wanted water but her voice came out crackly and distant, so she tried again and a female voice said she couldn't have water. So someone had heard her. She wished that someone would tell her what was happening. Why didn't Daddy tell her, or Mummy? She wanted to cry, but the blackness that had been coming and going descended again.

'We've done all we can here at casualty,' the doctor said. 'She is on morphine for the pain and fluids to rehydrate her. Now we're sending her straight up to the burns ward.' The doctor nodded to two nurses who had entered the room and were pushing the bed out into the corridor. With another nod and a quick smile she indicated to Mario, Jill and Sarah that they should follow the nurses.

Lucy could feel her bed moving. On and on they went. She drifted away then came back again but always it was the same – wide corridors with pale walls and bright lights. When the moving finally stopped, the room she was in was so glaringly white it hurt her eyes, so she scrunched them closed and listened carefully.

'This is the bath room,' she heard a woman say. Who is that? Lucy wondered. Why am I having a bath? Why doesn't someone would tell me what's happening?

Dazed, Jill looked around the bright sterile room where a stainless-steel bath took up most of the space. It was partially filled with warm water. Lucy appeared to be unconscious on the trolley beside it. An antiseptic smell hung in the air and heat lamps flooded the bath in a glare of light.

When the Burns Unit Manager introduced herself as Cathy and told Mario and Jill the staff liked to have a parent present with the child in the bath room they had quickly looked at each other, hoping the other would volunteer. Cathy warned them it was horrible to watch but comforting for the child to have a parent there. Mario didn't think he could cope with much more horror but felt he should be a man and do it; then he heard Jill saying she would do it and he felt her hand on his shoulder. 'I understand,' she had said quietly as she kissed him softly on the cheek.

In the bath room Cathy and another nurse quickly removed Lucy's soiled bandages and gently lowered her into the water. Cathy placed a mask feeding nitrous oxide over Lucy's mouth and started to trim away the excess skin and blisters with sterile cloths. Jill could now see the damage done by the fire. Lucy's left arm, the left side of her chest, up the left side of her face and across the top of her head were raw and blistered. She watched in horror as the nurses peeled off sheets of skin, exposing red raw flesh.

Lucy was moaning and crying out, so the nurses gave her a little more morphine.

'Why can't you just cover her in an antiseptic cream? Let her get over the shock before doing this!' Jill was appalled, unable to believe what she was seeing. The water in the bath was streaked with blood and pieces of skin floated to the top like scum on a stagnant pond.

'Because flame burns carry a lot of dirt so it's important we clean her thoroughly to prevent infection,' Cathy replied patiently.

'So you just do this once?'

'No, unfortunately.' Cathy worked on without looking up. 'This will be done many more times. It's essential to let the new skin grow. It keeps the area clean for grafting later on.'

After what seemed to Jill to be an unnecessary amount of peeling and cleaning, the nurses lifted Lucy gently from the bath and carried her to a small adjoining room dominated by a high table. The air in this room was clearer and Jill immediately felt better. She looked around. The walls were lined with cupboards and shelves neatly piled with bandages and jars of cream. Working swiftly, the nurses applied silver sulfadiazine cream to porous dressings cut to size to fit over the burn area, followed by a soft cottonwool-type fabric, then bandages. Jill watched in incredulity as the top half of Lucy was covered and wrapped like an Egyptian mummy.

'What happens now?' Jill asked.

'We'll take her to her the ward and she'll sleep.'

Lucy could hear their voices faintly but was too tired to respond. Occasionally she picked up on her mother's fear and anger. She wanted to ask what she had done wrong, to apologise, but she was too tired and the smells were making her feel sick.

Cathy gently guided Jill out of the dressing room. 'That was hard for you Mrs Borgetti but you stood up to it well. Now you must get some rest. We've made up a bed in the ward beside Lucy and will give you a sleeping pill. Please take it because we've got a long way to go.'

Jill sat on the edge of the narrow bed the nurses had made up beside Lucy. She looked up as Mario and Sarah entered.

'They told me a bit about the bathing procedure and I appreciate you going in there.' Mario took her hands and lifted Jill up off the bed so he could envelop her in his arms. 'How are you feeling?'

'She's so swollen. Cathy said her eyes are not damaged but the skin around them is puffy and peeling ...' Jill could not go on so she let herself go limp and dropped her head against his chest. Then she lifted her head and held out an arm for Sarah to join them.

'Are you all right?' she asked stroking Sarah's hair. 'It's all such a shock.'

Sarah did not answer. She was still trying to absorb everything that had happened.

After a while Jill sat back down on the bed and Mario guided Sarah out of the room and down the corridors to the car park. He could feel her thin childish shoulders and wondered how he had let this happen? Sarah so silent; Lucy frightened, maybe dying.

It was after midnight and there was very little traffic on the road, so they got home in less than an hour. Yama came out for a pat, but Mario led Sarah straight up to her room and told her to hop into bed and he would be back shortly to tuck her in.

In the narrow confines of the toilet he felt the floor starting to waver and its walls closed in on him, dank and cloying. Panic swelled like a black sea. He closed his eyes but couldn't erase the image of Lucy racing across the room, flames bursting out of her. He cried out in fright and had to sit for a while until his vision cleared and the shaking stopped.

He thought of the little birds that crashed into the large glass windows at the side of the house. Lucy would pick them up very tenderly, put them into a box and cover them with a dark cloth. 'It's frightened so it needs to be in a dark quiet place,' she would whisper, her fingers at her lips. Mario put his head in his hands and let himself cry.

Sarah was lying stiffly in bed staring at the ceiling when he returned to her room. She seemed calm but was so still he wondered if she was in extreme shock and he should call a doctor. Gently he lifted her shoulders to give her half of one of the sleeping pills Jill kept in their bathroom. How small and vulnerable she felt as he eased himself onto the bed beside her and gathered her into his arms.

At last he could think. He let the tears flow as his mind leapt from one thought to the next. Will Lucy live? Will she have a normal life? What will our family life be like? He must remember to phone his mother and Jill's parents in the morning. And work. He tried to concentrate on what else he needed to do tomorrow, but the warmth of Sarah's body and the sleeping pill did their job. It seemed indecent that he could sleep but it washed over him as a benevolent mist and gratefully he let it.

CHAPTER 7

The next morning, as Mario and Sarah walked into the hospital room, Jill leaped up. 'She won't talk.' Even with the sleeping pill, Jill had not slept well.

'Maybe she can't hear through all the bandages,' Mario suggested, taking her gently by the shoulders and sitting her down again.

'You don't understand.' Jill snapped 'The nurses say she can hear but she's angry with *ME*. And now she has to have another bath ... I can't do it again. You'll have to. It's your turn.'

'I don't think I can.' Mario looked across at Lucy. Her face had swollen even more during the night and the bandages seemed far too tight. 'Maybe we could ask them to skip this bath,' he suggested weakly.

But there was no reprieve. Jill went with Lucy while Mario took Sarah to the coffee shop for breakfast. The nurses would not allow a sibling near the bath room when a child was being treated and Jill trusted the medical profession enough to accept their judgement, but even so, she could not stay silent. 'I can barely recognise her,' she said when Cathy started to remove the bandages. 'Why don't you let the swelling go down a bit before doing all this?'

Cathy and her assistant kept working. There was nothing they could say to parents who had to be with their child during this terrible procedure. All parents suffered this combination of anger and disbelief.

The next day, as Jill and Mario sat beside Lucy, a woman they had not seen before entered the room. 'Hello, I'm Jane, Lucy's social worker,' she said with a bright smile. 'And you must be Jill and Mario Borgetti. The nurses told me you were here.' They shook hands.

Jane was a short dumpy woman with brown curly hair showing a few strands of grey. She wore comfy shoes, as did most of the hospital staff.

Jill fell on her with the speed of a diving vulture. 'She won't talk to me. The nurses say she can, but she won't.'

'That's understandable at this stage, Mrs Borgetti. Your daughter is frightened, in pain and probably angry. It may seem unreasonable but she's angry that you, her parents, let this happen to her. Of course, there's no blame in accidents like this, but she has to work this out, so do you. Blame is a damaging emotion that hinders recovery.'

'How long will her anger last?'

'Not long, usually. The best thing you can do is keep talking to her. She needs to hear you tell her you love her and that she is going to be fine. She needs to believe in a happy future.'

'Does she have a happy future?' Mario clung to these positive words.

'That's not for me to say. I look after her emotional health; the doctors and nurses look after her body.'

'Have they told you how long they'll be treating her?' Jill was hoping this would give an indication of how long Lucy would be in hospital.

'No. Not yet.'

'Will she have psychological problems?' This had been playing on Jill's mind and it just burst out of her.

'That's difficult to predict but our resident psychiatrist, Dr Kilter, will see her soon and you can ask him.' Jane smiled reassuringly. She had worked at this job long enough to know that it could be as disappointing as it was rewarding. 'We have a long road ahead. Getting better in here, returning home, returning to school; all that sort of thing. I prefer us to face each new phase as it comes. I believe Lucy has a twin?' Jane looked around as though Sarah would suddenly appear. 'If they're close, it would be good for Lucy to have her company as often as possible.'

For the next two days Mario and Jill sat with Lucy. They told her how much they loved her. They read aloud the "Get Well" cards and told her who had phoned with messages.

Sarah came too but said very little. When Sarah went out to the toilet Jill quickly asked Mario if she had spoken to him in the car or at home. 'No, I think she's still in shock and maybe, being a twin, is feeling some of Lucy's pain.'

Still Lucy refused to talk.

On the second afternoon Mario took Jill out into the hospital gardens for a walk in the fresh air. The brittle winter sun through the bare trees cast spiky shadows across the pavement and highlighted the dark shadows under her eyes. 'It's killing me seeing her in that awful bed,' Jill said. 'Her face is misshapen. Her left arm may never work again or could be deformed. Sometimes I'm not even sure it's really her inside all that swelling and bandages. And she won't talk. It's like she's never going to talk to us again.'

'She's young and strong. We have to trust the nurses and doctors.' Mario said, even though he had the same thoughts. 'I asked Cathy how Lucy was responding compared with other burns patients, but her answer was vague. Something like all burns patients respond differently. I don't think they really know,' he added, frustrated by the vagueness of the answers and his lack of ability to do anything about it.

The breakthrough came on the third day when Mario was sitting beside the bed singing softly. His beautiful tenor seeped through Lucy's wad of bandages and fear.

Lucy felt his voice flowing into her, subduing her feelings of anger like oil on rough waters. She wanted to feel his arms around her. Tentatively she raised the fingers of her right hand.

Mario's heart lurched. He wanted to grab her fingers but held back. Jane had said they must watch for little signals but not rush in. 'Give her time to reach. To want and then to receive.'

The effort it had taken to move her fingers alarmed Lucy and she withdrew back into herself. 'I must be really badly hurt,' she thought.

But her father's voice flowed on, gentle, persistent, soothing, penetrating her bandages and the pain, encouraging her to have hope.

Lucy lifted her fingers again and trembled when she felt his hand very gently envelop them.

'Thank you, Lucy darling. Thank you for coming back to me.' His tears splashed onto their fingers. How he longed to lift her up. To hold her in his arms, but her right arm and hand were the only parts of her upper body not wrapped in bandages. 'I've missed you and I love you so much.'

Lucy tightened her fingers a little and felt him lean down and lift her hand to his chest. She could feel his chest moving as he softly sang another Italian song she knew, of a mother's love for her newborn baby. She felt him put his lips against her fingers and for the first time since the accident, thought maybe she was going to get better.

She would ask Sarah if she was going to get better. Sarah would tell her the truth.

'That's great news,' Jane said when Mario told her about the fingers. 'It means she's getting ready to communicate.' Jane's round face beamed with satisfaction as she looked from Mario to Jill and Sarah. 'She'll speak soon. Just give her time. She's still working out her feelings. She could be reliving the fire, wondering what she looks like. Wondering about her future. You are all doing all the right things. Keep at it.'

'Is she really all right?' Jill's doubts increased with each day. 'She's been here three days and still the swelling continues. And those awful baths. I can't see what good they do. At the first bath Cathy told me the swelling would peak after about forty-eight hours, but we've gone over that time and it hasn't stopped.'

'I know it's difficult, but you have to trust the nurses. It's important for Lucy's mental state that you stay strong.'

Jill looked down at her own bandaged hands then back up at Jane with a rueful smile. 'You're right Jane. I have to trust, but it's not easy.'

'She could have a couple of good friends visit,' Jane said brightly. 'The hospital doesn't usually agree with me on this, but I believe the sooner we get friends in the better. Just close ones, you know, who can handle the situation and be gentle with her. Especially people who won't say anything that will upset her. She needs to be emotionally stronger before she will be able to cope with some of the problems she is going to have to deal with.'

LUCY

'Tell me again about the night of the fire.' Dr Singh's voice has an even cadence and his eyes are quietly questioning. 'The presence you say you saw; did it have a shape?'

'I've told you, it was just a fleeting thing. Probably nothing.'

For the first few weeks in the Rozelle Hospital I had refused to talk about that night. Just thinking about it would fill me with such weariness that it was an effort to open my mouth to speak. I felt a plug had been pulled and all my energy was running down a drain. I would beg Dr Singh to let me go back to my room to sleep.

'There's a clue there. If we can find it, we will be on the way to understanding your depression.'

Dr Singh goes on and on about wanting more details and gradually a few images do return and this pleases him.

I can still remember the day he was so pleased with me. Said we had learnt something new, something important.

'The colour blue?' he said. 'You have just told me you saw something blue and it was moving fast, and it frightened you. This could explain why you're having difficulty recalling it. Close your eyes Lucy and think very carefully. What was in the lounge that night that was blue?'

I remember saying that maybe the presence was blue and that exasperated him. 'The presence is in your mind Lucy. This thing. This something blue. It is real.'

'A leprechaun!'

'Lucy!' He is very patient, but sometimes I play on it to see how much he can take before he cracks. 'We have agreed that there were no leprechauns in the room, and no presence.'

I went too far that time and he became a bit angry with me.

When I first entered the psychiatric hospital at Rozelle, I was frightened of Dr Singh, but I was frightened of everyone and everything back then. Over the weeks I have grown to trust him and progressively he has learnt almost all there is to know about my life. He'll watch me with dark brown eyes that remind me of Daddy, except Daddy's lashes were long and curled up while Dr Singh's are short and straight. Also, he cares like Daddy did and I think this is why I tease him. It sounds silly, but sometimes when I'm with him I become a little girl again.

I felt safe in the hospital and after a while I tried to answer all Dr Singh's questions honestly. But there are holes in my life. It's like there's a padlock on those holes and I have lost the key. There are a lot of holes around my feelings, especially for Sarah. I loved her so much. Loved it when we would put our hands on each other's hearts to feel them beating ... twin hearts in tandem. But now I'm not so sure. I'm not sure I really understand her anymore, or if I ever did. My twin, my beautiful twin, is a complicated person. And now she's coming. I look again at the little clock – in ten minutes she will walk into the room.

As I pace the room I run through past conversations with Dr Singh, then I hear a noise and swivel around in fright to as the door swings open. It's Suzie, my favourite nurse. The nurses are supposed to knock but Suzie never does. She treats me like a child. There are times when this annoys me, but I'll miss her when I leave this place.

'Your sister will be here soon,' she says as her eyes sweep the room and she pats smooth the bedspread. 'Saw her photo in the paper yesterday ... stunning ... you don't expect a girl with her looks to be defending crooks. She could be a model.' Suzie is a passionate follower of celebrity gossip.

'Sarah relishes the challenge being a criminal lawyer gives her,' I reply more curtly than I mean to. I need to be alone and wish Suzie would leave.

'You all right Dearie?' Suzie's anxious eyes sweep over my bare face. 'Better put on a bit of lippy. Don't want her to think you don't care now, do you?'

CHAPTER 8

On her fourth day in hospital Lucy sensed a presence in the room near the door, breathing but not moving. Then it came towards her and she heard the chair beside the bed give a soft sigh as a light body settled onto it. She knew it wasn't Sarah. Lucy waited, a little nervous until long, finely boned fingers laced with scratches and cuts touched her bare right hand. In that instant she knew the nails would be chipped and dirty.

'Damon!' Lucy whispered as she opened her eyes carefully.

'I brought you a shell,' Damon said.

Lucy could hear the shock in his voice, the effort he was making to control it, his distaste for the confinement of the ward. His empathetic soul reaching out to her. She squeezed his fingers and felt his silent tears dripping onto her bandages.

Very few people understood Damon but she had found a quality in him that she liked. Their friendship had started one day when she was walking home from school and Sarah had stayed behind for a special maths class. Lucy was feeling restless and in need of an adventure when she saw Damon walking along the footpath. He was in her class and known to be an "odd one". Daggy Damon was what the kids called him behind his back. He had an older sister and she was a bit strange too. 'Tich can't wait to leave school,' he told her once. 'Wants to join a commune and live with nature, growing vegs and all that sorta stuff.'

'Where are you going?' she had asked, skipping along the footpath beside him.

'Fishin'.'

'Can I come?'

'S'pose so.' He strode along without looking at her and she had to jog to keep up with him. Without another word they crossed Birchgrove Oval where boys were kicking a football and onto the sandy crescent called Snail Bay. At the end of the wooden jetty, he made up a spare line, put a cube of sausage meat on the hook and showed her how to drop it into the water. It wasn't long before she was wondering what on earth she was doing sitting here beside the harbour, with him.

'What'll I do if a fish bites?'

Silence.

'Don't you ever talk?'

'Sometimes.'

'What do you catch here?'

'Tailor, flathead, crab.'

Suddenly she felt her line tug and was about to leap up when his hand came down firmly on her shoulder. He pressed his fingers to her lips to silence her silly squeals. With an intensity that surprised and excited her he wrapped his long slender fingers around her hands and helped her play the fish until they could flick it up onto the jetty. With a sharp knock on the head, it was dead. A few rapid flicks of a thin knife and it was filleted.

'Tell your mum to cook it quickly in butter and lemon,' he said.

Damon never invited her to join him, but she got into the habit of falling into step as he walked to the jetty. He still didn't talk much but she was comfortable with his silence and knew she was accepted when he started carrying a second line and extra bait. Sometimes his friend Billy joined them. Sarah did once.

'He's too daggy for words and the fish pong,' Sarah snorted as they walked home with two filleted fish in a plastic bag.

Lucy ignored the insult. 'He wants to be a sculptor,' she replied. Lucy knew Sarah well enough to know she wouldn't come fishing again. 'He collects driftwood and can see all sorts of things in it. One time he said he saw a dog in a piece we had just found in the rocks. I couldn't see a thing, so he sat down and carved it right there in front of me. It was amazing, it really was a dog, big like a boxer dog.'

'You sound like Loopy Lilly.' Sarah sneered. She did not like Damon and was irritated that Lucy was developing a friendship with him. Sarah didn't like Lilly, their art teacher, either. Lilly was always raving on about Damon's "artistic eye". She would say 'this boy is gifted' and 'he'll be a great artist one day'.

'If you put the shell against your ear you'll hear the sea,' Damon said as he leaned over the bed to place it awkwardly against Lucy's right ear where there were fewer bandages and she could hold it in place with her right hand. 'It'll remind you of Snail Bay and fishin'.'

Lying there listening to the roar in the shell reminded Lucy of more than Snail Bay. It made her think of home, of the little ripples that rolled up onto their little beach when a ferry went past, of Yama with his soft purr, and the lovely old brick school where she should be now. She couldn't speak for the fear that welled up inside her chest.

'Caught a black fish the other day,' Damon said as he watched her with his grey eyes, willing her to speak. 'And Billy says I gotta tell you he's doing a painting for you. He'll give it to you when you come out.' He faltered, 'or when it's finished'.

Lucy desperately wanted to tell him things – that the bandages around her throat were too tight and she was scared she might choke; that she was pleased he had caught a black fish; and grateful he had come to visit her. She wanted to tell him to thank Billy for doing a painting. But all did she was lie there listening to the sea roaring in the shell. It was beautiful and sad at the same time. She thought she might cry. The silence hung over them.

'I gotta go,' he said, his long thin frame unfolding as he stood.

Lucy flickered her eyes open without taking the shell away from her ear. She didn't hear him tiptoe out of the room.

When Sarah arrived later that day, she took one sniff of the shell and went straight to the bathroom to wash it in hot soapy water. The cleaning diluted the salty fishy smell but the sea still roared in her ear.

'Thank you for asking Damon to visit me,' Lucy said.

'I told Jane he was the one you would want to see,' Sarah replied.

Sarah had not suggested Damon. She did not even know he had visited until she saw the shell, but she wasn't going to admit this. She guessed Lilly their art teacher had suggested him. 'Did you tell him about the baths?'

'No.' Lucy reached for Sarah's hand. 'Have you spoken to Daddy yet? You promised you would tell him he had to tell the nurses to stop doing them. You know how to get around him.'

'I tried but he says he can't.'

'You didn't try hard enough.' Lucy wept, tears burning her eyes. 'Tell him you had a dream that I died in the bath.'

'Okay. I'll try again. But stop ... you must stop whingeing. The baths have to be done for you to get better,' she said sourly. Sarah was fed up with hearing how brave Lucy was when she had all these people running around after her and she, Sarah, was being ignored.

'When the bandages come off,' Lucy hesitated, 'What will I look like?'

'Just like before.' Sarah tore open a parcel from Nonna Borgetti.

'I'll be ugly, won't I?'

'You've got a present from Nonna. Look, a stuffed cat, same colour as Yama.'

'Tell me the truth.' Lucy knew Sarah wasn't paying attention but no one else would tell her anything. The uncertainty and fear of how she would look when the bandages came off never left her. Sometimes she wished she could stay asleep so she didn't have to think about it.

'You'll have a few scars,' Sarah admitted lightly, 'but Jill says you'll have plastic surgery to cover them.'

'What about my hair, will it grow again?'

Sarah reached over and took Lucy's hand gently into hers. 'You mustn't tell them I told you because I'm not supposed to say. Promise?'

'Promise. Cross my heart and hope to die.'

'Your hair will never grow again.'

Two days later Lucy got hold of a pair of scissors and was cutting up her bed sheets in a fit of anger when a nurse found her. It took two nurses to calm her down and they managed to persuade Lucy to tell them why she was so upset. When the nurses told Jane that Sarah had told Lucy her hair would never grow again, Jane was furious and told the hospital staff that Sarah must never be allowed in the room alone with Lucy. 'It's too upsetting for Sarah to see her twin in such pain,' she told the staff and if anyone disbelieved her, they didn't say so.

CHAPTER 9

When Mario returned from the canteen with coffee and soft drinks he was shocked by the look of horror in Lucy's eyes. He quickly put down the drinks and curled her right hand into his chest. 'What's happened darling?'

'I told her about Damon falling off his bike and it upset her.' Sarah said. 'You're all right now though aren't you LL?' Sarah looked directly into Lucy's eyes. Lucy gave a timid nod as she accepted Sarah's use of LL (Little Lucy) which she used when she wanted to assert her superiority.

Lucy's skin grafts started after she had been in hospital for five days. She had listened to the surgeon telling her parents how he would proceed and how pleased they would be with the results.

'He was telling them the baths were finished and *they* would be pleased with the results of the skin grafts,' she fumed to Sarah next time she visited. 'They think I'm just a kid, that I don't understand, but I do, it's my body. Without you I wouldn't know anything.'

Sarah stared at the nervous young nurse who was sitting in attendance behind her until she blushed and looked away. 'LL I'll never lie to you. You and me together, our pact, remember?'

But no one could help Lucy through next few weeks as she see-sawed between pain and oblivion. The skin for the grafts was taken from her thighs and this area was more painful than the burnt areas it covered. She received morphine intravenously when the grafts were being done and orally in times between. 'It's a fine balance between giving her enough morphine to control the pain but not so much she becomes addicted,' Cathy told Jill.

Lucy became sullen and aggressive, refusing to eat one minute then screaming for fruit and chocolate the next.

My life is like a chain, she thought after the second lot of surgery. There is a link for morphine, a link for baths, a link for boring meals, a link for pain, a link for exercises, a link for sick people, a link for visitors. She now believed the pain would never end. She lost the will to live and Jane pushed the family to ensure someone was always beside her bed throughout the day.

Mario didn't look forward to when it was his turn to be with her. He couldn't hug her because of all the grafts and bandages, and it ripped his heart out every time she asked him to stop the operations. He wished that they would but the surgeon had warned him that she needed two or three more graft operations. He said that if they stopped now they would be condemning Lucy to a life with horrendous scars.

'I hate him, I hate him, I hate him,' Lucy screamed, grasping at Mario. 'Daddy don't let him do it. You can stop him. Daddy, please.' She sobbed hysterically and Mario cried with her.

Mario and Jill agonised over what to do. The grafts were much more painful than they had expected, and they worried about the amount of morphine she was having. 'What more can we do to help her,' they asked Jane one afternoon after they had met Lucy's physiotherapist, Diane.

'Just stick to telling her good news,' Jane replied. 'Tell her the grafts are looking good. That her left arm is responding better than expected and will end up quite normal. Diane is a very experienced physio and you should work closely with her from now on.'

Diane, they learned, had started the exercises on Lucy two weeks earlier. 'Sorry we haven't met before this,' she said, 'but I have a lot of patients and move quickly from one to the other. Lucy's first exercises were done by the nurses while she was unconscious but I'm working more with her now when she is conscious. The exercises are very painful and intrusive but vitally important.'

Diane looked at Jill and Mario intently as though trying to read how helpful these parents would be. She was tall for a woman and very slim with long blond hair pulled back into a tidy bob. 'What we're doing is working to stretch the skin, not the muscles, as it's the layers of skin that have been damaged. The first six months are very important, but the exercises could go on for much longer, possibly two years, so we'll all get to know each other really well,' Diane flashed a quick smile, 'and she'll need to wear pressure garments. These will be tailored to fit her and apply the pressure normally applied by healthy skin to the maturing scars. She'll wear them all the time, except when bathing, until the hypertrophic scarring stops. Sorry, we can talk more later, but I have a patient waiting. Lovely to meet you.' And she was off down the corridor.

Sarah did not know why she was not allowed to be in the ward with Lucy without a nurse present, but she guessed it was an order from Jane. She resented this as she resented so many other things. Lucy was all Jill and Mario talked about. Lucy was all the kids at school cared about. They were always giving her cards they'd made and posies of flowers to take to Lucy in hospital. And after school she had to go next door with Kylie and her mum, Mary, until either Jill or Mario got home.

But one afternoon, three weeks after the fire, Sarah arrived home from school feeling angry and abandoned. Mary had taken Kylie to the dentist. Jill was at the hospital and she presumed Mario was at the newspaper.

But Mario was at home working in his library downstairs. He heard Sarah stomping upstairs then the toilet in the upstairs bathroom flushing again and again. The strange noises worried him, so he went upstairs and tapped on the door. The flushing continued so he pushed it open and there was Sarah standing beside the toilet holding down the lid. He could hear a frantic scratching noise inside the bowl.

'What's in there?'

'Nothing. I threw in too much paper and it's taking a while to go down.'

He knew she was lying. He pushed past her to lift the lid and couldn't believe what he saw. There, wet, terrified and frantically clawing for grip on the smooth sides of the bowl was Yama. He lifted the terrified cat out by the scruff of the neck and stared in disbelief at Sarah as they listened to it hurtle along the hallway, down the steps and out the open door to the safety of the garden.

'He'd rolled in a dead fish. I was just giving him a bath,' she said flippantly. 'He'll smell better now.' Without another look at Mario she stalked out of the bathroom and down the hall to her bedroom.

Sarah was furious with Mario. The cat needed to go and Mario shouldn't have interfered. For days it had been walking around the house meowing and looking for Lucy. She was Lucy's twin. She was all Lucy needed. I should have knocked it on the head first she thought angrily. But it put up a good fight, she mused, with begrudging admiration.

Sarah's lie was so blatant, Mario was struck dumb. He had never really understood Sarah. There were times when he worried about her long lethargic silences and the way she would look at him, as though assessing his presence. And there were those times when she would put a noose around the neck of one of Lucy's fairy dolls and hang it from a branch in the garden. She said she was teaching it to fly but she would hit it so hard its pretty dress would become shredded, or a leg or an arm would tear off.

He closed the toilet lid and sat down on it. What should I do? he asked himself. Tell Jill? Or Jane? Sarah's still a child. She's been left alone too much. It's not fair on her. I'll let it go until Lucy is home and Jill and I have time to talk.

He and Jill had started to alternate the days they went to

the hospital and Jill no longer slept there. This gave her time to go into the office to check how the staff were managing, and to make decisions on issues that needed her attention. It was easier for Mario because he could read the news anywhere and do his cartoons at home in his library with its big leather armchair and dark wood desk, or at the hospital.

Mario missed the camaraderie of being at the newspaper and the productive quietness of his office there. In recent years, the depictions of a mix of his Italian morality and bohemianism in his cartoons had become increasingly popular. Mario had even thought about producing an annual calendar of his favourite, and not so favourite, politicians. But that had gone on hold since Lucy's accident. Mario's editor was a hard man, but Mario was his star cartoonist so he let him do his cartoons anywhere and the company paid a courier to collect them.

'I need to have work to do,' he told Jane one day when she saw him working at his sketch pad. 'Keeping up with the news keeps me sane.' She patted him gently on the shoulder as he stared down at his sketch pad, fighting back tears.

'You could ask your mother to come in sometimes,' Jane said. 'Lucy often talks about her. I think she'd be a good influence.'

'Would that really be okay?' Mario felt warm pleasure rush though his body. 'You told us to limit visitors, so we've told all the grandparents they have to wait a bit. But my mother has desperately wanted to see Lucy. I pass close to her house on the way here so could easily pick her up.'

His childlike pleasure at the suggestion amused Jane. She wasn't sure about the other grandparents who sounded a bit stiff, but Lucy spoke so lovingly of Concettina – who she called Nonna.

From then on, Mario picked up Concettina on the way to the hospital. Wonderful aromas from the biscuits and cakes she baked for Lucy wafted around the car as he poured out his worries. 'All those sad little faces. Broken bodies. Ruined lives. I can't believe that one moment they're playing with a toy and the next they're screaming in pain. I'll be watching them laughing and playing, then they see a nurse coming and all those little faces freeze as they watch to see who she has come to collect. Some days I have to go outside to get away from it all.'

On the first day he had taken her hands in his and said he hoped she would be okay because it wasn't easy "in there". He need not have worried. Concettina spread her bags, took off her jacket and sat down with Lucy as though she was in her own home.

Many times he came close to telling her about Sarah putting Yama down the toilet, but he always stopped himself and he wondered why. Was he embarrassed that his daughter could display this kind of behaviour, or did he think his mother would have seen it all before and just shrug it off as a childish prank?

Lucy loved having Nonna there. She liked the click of her knitting needles, the music in her voice and the excitement of opening her many little containers. Lucy couldn't eat much but it made her feel loved to know Nonna had been in her kitchen creating them just for her. Lucy clung to any displays of love people gave her.

Four weeks after Lucy was admitted into the hospital, first in intensive care and now in a shared ward, she had become used to the routine of grafts, physiotherapy, meals, Jane, doctors … when a new patient who would change the course of her life arrived in the ward.

CHAPTER 10

The new arrival was a boy about Lucy's age. He was surrounded by his mother, father who pushed his wheelchair, two younger sisters, a stuffed black and white dog, a bag of games and a shoebox crammed with photos.

The family flowed into the silence of the room like a river in a raging flood. Lucy watched in astonishment as they gathered chairs, dropped bags and bundles on the floor, opened and shut drawers and arranged photos on the table beside the boy's bed. His father lifted him off the wheelchair and propped him up on pillows with his bandaged arms lying outside the blankets. He had a bandage around the top half of his head.

'Hello,' the mother said to Lucy once they had finally settled down. We're from out back of Camden. This is Tom McKenzie.' He flicked a look across to Lucy but didn't smile. Across his nose was the most astonishing splash of freckles Lucy had ever seen and his clear blue eyes were checking out the room with apprehension.

'He got burnt playing with kerosene on the farm,' Mrs McKenzie continued. 'Luckily, he had gloves on, so his hands weren't burnt but his hat fell off, so his hair got burnt. What did you do?'

'I was burnt by the fire at home.' Lucy said. She wanted to remain aloof, but the energy of the family drew her in.

'Why do you look like that?' One of the sisters had sidled up to Lucy's bed, her eyes wide with horror and amazement. Lucy had many more bandages around her face than her big brother Tom and one arm was sticking up in the air, held there with a splint, which made the fingers stick out like dead twigs on a tree.

'Daisy!' Mrs McKenzie dragged her back to Tom's bed. 'Don't mind her. They're just country kids. Always saying the first thing that comes into their silly heads.' While she reprimanded Daisy the other little girl, who she had introduced as Pixie, was peering across the top of the bed, every bit as fascinated and horrified as her younger sister.

The family stayed for about an hour and every time the mother's attention was distracted, the little girls would take the opportunity to scrutinise Lucy again.

This was the first time Lucy found herself exposed to people who hadn't seen her before or been schooled on how to act in front of her. In the confines of the hospital the children were used to seeing each other with pressure garments and splints. They all knew about pain and baths and operations. Sometimes they talked about it, but mostly they left each other alone when things were going bad and let them join in when they felt better.

Daisy's and Pixie's curiosity upset Lucy. For the first time she realised she would one day go outside and people "out there" would find her appearance strange.

As soon as the mother and girls left and their chatter and clatter had faded down the corridor, Lucy slipped off the bed and made her way carefully into the bathroom. She stood before the mirror for a long, long time seeing what the little girls had seen. What her school friends would see. What strangers on the street would see. She had looked in the mirror before, but never to see herself as another person would see her.

What she saw was her head encased in a beige-coloured-pressure garment which she had been told was to prevent scars and keloid tissue from forming. The only bits of her face showing were her eyes which glittered through puffy slits, her nose, and her mouth which was pink and still swollen. The top half of her torso was also encased in a pressure garment and a Jobst collar kept her neck steady. A splint held her left arm out to one side and there were more splints holding her fingers in place.

'I'm a freak.' She sobbed.

Mr McKenzie and Tom were watching a video on the television that hung from the ceiling when Lucy returned to the room. Mr McKenzie was going to ask her to join them but remained silent when he saw the tear stains on the pressure garment and the quivering lips. Another time, he thought.

The next morning, Mr McKenzie arrived early and put on another video. 'Want to join us?' he asked looking over at Lucy. She shook her head, but he disregarded her sulks and pulled up another chair which he patted for her to sit on.

'Hope you like cowboys and gangsters. They're our favourites.' He was a tall bony man with a deep voice that was surprisingly gentle. Lucy noticed he had a bent arm.

Lucy knew it was rude to ask personal questions, but her curiosity got the better of her. 'Why is your arm that way?'

'Got shot in Vietnam,' he replied and went back to the video. She watched to see how he managed it in case her left arm ended up bent like his.

Eventually the yahooing galloping hooves and wild shooting was too tempting so she slipped off her bed and across to the chair. When the video ended she edged closer to Tom to ask about his box of photos.

Mr McKenzie dragged the box closer so Tom could pick each photo out carefully with the bare fingers that protruded from his bandages. 'That's Shep – Dad's dog. This one's Snip – my dog and I trained him.'

'To do what?'

'Round up sheep 'n cows of course.' Tom looked at Lucy as though she was dumb. 'That's what dogs do. Some round up just sheep and some bring in the cows but I've trained Snip to do both.'

'I've got a cat.'

'We got lots of them. Mum has a spoilt one that lives in the house. The others stay outside and catch mice.'

Lucy had picked up a large framed photo of a white horse and was stroking the tip of its nose. 'Do you ride it?'

'Yeah, Blondie's really old but we still get onto her some-times. You can come out one day and ride her if you want to.'

'I've never been to a farm.' Lucy looked at the photograph showing the horse looking over a fence towards three dogs milling around steps leading up onto the deep veranda of a large single-storey house painted cream. People were sitting on a swing seat on the veranda and at a long table under a big tree on a mown lawn. It looked so peaceful.

Later Mr McKenzie dug out a shooting game from Tom's bag of toys and showed Lucy how to play. 'See them animals crossin' the screen,' he said. 'Well ... you look through here and shoot at them. The red spots are brains and hearts. You get the most points for hitting them.'

'Where are the bullets?'

'It's remote. See here, each shot you make is recorded on the scoreboard and at the end of the game you print it out on a score card.'

Lucy was shooting well after a few games. 'You've got a good eye ... a real feel for it. Have you done it before?' Mr McKenzie was amazed.

'Gosh no,' Lucy was warmed by his praise. 'Mum would be furious if I shot an animal.' She looked down at the score card he had handed her.

'We don't just shoot animals you know. At rifle clubs you shoot at targets. Tom here's got a .22 for shootin' rabbits and crows on the farm but he'll join my club soon as he's old enough.'

'Do shooting clubs have girls?'

'There's a girl 'bout your age in my group. She's so good, she could be representing Australia at the next Commonwealth Games. Now there's somethin' for you to aim for.'

'I bet she's been doing it for years,' Lucy scoffed but then asked 'Are there clubs in Sydney that will take girls?'

'Yeah, but you can't join till you're twelve. This girl's on a farm so she's played around with rifles since she took her first step.'

Lucy's interest was aroused. Before the fire she was in the school teams for netball and hockey, but she needed strong arms for both those games. She had been wondering what sports she would be able to do when she left the hospital. With Mr McKenzie saying she had "the eye", she started thinking she could take up shooting. I'll ask Daddy she decided.

But when she brought it up next time he visited her, Mario stared in disbelief. 'What! That's not something girls do.'

'Yes it is,' she snapped. 'Mr McKenzie knows girls who shoot in competitions, even the Commonwealth Games.'

'Maybe, but it's different for girls who grow up on farms.'

'He said there are schools in the city with shooting clubs that take girls. He said I could join one.'

'Have you spoken to your mother about this?' Mario looked sympathetically at Lucy as he imagined the disdain on Jill's face. 'To start with, she wouldn't let you shoot and secondly you're already booked into her old school. I'm sure those girls don't shoot.'

'So, what am I supposed to do when I leave here?' Lucy was disappointed and frustrated. 'I won't be able to catch a ball or hold a bat. The girls will laugh at me.' Tom, his family, the dogs, the white horse, the sheep, cows and green paddocks with wild rabbits had shown her a future full of possibilities. Now, in just a few words, her father had rejected that fascinating new world. She turned away from him and fell back onto her pillows.

Lucy was still sulking when Tom and his father returned from the treatment room. Mr McKenzie adjusted the blankets around Tom and sat stroking him as he cried softly. He looked at Lucy and raised an eyebrow at Mario. 'Problems?' Mario nodded.

After they had settled the children, each with their favourite computer game, they went outside to walk in the garden. The two fathers equally out of their depth over the pain of their child. 'My name's Neil by the way, and you're Mario aren't you?'

'Yes' Mario said as they shook hands. 'Lucy said she wants to join a shooting club. I told her she can't and it hasn't gone down well.'

'You city people think women shouldn't shoot but shooting's an Australian tradition. Some women are pretty good at it. I reckon Lucy's gonna need to do something that gives her a challenge when she gets outta here. She's going to have a rough time, you know. Kids are bloody cruel little monsters. At my club you can have two heads, just so long as you can shoot well.'

'Maybe,' Mario nodded. He heard the wisdom in the other man's words but had yet to find out how cruel children could be.

'I look at it this way,' Mr McKenzie went on. 'We all make plans for our children, then somethin' happens that sends those plans out to the back paddock. For my father, it was the war. My Tom got burnt just like your Lucy, maybe not as badly, but we've got to adjust and accept that things aren't going to be quite as we had planned.'

The two men got into the habit of walking together in the garden, speaking if there was something to say, or just in companionable silence. 'I've been thinking,' Mario said one day 'and you're right. Lucy will need something to challenge her when she comes home. She enjoys competing and although I don't think it should be shooting, however, if it was where would I find a club in Sydney?'

'You could try the ANZAC Rifle Range at Malabar.' Noticing Mario's dark brows knitted in concentration, he added. 'Don't go worrying yet. She can't get a minor's licence till she's twelve and even with that she can't carry the rifle. She has to have a parent or guardian to do that for her, so you've got time to chew it over. Guns don't make killers, you know,' he added with a grin. 'All country kids have 'em and they don't go around shooting people.' He chuckled as they strolled.

A week after he had arrived Tom was well enough to leave

the hospital to be treated by his local doctor. His arms
would need continuing treatment and his hair would grow
back because the burns were not deep enough to damage
the follicles. By then Lucy was shooting brains and hearts
regularly and couldn't wait to join a club. She hadn't spoken
to her mother but hoped Mario would because she had
talked him into joining the shooting game and he was
shooting almost as well as Mr McKenzie. This made him
more sympathetic to the whole idea of shooting, even to
Lucy joining a club.

Mr McKenzie stopped beside Lucy's bed as they were
leaving. 'As soon as you're ready, come out to the farm and
stay with us. I'll let you use Tom's .22 at targets, not rabbits,
you tell your Mum.' He winked. Tom gave her his photo of
the white horse.

'So's you'll remember to come out and ride it,' he said
shyly.

A week later, six weeks after she was admitted, Lucy also
left the hospital.

LUCY

'Tell me about your return home.' Dr Singh says. I am used to my sessions with him now and quite enjoy them. 'How did it feel to be back with Yama and your family all sleeping under the same roof?'

I tell him it was disappointing. I had spent most of July to September, the winter months, in hospital and it was early spring when I came home but I wasn't allowed out in the sun. I couldn't sit on our little beach and the veranda reflected the sun's rays too much for me to sit there. Also, my legs were weak. I could hardly get up the stairs to my bedroom. I bled easily, so everyone avoided touching me in case they opened a new wound.

'What about being back in your own bedroom?'

'It was too quiet. I'd got used to the other kids and the noises in the hospital, so I found it frightening being alone. Some nights I didn't dare close my eyes. Daddy understood and worried, but Sarah did something positive to help. Daddy had put her bed into another room to give me privacy but as soon as she saw that I was unhappy being alone, she dragged her mattress into my room and stayed there on the floor until I could cope.'

'Did she help you in other ways?'

'She was terrific. She read to me. Gave me the gossip from school. Helped me with my studies, which I was doing at home until I was well enough to go back.'

'Was she going to parties at this stage?'

'Not actual parties but she went to sleepovers. I had to stay home to do my exercises and anyway I didn't want anyone

to see me without the pressure garments on. She bought lots of new clothes for herself.'

'How did you feel about her buying clothes?'

'Horrible. Just horrible. My skin was covered in scabs. I hated everything about myself. When she bought her first bra I cried for hours.'

'Did she show you everything she bought?'

'Of course.'

'How did that make you feel?'

'I liked seeing all the new fashions,' I said, not wanting to talk about clothes. Thinking about clothes made me sad, especially that bra, which was lacy and blood-red. I knew my left breast was too badly burnt to ever develop properly but the other one was growing and becoming soft. At the time I was still trying to understand and accept what problems I would have. 'I remember being upset when Sarah said I must not ever have any babies,' I told him.

'Did you ask your doctor about this?'

'No.'

'Why not?'

'Because Sarah said it wouldn't be fair for me to have a baby because I wouldn't have enough milk so its growth would be stunted. I didn't know whether it was true, and I was too young to have even thought about having a baby. I still don't understand why she said that because babies weren't something we talked about.'

'So why did you accept it and let it upset you?'

'I don't remember. I was easily upset back then. I wasn't talking to other girls. Mummy was too busy to spend much time with me so Sarah was my main contact for life, other girls, my future, how I would look – for everything really.

'Also I felt a bit sorry for Sarah. I was getting all the attention and I'd been reading how the sibling of a badly injured child can become introverted, even aggressive, because the other child gets all the attention. Mummy sort of understood and I think tried to pay more attention to Sarah.

'Daddy cared. He tried to be understanding but he didn't know the things girls in their early teens talked about.'

'Did he and Sarah ever fight?'

'Often. After I started back at school they would fight about her not walking home with me; her letting other kids tease me; her going to sleepovers and not taking me; all sorts of things. I appreciated his concern, but I suppose she needed his love too. I remember her screaming at Daddy, 'I can't watch her all the time. Do I have babysitter written across my forehead?' I felt guilty about these arguments but I needed them both so didn't get involved.

'Then one day she yelled at him. "What about me? Don't I even rate in this house?"' This upset Daddy terribly. He ran after her and hugged her and said he was sorry over and over again. He really did try but she never got over it.'

'Would you have gone on sleepovers if one of the girls had invited you?' Dr Singh asks.

'I was invited sometimes, but I didn't go. The only people I saw outside of school were Kylie from next door and Damon. Kylie became a close friend to me, but at that age she idolised Sarah. She'd buy the same clothes, use the same words, even straightened her hair so it would fall like Sarah's. If I was talking to Kylie and Sarah appeared, Kylie would turn to her with all the attention of an adoring puppy.'

'What about Damon?'

'He would come over with fascinating shells and we'd fish from the jetty at our little beach. He wouldn't come in if Sarah was home and if she came home while he was there, he'd leave as soon as he could.'

'Why?'

'He wouldn't say. Then he stopped coming altogether.'

'Did he say why?'

'Not then, but many years later he told me Sarah had told him to stop hanging around – that he wasn't good enough for our family. That he'd never be allowed to marry me.'

'What did you do when you heard this.'

'It was years later and so many other things had happened between us that it didn't matter.'

CHAPTER 11

During Lucy's first few months back at home Yama avoided her, disconcerted by the new scents about her body; kids at school taunted her; strangers on the street would try not to stare but were so curious they couldn't help themselves. One woman stopped in her tracks when she saw Lucy sitting with the car window open and the pressure garment encasing her head. The woman was so intrigued she caught up with her friend and made her come back to have a look. Lucy felt subhuman, like some creature in a zoo.

Returning to school had not been as difficult as Lucy had feared it would be. Jane had visited the school before she left the hospital to explain to the students and teachers how burns affected the body. She had shown them a pressure garment and Jobst collar and explained why Lucy would be wearing them. She had explained to them that Lucy would be emotionally fragile. That she would need lots of kindness and help to regain her confidence. Most of the students took everything Jane had said to heart and were caring, but there were those who whispered "Kentucky Fried" and "Smith's Crisps" behind hands when Lucy was near enough to hear.

'You must learn to ignore these things,' Jane said.

'How can I?' Lucy retorted. 'What do I have to live for? It's okay for old people, they've had their lives. I haven't. I'll never have a boyfriend, never have a baby, can't wear short sleeves, can't swim, can't go out in the sun.'

'You'll be surprised Lucy. It'll all get better. What you're feeling now is because you are still wearing the pressure garment and having treatment. You can't see it ever ending. But it does end and you will wear beautiful clothes, you will drive a car and go to university and make lots of friends.

And, because you're strong and intelligent, you'll get a good job and fall in love.'

Jane stopped to let Lucy absorb this information. 'I've seen it all before. For now, you simply have to be patient and work at it.'

But Lucy slid inexorably into depression. She longed for extra attention but didn't know how to ask for it so sought it from her dolls, crushing them into her chest and piling them all under the blankets with her at night.

Walking home from school one day, Lucy began to cry. Through misty eyes, she watched her feet appear and disappear. First one foot came into view, flopped down and disappeared under her skirt, then the other foot appeared flopped down and disappeared under her skirt. On and on. Never changing. Her shoulders drooped, her hands hung down at her sides and she let her bag bounce over the uneven footpath. At home her footsteps echoed through the empty house as she called out to see if anyone was home. There was no response.

She knew Sarah had gone to see a friend's newly decorated bedroom but had expected Mario would home. He must have gone into the newspaper office she thought as she flopped onto her bed and stared at the wall, listening to the silence.

What's happening to me? She thought as self-pity flowed through her like dirty water. I'm drowning and nobody cares. One day I'll disappear and no one will even notice.

Lucy tucked up her knees and rocked. She let the sobs out; let them wrench at her body, tear at her throat and screw up her toes. After about an hour she was exhausted and a quiet peace slipped into the room. After weeks of pain, the torrent of emotion had washed her clean. She could smell the gum trees outside her window and hear the birds in the trees.

Lucy looked slowly around. Nothing had changed. The posters of cats and wild animals were still on the walls.

Clothes were still in messy heaps that annoyed her parents, and piles of books were still teetering in the corner. She had dumped her schoolbag near the door and Yama was crouched beside it watching her with his tawny eyes. He had heard her crying and come upstairs to investigate.

'Oh Yama, please come. Let me cuddle you.' He hesitated then rose up stretching, and walked tentatively across the room to sniff at her feet. Then he jumped onto her lap and pushed his nose into her hand as if nothing had ever been different.

Lucy cried with relief as she stroked his dark-brown fur. It was months since she had felt his panther-like body. As he stretched and squirmed under her hand, a stillness entered her soul and she knew her life was about to improve.

That was when she saw the piece of paper pinned to the end of her bedspread. It was torn from her father's sketchpad.

Hi Lucy.

Home six. All going pizza tonight – tell Sarah. Sat morn you-me visit Tom at Camden.

Love you.

Under the words was a cartoon of a young girl surrounded by farm animals and a big white horse.

CHAPTER 12

After the first visit with Mario, Lucy spent as many weekends as she could at the farm and blended comfortably into the fabric of the McKenzies' easy-going country life. She learnt how to herd sheep and cows, how to work the dogs, and how to tell when the hay was ready for bailing. She rose early to help with the milking. She even put the old white horse over simple jumps. Some evenings, Mrs McKenzie showed her how to bake a roast and small cakes. These evenings helping in the kitchen filled a need she had to feel she mattered and was worthy of affection.

Initially, Daisy and Pixie followed her around wide-eyed with a mixture of fear and curiosity. Tom always wore long-sleeved shirts to protect the scars on his arms and a hat to protect his head, but his burns had not been so bad that he ever needed to wear a pressure garment. To the five- and six-year-old girls Lucy, in her pressure garment, looked utterly weird. They would giggle behind their hands and run away screaming if she turned to look at them. Mrs McKenzie was too busy to keep calling them away and they took no notice of Tom, so Lucy devised a plan to get them to like her.

One evening after dinner Lucy went into their bedroom, sat down on one of the beds and told them a story. 'Once upon a time there was a pretty young girl who was burnt when a log fell out of the fire. She suffered terrible pain from the burns and became very sad. She was also very lonely because other girls wouldn't talk to her. Then one day she met two little girls who were blind. They couldn't see her face so they weren't frightened of her, but they could hear the magical stories she told. Every night they would sit beside her, so close they were touching, and beg for another story. And the pretty young girl with the terrible scars started to smile again because now she had friends who loved her.'

'That's you and us,' squeaked Daisy. 'But we're not blind.'

'I know, but if you were, you wouldn't be frightened of me and I could tell you my magical stories.'

'Do you know magical stories?' Pixie asked, sliding around the doorframe.

'Have you heard the magical story about the little boy who lives on a star and slides down the rainbow to visit his friends on earth?'

The girls shook their heads as they edged in closer.

'His name is Bobsy and one day he slid down a rainbow and landed at a little town called Camden near the big city of Sydney. He had never landed on earth before and ...' Bobsy's adventures mesmerised them. By the time Lucy finished Daisy and Pixie were sitting at her feet.

'Do you think Bobsy will come to our farm one day?' Daisy asked, eyes wide with hope.

'Don't be silly. Bobsy isn't real.' Pixie said. Even though she liked to act the big sister, she wanted to hear more about Bobsy too. 'Could you tell us another one?'

'Not tonight because you have to go to bed now. But next time I'm here I'll tell you what Bobsy did when he met a cow for the first time.'

On her weekend visits Lucy took Daisy and Pixie all over the world with the adventures of Bobsy. They visited children in other countries, rode trains up mountains, explored shipwrecks, met his rainbow friends Twinkle, Tweak and Tinsel.

Every evening, in the satiny twilight before dinner and story time, Mr McKenzie would unlock the gun safe and take Lucy and Tom out to shoot rabbits. At first, she refused to take the rifle. She watched their long furry ears and soft twitching noses through the binoculars. She admired the way one always stood guard to warn the others of approaching danger.

Mr McKenzie took her to areas where their burrows honeycombed the land and caused serious erosion. He showed her where they ate the tender young shoots of new grass so it never had a chance to grow tall enough to feed the farm animals.

'We don't shoot them for fun,' he told her, 'but there are so many. If we don't, the grass won't be able to grow to feed our cows and sheep. And remember, Lucy, we always check, we never leave any injured and hurting.'

His favourite saying was 'a good shooter is a clean shooter and a clean shooter is a controlled shooter'. He said it so often, Lucy and Tom would wait for it, then grin at each other. He saw their antics, but he repeated his mantra because he liked teaching them.

'It's important to wiggle your feet until you're well balanced and comfortable; and stay calm. That's it, steady breaths, not too deep, concentrate.'

To teach them how to stay in control he would get them to choose a rabbit and wait, gun barrel facing the ground, until he gave the signal to fire. Tom usually became too excited, but Lucy had learnt to endure. Her burns were deeper and covered more of her body than his. The discipline of the exercises, the taunts, the staring strangers and the never-ending pain had taught her to isolate her thoughts. When doing her exercises every day she had learnt to focus and exclude pain.

'I have peace at the farm,' she told Damon one evening as they sat on the jetty fishing. 'I'm away from staring eyes. I'm learning to live with this body and they like me,' she said feeling tears welling.

He took her hand gently and said softly, 'I like you too Lucy.'

When Mr McKenzie told her to think of nothing but the target, that is what she did. She was an extraordinarily controlled shooter. He sometimes had misgivings about this. He knew from his experiences in Vietnam that cold calculated control could be as destructive as it was advantageous.

But he never foresaw the dangerous places it would take Lucy.

CHAPTER 13

As Mary pushed through the well-worn gap in the hedge and up the steps onto the Borgetti's veranda, her heart skipped a beat. Mario was sitting in his old rocking chair leaning forward, tapping the tips of his fingers against each other. Silver threads in his thick, dark hair glistened where the sun touched them. How his broad shoulders had thinned since Lucy's accident. Mary's soft heart reached out to him and she longed to take him in her arms.

'You're brooding again,' she said as she handed over a cup of freshly brewed coffee. Since Lucy had come home from the hospital Mary had slipped easily into the habit of baking a cake or biscuits for the Borgetti household. 'I've only got Kylie to care for as James is away on navy manoeuvres most of the time,' she had said to dispel their objections.

'It's eighteen months and she's still struggling to work out where she fits,' Mario sighed. 'She can't swim. She is out of the netball team. The kids either tease her, ignore her, or are embarrassed by her and Damon seems to have faded from the scene. She loves the farm but there's no future for her there. If only I hadn't fallen asleep in front of that damn fire.'

'Not that guilt trip again, please,' Mary said. 'Jane's told you it's counterproductive.' Mary couldn't count the number of times they'd had this discussion.

Jill was travelling overseas more often now she had *The Teenager* up and running, along with a New Zealand-based lifestyle magazine. She also went to head office in New York every few months. Mario knew she loved the travel, but it left him with most of the responsibility for Lucy's treatment and tantrums. He was also finding Sarah's surly attitude to him puzzling and annoying.

'What is it this time?'

'Another skin graft. Apparently, she didn't do her exercises properly and the skin hasn't stretched enough for her left arm to move freely. She's begging me not to make her go through it, but what can I do?'

'Just comfort her. She's smart and knows it has to be done. I'm surprised though. I thought she was very conscientious about doing the exercises.'

'I thought so too. But maybe they were never going to be enough.'

They sipped their coffee in silence. Clouds overhead made shadowy patterns on the harbour and myna birds stalked through the grass. Summer's mugginess was damp on their skin and Mario's maleness seeped into Mary's consciousness.

'James gets home on Friday,' she said to dispel her unease. 'He's in town for six days. Would you all to come over for a barbecue on Saturday night?'

'Jill gets back from New Zealand on Friday, too, so Saturday works out well.'

He accepted that Jill often had to go overseas for her job, but he missed her. He missed the light touch of her fingers playing over his when they sat on the veranda to chat quietly as they watched the activity on the harbour. He twirled the coffee mug and thought back to how they came to own this house. Jill's parents had wanted to give them a house as a wedding gift, but his pride had bristled at the thought. He recalled saying this was a ridiculously expensive idea, that he was to be the man in the family and he would provide the home. He smiled when he remembered how Jill had convinced him that if he chose the suburb and the house, and her parents merely provided the money, then it would really be his. She was exquisite, very persuasive, and he was very much in love so, he caved in.

They chose this house for its classic lines, grand old trees standing tall in a bushy garden, and the little sweep of sandy beach at the edge of the harbour. The house was grander than he would have liked but he had consoled himself that the Balmain peninsula had started as a working-class area with a coal mine and ship repair yards.

Mario thought of how much Jill's mother had hated it, or maybe it was more the fact that it was a suburb on the *south* side of the harbour that she hated. Jill, in her inimitable style, had said: 'If you don't like it Mother, don't buy it. I'll get a loan.'

It reminded him of the time just after they had moved in together and Jill had sat up one morning after a passionate romp and said, 'I want to meet your mother'.

He had hesitated. 'I don't think that's a good idea.'

'Why?'

'Well ...' he had said, giving himself time to think. How could he tell her about his uncles and aunts and cousins who had already chosen the nice Italian girl he would marry. His people were not in Jill's class.

'I know what you're thinking,' Jill had said, sitting up and looking down at him with her steely green eyes. 'You think my rich family won't like your Italian family and you're right. But it's me talking. It's me who wants to meet your mother. It's the 1980s so stop over-thinking and arrange it.'

'Bossy bitch.'

'Get used to it. You know I'll always be the boss and you'll love me for it.'

He smiled as he remembered those words and how true they were. He had loved her so much its depth made him weak.

Yes, it would be nice to go next door for a barbecue. James always appeared rather formidable with his straight back and severe mouth, but he was good company and an intelligent sparring partner for Jill. Mario looked forward to an interesting night.

CHAPTER 14

James was pleased Mary had invited the Borgettis over. There would be lively conversation and it was good to have a break from official functions. He considered himself a good barbecue cook and was humming contentedly as he skewered prawns and scallops for the entree. He had sugar-cured a large fillet of steak for main course. Mary and Kylie were doing the salads and dessert. He cooked with the same precision he ran his ship – in neat lines, turned once only.

As he lined up the prawns, the last rays of sun warmed his skin and the contented hum of leisure boats heading home filled the air. James looked up at a swishing sound and watched Jill sashaying through the gap in the hedge between their houses. He had always had an eye for a good-looking woman. Mary had her mother's pale skin and soft brown eyes that reflected her moods in a way he found charming, but she was short, barely reaching his armpit, and a little overweight. She was more maternal than Jill, whose elegance always sent a tingle through him.

Tonight, Jill was wearing a simple towelling ankle-length black dress. A thin green scarf hung loosely around her neck and floated down her back. Her red toenails were like rubies in gold sandals and she wore no jewellery to detract from the impact of her green eyes above the scarf.

'Champagne in crystal for the lady with emerald eyes,' he said as she kissed him on both cheeks.

'Thank you.' She let her eyes linger on his as she raised her glass. Her mother would have liked her to marry a man like James. Handsome, urbane, socially well connected.

'And what part of the world have you been shooting up lately,' she teased lightly.

'None, my fair lady. We went to the Philippines to discuss tactics with the Americans and play war games with the Kiwis. And ...' He let the word hang in the air. 'I met the amazing Mrs Marcos.'

'Impressive. Was she as charming as they say?'

'Absolutely. Whatever else they may say about her she knows how to charm. And I took special note ... she does wear beautiful shoes.'

'Do I hear malicious gossip?' Mario slipped an arm around Jill's waist. 'Who is it this time?'

Straightening up from the oven Mary looked outside and thought how different the two men were. James was so cultivated and confident, Mario so passionate and handsome but a bit naïve.

Mary had met James in a pub in Ireland. He had come in with a group of navy cadets bursting with noise and bluster. He was lanky and blue eyed, and she was in love before closing time. He came and went for two years before he proposed. Mary knew he loved her before that, but he needed to assess her suitability as wife of the admiral he intended to become before he proposed.

They married in Ireland then settled in Sydney but, as the oldest of a boisterous family of six children growing up in a village with numerous relatives and neighbours, she was lonely in Australia. He was away a lot and her dream of several children, a dog, family picnics and holidays with friends didn't happen. She became quiet and pensive.

'You're daydreaming and everyone's starving,' Kylie said as she burst into the kitchen, her small pale face flushed. 'I've set the table under the frangipani tree and it looks gorgeous. The drinks and glasses are on the table on the veranda. I've seated Dad at the top with you and Jill on either side,' she said, giving her mother a quick hug as she picked up a salad to take outside to put on the table.

'You're sitting beside me,' she told Sarah, 'and Mario and Lucy are on the other side'.

'Can girls join the navy?' Sarah asked over dinner, looking along the table at James and visualising herself standing straight and courageous beside him on the deck of a big grey battleship, her braided captain's hat low over her eyes.

'Don't even think about it,' Jill answered before James could speak. 'It's not the career for you.'

'That's hardly fair.' James pretended to be prickled but he was used to women of Jill's social class thinking the navy was not for their daughters. 'Women in the navy have the same opportunities as men.'

'Name one female captain in our navy, or any navy for that matter,' Jill taunted.

'There will be,' James answered easily. 'Just give us time to get used to the idea. We're already training a few.'

'Said like a man.' The journalist in Jill was stirred. 'And what about the sexual harassment charges I've been reading about. Maybe there's a story in there for my magazine.'

James thought about stopping before he got in too deep but a favourable article in a leading lady's magazine would be excellent publicity. 'The navy's a bit sensitive about journalists but I could organise a visit. I'd have to get it cleared, but it's possible.'

'I would have to have complete freedom to speak to whomever I choose. And the women would have to be free to say whatever they liked without fear of reprisal.'

'Of course. We happen to have a two-day manoeuvre coming up. You could experience life on board firsthand,' James said. He would give her the run of the ship because he would choose the women to be rostered on.

'Jill wouldn't go. She'd send a staff writer,' Mario butted in. He didn't like the idea of Jill alone with James on a ship at sea.

'I'd need to bring a photographer,' Jill said, ignoring Mario's comment.

'Why would you go?' Mario snapped. 'You don't have time to spend two nights on a navy ship at sea.'

'It's my job,' Jill retorted, raising an eyebrow at Mario.

'Since when did the editor take on a job like that?'

Jill opened her mouth to reply but changed her mind. Mario had been touchy lately and had lost quite a bit of weight. 'You're right. Felicity would do a good job on a story like this.'

'Have you thought anymore about letting Lucy join a rifle club?' Mary asked to change the subject.

'Do you want to take up shooting?' James asked, looking down the table at Lucy. 'We've got men who are natural shots and others who couldn't hit the Opera House if it was ten metres away.'

Lucy told him about the shooting game with Tom McKenzie in hospital and how his father said she had a 'good eye'.

'But it's not for Lucy,' Jill said sharply.

'Like the navy isn't,' James said, with a wink at Lucy. 'Don't get me wrong Jill but I think Lucy could surprise you. For someone so young to go through what she has, and still be sane, says a lot. She has more steel in her than you realise.'

'She does need something,' Jill agreed as she thought back over the months since Lucy had come home from hospital – Lucy home alone while Sarah was out with her crowd shopping, coffee, boys, etcetera. All the steel in the world isn't going to help where boys are concerned, she thought.

'Why not let her give it a go?' James said. 'It can't do any harm and might do a lot of good.' James watched Jill tossing the idea around in her head. Pity about that altercation with Mario he thought. I would have found it interesting to have her on the ship for a couple of days.

'It's worth a try,' Jill said, turning to a stunned Mario. 'You could take her to that club Neil McKenzie told you about.'

CHAPTER 15

Lucy could hardly sit still as they left the clogged inner-city area and drove south through suburb after suburb of neat houses with tidy fences and mown lawns to the Malabar rifle range, a large open space adjacent to one of the wild ocean beaches of the southern suburbs. At long last – after much pleading and begging – she would see a fullbore rifle. Mr McKenzie had told her it was so heavy she would have to lie on the ground to aim it.

Sarah didn't share Lucy's enthusiasm for shooting but had come along rather than be left out.

As they approached Malabar they could see the long sandy beach with the surf rolling in. Slim figures carrying surfboards along the sand dunes appeared as dark silhouettes against the bright-blue backdrop of sky and sea.

The rifle range spread across a huge expanse of grass and scrub – its entrance a dirt track with a rickety gate.

'Look, the targets.' Mario said as he pointed to what looked like a row of small letterboxes along the top of a grassy ridge.

Lucy stared. They were so far away. How could a bullet travel that far?

'Look out, live targets!' Sarah squealed as a string of ponies trotted out from a row of bushes in front of them. 'Can you believe that? A pony club on a rifle range.'

Mario parked beside a cluster of old buildings which appeared to be deserted with most of the doors and windows boarded up. Grass was growing out of cracks in the concrete path, but this was where he'd been told to go, so he led the girls along the rows of buildings until he saw a faint light glowing from a doorway that was not boarded up. Peering in he could see a crumbling stone staircase which he went down into a basement dim with age and mould, its walls lined with the paraphernalia of shooters.

'Can I help?' He jumped in fright as a thin man with the stiff back of an old soldier emerged from a dingy back room.

'We're looking for the Besley Rifle Club,' Mario said.

'There are approximately thirty clubs here, sir.' The man waved for him to follow as he climbed stiffly up the stairs Mario had just come down. 'The one you want is over there in D Block. Each club has its name on its door.' He smiled thinly at Lucy and Sarah then turned and retreated down the stairs.

'Back to his lair the wily fox went,' Sarah said, rolling her eyes at his departing back.

'He looks like a soldier left over from when the army owned this range,' Mario said with a chuckle.

They found the Besley Rifle Club and entered a room where a big man with bright eyes under bushy eyebrows and a small plain- looking woman were sitting behind an old wooden table that was cluttered with piles of paper. Antiquated office machinery added to the clutter. The man, who looked to be in his sixties, rose and approached them, his hand outstretched.

'George,' he said with a welcoming smile. 'Can I help you?'

Mario shook his knobbly hand. 'We want to enquire about joining, getting a license and so on.'

'Certainly, certainly.' George beamed. 'We're always in need of new members.'

While they talked, Lucy directed Sarah over to the table across which lay a huge rifle. 'Look at the size of that, imagine how big the bullets must be.'

'That's a fullbore,' George said, interrupting his conversation with Mario. He recognised the pressure garment over the girl's head as the sort of mask worn by people who had been badly burnt. 'You'd like to see the size of its ammo, eh? By law we have to store it separately from the rifles ... wait a sec and I'll get a box.'

Even Sarah was impressed. The rifle was much bigger than she had expected.

George brought over a box of ammo and Lucy lifted out a cartridge and held it up. She liked the cool smoothness of the brass case. She let the cartridge drop into the palm of her hand. It felt heavy and powerful.

'Can I have a go now?' she asked Mario.

'Sorry, lassie,' George replied. 'You can't shoot on the range until you have a license and you need to be twelve. If you don't fill both these categories, you'd get me into trouble if an inspector came along.'

'But I can shoot. I've been shooting for a year ... longer.'

'It doesn't quite work like that.' But George was delighted with her enthusiasm. 'Take this safety awareness handbook and study it to get your license. Then come back here and you can start shooting.'

'But I know the safety rules.' Lucy was indignant. 'Mr McKenzie taught me.'

'I've got an idea,' George said, winking at Mario. 'The afternoon competition starts at one o'clock. Come back then and I'll show you what we do.'

When they returned, there was a scraggly line of cars, 4WDs and utes behind the 400-metre firing mound. George introduced them to various club members and gave them canvas stools to sit on while he went off to shoot.

Lucy paced up and down absorbing the activity, the smells, the shooters lying beside their rifles, and the spectators and competitors milling about. Most were men in bulky jackets and peaked caps. They compared rifles, peered through sights, studied scorecards, gossiped, sipped mugs of coffee, sat on stools or stood, legs apart, arms crossed, eyes squinting. When their turn came they went to their shooting position and fired their rounds.

A girl who looked to be in her twenties sauntered by with her black hair pulled back into a ponytail that swung out from the back of her cap. A rifle in a sling was hanging down, loosely looped over one arm. Lucy watched her stop to speak to a boy about the same age.

Lucy knew she had found her new sport.

'The person sitting on the stool beside each shooter is the score taker,' George said when he returned. 'Each shooter uses a telescope to see where the last shot went and decide what changes he needs to make for the next shot.' He handed Lucy a telescope. 'Watch the target. After each shot, the spotter in the safety ditch pulls it down and puts a marker where the projectile went through; watch and you'll see it come back up with the marker on. By the way, we call them projectiles, not bullets,' he said.

George handed Mario a rifle from the table and a set of earmuffs. 'Come on mate. Your turn.'

Envy and excitement flowed through Lucy as she watched them walk to the line of shooters. Her father wiggled into a comfortable position, slipped a cartridge into the breech, took aim and shot. Through the telescope she watched the target go down, then come back up and could see the red marker near the edge of the target. His next shot went through the bullseye and she shuddered as though it had entered her body.

When he had finished, Mario rose and walked triumphantly back to the row of cars. He was so busy grinning at Sarah that he didn't see Lucy creep around behind him and fall onto the ground he had left warm.

'Please,' she begged, her eyes owl-like in the pressure garment as she looked sideways at George still lying where he had been beside Mario. He realised immediately what she was doing, grinned and gave a tiny nod of agreement.

The barrel of the heavy rifle rested on a sandbag and she snuggled the butt into her shoulder as Mr McKenzie had taught her. Along the sights she could see the bullseye, small, black and beckoning. Through the ground she could feel the crack of other rifles going off.

It didn't matter that there was no cartridge in place. She

closed her eyes and, in her mind's eye, squeezed the trigger. The target went down then came up with the red marker shining in the centre – a V-bull. She heard muffled clapping from behind as her loyal team celebrated yet another winning shot from their emerging champion. When she opened her eyes, George gave her a subtle thumbs-up. It was a long time since he had seen so much excitement and burning ambition in such a young person.

LUCY

I am so agitated. I take another look at the little clock. Sarah should be at the lights at the Post Office corner by now, but she won't look up at the clock to check the time. She'll have it worked out to the split second.

And she'll be chic. She always is. I'm wearing jeans and a white cotton shirt with the collar flicked up … a combination I wear so often it's like a uniform. Should I change into something smarter? I peer into my small wardrobe to see if there is something else I could wear, but I'm comfortable in this.

This impulse to change out of clothes I feel comfortable in takes me back to when I was still wearing the pressure garments. After I left the hospital Jane, the social worker, would visit me at home and often said I was hiding behind them. About this time, I also realised I was missing school excursions because I didn't want to undress in front of other kids.

When I did finally bare my skin in front of another person, it changed my life. There was a school Adventure Weekend to the Blue Mountains that I desperately wanted to go to. Damon was not going because he didn't like sleeping crammed into a tent with other boys. Sarah and Kylie said they would shield me from other kids in the dormitory but I had fretted over it for days. It was Jane who finally convinced me.

'For the rest of your life you will meet people who can accept you the way you are and people who can't,' she had said. 'It's time to prepare yourself to walk away from those who

can't and befriend those who can. You're at the stage, Lucy, where you need to let someone outside the family see your scars. What about Kylie? She's been close to you through everything.'

I remember screeching at Jane. 'What do you expect me to do? Stand in front of her and open up my blouse? She'd freak out.'

Jane of course had heard it all before. 'You'd freak out too, the first time you saw something a bit strange,' she had said. 'But only the first time. You'll be amazed at how quickly others will get used to you. Remember what I've told you; it's the unknown that intrigues.'

I had developed complete trust in Jane's judgement and maybe it was time for that little push. I agreed on the spot, knowing that if I thought about it for too long I'd say no. I always needed a bit of a push to make decisions back then. But I knew enough to lay down a few rules: 'Just her and me, in my room, on a Friday night so there is no school the next day.' I didn't want it fresh in her mind when she was at school.

Kylie was nervous but proud I'd chosen her.

Before the designated Friday night, Jane had a meeting with Kylie and Mary to explain how my showing myself to Kylie would help me to move on. Kylie told me later that Jane had shown them photos of me throughout my treatment and had coached her a little on what to say and how to act.

It's strange looking back on the "F" night, as we called it. I was sitting on my bed all, the pressure garments off but clothes on. Mummy and Daddy had gone next door to Mary's for drinks. Sarah was sleeping over at a friend's place.

Kylie looked around nervously as she walked into the room. I literally jumped up and whipped off my blouse. It was the fatalistic act of a person full of defiance before a firing squad. I shudder now when I think of the shock for dear Kylie. My left arm, shoulder and chest were covered in a hard crocodile-like skin that was cracked and always seeping or bleeding from some small knock. My left breast was flat and crinkled and there was no nipple.

Kylie went rigid and I thought she was going to scream, but Jane had coached her well. 'I didn't expect it would look quite like that,' she stammered, forcing her eyes to keep looking at me.

Jane had coached her to show interest and encourage me to talk, so she did. 'What about your head?' She let her eyes leave my chest and up to the long blond wig I wore back then. I had planned to leave it on, but in a rash moment of 'what the hell', I wrenched it off and flicked it onto the bed beside the blouse.

'Will you always have to wear a wig?' she asked politely.

'Yes,' I replied just as politely.

'What fun. You'll be able to buy lots of different styles and change the colour whenever you like.'

As she began to relax, Kylie asked more personal questions, like could I smile? This was something that really worried me so I had been working extra hard on the face exercises – stretching the skin by making big oohs and moving my jaw like a man shaving. Most of my facial skin would move now but it was weirdly smooth, and the outside corner of my eyelid drooped horribly. I still hid behind the face mask, as people called it, but eventually all the pressure garments would have to go.

Kylie asked about the exercises, movement, bathing, the pain and so on until I was pouring it all out. I told her about the hospital, Damon bringing in the shell, Nonna's cakes, buying wigs, the teasing, boys, babies, things I hadn't even told Sarah. It surged out of me as I stormed around the room, wailing and crying, full of pain and self-pity that had built up since the fire.

'Look at me; I'm so ugly no one will ever marry me.'

I still wonder how that night would have ended if Kylie, in her most gentle and caring voice hadn't said: 'Of course you will. Everyone gets married … even funny looking people.'

As that last sentence came out she realised how terrible it sounded and she froze. I froze too. The words were awful but hearing them said so softly, without malice, diluted their impact and I started to giggle.

'That's so awful, Kylie, even Mr Bean wouldn't say that.'

I will always remember her look ... anxious and alarmed. Then she started to giggle and we couldn't stop. We became so weak with giggles we fell on the floor and held hands.

That night taught me so much about myself, about coping, about facing my future.

CHAPTER 16

Mary and Jill had agreed to be chaperones at the Blue Mountains Adventure Weekend but the night before they were due to leave, the computers at Jill's office crashed. 'I have to be there,' she said. 'I'm the only one who can get the computers sorted out and call in extra staff for the catch-up work. I'm sorry girls but this means I can't go to the mountains this weekend.'

'Daddy you'll have to come, the school won't go without enough chaperones,' Lucy begged.

'Don't be silly. They'll find a replacement and you've got Sarah and Kylie.'

'They don't know what to do. I can't do it without Mummy or you.' Lucy's eyes filled with tears and her bottom lip began to quiver. 'Who'll take my ointments and things? Mummy was going to bring them in our car.'

'Mary can take them in her car.'

'But she doesn't know what to do. Daddy I need you, please.'

'Other fathers are going,' Sarah said as she entered the room and took in the situation. 'It won't be easy to replace Jill this late. You could drive up with Mary.' She felt Lucy silently thanking her.

Mario hesitated. He had listened to the girls talking about this weekend for days and he wanted Lucy to do it. He believed it was the breakthrough she needed. It was also going to be a rare weekend at home alone for him that he was looking forward to.

'Please,' Lucy begged.

His heart melted along with his willpower as Sarah put an arm around Lucy.

The next day Mario and Mary loaded their gear into his Alfa Romeo and headed for the mountains. Rain earlier in the week had cleared the air of its cloying summer haze and the sun's rays glittered along the edges of the hills as they zig-zagged up and up, through villages that had sprung up last century. As Mario's Alfa Romeo zipped along the winding road he opened the windows to let fresh air toss at their hair. He pulled over at a lay-by so they could stretch their legs and admire the view.

'Aren't we lucky to live in such a city?' He gave a deep sigh of contentment as he arched his back. 'Look at that, a green canopy of trees screening the suburban developments all the way to the sea. Fantastic.'

'It's lovely.' Mary was relieved to get out of the car, which put her disturbingly close to him. When they set off again, his smell and the tenor of his voice each time he burst forth into song went through her like quivering fire. His lightness of mood made her want to throw back her head and laugh and sing along with him. She was tempted to reach over and stroke his brown fingers but instead forced her eyes to look out the window.

They drove through villages with houses that were built for the railway workers when the line was being laid but were now a home or business for a new era of retirees, city escapees, gallery and restaurant owners, antique and craft shops. Gorges gouged out by nature on both sides of the road fell away into valleys of dark-green trees with slashes of pale earth exposed by landslides and weather.

'I'd like to buy a house up here, but Jill won't leave the city,' Mario mused.

Mary was so on edge that his voice made her jump and squeal with shock. He looked across, surprised. In that split second, he saw the longing in her warm brown eyes, the softness of her body and her parted lips. Heat spread through his groin as his brain screamed, 'No, please no.'

He turned his eyes back to the road and drove as though

he could outrun this force that had just entered his life and threatened to destroy it. His senses were on fire. Her fragrance was so sweet and feminine. He could hear her breathing and her heart beating; or was it his? He would not let it happen.

His father had cheated on his mother before he left her with a baby and no financial support. His father had never visited his son. His father had denied his son the Italian family life his cousins enjoyed. He had vowed he would never do to his wife and children what his father had done to him and his mother.

Mario knew the situations were different. Jill never had to scrimp and save to put food on the table as his mother had, and the twins were older, but he could never forget the years he had spent watching the streets, seeking his father's face among the crowd, stepping off a bus or driving a car. He was well into his teens when his mother told him she didn't know whether his father was alive or dead.

Mary knew all this. She had watched him being the best father he could with Lucy and Sarah. She knew he loved Jill. She had long treasured her secret love for him, satisfying it with their neighbourly closeness and visits through the fence. She stared fixedly out the window wondering how she would get through the next two days.

CHAPTER 17

The coach which the students travelled in was already in the car park beside the camping ground when Mario turned in. He jumped out quickly and looked out across the rows of tents, hoping to see one of the girls. He saw a river sparkling at the base of a cliff with kids paddling and lots of movement among the tents but could not see Lucy, Sarah or Kylie.

'It's huge,' Mary said as she rose awkwardly from the low sports car. 'And it's already set up. Are we late?'

'No. I read in the information sheets the school sent out that all the camping, cooking, transport and abseiling was being organised by a specialist outdoor adventure company. 'It said there would be thirty kids, roughly half boys. We, the chaperones, just have to make sure they behave themselves.'

By mid-afternoon everyone had put their bags into their assigned tent and the leader of the outdoor company called them together at the long wooden dining tables. 'Welcome,' she said. 'I'm Kirsty your leader for the weekend and this is Harry my gorgeous assistant.' She laughed as the girls twittered and giggled. Harry was 185 centimetres tall, had deeply tanned sinewy arms and legs, slim hips, broad shoulders and a wicked smile.

'She looks too young to be our leader,' Mary whispered to Mario. 'I doubt she's had her twenty-first birthday and she's very slight.'

'Hm but she's an outdoor girl. Look at those strong shoulders and the short no-nonsense hairstyle.'

'Okay, kids into the coach and chaperones please follow in your cars. We're going to our shop in Katoomba village to get you all kitted out. It's chock-a-block with abseiling gear so please do as we say and we'll get this bit over as quickly as possible.'

Sarah led the way into the shop and came out rattling like a horse in harness, but Lucy stood back. She hadn't put on her face mask and the hat she had pulled down hard over her forehead didn't cover her face as much as she had hoped. Mary was also having her doubts but gave in when Kylie begged her to join in.

'This is the karabiner and this the descender,' Kirsty said as she buckled leather straps around Mary's waist and up between her legs.

With everyone in harness they piled back into the coach and were driven to a lightly treed area away from the village. Mary joked nervously as they all clanked in single file through tall wheat-coloured grass to a clearing where huge grey boulders lay scattered about like giant's marbles. Here Kirsty told them to divide themselves into two groups and Mario quickly gathered Mary and the three girls around him so they could stay together. The other group was led away by two other members of the outdoor company to a different pile of boulders.

Harry explained the safety rules then climbed up onto a boulder about the size of a two-storey house and demonstrated how to sit back into the rope 'so it takes your weight as you walk backwards down to the ground'.'

'Harry will stay below as our belayer – your safety valve,' Kirsty said. 'If anything happens on the way down he'll pull the rope, which will make the descender clamp shut on the rope and hold you safely until you're ready to move on again. Any questions?'

'Will we be abseiling down real cliffs or just these boulders,' Sarah asked, looking scornfully at a group of boys standing at the back, behind the girls

'Oh no, you have some serious cliffs coming up,' Kirsty replied. 'But first let's get you sitting back securely into your harness on the backwards walk. Okay, who's going first?' Sarah stepped forward.

They practised on the big boulder a few times, then went to a rock jutting out over a cave where they were shown how to drop down from top of the rock to the ground below without swinging about and banging their heads. Lucy did it all with quiet determination, thrilled that she could do it without needing to use her damaged left arm and hand.

'Okay that's it, all into the coach and back to the camp for a big cook up,' Kirsty called after a couple of hours. 'Tomorrow we'll go to the "real" cliffs as our champ Sarah calls them.' Kirsty waved at Sarah who was helping Harry gather up the ropes and other abseiling paraphernalia.

Mario was delighted to see Lucy outside without her pressure garments – but nothing could quell his inner turmoil over Mary. She's one of us, virtually part of our family, he thought as he watched Mary doggedly abseiling down the rocks.

That night Mary went to bed soon after dinner, pleading tiredness.

Mario stayed up until the all the students were in their tents then he walked over to the river. 'She is part of our family,' he told himself. 'My sounding board when Jill is away.' He thought of the many times she had put her arms around him, how he had perceived her kindness as neighbourly or a sign of the nurse in her. As he walked on, he reassessed those times. Do I enjoy her company more than I should? In the privacy of the moment he admitted that he did like the softness of her body against his when she put her arms around him.

The next morning they practised on a few medium-size cliffs until morning tea when Kirsty said: 'Okay you're ready to abseil the "real" cliffs above the sprawling Hartley Valley and we need some volunteers to help set up the ropes.'

Sarah called Lucy over. 'Let's walk along the ridge to see where we're going over.' Over dinner last night she had realised that Harry was more interested in Kirsty than her, so she was not going to help anymore. 'Look,' Sarah pointed to a body leaning over the cliff just in front of them.

It was Jack, one of the boys in their class. 'He could easily fall over,' Sarah whispered.

Lucy was about to call out a warning when Sarah's hand closed over her mouth. 'Don't be silly. Think of all the awful things he's been saying about your face. Wouldn't you like to see him go over?'

Lucy looked at Jack's stiff brown hair sticking out, grey with dust. If she were capable of hating anyone, it was Jack.

'Just a tiny push and he'd be gone,' Sarah whispered.

Lucy turned to share the joke, but Sarah wasn't laughing.

'And think about the things he does to his dog. Remember the time we had to stop him hitting it with that iron bar before he broke all its bones.' Sarah handed Lucy a strong stick.

Lucy's hand closed around it, but she didn't move. Jack was a despicable person and she was always wanting Sarah's approval ... but?

Fortunately for Lucy, Jack turned at that moment. 'What ya gonna do with the stick, Scarface?' he sneered. 'Pole vault yourself over the cliff so we don't have to look at you every day.' He guffawed as he walked off to join the others.

Lucy flung the stick away as though it was on fire.

'It's like a Gothic play,' Sarah said watching him walk away, her eyes devoid of any emotion. 'Evil skulks along the towering cliff as a pair of fledgling virgins plot against him,' she mutters. 'Pity he won this time.'

'You weren't serious, were you?'

'No LL,' Sarah laughed as she threw an arm around Lucy. 'I just needed to liven things up. I'd never have let you do it.'

'I'd never have done it.' Lucy spoke defiantly. Sarah was laughing at her and this angered her.

'Of course you wouldn't. Come on.'

Mario and Mary had finished their morning tea and were strolling towards the cliff edge. 'You're doing well,' he said.

'Only because of the girls. I wouldn't dream of doing this sort of thing normally. Look, my hands are shaking.'

'Mine too but not from the abseiling.' Mario held his hands out for her to see.

'Please. Don't talk like that.'

'What am I supposed to do? Pretend nothing's happened?'

'It hasn't and it's not going to.' Mary was about to move away from him when Kylie came bounding towards them.

'Mum, you're so cool,' she said hugging her. 'Isn't she Mr Borgetti, just cool.'

Together they walked over the to the edge of the escarpment and looked at the Hartley Valley spread out below them. The cliff of bare rock dropped steeply for the first fifty metres to a forest of dusty-green eucalypt trees interspersed with silvery waterfalls. From here the slope was more gradual as it continued on down to the valley floor where Mary could just make out farmhouses, paddocks and dams that seemed no larger than children's toys. 'We're not going to abseil down there, are we?' she asked.

'No. Just down the escarpment to the start of the trees,' Mario said. 'Now I know why people go around the world looking for the steepest cliffs, highest mountains, fastest rivers. What an adrenaline rush.'

'Your adrenaline may be rushing but mine stopped hours ago,' Mary whispered.

Mario felt a sudden rush of fear for her. 'It's time for you to stop,' he said more sharply than he meant to. 'You can join the others who aren't doing any more.'

'But you saw Kylie's face. She's so proud. I have to do it. At least once.'

Mario would have said more but his name was called. Once he backed over the rim, he forgot everything in the sheer ecstasy of the descent. His body heat spiked. Then there was a moment of fear when a rock came adrift under his foot, and he had a fleeting thought of the rope breaking, but he felt secure in the harness. He owned the world. Birds flew below and clouds floated above like balloons without string. It was so quiet. He thought he would like to hang there forever but Harry called him down.

'That was bloody marvellous,' he said as his feet touched the ground.

'Here comes Mary,' Harry said, flicking the ropes into a better position.

'Watch her. She's nervous.'

'I'm not surprised. We don't get many older women. She's got guts. But don't worry, we know how to get her down safely.' He ducked as bits of rock dislodged by her feet floated down and a kookaburra laughed in the trees below.

Mary felt quite confident until about halfway when she had to scramble her legs to get leverage. Then she panicked and thought she was going to die. She felt herself losing control as she grabbed at the air and swung around, banging hard against the cliff. Harry pulled on the safety rope, the descender clamped down and Mary stopped, but she was hanging upside down in spine-chilling silence. It was like waking from a bad dream, but in a moment of clarity she knew she was going to be okay.

'Okay, Mary. I've got you. Everything's okay.' Harry called clearly and calmly. 'What I want you to do now is to put both feet carefully flat against the cliff and push your body out ... that's it ... now let your weight ease back into the harness. That's it. Good. When you're ready, just walk down slowly, one foot after the other, like you were doing before. There's nothing to worry about. I'm holding you.'

'Keep your shoulders level with your feet,' Mario croaked. 'Don't let them drop below your feet.'

Being upside down had filled Mary's head with blood and Harry's and Mario's voices seemed far away. She listened intently and followed Harry's instructions like a robot as Mario's soothing voice encouraged her.

Slowly she walked backwards down the cliff until her feet touched the ground and Mario's big strong arms wrapped around her. Only then did she let herself collapse into him and burst into tears.

Harry had seen before the powerful emotions that danger could arouse and discreetly moved away. He would look for any cuts and bruises later.

Sarah was further along the base of the cliff, scrambling up the fissure back to the top, when she decided to return to Harry to learn what a belayer did, and to flirt a little. As she came around the cliff, she saw Mary reach the ground and Mario pull her into a very a passionate hug which went on for a very long time. What is this? she thought? She would store this information for when it might be useful.

That night, after the kids and chaperones had disappeared into their tents, Mario left his to walk beside the river. The moon was like a fingernail cutting and stars filled the sky with their beauty. Mario savoured the silence broken only by the tinkling of the shallow water over the river rocks and the hoot of an owl in a tree. He sat to watch stars reflected in the water. It was some minutes before he realised that Mary was sitting hunched on the bank a bit further up.

Without speaking he went and sat down beside her. Gently he took her hand and rolled her fingers between his. He could smell wafts of perfume mixed with smoke from the campfire in her hair. He noticed three deep lines at each of the knuckles on her fingers.

'I don't know what to say,' he said, his throat so tight he could hardly get the words out.

'I've loved you for a long time,' she said so softly he strained to hear. 'I've just not admitted it, even to myself.'

His fingers gently smoothed the lines over her knuckles. 'This is a shock to me.' He lifted her fingers to his lips and kissed them one by one. 'But, Mary,' he choked and waited until he had regained control of his voice. 'Please understand. I can't start something I wouldn't know how to stop.'

They sat watching the stars' reflections bounce over the ripples. The owl hooted again. A child coughed. They rose and walked separately to their tents.

CHAPTER 18

That weekend in the Blue Mountains changed Mario's life. He and Mary couldn't avoid seeing each other at Christmas parties and end-of-year school activities but they no longer pushed through the gap in the fence for morning coffee.

When Mario stood on his veranda and heard Mary moving about next door, his loins would burn. When James was home, he was tormented with such an unreasonable anger that he would go out onto the street and walk until he was exhausted.

Jill saw his restlessness and teasingly accused him of going through male menopause. Her solution was a good stiff Scotch and a pat on the back. Mario stopped working in his library at home and went into the newspaper every day.

Mary saw his anguish, but she had her own. She started art classes to get away from the house and became a regular at the cafés along Darling Street. For the first time, she understood why people frequented these cafés. Sitting there, she would think of her mother's advice. 'You'll never get everything you want in life so learn to be satisfied with what you do get,' her mother had said as she waved Mary goodbye. 'There'll be good and there'll be bad. Concentrate on the good and the bad will take care of itself.'

About four months after their return, Mario was sitting on the veranda so tense he wanted to punch something. The twins and Kylie were at a birthday sleepover, Jill was at a furniture show in Milan and, as usual, James was somewhere at sea. His thoughts drifted back to when he was a child and he would sit on the step trying to decide whether to do something or not, and the relief he felt when his mother would lean out the door to say 'do it'. It was often just a small thing like going with the other kids to watch the circus putting up its tents, or a big thing like asking for money for a school trip. The size of the decision didn't matter; it was the relief he got when he heard those words 'do it'. He thought of the way those words released the tension in his muscles, washed away the worries in his head, made the day seem brighter.

'Do it,' he said out loud as he banged down his whisky glass on the table, strode across the veranda, down the steps and through the gap in the fence. He entered without knocking. Mary was curled up in a large floral armchair, shoes off, watching television. He stood for a moment absorbing the comfort of the room, the paintings of ships on the walls, the colonial sideboard covered with photos of Mary's family in Ireland, the vase of flowers.

Mary jumped up and spun around.

She watched him cross the room.

The waiting was over.

He tenderly placed his hands on her shoulders. She was so short with her shoes off. Her eyes were soft, brown and misty. Quivering he drew her gently towards his body and stroked her hair. 'I love you Mary.'

'I know.' Her breath brushed his chest.

They removed each other's clothes, slowly, letting each piece fall like petals from a flower in the flicker of the television. There was no rush. His hands caressed each new curve, marvelling at the softness of her body.

Shuddering but strong now, she scraped her fingers through the curly hairs on his chest and over his flat stomach to his swollen penis. Taking it in her small hand she bent and kissed it. Only then did she lead him upstairs to her bedroom. There were no photos beside the bed to watch them as they fell across the patchwork quilt. Impatient now, she took his face in her hands and explored his mouth with her tongue. He arched his body over hers.

He felt he would explode but he kept kissing and stroking, waiting for her to be ready.

She had never felt so completely loved.

Afterwards, they sipped red wine. Talked. Stroked. Caressed. Rested and rolled about like puppies let outside for the first time. Eventually they fell asleep wrapped in each other's arms and that was how the sun found them next morning.

'My God I'm hungry.' Mario sat up shielding his eyes.

'Is that the only thing you can say after last night?' Mary's hair was dishevelled and her eyes were still bright from their lovemaking.

He lay back and looked at her for a long time. 'I love you,' he said softly. 'And when I look at you now, I see a woman so desirable my heart wants to cry it out to the world.' He pulled her into him. 'Can you feel it beating out my love for you?'

'Yes and something else tells me you love me,' she said as she slid her hands down his body.

After making love, they went downstairs and cooked eggs, bacon, tomatoes, toast and freshly brewed coffee, which they carried onto the veranda to watch the harbour come awake. Yachts rocked lightly against their moorings. The green and yellow Sydney ferries splashed along through the light chop on the water and a few early fishermen were out in their dinghies.

Mary knew she would leave James if Mario asked.

He smoothed the wrinkles over her knuckles. 'A penny for them.'

'I was thinking about James. About us.'

'Don't.'

'I know. But my dearest I have loved you for such a long time. Just having you next door has made my life here in Sydney worth living.'

'I've been fighting it, haven't I?'

'Yes.'

'I think I have known but haven't wanted to. Like, if I didn't admit it, then maybe it wasn't true.' He turned his head to watch the boats. 'It must be our secret for a while longer,' he whispered. 'We will be together Mary. One day. We will. Just not yet.'

After Mario returned to his empty home, Mary dragged herself slowly upstairs and fell across the bed. His smell lingered on the sheets as she wept.

CHAPTER 19

Mario didn't want their love to be soiled by grabbed moments and clandestine meetings in grubby motels. He remembered his mentor from his cadet days, Bill, who had bragged about his and his wife's open relationship. 'She does her thing, I do mine and no one gets hurt,' he would say.

Mario often met up with Bill at the Press Club and had been trying to get up the courage to say something when Bill leaned forward: 'What's up, boy? You're as jumpy as hell. I'm willing to listen if you want to spill it over me.'

As Mario spoke, Bill sat sipping his beer and nodding sagely. 'And now, my boy, you need somewhere for your trysts. No. Don't deny it, I've been there. Anyway, that's none of my business but I can give you what you need. We have a boatshed which we turned into a flat for young Flic when she was home. Since she's gone off to London, it never gets used.'

The boatshed was down a driveway that ran alongside Bill's house in Hunters Hill but was hidden from the house by a high hedge. Mary was doubtful at first but quickly fell in love with it and spent the first week filling the single cupboard with sarongs and towelling robes and decorating the furniture with blue and yellow striped linen cushions.

They popped a bottle of champagne and christened it their "Refuge".

'We'll never wear clothes when we're here,' she said as she tied a sarong around his waist.

Mario filled the fridge with wine, cheeses and jars of olives, so they could arrive at any time and stay as long as other commitments allowed.

Now it had started they were powerless to stem the flow of their desire.

'I don't know what real is anymore,' Mary said one day as the sun warmed her shoulders and the water lapped at the pylons below the jetty. 'I no longer know how to act when I'm with other people. How do I dull the sparkle in my eyes? How can I eat cheese without thinking about our little fridge? I started art classes to get away from you and now I'm using them to be with you.' She looked pensive for a moment. 'A few of my friends are suspicious, they think it's a man at art classes. I don't admit it, nor do I deny it.'

'I have to be careful, too. Jill keeps saying how happy I am, and I have to stop myself from telling her why. I have to stop singing around the house, stop from laughing out loud when I think of some wonderful thing you've said.' Mario took a sip of wine and looked out across the harbour. 'Do you think Kylie suspects?'

'No. She's pleased I'm out of her hair. With James away so much it gives her free run of the house and she likes that.'

'I think Sarah suspects,' Mario took a bigger sip. 'She's got this defiant edge now, like she's challenging me to deny her anything.'

'Do you think she would tell Lucy?'

'If it suited her and that worries me. Lucy's still very dependent. She might see it as a form of desertion. When she's older she'll be able to cope. But not yet.'

CHAPTER 20

The Birchgrove School end-of-year disco was fast approaching and everyone was going. Lucy wandered across the playground musing over whether to go. The other girls were wearing lipstick and trendy clothes and drooling over photos of celebrities. Lucy was still self-conscious. Her skin still looked ugly. Her left eye still drooped. She felt vulnerable in crowds. Sarah would be there, but she would be busy socialising. Lucy wanted it to not matter whether she went or not – but it did.

If only Daddy could come so she would have a special person with her.

'Hey Lucy, come and join us,' Kylie called.

She walked over to the group of girls and sat down before she saw Claudia. Her heart sank. Claudia was Sarah's fiercest competitor as the most popular girl at school. Her raven hair cascaded magnificently to her waist and her dark eyes glittered with malice as Lucy sat down.

'Don't suppose you'll be going to the disco.' she declared.

'I haven't made up my mind,' Lucy replied.

'Haven't made up my mind,' Claudia copycatted as she brought her hand up to her mouth and made chewing sounds in a crude imitation of the boys who would mumble "Kentucky Fried" to Lucy as she walked past.

There was a collective shocked intake of breath from the girls sitting around Claudia. The headmistress had threatened to expel anyone heard using these words, but mimicking chewing on a chicken bone became a sneaky habit used by some of the nastiest students.

Lucy felt her face flush, then she thought back to Jane's advice on not succumbing to self-pity. 'You think you're so

smart,' she retorted. 'I suppose you'll be hanging around
Matt Walgate now you've let him touch you down there.'

She had the satisfaction of seeing the colour drain from
Claudia's face. 'Don't look so shocked, he's told everyone,'
she added before striding off. Lucy was pleased she had
fought back but her legs were shaking. Matt had told Sarah,
but he fancied Sarah and could have just been bragging.

Damon had seen the altercation with Claudia and followed
Lucy. 'Don't worry about her. I'm going to Snails Bay after
school to see what the high tides have washed up. Wanna
come?'

She spun around stared at him. Why hadn't she thought
of it before? 'Damon! Will you come with me to the dance?
Please, I need a special person with me. You can bike over
to our place and Daddy will take you, me and Sarah and
Kylie in the car.'

'Me?'

'Yes, you!' She grabbed his arm, the idea growing better by
the second. 'Please. You're my best friend and I'll die if you
don't.'

'You know I don't do parties,' he said. But even as he
spoke, he knew he would. She was his best friend after Billy.
She never judged him and never asked more of him than he
could give easily. He looked down into her moist brown eyes.
'Okay. But you make all the arrangements,' he grunted as
he turned and strode away.

'I'm so sorry.' Kylie puffed as she caught up with Lucy and
grabbed her arm. 'When I called you over I didn't think
about Claudia being there. The bitch.'

'Doesn't matter,' Lucy tittered, patting Kylie's hand.
'Damon's coming with us. 'Will you help me design a dress
to cover all these?' she waved her hands over her scars.

When the girls who had heard the altercation between
Claudia and Lucy filed into class they were surprised to see
Kylie and Lucy huddled over a notepad, scribbling excitedly.

Claudia was about to saunter over to see what they were

doing when Sarah beat her to it. She listened intently to Lucy then straightened her back and looked directly at Claudia, her eyes hard with menace.

Sarah was the supremo of this class and of Lucy. She did not intend to let Claudia usurp her or denigrate Lucy, ever.

On the night of the dance Damon arrived a bit late but his hair was combed, he was wearing long pants and his T-shirt was clean and ironed. Only his smile was strained and his grey eyes wary.

'Hello, Mr Borgetti,' he said. Then he looked past Mario to where Lucy was standing in the hallway. 'Wow!'

Lucy wore a plum-coloured satin dress that was fitted at the waist, had fitted sleeves to cover the scars on her left arm, and was short to show off long slim legs. Her wig had been set to cascade down the left side of her face where most of the damage was.

'You look terrific.'

'Thank you,' Lucy said as she took Damon's arm to lead him out onto the veranda where Jill, Sarah and Kylie had gathered.

Mario was deeply grateful to Damon for going with the girls. He knew they would be in a group, but the others would probably wander off during the night leaving Lucy standing alone and feeling embarrassed. Damon, he knew, would stay with her all night.

Jill also appreciated Damon's generous show of kindness and immediately forgave him his dirty fingernails and mismatched shoelaces. She had not seen very much of him since Lucy came out of hospital and noted that he was filling out and showed signs of becoming a handsome young man.

The narrow streets near the school were crammed with cars and parents giving last-minute warnings. For the older residents who still lived in the old workers' cottages that had not been renovated, the red brick school festooned with coloured lights was their last link with their past.

Sarah led Kylie, Lucy and Damon through the throng of

students like a hot knife through honey. She had organised a select group of her friends to meet inside. Black was the favourite colour for the girls along with short skirts, dangling earrings and chunky high-heeled shoes. Only Sarah was different. She wore a dress of golden fabric that floated almost to her ankles, just short enough to show off her gold Italian sandals. Her hair was meticulously sculptured to look messy.

Following tradition, the Year Five students catered for the Year Six's end of school dance. They had set up coloured lights and long tables on the flat roof above the school hall and a disco was being assembled. From the barbecue delicious aromas of roasting beef and ham and vegetables wafted on the warm December air.

'You should see Claudia,' Lucy said, hugging Sarah. 'She's in boring black.'

Sarah stood at the top of the steps with Lucy, Kylie and Damon beside her. Her dress shimmered like molten gold as a light breeze blew it against her long slim body. She watched Claudia hesitate at the bottom of the steps. Claudia didn't want to walk past the Borgetti group which was exactly why she had positioned them here. She felt the flush of triumph as she watched Claudia set her resolve, tilt her chin high and lead her group of six up the steps towards them.

'Evening Claudia,' Sarah said as she stepped aside so Claudia could see Matt Walgate's face leering over her shoulder. 'I think you know my friend. He thought you might need this later on tonight.'

Sarah held torn and stained scarlet panties high so everyone could see them clearly before she opened her fingers to let them float down to land in a crumpled pile at Claudia's feet.

L U C Y

I look at the little bedside clock – if Sarah get the lights at Victoria Road, she'll be here in seven minutes. I hurry into the bathroom to check myself again. I don't know why it matters, but I want her to be proud of me.

While I wait I think back to the time I told Dr Singh how much I hated Abbotsfield, the secondary school Mummy insisted we go to. 'It's a school for rich girls who spend their awake hours buying clothes and sharing secrets about boys and periods – things they wouldn't share with me,' I told him. 'And we'd just started there when Sarah told me Daddy was having an affair with Mary.'

'Did you believe Sarah?'

'Not at first, I suppose. But she told me to watch how their guilt made them avoid each other, and she was right. They had stopped having coffee, stopped crossing the fence for chats; Mary even stopped cooking cakes for us. Sarah pointed out how they would stand on different sides of a room. She would bring them together with some clever pretext so we could note how they would talk but wouldn't look each other in the eye.'

'Did you feel sorry for your mother?'

'Not that I remember. At that time, I took everything personally. My periods hadn't started, I couldn't share shopping jaunts with the girls, my eye would weep and my skin was ghastly to look at.'

'Do you think Sarah understood what school was like for you?'

'Why would she? She was the best-looking girl at school, a prefect, our champion tennis player, leader of the debating

team and always top of the class. She charmed everyone so I kept out of her way. I didn't want to be the deformed twin.'

'But the records show you regularly made high marks, even won prizes.'

'Academically yes. And I wrote for the school newspaper; reviews on theatre productions etcetera. Anything I could do alone. I lived for the weekends when I could go to the farm or the rifle range.'

'What about Kylie?'

'She's a Catholic so she went to a different secondary school.

'Tell me how you felt when you were at the rifle range?'

'Shooting was everything. When I was there nothing else mattered; not school, not scars, not even Daddy and Mary. With a fullbore thundering beside me, I was in control and they all liked me because I was young and I was good. George used to say that shooting was ninety per cent psychological and ten per cent the rest. He would tell me that I was a one hundred-per-center and would one day represent Australia at the famous Bisley Range in England. I lapped it all up.'

After this session with Lucy, Dr Singh sat for a long time thinking. What was he missing? He was beginning to think Sarah had psychopathic tendencies but there was something else, something very deep in her core where Lucy dwelled. Her actions went beyond manipulating people – Sarah had crossed the barrier of decency with Lucy. Why did she tell Lucy her hair would never grow back? Why did she send Damon away from the house? Why did she show Lucy her red bra? Why did she tell Lucy about Mario and Mary when she knew how central he was to her happiness?

Dr Singh sighed as he put away Lucy's file. If only he could get Sarah into his office and talk to her face-to-face. Find out what drove her, what she was harbouring. He sensed there was a secret, an anger, a resentment; something driving her to manipulate Lucy in such hurtful ways.

He would not know until some years later how close he had

come to understanding Sarah and the enigma that lurked deep in her psyche.

CHAPTER 21

George had never coached anyone like Lucy. He saw that Sarah also had a surprising natural ability, but surmised she only wanted to shoot to keep an eye on Lucy. She skipped a lot of training sessions. Mario would arrive with Lucy and an excuse why Sarah could not come.

'That Sarah's a charmer, but she gives me the creeps,' he told his wife. 'They might be twins but those girls are chalk and cheese. Lucy is polite but that other one would shoot her mother for her lipstick.'

Lucy absorbed knowledge like a sponge.

'One rabbit at a time,' Mr McKenzie would tell her.

'One shot at a time, girl,' George would say.

'Shuffle your feet until you're comfortable,' was another of Mr McKenzie's regular sayings.

'Wiggle about until you're comfortable,' George would say as they lay on the ground with the rifle. 'Shut your eyes, take aim, open them, check your aim. If the rifle isn't pointing at the target, then your body isn't lying the right way.'

After a few lessons George started to teach her more specific features, such as how light and wind affect a shooter's judgement.

'Your eyes can take up to half an hour to adjust to changes in light,' he said. 'Any cloud movement or sunburst will affect them. Practise with the rear sight open, then closed to get a dull light.'

'You can't control the wind,' he said another day. 'So you have to understand it. Eight per cent of good shooting is being able to read the wind. It affects the round in three ways – by its force, its direction and the length of time the round is in the air.'

Lucy took the wind chart home and studied the way the flags fluttered in every wind variable until it was imprinted on her brain. Then George told her all that knowledge was useless if it was a bad wind day.

He chuckled when he relayed this story to his wife. 'I threw it at her because I knew she could take it. She looked me straight in the eye and said, "Okay, now teach me about bad days".'

George gave Lucy some flags. 'Feel these. One day they could be wet and dangling like the wife's washing. Or they might be made of a lighter fabric than the chart allows for, meaning they'll pick up the slightest breeze. If the wind fishtails, the flags might flap in all directions and change just when you think you have adjusted correctly. A wind from the front will tend to lift your projectile, while from behind the wind will tend to drop it, A champion reads the wind with his guts.'

'Okay. Teach me to read with my guts.'

George took Lucy to Gosford and Canberra where she learnt to shoot with capricious winds. Then other ranges where he showed her how the lie of the land, ditches, trees and obstacles affected the direction and the force of the wind. 'Watch for bits of paper or dry leaves rolling about close to the ground where the round travels,' he said.

He taught her how to find the mirage through her spotting-scope. He explained the mirage was about density differences in the air and how it was usually close to the ground and how it changed according to time of day, the lay of land, the seasons, even a sea breeze suddenly coming in.

'You can only learn to read the signs by studying, practising, and more practising. I want you to study the mirage until you can find it in seconds. As soon as you see it, shoot, because it's telling you what's happening right now, this second, on the ground.'

Jill never went to the rifle range and when her mother, Catherine, found out the girls were shooting she was incensed. 'Only terrorists and kangaroo hunters use guns,' Catherine snorted. 'You must discourage this silly idea of Lucy's and get her into a proper sport.'

'She can't really play many others with her injuries,' Jill had replied.

'Well a hobby of some sort. What about the art gallery? She and Sarah could join me there as a volunteer. I know they'd like some younger volunteers.'

Jill knew her daughters well enough to know that Sarah would never be a volunteer, she only did things with a purpose, and Lucy was not yet ready to expose herself to all those curious eyes. She did not like the girls shooting, but she knew Lucy had to have something that interested her outside school hours. She was at that age where she was still too young to start working with her on the magazines and too old for childish hobbies.

One cool autumn morning, Jill poured coffee into a fine china mug and sauntered onto the veranda. She thought about how little they did as a family these days, how they used to sail, bat a ball over a net in the garden, barbecue, go to the movies.

'Is that coffee I smell?' Mario said as he strolled unwittingly into Jill's unquiet thoughts. He poured himself a coffee and stood beside her, watching Lucy aiming at a target hooked onto a tree across the lawn.

'This has got to stop,' Jill said. 'It's becoming an obsession.'

'It's just a hobby. This is her way of practising what she's learning from George when she can't get to the range; things like positioning and breathing techniques.'

'Hobbies fit into one's "real" life. This rifle club is taking over hers.'

'Why don't you come out and see how good she is? She's gone from C grade to B in eight months and she'll make A soon. They say at the club she'll make the National Ladies Team before she's eighteen.'

'As if that matters. What matters is her future, her career, the friends she's making now and will have for the rest of her life.'

'I worried about all that,' Mario said. 'Then I realised if she can't play other sports and this one gives her pleasure, then why not? Maybe these will be her friends for life. Maybe shooting will be her career.'

If he'd said Lucy would become a murderer, he wouldn't have infuriated Jill more. 'Shooting a career?' she spat, spinning around to look at him. 'I wish she'd never met that boy in hospital.'

'Jill darling, please just come out once and see for yourself.' Mario cringed at his pleading tone. 'You've no idea how big this sport is. Australian shooters win more medals per head in the Commonwealth Games than any other country. It's an untold story. In fact, you could write an article on it.'

As they stood there, Jill thought about how much she still loved Mario and how she missed the closeness they once had. Had bringing up children been easier for her parents? She couldn't remember she or her brother giving them any big worries. 'Nothing prepared us for a damaged child, did it?' she said moving closer to him. 'There are no handbooks to follow. We're floundering about like beached whales. I don't mean to be hard on her, but I worry about where she's heading.'

'I know.' Mario knew he should take her in his arms. She looked slight and vulnerable in her cream cashmere jumper with the pearls he had bought her for a birthday a few years back. Instead he took another sip of coffee and mumbled, 'Why don't you come out this afternoon? They're both competing.'

'I can't. A contributor failed to deliver, and I have to find something to fill the hole.'

Mario shrugged. Lucy was using his rifle because she didn't have her own yet. She lay on a rug with her right leg bent the way she liked. He preferred to lie flat. Lucy was dry-firing at a target nailed to a tree to ascertain whether she "pushed the barrel" off aim, a common fault among shooters.

Mario would have liked to join her but there was already enough friction in the house with the double life he was leading. When he and Jill had first met they discussed absolutely everything. Even though they came from very different backgrounds this had not worried her.

'Love is a meeting of body and mind,' she would say. 'We may be the product of our backgrounds, but you and I can rise above that.'

Could he rise above what he was doing to the people he loved?

CHAPTER 22

By the time Lucy was ready to attend Sydney University she had made the National Ladies Team, competed in Tasmania at the Oceania competition and won more medals than any person her age at the highly regarded state Queen's competitions. Buoyed with all this success she was hoping to make the university's top team.

Opening day was in February and Lucy was walking across the university campus with Sarah when Tracy Johnson grabbed her.

'Remember me? I'm with the Windsor club.'

'How could I forget? You beat me at Canberra.'

'The only time ever. You going to join us here?'

'We both intend to and to go to Bisley to compete in The Imperial Meeting and win the Queen's Prize.' Lucy laughed as Tracy fell back in mock amazement.

'Then you'd better let me introduce you to our captain.' Tracy strode off across the campus and they followed, skipping every few steps to keep up with her. Tracy stopped many times to chat, but eventually they came to three boys chatting under a tree.

'Hey guys, meet Lucy Borgetti, shooter extraordinaire.'

'I heard you were here,' a stocky man with a receding hairline turned and stepped forward to shake her hand. 'I'm David,' he said as he turned to include, 'Brad and John, top-grade shooters.'

'My sister, Sarah, and she's A grade too,' Lucy said moving to stand beside her.

'Welcome both.' David beamed. 'But be warned, this university is very competitive. Lots of training, lots of competitions and Bisley every year.'

'Lucy intends to win Queen's.' Tracy said as she flung an arm over Lucy and nodded in admiration.

David looked at Lucy. 'Nothing's impossible. Bisley's in July and we start picking the team over the next few months. I'll be looking for the best shooters, people who work well in a team.'

'I think they'll fit in very well.' John said, appraising Sarah. She flicked him a little wink. He was a handsome creature.

Lucy was in her element at university. She wanted to be a journalist in the arts area so was studying English and arts law. She liked the casual dress, the irregular lectures and the camaraderie of the rifle club. Tracy was the rifle club's self-appointed social secretary and a font of information about cheap and cheerful restaurants. John was the organiser of weekend shoots with other universities and clubs. David held them together with a mixture of fun and serious discipline. Sarah was accepted as part of the team but after a few weeks spent more time with her law studies group.

'If Tracy would stop organising parties and John would stop chasing women, they'd be my best shooters,' David told Lucy one day as they stood behind the line watching the others practise. 'They both lose concentration and "drop the last".'

'And I can tell you now,' he said, 'you're in the team for Bisley.'

'Wow.' She threw her arms around him and jumped up and down. 'And Sarah?'

'She hardly ever comes to practise,' David said carefully. He sensed he wouldn't get Lucy without Sarah. 'She's good enough but she's not dedicated. I owe it to those who put in the effort.'

'I'll talk to her.'

David nodded. He hadn't warmed to Sarah. He felt she only joined the club to keep track of Lucy and he couldn't fathom why. She was extremely popular but was studying law so moved with a much faster crowd than most of the members of the rifle club. Also, he did not like the way she manipulated people. She made Lucy insecure and distracted John. But Lucy was a potential winner and he had to have her on the team ... was he prepared to take Sarah to get Lucy?

'What on earth is a Bisley?' Jill asked that evening when Lucy announced that she was in the university team to go to Bisley. Jill sat beside Mario, a long slender hand resting lightly on his knee.

'It's the St Andrews of golf. The Wimbledon of tennis. The gold of the Olympics.' Lucy replied, palms facing up to emphasise its importance.

'Is it a prize? A place?'

'It's the most revered shooting range in the world, and the most pukka.'

'So, it's British.' Jill lifted an eyebrow at Mario as she reached across the arm of the couch to pick up her wine glass from the side table.

'Very,' Mario responded. 'In July 1860 Queen Victoria fired the first shot in a competition on Wimbledon Common. She was so pleased with herself that, on the spot, she gave two hundred and fifty pounds for the best individual marksman in a competition that was to be called the Queen's Prize. It's still called that, the prize is still two hundred and fifty pounds and it's still held every July, attracting two thousand shooters from around the world.'

'So why is it called Bisley if it's held at Wimbledon?'

'Wimbledon was becoming overdeveloped, so they shifted the competition to Bisley in 1890. That's less than an hour from London on the train.' Lucy had devoured everything she could find on Bisley and took over from Mario. 'After Queen Victoria gave it the royal seal of approval, it attracted the cream of British society with ladies in high fashion travelling from London. They even named the train the Bisley Bullet.'

Although Jill still didn't approve of the girls shooting, she was impressed. 'What can we do to help? Do you need a sponsor, money, clothes?'

Mario nodded, pleased that Jill was taking an interest.

'Not all the shooters have been announced yet, but David told me I'm in. Sarah will be if she comes to practise more often and she's promised me she will.'

In July, Lucy flew to London with the team of eight, which included David, Tracy, John and Lucy. Sarah was a reserve. Three coaches and Sally, the team's capable psychologist, completed the entourage.

CHAPTER 23

Bisley in 2004 was everything Lucy had imagined. Frightfully English with heathland rolling out as far as she could see. The grass was kept short on the wide ranges. The old roads were lined with huge trees which spread their leafy shade over lawns and meticulously restored old buildings, some with red roofs and white painted verandas and window frames.

Lucy hungrily took it all in – the national flags fluttering on white poles, the accommodation provided in barracks, clubhouses, caravans, huts and tents, some gaily striped.

'Don't you just love it?' Tracy bubbled, clinging to Lucy's arm as they drove into the grounds. 'And we've got to go to Fulton's, the most famous gun shop in England.'

White signs pointed to ranges with names like Century Range, Running Deer Range and Stickledown, the most famous long-distance range in the world.

'We'll be shooting at Century, the short range for 300, 500 and 600 yards and Stickledown for 900 and 1000,' David explained as he drove the hired van slowly to allow them time to absorb the atmosphere. He pulled up in front of Crawford Lines, a building dating from the late 1800s. 'This is us. Home for the next three weeks. The rooms are basic and we have to share a bathroom, but it's right on the grounds. Find your rooms, dump your bags and we'll go for a walk before it gets dark.'

'I feel like Alice in Wonderland,' Lucy whispered to Sarah as they walked with the team taking their first look around. She wanted to remember this moment for the rest of her life. She could hear what she imagined was every language in the world. Old men were sporting chests of medals. People in shorts, shooting jackets, jeans, suits, mackintosh trousers and army uniforms, and teams in matching blazers. It was an intermingling of young, old, bent over, ramrod straight; even people in wheelchairs.

As the team strolled along Queen's Way, a Range Rover hurtled around the corner nearly hitting John, causing him to wave his fist and hurl a few words of abuse.

'Frightfully sorry chaps,' the driver said leaping out. 'Going a bit fast. Just a bit excited. Andrew Braybrook.' He leaned forward from the waist offering his hand to David who had quickly stepped forward.

'That's okay mate, David Bryson.'

'Golly, Australians. My favourite country. Went out there last year to visit my uncle. Pleased to meet you. Sorry.' And he was gone.

'Andrew Braybrook.' Lucy squealed as she grabbed Sarah.

'Who's he?' asked Sarah, her interest piqued by the toffy accent.

'Only the greatest young shooter in England and last year's Queen's winner,' Lucy replied, bowing elaborately to the departing Range Rover. Although she joked her heart was thumping. As far as she knew, there wasn't an international competition he hadn't won, and he was a hot favourite again this year. Wish he wasn't so gorgeous, she thought as they walked on.

'Cool down kiddo.' John laughed, throwing an arm over her shoulders. 'Don't go soppy over the opposition. He's your nemesis, remember.'

The sun rose over Bisley at about 4 am in July. Most first-time competitors from the team were so excited they didn't sleep well. They would wake with the sun, then fall back into a deep sleep until seven when the team conference started.

David had learnt over the four years he'd attended Bisley that the team needed a good motivator. This was the reason he had invited Sally along. She was a psychologist, but her forte was motivation. She knew how to be a friend but never lost sight of the end goal, which was to win.

Sally had the team up and in the designated conference room by 7 am the first morning. 'It's vitally important you sit quietly and at least have a cup of tea or a full glass of water before you step out of this room. It's a madhouse out there.' She ignored grumbles about jet lag and stony looks from those who had looked outside at the dappled lanes where there was not a soul in sight.

'Okay, it's a bit empty now but there'll be fifteen hundred shooters moving around every day. Bisley works on precision timing, rigid protocol and no waiting for latecomers. If you're not there, you're out. But you will be there because the coaches will have your daily program in your room the evening before.'

'Three main rules,' David said as he put his arms up for silence. 'We've been through them before but they'll sink in better now you're here. First, ranges are measured in yards, not metres so remember to change your sights and elevation. Second, absolutely no rounds are to be taken off the range. Third, you'll be shooting the Bisley style we have been practising for the past few weeks.'

For the next ten minutes they sat cross-legged on the floor listening to Sally's calming but persuasive voice. 'You will be inundated with invitations. Every country throws a party and believe me, beer and champagne flow like rivers. Enjoy yourselves but don't lose sight of the fact that you're here representing your university and you're here to win.' She let her words sink in. 'We've won many medals here and I believe this is the best team we've ever brought over. Not only for the team events, but I believe the Queen's Prize is within our grasp. I want to see an Australian carried on the chair.'

The team gathered their gear and Graeme, one of the coaches, drove them to the Century Range where hundreds of people milled about.

'Bit proper isn't it,' Sarah said as she stood beside Lucy. 'Jill would approve of those officials in suits and ties.'

Lucy nodded then moved to compete but was so overwhelmed she was down into position before realising she hadn't collected her ammunition from the officials. Hot with embarrassment she went to get her allocation.

She cringed for being such an obvious first timer, but the other competitors nodded their understanding. She tried to concentrate but her brain fluffed about like feathers in a bag. The flags were difficult to see and the light changed from dull to duller and back to dull. She looked through the spotting-scope to check the target, adjusted the wind-gauge on her rifle and shot her two free sighters. This helped settle her down for the fifteen counting shots. She achieved several bullseyes but missed the small circle in the centre that would have given her a V-bull.

A V-bull didn't earn extra points but if two competitors ended up with the same score, the one with the most Vs won.

No one did well that day. John shot at the wrong target, which they sympathised with. Tracy had forgotten to bring her sports bra and her normal bra dug in where the stock sat into her shoulder. David had forgotten his lucky talisman and Brad and Doug, like Lucy, had forgotten to collect their ammo before settling down to shoot.

'Cheer up,' David said as they gathered for dinner. 'The first day is always difficult. We're going to the German party tonight. Remember the protocol; collar and tie for men, skirts for women.'

'I'm the size of a horse in a skirt,' Tracy wailed as John grabbed her from behind and pretended to ride her.

As they settled in, the trophies mounted and their spirits soared. David came first in the Monro Memorial Match and third in the Daily Telegraph. Tracy excelled and won the Donaldson Memorial and the Imp, with Sarah filling in as reserve coming third; both matches were for ladies only.

Lucy beat John to first place in The Kenya, a competition for overseas competitors, with Brad close behind in a shoot-off for fourth place.

As the individual events heated up Lucy stopped going to the parties. She felt as though everything that had happened in her life had been leading to this – the Queen's Prize.

CHAPTER 24

Day one of the Queen's Prize, which every competitor could enter, dawned bright and sunny.

Lucy walked to the ranges with the seashell Damon had given her in hospital against her ear. She visualised the peace of Snail Bay with its jetty where they fished and the sandy corner where dogs were allowed to run free.

She studied the Century Range flags as she walked towards it.

'You're with Andrew Braybrook,' David said, and her mouth went dry. She watched Andrew change from his tweed into his shooting jacket, take his rifle from his butler and move towards his firing position. As the only shooter with a butler, he was equally admired and ridiculed for it. Lucy visualised his silky blond hair gleaming like a halo under his cap.

'Lucy.' He tilted his head and touched the rim of his cap with one finger as she came up alongside him. 'I've been looking forward to this day. Come.'

They walked together to collect their ammunition and returned to lie down at the 300-yard range. Lucy found it difficult to concentrate with him beside her but did better at the 500- and 600-yard ranges where they were not together.

She had been so focused on her events all day that she was feeling a bit dazed when David bounded up and gave her a big hug. 'Congratulations, you've made the top three hundred so you're in for day two. John's in too and Tracy won the Donaldson Memorial.'

'You and me against the blond Adonis.' John said as he grabbed her and spun her round. 'Did you see he won the bronze medal for the day. I don't know who won the other medals but getting into the three hundred is all that matters.'

'Really? Sorry John, but I was so wrapped up in it all I didn't even see your score.'

'Just one V under you,' John raised his eyebrows to show his surprise. 'I was so nervous I couldn't eat so I'm going off to find a place that sells traditional English pork pies or fish 'n chips. Want to come?'

'I couldn't eat a thing.'

'But before I go I've learnt something that will interest you. Your rich boyfriend loses his cool if things don't go his way.'

'He's not my boyfriend.'

'Don't interrupt. Just pray that a blackbird poops on him as he's about to shoot.' John roared with laughter. 'You should come to more parties. It's amazing the gossip you pick up. But you'd better be quick, because Sarah is sniffing around your Adonis, like a bitch in heat.'

Lucy laughed as John walked away. She liked him despite his loudness. He made her feel life was worth living and decided to break her "no parties" rule that night. She felt comfortable with the team at the party but soon John was off dancing with a brunette from the Canadian team and Tracy was chatting to a handsome Jamaican. She couldn't find Sarah in the crowded room but as she left, she saw her sitting on a bar stool surrounded by the British team.

Before David left the party he took John aside. 'You're shooting so well this year you have a real chance to win the Queen's. Don't muck it up, tomorrow you need to ensure you make it into the final one hundred.'

'I know. I know. I've been thinking about it and it's early to bed tonight.' John meant what he said but later that night, as Lucy sat quietly in her room listening to the waves on Snail Bay, the Canadian girl was teaching him to bootscoot.

'Anyone seen John?' David asked the next morning at coffee. The second day of the Queen's didn't start until after lunch, so he hadn't been too concerned. 'Anyone?' He felt the first stirrings of concern as bleary eyes squinted blankly at him.

'Try his room.' Tracy suggested pointing her thumbs down.

Without another word, David and Sally took off.

They found John flopped across his bed face-up and snoring. He was fully dressed except for a shoe and his tie. His club jacket lay scrunched on the floor. Flies buzzed around a half-eaten hot dog, the room was hot and stuffy.

'You bastard,' David shouted as he flung open the windows, heaved John off the bed and down to the showers. He turned the water on cold and held John there while Sally ran to get aspirin and coffee.

'Shit it's freezing,' John grumbled.

'Don't move or I'll bloody kill you.'

'And I'll help him,' Sally snarled as she handed a glass of fizzing aspirin into the shower.

The others were already at Century when David and Sally arrived with John. They had put him into uniform, and he was walking okay, but he looked as though he could throw up at any moment.

Lucy had already had her turn at the 300 range and shot a better score than yesterday, but John's hands were shaking and as soon as he lay down, he knew it was over for him. He could hardly see the flags, let alone read the damn things. Furious with himself, he lined up and shot the worst score of his life.

All hopes were now on Lucy.

She got another good score at the 500 and knew she would have to do something incredibly stupid at the 600 to not be in the final one hundred competitors for the third day, the Queen's final. Her first sighter went left and she corrected for this. The next was a V and she asked for this to be counted. She overcorrected with the next shot, earning only four points. Calm down. Concentrate. Breathe. The competitor beside her wiggled but she ignored him. She took control and the next eight shots tore through the centre giving her eight Vs.

Lucy could feel her legs shaking as she stood up to walk over to David and the team who had been anxiously counting her every shot. 'Onya kiddo.' John said as he lay his head on her shoulder and pretended to cry.

She was so overwhelmed she just folded her hands and held them hard against her lips.

'Cry if you want.' John said. 'You're through to the final with a very strong score to carry over from today. Come over here Sarah and give you sister a hug.'

'Andrew?' Lucy asked looking at David.

'Andrew's in twenty-fifth place with 149.8 out of a possible 150.30. The Canadian, Philip Brightwell, leads with 150.26. You're sixty-seventh with 148.20. With today's score being carried through to the final you're trailing, but with good shooting and a bit of luck tomorrow, you can do it.'

'I'll come to your room later,' Sally gave Lucy a knowing wink.

After dinner, Sally went to Lucy's room where they sat on the floor and discussed Andrew, Philip and the other shooters who would be competing on the final day. They analysed their style, their history and each shooter's chances of doing well at the longer 900 and 1000 yards. They talked about Andrew's butler who treated other shooters with more disdain than his master did.

Then out of the blue, Sally reached over to swipe at Lucy's shoulders as though brushing off dandruff. 'What are you doing?'

'Wiping all those people off your shoulders.'

'What people?' Lucy looked around, alarmed.

'Andrew, Philip and the other ninety-seven.'

Lucy laughed and started swiping too. 'Billy, James, John, Colleen,' she called out sweeping them across the room and out the open window. They swiped and laughed, calling out names until they were both exhausted. By the time Sally left, Lucy knew she would sleep well. But before crawling into bed she made a phone call: 'Mummy. I've made the finals.'

'We know! George told us. Mary and Kylie are coming over

for dinner and we're going to watch videos until we hear from you. We'll be sitting beside the phone so you must ring whatever the time is – or get David to if you can't. What distances are you shooting tomorrow?'

'The 900 and 1000 at Stickledown.'

'That's good. You like those longer distances. How many shots do you have?' Jill had been reading up on women shooters and the Queen's Prize with a view to doing a story in the lifestyle magazine.

Lucy couldn't believe this was her mother. 'We have fifteen shots each with a possible score of 75.15 for each distance. I need to shoot a minimum of seventy-five at both distances ... and a lot of Vs.'

'Dad's been telling me that the harder the competition the more control you muster. George has a friend at Bisley who is reporting back to him, so Dad and George have been on the phone analysing your chances.' They both laughed. 'Who are your main competitors?'

'The two I'm most worried about are Philip, who's in the lead and shooting really well, and Andrew Braybrook, last year's winner.'

'Is that the Andrew Sarah's been telling me about?'

Lucy's hands went clammy. She hadn't seen much of Sarah and had assumed she had met up with someone who interested her.

Her mother was still talking, '... said his uncle has a big cattle property in Queensland. She's going up to stay with him in October when he comes over. He sounds nice. Dad thought you might take him out to the range at Malabar when he's here.'

Lucy didn't register the rest of the conversation. After putting the phone down, she paced the room banging her fist into her palm. Was Andrew using Sarah to learn her weaknesses? Did it matter? All shooters had superstitions. She tried to convince herself she didn't, but it upset her to think Sarah might be sleeping with her main opponent.

Knowing she had to have a good sleep, Lucy took a long hot shower and curled up in bed with the shell against her ear. The roar of waves helped her drop into a fitful sleep.

CHAPTER 25

The next morning was the final of the Queen's Prize and there was no wind. David had taken Lucy's gear to Stickledown and she and Sally were planning to walk over together.

Low clouds threatened as she picked up her jacket and searched the bed for Damon's shell. She dragged off the sheets and flung them onto the floor. Then she searched drawers and shelves. By the time Sally arrived the room was in a shambles.

'My shell. I can't find my shell. I had it last night and now it's gone.'

Frantically they searched the room until there was no more time to spare. 'I'm sorry Lucy but we have to go now if we want to walk to Stickledown and have time to adjust to the atmosphere.'

'I can't go without my shell,' Lucy wailed. 'I never shoot without it.'

'I understand but we have to go or we'll be late. Maybe Sarah has taken it for you.' Even as she said this, Sally knew it wasn't possible. The whole team had been scheming carefully to prevent Lucy finding out about Sarah and Andrew. Sally knew perfectly well that Sarah would not have taken the shell to the range for Lucy, but she had to get her out of the room and across to Stickledown.

With one last hopeful look through the bedclothes Lucy let herself be led from the room. Sally held her hand as they walked, but Lucy missed the soothing sounds of the sea. She looked up at the shadows drifting across the clock tower and tried to visualise the puffy white clouds that cast soft shadows over Snail Bay.

They were awed when they arrived at Stickledown. Even though Lucy had seen it many times over the past week the place had never been as crowded. She guessed the crowd under a multitude of coloured umbrellas to be five thousand. They wore windbreakers, hats and comfortable shoes – stoic under a multitude of coloured umbrellas opened against the foggy dampness.

'I think every Pom must own a spaniel,' Sally said to break Lucy's silence. 'And look, there's the winner's dais.'

Lucy glanced over at the platform bitterly then back at the shooters who looked the same anywhere in the world as they scrutinised rifles, checked sights and mumbled to each other.

'I can do it, can't I?' she hissed as she clung to Sally's hand.

'You can, and you will,' Sally squeezed Lucy's hand. 'This is what you've been training for. Your greatest wish. Today you will make it happen.'

As they approached their team, Sarah came forward and crushed Lucy to her. 'You're going to win today LL. I just know it.'

Then the others were there, wishing her well, saying she could do it. David cupped her face in his hands and said quietly 'Go do it, champ'.

In the final all competitors shoot at the same time Bisley style, two to a target.

'Help me, dear friend,' Lucy whispered to her rifle as she lay beside it. The confidence of her teammates buoyed her but she still felt terribly vulnerable. Her first "counting" shot at the 900-yard range went wide, giving her only four starting points.

Tracy and John clung to each other. David grasped Sally's hand. Sarah stood apart.

Lucy could not afford another miss. She closed her eyes and imagined George's deep rumbling voice. 'Concentrate girl. You can do it.' Lucy's final score at this range was just behind Andrew. Philip had dropped two Vs but held his lead.

Only a perfect score on the 1000-yard range would enable Lucy or Andrew to beat Philip.

The drizzle had become a light rain and a fickle wind was sending scurries of mist across the targets when Andrew went over to his butler. 'I need my grandfather's green jacket from the 4WD,' he ordered.

'Sorry, sir, but we didn't bring that one. Your father took it to Scotland.'

'But I told him I needed it for Bisley.'

'Yes, sir, but he took it anyway.'

'Damn him. Grandfather said it was mine for as long as I shoot at Bisley. So what else have I got to wear?'

'What about the Driza-Bone your uncle sent from Australia? It's waterproof and windproof.'

'It's too heavy.' His father had obviously taken his grandfather's jacket to Scotland for his older brother, Bradley, the favourite. He stalked over to the 4WD and ferociously rummaged through the jackets lying across the back seat.

'Don't go upsetting yourself, sir,' his butler pleaded. 'You must stay calm to beat that Canadian chap.'

'Bugger the Canadian. It's that girl from Sydney with the sexy sister I'm concerned about. I could bloody shoot my father.' By the time Andrew reached his firing point his concentration was in disarray. He lay down and looked at the soggy flags. 'How do I read those,' he grumbled. 'I should be wearing grandfather's jacket. He wanted me to wear it here.' Andrew tried to concentrate but his mind seethed over the unfairness of his father taking the jacket. He lined up the targets but shot badly and was out of the contest.

With the flags thoroughly soaked and a mist playing games across the range, all the competitors were in trouble. Lucy stood quietly watching the flags, trying to find a pattern in the wind which was sweeping across the barren ground.

Philip had grown up in the cold windy wilds of northern Canada. The rain didn't bother him, but he wasn't accustomed to such fickle winds. Like Lucy, he was intensely controlled. He calmly settled onto the damp ground and shot to finish with 297.44.

Lucy's first "sighter" went wide and the crowd gasped. But Lucy didn't hear anything as she reloaded and bent to the sights. The next projectile ripped through the V. With calm precision she loaded and shot, loaded and shot, sending projectile after projectile through the centre. She didn't think of the team, or Sarah, or the projectile, or the weather. Load, aim, squeeze. When she completed all fifteen shots, she looked up at the huge scoreboard and let the tears flow.

She had a score of 297.46; two V-bulls better than Philip.

According to tradition, Lucy mounted the dais to have the Queen's badge pinned to her sleeve while the crowd cheered. Then, holding her rifle, she sat on the ceremonial chair that would be carried on the shoulders of her team for the rest of the night. Little had changed since Queen Victoria shot that first competitive round in 1860.

Their first stop was the National Rifle Association Headquarters where the bigwigs gathered for drinks. There was the winner's first sip of champagne, the signing of the book at the NRA museum, scones and cream at the Commonwealth Club, the traditional firing of the cannon, speeches, drinks at private clubs and so on until the first hint of dawn could be seen through the trees. The team complained of sore shoulders, but still argued over who would have the honour of carrying her when it was time to move on.

Sometime during the night Lucy rang home and when George came on the phone, he told her he was drinking champagne. This made her laugh out loud because he always called champagne the "piss of toffs".

Sarah moved along with them but scorned their pitiful world. Real power was not winning a few prizes at a shooting competition. Real power was influence, absolute control and getting what you wanted. She had arranged with Andrew that he would visit her in Australia, and they would fly up to his uncle's property where the pony paddock was bigger than that farm at Camden Lucy was so fond of. She sipped her drinks and avoided Sally, who had found the shell.

On a hunch Sally had gone into Sarah's room while the speeches were on and found the shell hidden behind shoes in the wardrobe. Incensed, she had confronted Sarah. 'How could you do that to your sister?' she asked, barely able to contain her anger. 'Lucy could have lost today because of you. Is that what you wanted? Her to lose and your new boyfriend to win? Eh?'

Sarah looked into Sally's eyes with silent contempt – saw a pathetic little person who would never be anything more than a suburban psychologist with a university shooting club as her greatest achievement – turned and walked away.

L U C Y

I force myself to stop thinking of Sarah driving towards me and let my mind drift back to Bisley.

I had never known such confidence and contentment as I did after that trip. I received congratulatory letters from shooters I didn't know. I was asked to give speeches. Now, every time I enter a competition, people from other clubs want to talk to me, ask my advice, study my rifle.

George bought a new cap to celebrate and made me wear my badges so he could boast about his "protégé". His eyes under those bushy brows twinkled brighter than ever.

And Damon, dear Damon. When I returned to Sydney, he held me in a long gentle embrace and said: 'I always knew you had an inner strength. So did your dad. Now you know it so you can start to believe in yourself and stand on your own.'

I should have written down those words and read them every morning before I got up. The trouble was, every time I started to believe in myself something happened to crush me again.

Like the night of our twentieth birthday party.

CHAPTER 26

'We should let Lucy fly a little now that she is feeling so good,' Jill said to Mario as they sat on the veranda enjoying the unexpected warmth of a late winter evening. Their twentieth is coming up and I've decided to give them the house for the weekend so they can have a party and invite whoever they want. We'll pay for the security and caterers and disappear for the night. Let them "do their thing" as Sarah would say,' she said with a raised eyebrow.

'What about us?' Mario was cross. 'I was looking forward to celebrating it with our families – our parents, your brother, my uncles and cousins. Mum would love to cook up a festive Italian meal.'

'We can do that during the week. The weekend should be for their own crowd. As it happens, I'll be on the Great Barrier Reef for a fashion shoot that weekend. You could go to your Mum's? She loves having you to herself.'

'When I was a kid, everyone came to special birthdays.' Mario said, hurt by Jill's unexpected decision. He'd been looking forward to putting on a big party for his girls. 'And how do we know what they'll get up to in the house on their own?'

'Darling, don't be so old-fashioned. What do you think they "get up to" when they go skiing and to the beach house at Palm Beach? Their friends can stay over so there will be no drink-driving and Lucy can share the hosting with Sarah. They haven't done much together lately.'

Mario could still be surprised by what Jill perceived, even when she didn't seem to be taking any notice. 'Hmm, they have drifted apart lately.'

'It's to be expected. Sarah needs her freedom and Lucy has

her shooting friends. Get used to it my darling; women are naturally competitive. They're discovering their own paths in life, but it's important for them to do things together occasionally.

When Lucy and Sarah were told they would have the house to themselves they smacked their hands together in a high-five and started planning. Sarah would invite her legal crowd from university and some girls from Abbotsfield ... Lucy her shooting mates, Damon and Billy. Sarah would organise food and drinks ... Lucy music and decorations. Mario agreed to design the invitations. Other than suggesting a good caterer, Jill left them alone.

In the weeks leading up to the party Lucy floated on air. Some days she was encased in headphones and swaying to the beat, others she was climbing trees with Mario to string up fairy lights. She sorted the family's extensive CD collection into dancing, romancing and conversation, which, according to her favourite radio station, was the way to party success. She bought small squat candles for the path leading to the front door and gold ones to float on the fishpond.

The evening of the party they stood together regarding a large cake moulded into a mountain scene topped with a carving of two girls holding hands. 'It's a bit kitsch, isn't it?' Sarah decreed. 'It looks different in our house to the picture the baker showed me.' The cake sat in the middle of a small square table at the end of a long table laden with platters of seafood, meats, salads, cheeses and exotic fruits. 'The staff will stay on until after coffee and I've filled the fridge for a barbecue breakfast tomorrow.'

'I love it all.' Lucy squeezed Sarah's hand as they grinned at each other. Still holding hands, they walked onto the veranda.

'You've done a wonderful job with the lights and candles,' Sarah stated. 'Our prince could come galloping up along that path lined with candles.' As little girls their favourite story had been about a beautiful princess who was saved from a horribly cruel uncle by a handsome prince on a magnificent white horse.

Sarah shimmered in a short silver dress with spaghetti shoulder straps and matching shoes with long, fine metal heels. Silver bands held her hair in a sophisticated pile.

Lucy was all loose glimmer in a sheer material of muted gold with bronze and yellow swirls that floated over a fitted black dress. Her gold shoes had soft leather straps that wrapped around her ankles.

They listened as the security guard, who their father had insisted on, checked the names off his list and ushered in their first guests.

Lucy and Sarah, with help from Mario and Jill, had cleared the lounge of furniture for dancing and by midnight the party was in full swing. Lucy put on dance music that pulsated through the floorboards. She'd had a couple of puffs of a joint and her senses were electrified. She soared over the tide of bodies, rose and fell with each instrument, pranced like a horse in the wild. As the dancers tired she put on a slower beat and sat happily watching romance drift in.

'I'm getting something sweet to eat,' Kylie whispered, leaning over to speak in Lucy's ear. 'I think it's the grass.' She giggled as she dragged Lucy towards the heavily laden dining table.

On the way, she asked why Damon hadn't turned up and Lucy shrugged. 'You know him, hates parties. His family moved to the south coast so he's down there studying at lot. You're lucky to have Pete here. He's gorgeous.'

'Yes, but he's a bit mixed up,' Kylie said reflectively. 'Did you know his father's a politician and never home and his mother's a socialite on her way to becoming an alcoholic. He's an only child and as long as he keeps out of trouble, they keep his allowance going. Who's the guy Sarah's with?' she said to change the subject. 'I haven't seen him before.'

'Andrew Braybrook,' Lucy said, pushing up the end of her nose with the tip of her finger. 'He's the guy I told you about at Bisley. The one I had to beat. We didn't know whether he would be in Australia until a couple of days ago. I suspect he planned it so he could. He and Sarah sort of got together over there.'

Kylie listened closely. John had told her how angry the team had been with Sarah but she couldn't detect any bitterness in Lucy's tone. 'He's a bit pasty for Sarah, isn't he?'

'He looked much spunkier at Bisley in his shooting gear with a toffy butler panting at his heels.' Laughing, they walked outside to join Pete.

'Fantastic music.' Pete said as he kissed Lucy. The three sat at the edge of the veranda to eat their cake.

Lucy let her gaze wander. Her romantic music was working well. A couple leaned against each other on a seat near the fernery and another couple were softly paddling on the beach. Jasmine wafted in the air and two girls sat giggling under the hedge where it was growing. Sarah and Andrew had joined a group sitting around the edge of the fishpond, trailing their fingers to make the floating candles wobble and cast ghostly shadows over their faces. Lucy could see couples all over the lawn swaying softly to her music drifting out from the lounge.

And that's when her mood crashed. It dropped like a stone hitting the ground as she recognised the unspeakable – she was the only girl without a guy. Dazed, she stumbled inside pushing her way through swaying couples. Close to tears, she fumbled through the CDs for a loud dance beat. I'll get them dancing, stop this romantic rubbish she mumbled to herself as tears threatened.

'Don't change it.' Sarah had come inside and guessed what Lucy was about to do. 'Everyone's enjoying a bit of you know what!'

Lucy leaned against the wall and watched Sarah float into the darkness with John from the university team. Where's

Andrew, she wondered? The romantic tune slunk into her body, caressing her mind. Oh, God, I want a guy. I want to feel his arms around me, his hard belly against mine, his lips ... she let the tears flow.

The scent of heated bodies sent such a longing through her she wanted to cry out. The music throbbed and the dancers swayed like ghouls taunting her.

A deep agonised longing turned her thoughts bitter.

'Don't let yourself become bitter,' Jane had told her many times. 'Move away from any people, or any place, that makes you feel that way.'

But where could she go? Not the garden. Not upstairs where couples had tiptoed, stifling their giggles. Not the kitchen with its plates of half-eaten food and bright lights. Then she thought of her father's library discretely tucked away off the kitchen. No one would be there because they had stuck a "Do Not Enter" sign on the door to protect his privacy. She put the player onto automatic then slipped into the dark room, where she curled up in the big leather armchair and fell asleep. Lucy had no idea of the time when she woke with fright at the sound of the door bursting open.

'You got a condom?' John's guttural whisper pierced the darkness.

'Of course,' came Sarah's teasing tone.

'Get out. Get out. Get out.' Lucy screamed.

In shocked silence, they fled.

Lucy curled her arms around her body and felt a satanic blackness envelop her as she sobbed. She was vaguely aware of the dance music starting up again and voices laughing and getting louder as the party continued. Later, she heard a few people going, calling out their thanks, some asking for her.

'Leave her. She's asleep,' she heard Sarah reply.

CHAPTER 27

The next morning John was first up. He stepped carefully over debris and sleeping bodies to the veranda where he found David and a couple of other guys draped over camp beds, mouths open and snoring. He poured himself a tall glass of tomato juice, spiced it with Tabasco and walked down to the boatshed where there was more snoring. He sat on the grass under the tree with Lucy's target nailed above his head.

What a dick I am, he thought, as he recalled the scene in the library. Sarah had suggested it on the spur of the moment, and he had gone along with her even though he knew she was with Andrew. David's right, I've got to cut down on my drinking. I should have gone back and apologised to Lucy, but Sarah said not to. John put his head in his hands and gingerly rubbed his temples.

Lucy had dozed fitfully in the big armchair until the rising sun stabbed through the wooden slats directly into her eyes. She despondently moved to another chair away from its glare.

Memories of the night were a disjointed jumble, but the library scene was vivid. What did it matter? They were free to do as they liked, she told herself as she recalled Jane's words, 'Don't let yourself become jealous of Sarah.'

Guys will talk to me, but none want to touch me, she thought as she slumped into the chair, all the excitement of the night before gone.

Was it minutes or hours later when she woke with a start to feel hands resting lightly on her shoulders? 'Lucy.' she heard a gentle voice say as she struggled awake and looked up into a pair of caring grey eyes.

'Morning.'

'Damon!'

Lucy stared in disbelief. In the months since she had last seen him, he had changed so much. He was finely honed with broad shoulders and not an ounce of excess fat. He knelt in front of her as he slid his long slim fingers down her arms to rest lightly on her knees.

'How was the party?' he asked.

Damon didn't tell Lucy he had already spoken to John. He would let her tell him if she wanted to.

Lucy wanted to tell him about the longing; he would understand her aching need to be held close. But instead she told him about the music she had played, the food, the presents, the candles in the fishpond and how she had crept into the library for a few minutes' peace then fallen asleep.

'Look at silly me, still here,' she laughed nervously. 'I missed half the party.'

He looked around. 'Your dad said I could come here and use his books.'

'I didn't know that,' Lucy said. 'When?'

''Bout a year ago. I was working in that framing shop in Rozelle at the time and he came in to buy some art stuff.'

'Why did he offer you the use of this room?'

'I told him I was about to start classes to be a sculptor and he said he had some books that might be useful.'

Lucy realised she had lost touch with Damon and didn't know he was studying to be a sculptor. Her shooting and university studies, along with his move to the south coast, had separated them. The last time they met was just after she had returned from Bisley. 'And are you a sculptor?'

'I've been accepted for a three-year Advanced Diploma at the National Art School next year.' Damon didn't elaborate but Lucy heard the excitement in his voice. 'I can major in sculpture in the last year. Billy got in too.' He walked around the room looking at books. His dark-brown hair was bleached blond by the sun and he had let it grow long so he could drag it back into a ponytail held with a thick rubber band.

'You can still use the library, you know,' Lucy said. She wanted to tell him he should use a proper hair band because rubber bands split the ends of the hair.

'They've got the barbecue going outside. Want breakfast?' he asked. He came over and held out his hands to lift her from the chair. It was the sort of old-fashioned gesture her father would make and she was flustered by the overwhelming need she had to be cuddled. Embarrassed, she stammered 'I've got to go to the bathroom'.

'I'll wait for you.' He gave her a little hug before she left the room. He knew instinctively that it would boost her morale to be seen walking across the lawn with him at her side.

He knew her pain, because he was learning that he too was an outsider.

CHAPTER 28

Jill had scheduled an excellent piece on infidelity for the next issue of the lifestyle magazine. The article had experts describing the signs to look for, advising how to catch a cheating partner, and what to do once you had. She shuddered at the thought of laying a trap, but recognised herself in parts of the story. Mario seemed distracted lately. He didn't look at her with the adoration and admiration that went with his passionate nature. He was working late more often and when he worked at home, he stayed in his library until after she was asleep. He didn't initiate sex anymore.

Jill walked to the window and looked down on the toy-sized cars moving along the canyons the city's office towers created. Straight ahead, on the harbour, ferries and luxury craft sped along leaving bubbling white wakes behind, but she didn't register any of this. She was thinking back on her marriage. How much she still loved Mario. How she had never doubted his love for her.

Okay, so she had indulged in a couple of affairs on overseas trips, but nothing serious. He may have too? They were, after all, a modern-day couple.

'So why has this story disturbed me so much?' she deliberated as she returned to her desk. She had another look at the article and flicked her pen over a few points: has your husband/partner stopped looking at you the way he used to – tick; has he lost interest in sex – tick; does he seem to be avoiding you – tick. Could Mario be having an affair? she asked herself with growing unease.

I'll ask Mary, she decided. Although I've hardly seen her at home since she started those art classes. She must be enjoying them, she thought fondly, because she's never looked better.

'I sound like those women in the article', she reprimanded herself and made a resolution to stay home more often.

Jill would have liked to screw up the article and toss it in the bin, but it was a good story so she marked it up for publication.

A week later, she received an invitation from the NZ lifestyle magazine to send a journalist do a story on a wilderness lodge in Arnhem Land and she called them immediately. 'I'll do it myself and bring my husband,' she told the delighted public relations girl.

That night she placed the brochure in front of Mario with a knowing look and an arched eyebrow. 'You'll just love it darling. Remote, luxurious, deep-sea fishing, wildlife, a bona fide break from the city. The resort has received approval from the local Aboriginal people and you've always wanted to learn more about them. And look at the cabins!' She ran her fingers over a photo of a hexagonal cabin with louvred glass walls that opened so there was no visible barrier between the inside and the bush.

All Mario saw was the king-sized bed in the middle of the room. How could he explain this to Mary? A business trip to a city somewhere, maybe. But a romantic tropical resort?

'Why don't you take the girls?' he said with a sudden brainwave. 'They'll love it. And Lucy would benefit so much from a trip out of the city.'

Jill came around the table and, putting her arms over his shoulders, nibbled at his neck. 'No, darling. This is our holiday. It's years since you and I have gone somewhere special without the girls.'

Mario tossed and turned all night and the next morning he drove to work with his thoughts in a jumble. His love for Mary was the purest emotion he had ever experienced for another adult, but he loved his children too and he did not want them to know the pain of a broken marriage before they were safely married.

When he was with Mary, he had no doubts about their love

but when they were apart he chastised himself. He played his early years with Jill over and over in his mind. They were magic and she was still that same exquisite woman who never complained. She had a driving ambition, but she was not a complex person. She went for what she wanted and stayed with those she loved.

It was not until two days before they left for Arnhem Land that he found the courage to tell Mary. They were lying in the sun at their Refuge after a long session of lovemaking. 'I have to go to Arnhem Land, to a remote resort, with Jill for her work,' he said lamely.

She sat bolt upright and stared at him. 'How long have you known?'

'A week, maybe two.' How easily one learns to lie, he thought.

'The two of you at a remote tropical resort, swimming, drinking G&Ts beside the pool.' Mary shivered as she pulled a towel around her shoulders. 'I knew this day would come. That Jill would suspect something and reclaim you. That's what this is, you know,' she said, feeling the first pains of their break-up.

'It's not like that,' he said reaching for her. 'It's on Aboriginal land. We'll be learning about the wildlife and bush tucker and their culture, that sort of thing,' He trailed off.

'Bullshit!' Mary's eyes were blazing. 'Aboriginals and bush tucker are not Jill's scene and you know it. I'll bet it's that place I saw in a flash magazine ad recently – gourmet chef, hexagonal cabins with glass walls, candlelit dinners by the pool. She's claiming you back. She may not know it's me, but she damn well knows it's someone.' Tears streamed down her cheeks but when he tried to take her in his arms, she shoved him away.

'Please don't do this to me,' she begged as his heart thumped. She could call for a showdown, but she had known all along his loyalties were tearing him apart and that this day would come. Shaking but resolute she dressed, marched out the door and down the driveway to her car.

The next morning, after everyone had left, he pushed through the gap in the fence. 'I just want you to listen,' he cautioned with his hands up. 'I love you more than anyone else in the world. I just need time to work it out. And I will, Mary, I just don't know how yet.'

They clung to each other and let their emotions take them upstairs. Afterwards they lay spent but not satisfied. He left feeling shamed for soiling the woman he loved.

CHAPTER 29

The flight from Sydney to Darwin renewed Mario's interest in the vast deserts of Australia that he longed to one day explore. They boarded a light aircraft in Darwin and flew low enough to see the northern wetlands, home to thousands of water birds and crocodiles. Despite his good intentions, Mario was swept up in the wonder and excitement as they flew over Arnhem Land. Jill's slim hand rested lightly on his knee as she leaned close to gaze out the window.

Mario took a sick bag from the seat pocket and sketched the aircraft's door bursting open with undies, bras and shirts fluttering down like dying seagulls to drop over the noses of wild buffalo and startled crocodiles. Jill admired it and passed it on to the four American tourists travelling with them.

They laughed and nodded. They had all watched as their luggage was crushed into a very small hold at the front of the plane and the door was closed with considerable difficulty.

'That's the Cobourg Peninsula below,' the pilot called above the noise of the engine. 'It's about the size of Portugal. And there's the Arafura Sea.'

Mario marvelled at the pilot's skill as he landed on the dusty airstrip slashed from the bush, and the driver's expertise as he steered the 4WD on the bone-shattering track to the resort. He walked around their cabin stunned by its size, the wild bush that surrounded it, and the turquoise water twinkling through the trees. 'You can't even see another cabin,' he said as he pulled the cord to open the louvres.

Jill smiled, pleased about deciding to do this trip.

Over the next two days Mario gave himself completely to the burning land, the hum of insects, the coolness of the pool and the excitement of a big fish on the end of his line. Inertia fell softly as Sydney slipped away.

Jill needed copy for her story, so she followed the Aboriginal guide into the bush where she took photos and notes. At the ruins of a British settlement he explained: 'White people tried to settle here two hundred years ago but they wouldn't learn from the blackfella, so they died from heat, malaria and poor soil. Those that survived fled and the army closed the settlement.' Jill read the inscriptions carved into the crumbling headstones, appalled at the number of mothers and babies that died on the same day.

She wanted to photograph a horned water buffalo, like she had seen in the movie *Crocodile Dundee*, so the guide found one for her. It was contentedly ripping up and eating long strands of scraggy grass and would not stop even though the guide waved his arms about and shouted at it. 'I thought game hunters came from around the world to stalk and shoot these beasts,' she said. 'You can't even get that one to look up.'

'Don't tell the big white hunters that,' the Aboriginal guide chuckled. 'Sometimes they run. If we know a hunter is coming with a gun and camera for trophy photos, we will chase them with a big stick for a few days.' Jill thought the guide would never stop laughing.

'Don't you write that, lady. Those hunters bring in big bucks and it means the rangers don't have to cull them. Cheaper for the taxpayer.'

While the other tourists wilted in the heat, Jill thrived. Before leaving Sydney, she'd had her blond hair cut very short and it framed her fine-boned face like a cap of gold. She and Mario swam in the pool before breakfast and met back there in the late afternoon.

The outdoors and the fishing rejuvenated Mario. He returned each afternoon with stories of fish caught and others taken off the lines by sharks that glided like grey submarines around the boat.

Jill watched with satisfaction the reduced tension in Mario's arms and shoulders and the jaunty angle of his hat as he settled into the pattern of tropical time.

On their last night the chef baked Mario's catch of the day in banana leaves over the barbecue. Jill had put on a loose silk dress and Mario, tanned and relaxed, laughed uproariously as she told him the story of the buffalo hunters. After dinner they took a bottle of champagne to the pool, where they sat dangling their feet in the water. The full moon cast an orange light along the water, which shimmered as they wiggled their toes.

Jill, knowing the moment was right, lifted his hand to her lips, kissing it softly. 'I've been worrying about you. You've seemed detached. Is anything wrong?'

'Of course not.'

The snap in his reply alarmed her. 'There is something bothering you, isn't there?'

'Don't start on this now and ruin a perfect evening.'

'Is it work?'

'No.'

'Lucy?'

'Of course, I worry about Lucy, but so do you. Don't get all serious and ruin the night.'

Jill sat up a little straighter, realising her worries were not just in her imagination. 'Don't shut me up. Whatever it is, I want you to know I'm with you. That I love you as much now as I ever did, and I will do anything I can to help. If it's Lucy, let us work it out together.' She hesitated then said the words she never thought she would hear herself say. 'You do still love me, don't you?'

Mario stared into the water, his mind racing as he tried to think what to say.

Jill leaned forward and the folds of her dress fell open enough to expose her firm breasts. 'You know I have never loved anyone but you. Maybe I've been away too much and maybe I should have helped more with Lucy, but I've never stopped loving you. You're the only man I have ever wanted,' she finished, feeling she might weep.

Mario looked into the face of the woman he had married twenty-three years ago and who he had been cheating for the last few years. Her green eyes were looking at him with such honest love, that guilt and regret burned through his body and he knew, in that instant, that he still loved her. 'I love you now as I have always loved you,' he whispered.

'You give me my life,' Jill replied as she felt the tension leave her body and rested her head lightly on his shoulder. 'Knowing you're there gives me the confidence to walk into that publishing house and fight the battles I have to fight. Never, ever, my darling doubt my love for you.'

They swirled the water with their feet as they sipped their champagne in silence. Small animals scuffled in the dry grass behind them. Jill slipped her hand up under his shirt and ran her fingers in light scratchy strokes over his back. He put an arm around her shoulder and let his hand drop over a breast. The nipple rose expectantly.

After a while they stood and walked along the shadowy path to their cabin. The moon was high and it cast shadow lines through the open louvres across Jill's body as she let her dress fall from her shoulders. Naked, she glided towards him and he felt the heat rise in his body as she stretched up against him ... the flat tummy, soft breasts and slim hips that were so familiar. That night he made love to her with all the wild passion of their first nights together. As they had in those days, Jill lay her head in the hollow of his shoulder and he stroked her tenderly until she was asleep. In the silence of the room he thought back over the past five years, but he had no answer to the overwhelming lust he had felt tonight.

Back in Sydney, Mary had enrolled in a short watercolour painting course in the Blue Mountains while Mario was in

Arnhem Land with Jill. She had hoped a few days away with a new style of painting would ease her tension, but she returned just as depressed as she had left.

Jaded, she opened the wardrobe for her comfy slippers and stared at her clothes in shock. At first, she couldn't comprehend what she was seeing. Then she screamed.

Kylie leaped out of her chair and rushed upstairs to her mother's room.

'Oh no,' Kylie cried as she stood beside her mother staring into the wardrobe. 'It's Lucy.'

'What do you mean, it's Lucy?' Mary spluttered.

'She did that to Sarah's clothes, too.'

'Did what?'

'Cut the legs off her trousers and the sleeves off her jackets.'

'No one told me.'

'They all agreed not to tell anyone.' Kylie put her arm around her mother and led her over to the bed so they could sit close together. 'Sarah told me, but I didn't tell you because she asked me not to. Jane was going to talk to Dr Kilter, the psychiatrist who treated Lucy at the hospital at Westmead. She thought all the excitement and attention of Bisley built up Lucy's expectations, then nothing really changed. Jane thinks it might have even started at their twentieth and now Lucy's on a massive downer. She thinks Lucy cut up Sarah's clothes in a fit of jealousy or anger, but I don't know why she would come over here and cut up your clothes. Why would she be angry with you?'

Mary turned towards Kylie and took up her hands. 'You must promise that you will never tell anyone, absolutely no one what I am going to tell you. Most definitely not Sarah.'

CHAPTER 30

'Can we meet at Gladesville Park near the Banjo Paterson restaurant?' Mario's voice over the phone was strained and unsure. He did not suggest the Refuge because what he had to tell her demanded all his control.

As she walked along the disused road to their meeting place, she saw him standing on a little rise looking out across the bay. The breeze coming off the water tossed his dark curls about and pressed his shirt against his body. Her legs went weak at the thought of the curls spread like a mat over his chest and the strange knot of his belly button.

He turned at her puffed approach and the desperation in her eyes electrified the air.

He looked away, ashamed.

They stood side by side like poles in the wind, close but not touching.

'Jill still loves me,' he muttered as he looked at the water.

'So do I.' The wind snatched at her words and he strained to hear them.

'I didn't realise how important I am to her.'

'You're important to me, too. Your love has changed my world.'

'I can't leave her.'

'I know.'

'You know?' Surprised, he looked down at her. He had expected tears or anger. Not this quiet acceptance.

'I know, and I won't ask you to leave her.' She looked out over the water, letting the wind blow her hair back from her face.

'Your being away gave me time to think. I don't want to share you anymore. I don't have the emotional stamina to live a double life and neither do you.'

Mario gathered up her hands and rolled her fingers between his. 'We can still see each other sometimes.' He was frightened by what her words implied. 'We've still got our Refuge.'

'I don't want borrowed time with you. I want to be with you all the time and have friends over for long lunches. If I can't have it all, I'll have nothing.' She felt his hands shaking as she snatched hers away.

'Mary,' Mario's voice trembled. 'We just need a bit more time.'

'I knew what it meant when you asked me to meet you here.' She spoke so softly he had to watch her lips to catch the words. 'You can't do it, but I can. In fact, I've done it. James is on manoeuvres in the North Sea for the next six months so I'm going to Ireland to visit Mum. When he has time off, we're going to drive around Ireland and France. Kylie is getting a girlfriend to keep her company and Jill has agreed to keep an eye on them. My flight leaves on Monday.'

Tears spilled over Mary's cheeks and dripped from her chin as she stumbled back down the path, her light denim skirt flapping against her bare legs.

CHAPTER 31

'Liam's about to double-cross me.' Jill said as she stormed into the house, dumped her bag and gave Mario a cursory kiss on the cheek. 'He's asked the marketing department to assess the benefits of a new strategy he's interested in for the Asia/Pacific – my publications – and to report back to Dwight.'

'How do you know all this?' Mario asked, looking up from the curry he was stirring.

'My spy in sales and marketing phoned.' Whenever she went to New York she took Alex half-a-dozen of the latest most talked about Australian wines to present at his wine club. She regularly sent him newspaper and magazine articles, as well as the annual digest on the Australian wine industry.

'Alex said Dwight is back from Europe and looking for a challenge. In Europe he took several of Liam's magazines to the top and started *The Teenager*, copied after mine I might add. It's a huge success and on top of that he married that rich New Yorker he was dating, and they have two boys who get on famously with Liam and Nuala's kids. He's too damn perfect for words.'

'He's a success but so are you, with the biggest-selling lifestyle magazines in Japan, Australia and NZ. *The Teenager* has put all your rivals out of print. Liam's not about to interfere with that sort of success.'

'I've got to go to America immediately.'

'We could meet you in Aspen after your meetings,' Sarah said as she sauntered into the room. 'We haven't skied there for ages. It would be great for Lucy; get her away from the glums.'

'Good idea.' Mario was prepared to grab at anything that might help Lucy. 'She loves skiing and I'd like to see Aspen again.'

'And I've just worked out a reason why I need to go to New York.' Jill smiled to herself as she walked over to her writing bureau.

Mario, Lucy and Sarah arrived at Aspen the second week of January, one day before Jill. They had booked into a lodge recommended by a friend, in the middle of Aspen village which was located below the ski runs on Aspen Mountain. 'It's decorated with American Indian artefacts and has tall Indian drums as bar stools,' the friend had told them. Lucy was beating on one of these drums when Jill stalked in, frowning and letting her bag bang on the floor. 'He's gone,' she said.

'Who?' Mario jumped up, waving at Lucy to stop beating the drum.

'Dwight.'

'Gone?'

'Yes. Gone.'

'What? Dead?'

'No. He left the company. Been purloined by Mortlock Publishing with the promise of total control over its international magazine division. More power. More money. More everything.' Jill threw down her bags and twirled around the room laughing at their puzzled faces.

'What about Liam's plans for Asia/Pacific?' Sarah asked. Jill's managing and opening new magazines had fitted in well with her studies of corporate law and takeovers.

'I didn't ask. Liam likes my idea of expanding into Hong Kong and has given me a substantial budget to do a feasibility study. He sends his love and wishes he was here to chase you girls over the slopes.'

'Did you see Dwight?' Sarah couldn't understand why he would leave a company where he had such a promising future.

'Oh yes. He took me to lunch at the trendiest restaurant in town. He hedged around making me a proposition, sussed out whether I'm open to offers. My spies tell me it was common knowledge around New York publishing circles that Mortlock wanted to expand beyond America and Canada. Buying Dwight is a smart move.'

'Would you listen to an offer if he made one?'

'What do you think, Sarah?' Jill asked. 'I might not accept it, but I'd be a fool not to listen, don't you think.' Jill often had Sarah in her office working on the legal side of opening the new magazines. She was impressed by how razor-sharp Sarah was and how much the staff liked her. 'Where are we skiing tomorrow?'

'Early start on Aspen Mountain then I'm taking you to lunch,' Mario grinned. 'The girls are leaving us at lunchtime to ski Snowmass with some of Sarah's friends from Abbotsfield.'

In truth it wasn't girls from Abbotsfield but a group of boys from university. Sarah didn't see the need to tell her parents every detail of her life.

The next morning, they skied together until lunchtime when Mario took Jill to lunch and the twins skied across to the boys' unit, arriving just as the pizzas were being delivered. Lucy hesitated at the door, reluctant to go into such a hot crowded room where everyone had stripped down to their T-shirts. Sarah tossed her head at Lucy's timidity and pushed on into the room to a raucous welcome and high-fives.

'She seems to know everyone in there,' a voice behind Lucy drawled softly. She turned to look into the blackest eyes she had ever seen.

'They're all doing law at university in Sydney.'

'You coming in?' He smiled as he pointed inside and Lucy found herself wanting to smile back. For a moment she hesitated then turned and quickly walked away.

'I don't bite,' he called as he ran to catch up with her. 'I don't even bark very loud.'

'I ... I'm sorry, it wasn't you,' Lucy stammered, overcome with embarrassment. 'I get nervous in crowds. I'm not hungry so I'm going to ski some more.'

'Mind if I join you? I hardly know anyone in there myself and the forecast is for bad weather tomorrow so we may only have today to ski. By the way, I'm Michael and I've never had anyone run away so soon after meeting me.'

Lucy's heart hammered as they rode the chairlifts up and skied down together, Michael leading the way. She had never met a guy who was so open and easy to talk to.

'Do you ski a lot in Australia?' he asked after they had skied most of the difficult runs he knew.

'A bit. Our snow's not very good and the runs are short compared with here, and tricky. You have to be in control all the time.'

'You're exceptionally brave for a girl,' he said after a very difficult black run.

'Not so much brave,' Lucy said self-consciously. 'It's control. I ski with my head, not just my body.'

'But you need skill as well; skiing is after all a physical activity.'

'Yes, true, but think of all the people who have never got past a certain level. They can go fast, do bumps, trees, even the Wall ... but they're not quite good enough to compete.' Lucy could feel herself glowing. The fast skiing and Michael's attention had lifted her spirits and she knew she was being very verbose, but she didn't care. 'And that's because they're not positive and can't hold their concentration.'

'I can concentrate,' Michael laughed. 'But if you come flying around a bend and are suddenly on a steep slope with rocks at the bottom, there's not a lot you can do.'

'That depends. If you see rocks as something that will hurt you, that's a negative thought, so you panic. But what if you saw them as a challenge and concentrated on how to negotiate them successfully? That's what extreme skiers do.

They don't know what's ahead, so they think positively, focus hard, concentrate and stay in control.

'Okay then, let's go. I've got a few more runs to show you.' He was impressed with this tall slim girl who spoke her mind in a warm, husky voice.

At times she was hard pushed to keep up with him, but her blood was up and nothing would let her give in before this guy. His soft drawl and light humour lifted her spirits. She like the way he openly admired her skiing style and he had made subtle comments on her fine figure. She recognised he was flirting and it made her even more daring. She was in her twenties and still a virgin. It bothered her that she had never been kissed romantically.

All too soon the afternoon was over. They made their final run and as they skidded to a stop at the bottom he pushed back his goggles. 'How about a drink with the others back at the unit?'

Lucy followed him reluctantly. She would have to remove her hat and goggles. As they clumped along amongst the colourful river of skiers coming off the slopes, she let herself drop back until the gap between them filled with bodies. Once he was out of sight, she ran to the bus stop and took the shuttle back to Aspen village.

An hour after she got back to the unit the phone rang.

'Where did you get to?' She felt her face flush when she heard Michael's voice.

'Lost in the crowd. I couldn't remember where the unit was so I just came home. How did you get this number?'

'Your sister gave it to me. Listen, we're all meeting at Tippler's tonight about 10.30. I'd like to buy you a drink and see if you dance as well as you ski. Sarah said she's going home to change and can bring you along.'

'I'll think about it.'

'No, baby doll. You talk about being positive ... well I want positive.'

'Okay,' she said, her heart thumping. As she put the

phone down she turned to find Mario watching her. 'He's drop-dead gorgeous.'

'I can tell. Want to talk?'

'He's a little bit funny and a little bit serious and has dark eyes and the cutest smile.'

Sarah and Lucy were at the club when Michael arrived, wearing a fawn shirt over a black skivvy and blue denims around the slimmest hips Lucy had ever seen.

'I feel weak just looking at him,' Lucy said, nudging Sarah. They watched as he started to walk their way but was stopped when two girls called to him. He smiled and stooped to kiss them. 'What's he doing? I'm going to die.'

'Don't worry. He hasn't seen us yet.' Sarah recognised the body language of a man confident in his own skin. Gradually the law students from the unit began to arrive with girls they had met on the slopes and at bars until there was quite a crowd around the twins. But still no Michael. It was half an hour before he materialised before them carrying a bottle of French champagne and two glasses.

'For Lucy, the hotshot skier,' he said winking at the others as he nodded his head towards her.

Michael and Lucy moved on to a disco later, still drinking champagne and margaritas until Lucy couldn't tell the difference. She had covered her face with thick make-up so she felt confident her scars couldn't be seen in the endlessly flashing disco lights. Michael knew everyone, but even as he greeted old friends he hadn't seen since the previous ski season, his hand was always reaching for her to keep her near him. Having never experienced such a boisterous place with such a considerate person before, Lucy forgot her scars as she laughed along with everyone else.

Towards the end of the night Michael led Lucy into Eric's. 'This is the secret den where the locals come to play billiards and smoke cigars. We're going into the Cigar Bar where we can talk.'

The room reeked of cigars and was so dim she could only

just make out the bar in one corner and armchairs and couches covered in dark material, placed strategically for large and small conversation groups. 'It's like a gangsters' den,' she said, relieved he didn't want to play billiards under the overhead lights.

They found two armchairs and he bought thin cigars that tasted sweet and cognac that burned her throat.

'Cheers to an amazing girl,' he said, leaning close as he clinked his glass against hers. 'Now we're here, I'd like you to tell me how you developed this ability to concentrate so well.'

Relaxed by his manner along, with more than alcohol than she was used to, she opened up in a way she had never done before. She told him about her love of shooting and how Mr McKenzie and George had taught her the importance of concentration. She told of winning the Queen's Prize at Bisley. He was impressed because his father had competed there. They talked about university life, friends, Yama and skiing together tomorrow. She didn't mention the fire.

When the bar manager announced they were closing, he took her glass and put it on the table. 'We ski so well together I want to ski with you every day until my family gets here.'

Lucy was so high in the clouds she did not hear, or register, his last words.

It was so cold outside their breath floated in puffs before their faces and ice on the ground made walking dangerous. Michael held her protectively against his body and asked, 'Would you like to come to my place for coffee?'

This was the moment Lucy had been both dreading and praying for all night. She desperately wanted him to invite her home, to hear the desire in his voice, but at the last minute her courage failed her. 'I can't tonight. Don't get me wrong, I want to, I just can't.'

'That's okay, don't look so worried. In America, we don't push women to do anything they don't want to do. You're such a cool chick there has to be another man somewhere.

'And,' he looked down at her thoughtfully, 'I believe there is something you're holding back from me, but we can talk about that when you're ready. Right now, I'm going to see you safely home.'

They walked arm in arm in contented silence until they reached Lucy's door.

'Remember we're meeting at nine at Snowmass, whatever the weather.' He kissed her with his tongue gently probing then stepped back. 'Nine tomorrow.' He waved and was gone.

'I didn't expect to see you home tonight.' Sarah said as Lucy slipped quietly into the room.

'Sorry, I didn't mean to wake you.'

'He's obviously fascinated by you.'

'I've never wanted anything so much in my life.' Lucy perched on the end of Sarah's bed and hugged her knees. 'I get goosebumps just thinking about him. What should I do?'

'He's a hunk, but you had better watch yourself. The boys tell me his father is a multi-millionaire. With his looks, and money, he'll have hundreds of girls after him. Do what you like but don't fall for him,' she cautioned. 'And don't even think about living on the other side of the world away from me.' Although Sarah said this jokingly, she was not smiling. She would stop the affair if it looked like getting serious.

'Don't you think I'm good enough for him?' Lucy was annoyed by Sarah's comment about other girls.

'Snow and sex go together. Just don't think you're the only chick on his plate.'

The next morning dawned dull and grey with forecasters predicting strong winds to arrive around midday. Sarah and Lucy met the law students and Michael at Snowmass at nine and started skiing as a group, but the wind increased and the temperature dropped below zero.

'This is ridiculous,' Sarah said at the top of Big Burn as snow gusts swirled and stung their bare cheeks. 'Let's go back to the unit and play cards.'

'It's too early to go in,' Lucy said, desperate to stay outside where she could keep her eyes covered. 'It's not that bad.'

But Sarah took off and the rest of the group followed. Despondent, Lucy was watching them disappear down the slope when suddenly Michael's voice made her jump. 'I'm still here but I need a kiss to keep skiing.' He had moved closer and leaned over to push up her goggles and pull down her scarf so he could kiss her on the lips.

His eyes opened wide with shock as he looked down at her scarred face and drooping eye.

CHAPTER 32

Michael stood stock still while his mind collated the images that were assailing him – Lucy with scars. Confident controlled Lucy crying. The secret he had imagined she was hiding from him was that she loved a guy who didn't love her, or some guy in Sydney had just dumped her. It had never entered his mind that she might be physically damaged. Michael's parents had taught their children not everyone enjoyed their privileges. His father gave generously to several charities and his mother was independently wealthy as a result of her small legal practice for the underprivileged in a poor part of Boston. She had often taken him to hospitals when he was a child, where he had seen accident victims badly scarred and crippled.

When he studied law, Michael had helped her in her practice, so scars didn't frighten him. Gently he replaced Lucy's goggles and lifted her scarf back over her mouth. 'Let's go someplace where we can talk.'

She nodded.

He led her halfway down the slope to a barely discernible track that he followed into the trees. Breathless with anxiety, Lucy followed him to a clearing where they unclipped their skis and sat on a large flat rock. They looked out over the valley that spread like a dark and brooding beast in an uneasy silence. Skinny threads of sun pierced through clouds and lit up a tree, a house, a car moving along the road. The wind howled above the trees and music drifted faintly from the village far below.

'It's beautiful,' Lucy's voice came out as a tight squeak.

'So are you.'

Michael pulled her into his arms and held her close as she

cried. His experience told him this was a time for listening. After a while Lucy started to talk in short jerky sentences. She told him about the fire, the years of treatment, the ugly pressure garments, the ridicule from kids, the scars, and finally the night she had shown herself to Kylie.

'I'd be honoured to be the first man,' he said as he lifted her chin and watched her eyes go from fear to acceptance.

As they entered his parents' house in the fashionable West End, he flicked on a CD and sat her down while he went to the kitchen for a bottle of wine. She appreciated that he left the lights off so the only light, apart from the CD player, filtered through fine drapes.

Lucy let herself relax as they sipped a Californian red and talked quietly.

When Michael began to remove her clothes, she experienced the familiar sense of fatalism that overcame her whenever she had to expose herself to a new doctor. When he had removed everything, except her panties, he ran his hands over her body, one breast firm and rounded, the other flat with coarse skin. Down his hands went over her flat belly, the swell of her hips and buttocks to the silky panties that he removed tenderly.

'You have a tantalising body and skin the colour of honey,' he said, gently taking her hands and placing them on his chest.

She felt the soft curly hairs over hard muscles. Her thighs gave little jerks. His masculine odour assailed her senses and wild sensations seared through her body as she felt him lean over her. Michael's hands were gentle but relentless as they awakened the woman in her.

'Are you on the pill?' he asked quietly.

She shook her head.

'Are you a virgin?'

She nodded.

He rose and came back with a condom. They didn't leave the house for the rest of the day, nor that night. Lucy phoned her parents to leave a message saying she didn't know when she would be home.

'It's time,' Jill said to Mario as he paced the room.

'I'd like to have met him first.'

'What would you do, look into his eyes and read the man within?'

'It's not a joking matter. She's a special case.' Lucy wasn't someone Mario could joke about.

The next day, Michael took her to the Krabloonik Kennels where they wrapped themselves in blankets, and tail-wagging huskies pulled them through the mountains on hand-crafted sleds. They lunched on wild game and blood-red wine in a log cabin then went back to his house to make love. Later that day Michael took skidoos out of the garage and they hurtled across the snow. That night he took her to a restaurant with candles on the table and politely asked the waiter to take them away. He held her hands, told her she was beautiful, and she felt beautiful.

'I wish we'd met earlier,' he said when they were back at the house.

'Why? We have our lives ahead of us.'

He wanted to say more but she was kissing him from the toes up, so he didn't get around to it. Later, before they went to sleep, he tried again. 'I'm a bit worried because I'm your first and I don't want to hurt you.'

'You never could. I'm invincible. You make me that way.'

'But Lucy, we need to talk. The day after tomorrow my parents and everyone arrive.'

But she was already asleep.

Michael wrapped her in his arms and lay there looking at up at the ceiling. 'What have I done?' he thought miserably. 'I should have told her right at the start. Oh God, she was a virgin and now this.'

The next day Michael and Lucy caught up with Sarah's group and skied with them until it was time to go back to the Snowmass unit. This time Lucy went inside. After three days with Michael beside her she felt so confident she could face anyone.

But that night as they cooked dinner at his place, she wondered briefly why he was so quiet. She thought about asking him but didn't want to do anything that would break the spell of cooking together. Looking back years later she realised he was trying to tell her, but she wasn't listening.

The next morning when she went to make the bed, he said, 'Leave it. I have to wash everything and tidy up before my family arrives. They are flying in at two so I can't ski today.'

'I'll help. We could have the house done and ski until they arrive.'

'No. But thanks for the offer. I need to do it alone.' He was stammering, and she felt the first stirrings of alarm. 'I can't ski today ... or again ... with you that is.'

'You mean ...' Her mind was racing through all the possibilities.

'Yes.'

'You're breaking it off?' Her voice was light, but damp clouds were closing in. 'You've finished with me.' Despair caught hold, slobbering like a rabid dog.

'Don't say it like that. I thought you understood.'

'Understood what? What was there to understand?' The dog strained forward, saliva dripping.

'I thought you understood we were on holiday and having fun. I wanted to make you happy. Please, sit down please. I need to explain.'

'Explain what? That I'm not good enough for you. That a handsome stud like you can't have a freak like me around?' she screamed as she raced around the room gathering up her things, shoving them into her backpack.

'Don't touch me.' She lashed out at him when he tried to take hold of her as she ran past him and out the door.

He stood tormented as the front door slammed.

CHAPTER 33

'I'll kill the bastard.' Mario shouted, as Lucy stormed through the unit and slammed her bedroom door shut.

'You can't blame him.' Jill was pleased Lucy had finally known love but had not really expected it to last beyond Aspen. 'It's her first love and it won't be her last.'

'You don't play first-love games with someone like Lucy. Unless he's a moron he could easily work out what she's been through.'

'True, but Lucy gives off an aura of such confidence on the slopes that no one would guess how fragile she really is.'

Mario ignored her as he scrabbled angrily though the papers beside the phone for the number Lucy had left for Michael's house. 'I should've stopped it.'

'Let it go,' Jill said as she grabbed the piece of paper out of his hand. 'We've discussed this each time she's gone out with him and agreed that Jane would have said to let her have the experience.'

'You agreed, not me. It's taken her twenty-one years to find love and he dumps her after three days.' Mario stormed up and down until he had himself under control then he tapped gently on Lucy's door, but she screamed at him to go away.

Jill sent Mario off to the shops, hoping Lucy would come out before he got back.

Lucy heard Mario storming out and crept out of the room looking lost and frightened. She flopped onto the couch. 'He doesn't want to see me anymore.'

'Did he give a reason?' Jill asked as she put her book down.

'Said his parents were arriving and he couldn't see me again.'

'That's strange.' Jill was puzzled. Kids nowadays didn't stop doing things just because their parents were around.

'Said he'd be busy with them. But that's a lie, isn't it?'

'It's certainly a weak excuse. But men are weak when it comes to breaking off relationships. They never do it with dignity.'

Jill handed Lucy a glass of wine and sat beside her on the couch, letting her sob until she was ready to speak again.

'He used me. Pretended my looks didn't matter. He's probably laughing now, telling his mates about this freak he had. I hate him so much I could kill him.'

Jill wondered if Lucy was right, but she wasn't going to say so. 'In a way, darling, you also used him. After all, he was the first boy you've shown yourself to and I gather he treated you very well for a while. Look at it as an experience, a stepping-stone into womanhood.'

'An experience?' Lucy leaped up and glared at her mother. 'What a sick thing to say. I loved him. I trusted him.'

'Did he ever say he loved you?'

'Can't remember.'

'So maybe he wasn't being deceitful. Maybe he really did like you and thought you'd both have a good time for a few days while on holiday.'

'But I want to see him again.' Lucy slumped as she sat down close to Jill.

'Why don't we give it a few days and if he doesn't call, you can come to the fashion shoot at Telluride with me.' Jill knew this was not what Lucy wanted to hear but she could not think of anything better to suggest.

Three days later, Lucy boarded the chartered jet with Jill, dressed well for the trip but sullen. Her only slight consolation was Mario's promise to contact her immediately if Michael called.

Delia, Jill's glamorous fashion editor from Sydney, met them as they landed at the airport. 'This place is to die for,' she enthused. 'They say Butch Cassidy and his gang robbed their first bank here. Kas is over the moon. He's had the models walking along the wooden boardwalks with gorgeous-looking horses and wild-looking latchkey teens with Rastafarian hair. And at the amazing bar which has sloping mirrors above it so the goldminers could see if anyone was sneaking up behind them to pick their pockets. It's all very cowboys and Indians … not that I've seen any Indians,' she said with a light laugh.

The three were driven past meticulously restored colonial-era houses with wooden verandas and attic windows painted in pretty colours. Tall mountains lined both sides of the valley.

'We can explore those slopes before we leave,' Jill told Lucy. 'Telluride has some of the steepest runs in Colorado.'

'Michael and I would do them easily,' Lucy grunted, wishing she hadn't come.

Kas was photographing along the main street. 'Hello, darlings,' he said as he kissed Jill and Lucy on both cheeks. 'This place may be paradise if you ski, but it's a freezing hell-hole if you don't. Quick! Inside before you all get pneumonia.' He bustled up his cameras and shooed them inside the bar belonging to the unit block where Delia had booked their accommodation. 'Drinkies time. Can you believe it, not one of these Sydney models is a good skier? How am I going to get any good action shots?'

'What size are the clothes?' Jill asked as they waited for their margaritas to arrive.

'Eights and tens. The models you've booked are all gorgeous, darling. But they would probably fall in a faint if I asked them to ski down these steep slopes.'

Kas accepted a margarita with crushed salt gleaming around the edge of the fine-stemmed glass as he winked at the sassy waiter.

'Use Lucy. She's a ten and the prettiest skier you'll ever see.'

Lucy looked at her mother in disbelief while Kas looked across at Lucy with renewed interest. He had thought her surly, but she was tall, slim and her long blond hair would fly out nicely. Also, she was the boss's daughter and it paid to keep in with the boss.

'Don't be stupid Mummy. I'm not a model.'

'You don't have to be,' Jill said. She could already see the shots in her lifestyle magazine, maybe even *Sporting Life*. 'All you have to do is ski and look good. Instead of tucking your long hair up under your beanie and goggles, leave it down so it can fly, and add a few jumps for drama.'

'Jumps! Oh, wonderful, darlings!' Kas took a closer look at Lucy. He knew about the fire and that she wore a wig but from what Jill said that was not a problem. He could shoot from the right-hand side with maybe a scarf flying across the damaged side of her face, although big ski goggles would probably cover most of that. The emphasis of the shot would be on the action, the clothes and the light. As a fashion photographer he was adept with difficult petulant women. 'Could you really do that?' He leaned forward making eye contact with Lucy.

His enthusiasm disarmed Lucy, drawing her in. 'We'd have to find powdery snow. If you set up the camera below a rise, I could come flying over and do a twist to kick up a spray of snow. With the sun was behind me I'd be silhouetted and the spray would glitter,' she added.

'Hmm, but I'd need a clear line and light on you to show off the clothes.'

'If the light's on me, it won't be as dramatic.'

Kas grabbed a scrap of paper and they bent over it as he sketched. Lucy didn't think of Michael again until she was in her room and the sound of hot water running reminded her of the baths he had filled with bubbles and sweet-smelling oils. The excitement that had built up while making plans with Kas slid away like a snake as she lay across the bed and cried.

The next morning, she refused to respond to her mother's knocking.

'Give me her room number,' Kas said as Jill stormed into the dining room where everyone had gathered for breakfast. 'You chappies go on and get ready. I'll find Lucy and bring her with me.'

Jill watched Kas stalk off across the foyer, his slight body pushing skiers out of his way, his blond hair spiked with gel, making it stick out like stalactites. 'David and Goliath,' she mumbled to no one in particular. 'And I wonder who will win?'

The models were all made up and lounging around in a small conference room Delia had rented for the day when Kas walked in with Lucy.

Jill recognised the defiant set to Lucy's mouth but there was resignation there as well. 'What do you have that I don't?' she whispered to Kas.

'Easy, Darling. I'm not her mother for starters. I just agreed with her that all boys are shits and she's better off sticking with me. I'm safe.' He rolled his eyes. 'Then we talked about rifle shooting and photography and agreed they're captivating but cruel masters.'

He didn't tell Jill they'd also discussed how difficult it was to make a living out of fashion photography. How important it was for him to do a great job on a commission like this. He was already a renowned fashion photographer but great photos in one of Jill's upmarket magazines would attract all the right attention and keep the work coming in.

'She's a softie. A bit naïve, which is why that Michael chap has upset her so much. He kicked her in the guts and now won't even listen to her. In her book, that's not fair.'

'I don't think Telluride helped', Jill said. 'She's still down in the dumps.' They had arrived back in Aspen to find Mario still brooding over the Michael debacle.

'It took her mind off Michael for a few days and she got on well with Kas. He will be a good contact for her in Sydney; he knows absolutely everyone in the arts and theatre.'

'Do you know, she keeps walking past his house and standing at the bottom of the lifts hoping to see him?' Mario was still seething. 'I wish to hell I knew what he looked like. I'd ask him what he thinks he's bloody well doing.'

Lucy was not only looking for Michael, she was phoning as well, but every time a woman answered she quietly replaced the receiver.

She just wanted to talk to him. To explain that she had thought it through and realised she had expected too much too quickly. That she was prepared to slow down but wanted to keep in touch. He had said he wanted to see Sydney and she would show it to him. He could even stay with them. 'I just want to tell him these things,' she sobbed into her pillow.

Then, like a door closing, it was their last day in Aspen. They were catching the afternoon shuttle to Los Angeles. Lucy was desperate. She had to talk to Michael and tell him all the things that were boiling around in her head.

Steeling herself, she rang his home number and this time when the woman answered she took a deep breath and said in her calmest voice, 'Could I speak to Michael, please?'

'I'm sorry. He and Michelle are in Vail making the final arrangements for their wedding. They'll be back tomorrow if you would like to leave your number.'

Lucy placed the phone carefully in its cradle as she slid down the wall and collapsed onto the floor.

L U C Y

As I pace the room waiting for Sarah to arrive, I think back on all the episodes of our lives. Aspen, for example. As soon as we arrived home Daddy made an appointment for me to return to Dr Kilter, my psychiatrist from the kids' hospital.

'You refused to speak to your father for several weeks,' Dr Singh said softly. 'Was that because he made you go back to Dr Kilter?'

'No. Because he was a man and I was full of loathing for men. I had decided all men were cheats and I'd never speak to any of them again.'

'Wasn't that a bit harsh on the species? After all, Michael was the only man who had let you down.'

'And Daddy.' I wasn't about to let him forget that he had cheated on me with Mary. 'And Pete.'

'Do you mean Kylie's Pete? Tell me about that.'

'Just before we went to Aspen, Kylie won a scholarship with a mining company that sent her out to Kalgoorlie for six months. She planned to get her mining qualifications then go overseas, helping out in third world countries.

'As soon as Kylie was out of sight, Pete started seeing Sarah. Then he turned up in Aspen because Sarah had rented them a one-bedder in the building where the law students were staying.'

'What did your parents say about that?'

'They were furious but what could they say? Sarah had an allowance and did her own thing.'

'You have often told me that Pete is one of the nicest, most caring guys you know. For him to do this with Sarah seems out of character.'

'He was lonely and mixed up. His father only contacted him when he needed publicity photos for his political career.'

'What was his relationship with his mother?'

'She was away with the fairies. Her family were wealthy graziers. They were furious when she married a chap from the city; a Labor politician to boot.'

'Do you think he was in love with Sarah?'

'He probably thought he was, but Sarah knew how to make people feel wanted and fabulous.'

'Did you think Sarah was cheating on Kylie when she did this?'

'Sarah wasn't the cheat, he was. Or that's what I thought at the time. I also went next door to apologise to Mary for cutting up her clothes.'

'Was that Mary your neighbour? Tell me about that.'

'She and Daddy were having an affair. I don't think Mummy knew but she had taken him to Arnhem Land and I didn't want Mary to take him back when they returned. I was so angry I wanted her to hate him and break it up. I wanted him to suffer.'

'Do you still believe it's only the guys who do the cheating?'

Dr Singh steepled his fingers and rested his chin on them. I don't remember how I answered him.

Even now, years later, I'm still not sure how I feel about men. They seem to come and go, in and out of my life. I wish Daddy was here so I could apologise for everything. I just want to feel his big warm arms around me.

'I remember Kylie was devastated when she found out about Aspen. She never spoke to Sarah again if she could avoid it and she stopped going out with Pete. It took me a while to convince her I wasn't involved, but I did, and our friendship became stronger.'

'Did it upset Sarah to lose a good friend like Kylie?'

'Not at all.' This question made me realise how little Dr Singh understood Sarah. He couldn't come to grips with how easily she could shut someone out of her life. Or how easy it was for her to charm people.

Dr Singh would be flabbergasted if he knew how often Sarah's friends would shut another friend out of their lives, simply because she had shut them out of hers.

It's bizarre how interested he is in Sarah but how little he understands her.

CHAPTER 34

'You can't wear that, you look ridiculous,' Sarah shrieked as Mario ran around the room waving his arms in a Superman costume.

'Why not?' Jill asked as she entered the room wearing a slinky red dress, red high-heeled sandals and a red headscarf with a splendid red feather floating out from it. 'It's a fireball party so everyone's expected to wear red.'

It was almost a year since their return from Aspen and Jill and Mario were going to a New Year's Eve party at a friend's home on the lower north shore.

Sarah was going to a party at Pete's unit at Kirribilli, which had fabulous views of the Harbour Bridge and the fireworks. Lucy was going next door. Mary and James were back from Ireland and were having a few friends over for a barbecue.

Mario prepared a soda and bitters for Jill and flutes of champagne for himself and the girls.

'It's impossible to get a taxi after midnight on New Year's Eve and it's my turn to drive,' Jill said ruefully before the twins could comment.

'Your friends serve the best French champagne in the world and you're not going to drink any?' Sarah asked, incredulous. 'Why don't you get a water taxi?'

'Because I've had so much champagne over Christmas that I've sworn off it until next year.'

'Huh. Only a few hours away,' Sarah said coolly as she kissed everyone goodbye and went out to the waiting taxi.

'Will Kylie be home?' Mario asked Lucy.

'Yes. She won't go to Pete's party with Sarah there.'

'So she still isn't talking to Sarah?'

'It's not so much that. I think it's more that Kylie idolised Sarah and now she feels she's been made to look a fool.'

Mario had felt despondent after their return from Aspen. The rift between Kylie and Sarah had kept the families apart and time had not diminished his feelings for Mary. When she returned from Ireland, he would see her walking down the path next door and feel a need so great it was all he could do to not call out. The gap in the fence still beckoned when everyone else was out and he often wondered how much longer he could control himself.

Also, he worried about Lucy's pessimism after the Michael affair. He had taken her to meet the Arts Editor at *The Australian* newspaper, where he worked, and this had led to fairly regular freelance work writing theatre reviews. It wasn't favouritism. The editor told Mario that Lucy was very perceptive and wrote with remarkable depth and style. She was also doing some work with Kas, promoting photographic exhibitions. But she had not returned to shooting and was still resisting Jill's suggestion that she have a breast reconstruction.

'I'm pleased Kylie's back,' he said, giving Lucy a big hug. 'She's a good friend. I've put two white wines in the fridge for you to take next door and a special cognac for James.'

'Have fun. Give them all a big kiss from me at midnight,' Jill said as she looped her arm through Mario's, and they skipped out the door.

'See you next year,' Lucy called, laughing as Mario pushed his Superman cape out the window so it flapped madly outside the car.

CHAPTER 35

At 4 am on New Year's Day, two young police officers knocked on the front door of the Borgetti's house. They were at the station when the call came in and had been sent to speak to a member of the family about a car accident.

Lucy had not been home long. She was watching an old movie on television when she heard the knock and stumbled to the door, tired and bleary.

'Lost your key?' she called out, expecting to see Jill or Mario. But when she opened the door she rubbed her eyes trying to clear her brain.

'Are you Miss Borgetti?' one asked formally, looking ill at ease.

She nodded.

'Is anyone here with you?'

'No. My parents are at a party on the north shore and my sister is out.' She noticed the sky was quite light as she waved at James who was seeing off the last of their guests.

'May we come in?'

Lucy waved them in. Her head was clearing and she felt the first stirrings of alarm. She led them into the lounge and, picking up the remote, switched off the television. She indicated for them to sit, which they didn't do, so she perched herself on the arm of a chair.

'What's happened?'

After a bit of shuffling the male officer spoke. 'Do your parents drive a gold Mercedes with red upholstery?'

She nodded.

'Are they called Mario and Jillian Borgetti?'

She nodded again.

'Well, I am very sorry to have to tell you this but, um, there has been a car accident.'

She stared at them, her brain suddenly racing. 'Are they all right?'

'No.' The officer looked around as though help would appear from another room. 'Are you sure these isn't anyone else here?'

'No. What are you saying? What's happened?' Lucy felt as though her muscles had stopped working.

'We're very sorry to tell you this ... but your parents ... are dead.'

'Dead?' Lucy looked at them as though they were from another planet.

CHAPTER 36

'They were driving onto the north side of the harbour when another car, travelling at speed, allegedly hit them. Mr and Mrs Borgetti's car rolled and hit into the side of the bridge. The paramedics think the occupants would have died instantly. We need a relative to come with us to identify them.'

Lucy stared at him.

'Is there someone you would like us to contact? That man next door who you just waved to? Would you like my partner to go and get him?'

Lucy looked over at his partner and gave a little nod as she felt her hands shake.

Dead.

She could see her father's red cape fluttering out the car window. Her mother at the wheel, not drinking.

See you next year.

A part very deep down inside her knew the policeman was telling the truth, but with the familiar furniture around her and Yama meowing at her feet, it didn't feel real.

Then Mary was there holding her. Kylie was crying with her. James was talking to the police. About an hour later Sarah and Pete came bursting in – their faces pale, eyes wide with disbelief.

PART TWO

CHAPTER 37

Two weeks after the funeral, Lucy walked into Mary's kitchen without knocking. She had waited until Kylie's car pulled out of the garage. Mary was sitting at the table, blank eyes watching her fingers. Kylie's breakfast bowl was soaking in the sink.

Lucy sat opposite Mary and slid a gold pen across the table into Mary's hand. 'It was his favourite. The one he signed all his best work with.' She had planned this speech and was stiff with resolve to do it properly. Lucy's eyes were moist, but she wasn't crying.

Mary gave a little whimper as she blinked several times trying to focus on the pen – his pen. She rolled it between her fingers, her throat tight with pain.

'I know you loved Daddy and I want you to know I'm okay with that now. He needed lots of love. Mummy loved him too. Some people thought she was cold but it was just her way and Daddy knew that. We all loved him.' Lucy took a few deep breaths to regain her composure. 'I just want you to know that I'd like you to have his pen as a remembrance.'

Mary rose stiffly and shuffled around the table to put an arm across Lucy's shoulders.

Lucy melted under her sympathy and wept. The police, the questions, the funeral arrangements, the funeral. People arriving – relations, workmates, friends, neighbours, associates, strangers. Kind caring people bringing food, cards, flowers, their own shock and grief.

'The flowers have stopped.' Lucy blurted out as though it was important that Mary know this. 'No one comes anymore.'

The pen lay neglected on the table.

'That's what happens,' Mary said, thinking back to when her mother died. 'It is frantic for a while, then it goes quiet. Actually ... I liked the quiet. It gave me time to adjust.'

They let themselves cry. After a while Mary blew her nose and rose to put on the kettle. Lucy jumped at the noise of the coffee grinder, but the aroma of the freshly ground beans was a panacea to her nerves.

'We didn't want it to happen, but it was bigger than both of us. And you're right, he did love Jill. He loved us both. He just didn't know what to do about it.' Mary put the coffee on the table and sat down. 'I would have left James for him. Oh, my God, I would have. You must know Lucy it was very special. Love later in life is more satisfying than all your first loves. For me it was the highpoint of my life, it showed me what love was meant to be.' Sniffing, she took up the pen and rolled it between her fingers. 'He loved you two so much. What are you and Sarah going to do now?'

'Sarah's got another year at uni so she is going to stay with Grandma and Grandpa Pedersen for a bit then probably come back here to Birchgrove. I'm taking some time off work to spend a couple of weeks at Coalcliff on the south coast with Damon and his parents. I hardly know his dad Bob, but I've met Dot when I've gone home with him and at the Orange Grove Market where she has a stall for selling her ceramics,' Lucy said. 'We haven't thought further than that.'

'I've met Dot at that stall,' Mary replied, pleased to hear Lucy was going away for a while. 'Like everyone around here, I go to the Orange Grove Market every weekend for its organic fruit and veges. Kylie comes with me sometimes and introduced me to Dot. I fell in love with her ceramics with those exquisite paintings of Australian birds. You'll have a nice time down there. Have you thought about selling Birchgrove?'

'Grandpa is our trustee. He thinks we shouldn't sell, not yet anyway. Sarah wants to live there but the house gives me the creeps.' Tears welled up again.

Mary patted her hand. 'Will you keep working for the newspaper?'

'Yes and Liam has said that when I'm ready he'd like me to do profile interviews with actors and singers from this part of the world for his American mags.'

'Jill would be pleased. She used to tell me that you would be a writer, maybe write a book one day? She worried about you.' Mary thought back to one afternoon after the trip to Arnhem Land when she and Jill were chatting. Jill had said: 'Lucy's not strong like Sarah. It amazes me that she can shoot rabbits – yes I know about that – when she's so sensitive about everything else.'

'The reason she thought I should be writer was because it meant I could work at home,' Lucy snapped, 'hidden where no one had to look at me.'

Alarmed at Lucy's bitter tone, Mary changed the subject. 'When you come back from the south coast, come and stay here for a while. We'd love to have you.'

'I thought Kylie was going to London?'

'The company's sending her to the Royal School of Mines on a six-month course, but she doesn't go for a few weeks. Even after she's gone, I'd be thankful for company. James is away so much.'

'Grandma and Grandpa want us to go to Scandinavia and Italy to visit their families, but I'm not going. I can see all those relations I've never met, dragging out photos our grandparents have sent them over the years and discussing how we all looked as a happy family.' Lucy screwed up her face as she stood to leave. 'How appalling looking at photos of dead people!'

Mary looked up quickly, disturbed by the anger in Lucy's voice. Mario had told her that Jane always said that people who suffer extreme trauma need strong relationships to rebuild confidence in themselves and the world in general. Alone, they seldom make it.

CHAPTER 38

As Lucy pushed back through the gap in the fence and climbed the steps onto the veranda, she tilted her head to better listen for the sound of his voice singing. Mario's favourite old rocking chair beckoned. She sat down on it, humming and rocking back and forth. She imagined his warm arms around her, the vibrations of his deep voice calming her soul. She hugged herself and rocked more furiously. Her eyes stared at the harbour, seeing nothing.

Then she shivered even though it was the middle of summer. 'Daddy's not here and he's not coming back' she sang softly to Yami who had jumped onto her lap. 'Mummy's gone too and she won't be back.' She patted Yami who purred.

When Yama had died unexpectedly of choking, Mario had bought her a Burmese kitten, which she named Yami because Yama and Yami were mythical twins who became rulers of the Indian underworld. It is said that Yami wooed her brother Yama, in what could have been the first case of incest ever reported.

'Where's your twin brother?' she shouted, suddenly overwhelmed with a raging anger. Yami looked up startled and stopped purring. 'Dead. Gone. Left you. That's what guys do.' She yelled as she yanked Yami off her lap and threw her across the veranda. 'Yeah go on. Run. You stupid bitch.'

Wild-eyed, Lucy stormed into the house and froze, glaring at the hateful things everywhere: couches stuffed like bloated pigs; flowers dying in their vases; photos of their yacht, now for sale. How stupid of people to send flowers which would wither, go black and smell like dead bodies.

'Idiots,' she howled as she swept a vase across the room. Coloured petals on long stems, water and bits of broken vase scattered like jigsaw pieces.

'Stupid asinine idiots.' Lucy ran through the downstairs, letting loose a torrent of curses as she swept vases off tables and threw baskets of fruit and flowers against walls. In a mad frenzy, she stomped the fallen petals, smudging them into the carpet, leaving stains that would never come out.

When all the surfaces were clear she stood puffing and wild-eyed. Then she spied the heater that had been set into the fireplace. After her accident, anything with flames was removed. Coal replaced with electricity. Candles banned except for birthday parties. Lucy tried to wrench the heater from its place, but it was firmly bolted. She kicked it again and again, swearing and yelling all the foul words she could muster. She couldn't break the glass on the front of the heater but the dents she had made formed into faces that mocked her. She twirled around, faster and faster. Desperate to hurt and destroy, she grabbed armfuls of cushions to stuff up against the heater. She pulled down the drapes, raced about bringing in more cushions from other rooms and piled them against the heater until it was buried behind a mountain of fabric.

Sweating and frightened, she raced upstairs. 'Must tidy my room,' she panted. 'Daddy won't like me if it's not tidy.' Frantically she grabbed clothes and books from the floor and stuffed them into cupboards, bags went under the bed, shooting photos and trophies out the window. The model of the family yacht, which Damon had made, was an awkward shape. As she carried it across the room towards the window she tripped and crashed to the floor. The model shattered into shards of splintered timber. Only then, sitting on the floor with the hull gaping and the little flag bent, did her eyes begin to lose their mad glitter.

'I'm sorry Damon,' she sobbed as she tried to straighten the green tie wire he had used to make the flagpole. Holding the little flag to her chest she crawled onto the bed, curled up into foetal position and put her thumb into her mouth.

When Sarah arrived home she thought the house had been burgled. She walked through trying to work out what was missing, then sprinted upstairs calling to Lucy. It wasn't until she reached the landing that it crossed her mind that the intruder might still be in the house. She crept carefully forward. From the hall, she could see Lucy curled up on her bed, asleep or unconscious she wondered and waited before tentatively entering the room.

'You're home,' Lucy mumbled.

Sarah moved carefully into the room, looking around to make sure no one was hiding behind the door. 'What happened?'

'Yami ran away.'

Sarah sat on the bed and patted her twin's shoulder – this was the game-changing moment she had been waiting for. Lucy was hers now.

Very gently she took the little flag from Lucy's fingers. 'Never mind,' she said softly. 'You can have a bath while I do dinner,' Sarah said with a satisfied smile.

'It's okay to let her bathe often, so long as it doesn't become an obsession,' Jane had said. 'Water can be a balm to people badly burnt by flames.'

Sarah led Lucy across the landing and sat her on the bathroom stool while she ran the water and added pine-scented oil.

'It's a balmy night outside and I'm going to cook us a special dinner to have on the veranda. We can watch the ferries on the harbour. Just you and me.' She helped Lucy undress then guided her into the bath. 'I'll come to get you as soon as dinner is ready.'

While Lucy lay in the bath, Sarah put a frozen dinner into the microwave. Her parents had done their duty and she felt no loss in their passing – their time was up. She would care for Lucy now. Sarah needed no counsel. Asked for no advice.

Sarah realised Lucy wasn't aware of what she had done to the house, so she would use this to strengthen her hold over her. She set the table outside with a white tablecloth and colourful napkins then went upstairs to the bathroom.

'Out you get,' she said as she helped Lucy up and wrapped her in a big fluffy robe. 'Just you and me, it's all we need isn't it.'

As they walked downstairs Lucy stared wide-eyed at the destruction in the house and stammered. 'Yes, my dear twin, you made that mess. But don't worry. I'll clean it up and I'll protect you from the police as well as our snoopy grandparents. It will be our secret.' Sarah squeezed Lucy's hand and seated her before a plate of steaming pasta. She had no intention of telling Grandpa Pedersen, who was very protective of his family and would try to take control of Lucy. They sat and watched Sydney's iconic green and yellow harbour ferries glide past their small private beach.

Yami stalked up and Lucy tucked her under her chin. Annoyed, Sarah snorted. She hadn't decided what to do about that cat. After several failures she had finally managed to poison Yama, then Mario had gone out and bought Yami.

LUCY

'Do you feel self-conscious about wearing a wig?' Dr Singh hasn't asked me this before.

'I did for a long time, but I got used to it. Jane told me to think of it like a man having to shave every day – they take their whiskers off – I put mine on.'

'Jane was very good for you, wouldn't you agree?'

'Yes.'

'Did you keep seeing her after you left the hospital?'

'For a while.'

'How long?'

'A while.' Dr Singh looks at me, long and steady. He always knows when I'm avoiding a subject and if he thinks there is more to it, he will persist.

'Why did you stop seeing her?'

I don't answer.

'Did you decide she had done all she could for you?'

I don't want to even think about this.

'Did Sarah tell you to stop seeing Jane?'

It annoys me when he shows how perceptive he is and I'm forced to give an answer. 'Sarah said she was a lesbian and we shouldn't have anything more to do with her.' I remember I didn't want to say anything about this episode, but he can get everything out of me.

'From what you've told me, she was very professional. How did her sexual preference affect her working with you?' Dr Singh's chin is resting on his steepled fingers as he watches me.

'Jane never touched me, never even suggested anything,' I say.

Dr Singh continues to watch me as I struggle to hold back tears of frustration.

I finally blurt, 'It was Sarah.'

'I see. So, Jane made a pass at Sarah?'

'No … at Kylie.'

'Why do I feel you're holding something back?'

I can't answer. I want him to stop this inquisition.

'What exactly did Kylie say Jane did?'

'It wasn't quite Kylie … exactly.' I take a deep breath before going on. 'Sarah told Mummy that Jane had touched Kylie improperly when she was coaching her on how to act that night when I was going strip off to show her my scars. She said Kylie couldn't tell Mary because she was too upset.'

'Did your mother speak to Kylie and did Kylie concur?'

'Eventually.'

'Eventually? That was a long time ago, when Kylie still wanted to be Sarah's best friend. Do you think she agreed because of this?'

I look away, unable to meet his eyes. I still feel terribly guilty about what I allowed to happen to Jane.

'How much back then did you and Sarah know about lesbians and other issues of sexuality?'

'Sarah was fascinated by sex. She would sneak books out of Daddy's library and she bought grubby-looking books from secondhand shops.'

'Did Sarah dislike Jane?' Dr Singh continues the inquisition.

'I know you're trying to suggest Sarah wanted to get Jane into trouble.' I hesitate, embarrassed, because he's so near the truth. 'And maybe she did. Sarah found out that Jane had learnt that she had told me in hospital that I'd always be bald like an old man, so Jane put a ban on Sarah being in my room without a nurse or an adult present. This infuriated Sarah.'

'Why do you think Sarah told you that when she knew you needed to be encouraged and comforted?'

'She believed I should know the truth about my future, not the rubbish the adults were telling me.'

'So, what happened to Jane?'

'I never did find out who told the hospital but there was an enquiry and Jane lost her job.'

'Did they question you?'

'Yes. They came to our house one day.'

'And what did you say.'

'I told them Jane would ask about the exercises the physio had given me ... that she sometimes asked me to take off my top so she could see if my skin was stretching as it should. I told them she would admire my good breast and sometimes touch it.'

'So, they believed you and Kylie – and Jane lost her job. Did you ever see Jane again.?'

'No. But later, after I left university, I tried to find her because it was such a horrible lie. I just wanted to speak to her to tell her I was sorry.'

'What part of it was a lie?'

'All of it.' I never did find Jane and I still feel guilty about that.

CHAPTER 39

Two weeks after her meltdown, Lucy put a small bag into her car and set off for the south coast. Sarah had not wanted her to go. Had turned away when she tried to kiss her goodbye. Lucy held back tears as she drove through the cacophony of cars, trucks and cyclists. She nearly turned back many times, but eventually the suburbs were behind her and she entered the wilderness of the Royal National Park where the tension in her shoulders began to ease. She gave a silent thank you to the government who'd had the foresight to declare this vast area a national park, the second in the world.

Lucy felt the strain of the past weeks dissipate as her car zipped through the park's scrubby plains and deep gorges, splashed through low fords and along the tops of creamy sandstone cliffs that rose dramatically from the sea below. The park's wildness seeped into her soul. She pulled into a parking bay at the top of a cliff and stood mesmerised by the blue of the Tasman Sea and the crispness of the salty air. Grandpa Pedersen as the trustee of the family estate had bought her a new Saab convertible to replace her dying Mini. She knew probate would not yet be settled so he must have used his own money. That he cared so much he would do this for her lifted her spirits. The car was very peppy and there was little traffic in the park on a weekday so she wound down the windows, put her foot down and let the fresh air swirl around inside the car. As she drove, the sun flashed on and off through the gaps between tall ghost gums lining the road.

After the park came the coast road that flowed like a grey ribbon around precipitous cliffs and down steep inclines to small towns that nestled around sandy bays like friends gathered for a picnic.

These towns developed from the 1880s when the demand for coal grew as industry expanded in the port of Wollongong a little further south down the coast. Damon said the coal was all but depleted but he would hear an occasional blast of explosives.

Lucy drove slowly around Coalcliff. Damon had told her his parents sold their Sydney home to live a quieter life and to take advantage of the cheaper house prices. After the mine reduced its output most of the houses were left to the wind and the rain, but in recent years a dribble of city people had discovered the pretty beaches less than an hour and a half south of Sydney. They came, liked what they saw, and were buying the old houses as an escape from city living. Damon had told her to look for a yellow gate.

The town was small, so it wasn't long before she saw Dot standing beside a yellow gate. Lucy always found comfort in Dot's ample body wrapped in a loose flowing dress and her mass of dark hair, streaked with grey, piled on top of her head and held loosely with an assortment of combs.

As Lucy stepped from the car she swayed and Dot waddled over to catch her. 'You okay?'

'Just stood up too quickly.' Lucy always felt like a skinny chick beside a fluffed-up mother hen when she was hugged by Dot.

They embraced quietly and walked into the classic weatherboard house with a veranda, a chimney and a tin roof that would be noisy on rainy days. Parallel tyre tracks with grass growing between them ran along one side of the house to a wooden garage, so decrepit it was in danger of falling in on itself. The picket fence needed painting.

The house creaked as Dot led the way down the long central hall with doors to rooms on both sides.

'Tich is at Byron Bay communing with nature and her boyfriend so you have her room.' Dot said as she opened one of the doors off the hall. 'Damon's in the mountains, but of course you know that.'

Lucy smiled. Damon had told her he was having lessons from a sculptor in return for working in his garden. He was embarrassed about not being home, especially as she hadn't visited the house before, but the offer from such a famous sculptor was too good for him to turn down.

Lucy let out an involuntary gasp at the red and orange flames that seemed to float out from Tich's ceiling. She stumbled back into the hall.

'Sorry love,' Dot mumbled as she rushed around dragging down the flaming red and orange fabrics that hung from the ceiling. 'Tich was going through an Eastern enlightenment period,' she said as she piled the fabric into a soft lump in a corner. 'I should have pulled that stuff down ages ago.'

Lucy dropped her bag then followed Dot out through the back door and along an unkempt garden path to where an old lean-to shed had been converted into a light-filled studio. Bob, Dot's husband, had put a skylight into the roof and knocked out the back wall for sliding glass doors onto a little deck. Bob had followed his father into the boat repair business in Balmain and was a capable handyman. In the middle of the room under the skylight he had built a solid workbench that was littered with fine ceramic teapots and lids, paints and paint brushes. The room was comfortably cluttered.

Lucy let her gaze wander around the unpainted ceramic ware, chipped and broken fragments, rags and magazines. She liked the bright lived-in feeling of the room and made her way across to the back shelves that were lined with vases and teapots intricately painted with native birds. 'These are awesome,' she said 'and so delicate. Have you ever thought of doing a book on native Australian birds?'

'No,' Dot laughed. 'People are always suggesting I do one. Your Dad asked me about doing a book you know. I think one of those publishers who produce coffee table books wanted it and talked him into asking me. They worked together or something.' She chuckled. 'Nah ... I work at my own speed and I like selling at the weekend markets. Bin doing it for years.

'Now, I'd like to do a bit of work so why don't you just make yourself at home love. Around here Bob goes to work, I go to my studio and everyone else does whatever they feel like.'

'I'll go for a walk on the beach,' Lucy said as she watched Dot pick up a nearly finished ceramic mug. She was pleased Dot and her father had talked about art. Many times since the car accident she wished she had taken more notice of his cartoons and where they were published.

Back in Tich's room Lucy changed into shorts and a T-shirt and found a well-worn path leading to the beach. A light sea breeze ruffled the hot air as cockatoos screeched and flew in agitated groups from tree to tree. Lucy sniffed the fragrance of green bushes, the wildflowers, the salty air and wondered what it would be like to live here.

She was still self-conscious about exposing her scarred body, but there was only one family group on the beach building sandcastles, so she kicked off her shoes and paddled, enjoying the tickle of the waves and the grittiness of the sand. Seagulls swooped around her but decided she didn't have any food so returned to the family who had previously thrown them a few scraps.

Lucy's euphoria from the drive through the national park and being in Dot's sun-filled studio faded as she walked. By the time she reached the steep rocky outcrop at the end of the beach she felt the loss of the past few weeks engulfing her. She sat wearily on a rock and watched little waves rush over her feet then sulk away, leaving strands of seaweed and empty shells on the drying bubbling sand. Just like my life she thought. People come, destroy, then go.

Mesmerised by the motion she rose and walked slowly into the water, following the outgoing waves. Further and further she followed them until they were no longer breaking, but heaving like soft hills around her hips, rising to her waist, sloshing into her armpits then up over her shoulders.

A man from the family group had seen Lucy walking along the beach as though in a trance. When he realised the strange young woman had walked into the water fully dressed with her towel hanging over her shoulder, he became concerned and stood up so he could see her better. He had a paunch and didn't want to go into the water, but he put down his sandwich and waved at his children to stay with their mother.

Lucy was a strong swimmer. As the water came up to her chin, she lifted her legs and lay back so she could float and quietly observe the beach and Coalcliff rising up the hillside. Then she saw the man standing tall so he could see her. He had his chin up so he could see her over the swell, just like Daddy would do she thought. She put her head under the water, held her breath for as long as she could and when she came up again, he had moved a little closer. It was comforting, like old times when Daddy would be watching out for her. She went under again, letting the current take her out a little further. When she came up again, he was still watching but had not moved any closer.

After the sixth time of going under she came up and saw he was walking away, back to his family. She knew he had worked out that she was a good swimmer and was perfectly safe on this calm day. Even though he was a stranger, he had cared, and this made her feel less alone as she swam strongly to shore.

That evening, Lucy, Dot and Bob sat on the veranda sipping wine as they watched the setting sun turn the sky pink, then red, then a threatening shade of mauve.

Dot had seen Lucy come home with her clothes and hair dripping wet and wondered if she should ring Mary. She knew Mary from the Orange Grove Market and knew her daughter Kylie was a good friend of Lucy and Damon. And at the funeral Mary had confided to Dot that she was worried about Lucy's state of mind. 'With Kylie away she's going to need Damon to help her over the next few weeks,' Mary had told Dot.

'He's away quite a bit these days,' Dot had replied, 'but I'll see if she'd like to come down and stay with us at Coalcliff. It's quiet down there and would get her away from the city for a bit.' They exchanged phone numbers with a knowing nod.

She thought about that phone number still in her wallet but what did she know about these things? Maybe Lucy swam in her clothes because of her scars.

CHAPTER 40

Damon returned the next day and in his quiet gentle way cosseted Lucy like a special child. He took her swimming and fishing off the rocks. Sometimes he would fling off his shoes and dance for her on the sand. He moved with a languid easy flow, as graceful as a gazelle free on the plains. He took her to his favourite walking trails in the national park. At night he sat on the end of her bed and they talked until she fell asleep.

By the time Lucy returned to Birchgrove, she was smitten with the idea of beach living and couldn't wait to tell Sarah. 'It's such a different way,' she said, her eyes warm as memories of the last few days flooded her thoughts. 'I've never known such quietness, such peace. Do you think we could buy a beach house and live there for a while, just a while? You and me, the beach and the birds.' She wanted it so much she was prepared to beg if necessary.

'What would I do down there?' Sarah said, her voice flat. 'This is my last year at uni and I'll join a city law firm when I finish. I've already had some impressive offers.'

'You could commute to Sydney like Bob and lots of people do. There's a freeway and a regular train service.'

'And what about dinners, parties, dates, all that? I don't intend to be stuck down there at some southern beach with all those boring tree huggers and retirees! You've had a mind-blowing week with Damon, fine – but we're city girls. We'll do our sea change when we're old, not now.'

The feeling that this was what she needed didn't leave Lucy and when she told Grandpa Pedersen he was all for it. The sudden death of their only daughter had shattered him and Catherine. He knew Catherine found some solace in her many friends, but he was more solitary. Like Lucy, he found the house at Birchgrove crowded with memories. One day he might appreciate these memories, but not yet.

'I think it's a good idea for you to get away for a while Lucy,' he said, his eyes soft. 'If you prefer to stay in Birchgrove,' he said, turning to Sarah, 'then why not buy a place together so Lucy can live down there and you can visit whenever. I'll guarantee your mortgage until probate is through and property is a good investment, especially in coastal towns within a couple of hours' drive of the city.'

'We shouldn't be separated,' Sarah said, looking at him with contempt. 'Lucy needs me and shouldn't be down there on her own. Anything could happen.'

'That may be so, but she can't relax in this house. She thinks she'd be happy down there and she needs to be where she can feel at peace.'

Grandpa Pedersen had a gut feeling that Lucy would benefit from some time away to think and dream a little without Sarah's influence. When he had migrated from Denmark with his young wife Catherine and very little money, he had found a willing financial partner and set out to convince the Australian people that they needed to chuck out all the heavy colonial furniture they had inherited from their British background and replace it with light Danish furniture. Through clever advertising he showed them that clean lines with pale colours were much more suited to terraces and harbourfront houses with sliding glass doors that opened out into the bright Australian sunshine. They saw the truth in his ads, trusted this tall blond man and sales rose steadily. Once the business was established, and before the sales figures were too high, he bought out his partner and the Pedersen Furniture stores were his. Today, these stores were in every city and big country town.

'Lucy takes after Mario and me,' he would tell people. 'We're the lovers of the good life and peace at home.' He never told anyone, not even Catherine, how much he worried about Sarah. He watched Sarah do all the right things, but he found her cold indifference to other people's needs and feelings unnerving.

Listening to the twins now, he realised how much he had stood back and let Mario and Jill deal with Lucy's rehabilitation and Sarah's wilfulness. Maybe he should have offered to help more. It was too late now, but they had trusted him with their money and their two girls and this he would do with all his being. Money and investment he understood. These he could do with confidence and he resolved he would also take more interest in the twins' welfare. He had watched the roller coaster that had tossed Lucy about after the fire and now she had lost the stability of her home, her parents. He empathised with her need to get away from Birchgrove for a while. While Lucy was down the south coast, Sarah had stayed with them for a few days, then she'd just upped and returned to Birchgrove. He knew Sarah would cope well on her own.

'Lucy and I will take a run down to Coalcliff next weekend for a look around,' he said, looking severely at Sarah.

Sarah scowled.

For Lucy, the return to Coalcliff filled her with a sense of wellbeing. The air was perfumed by wild and cultivated flowers, the sand crisp under her feet, and the sea breezes gentle against her skin.

They didn't find anything suitable on their first visit, so the second time they called in to discuss their search with Dot and Bob. Grandpa Pedersen accepted a beer and eased his long frame down into a chair on the veranda. He liked the area but finding a house was not as easy as he had expected.

'There's not much for sale and what's available is so dilapidated,' he said. 'I wouldn't like to see the twins in some of these crumbling places.'

'People don't shift once they got an 'ouse down 'ere,' Bob said, easing another beer into his stubby holder. 'They 'ang on to it. We looked for a long time didn' we, love? Came down weekend after weekend. Bit of a bugger it was with work an' all that.'

Dot pointed to the northern headland where Lucy had walked into the water. 'Try Stanwell Park, just around that big headland. It's got a lovely sandy beach like Coalcliff, but the homes are posher. They cost a lot more but there's a store and a gallery with some good works in it. The owners want to sell my ceramics and I might let them one day, when I'm too old to go to the markets.' Dot chuckled at the very thought of being too old.

'Perfect for the girls.' Bob agreed. 'More trendy. Less of us old codgers. We don' want flash 'ouses an' sealed roads. We like the grasses grow'n wild.'

The following weekend Grandpa Pedersen drove the twins down again. 'So, this is Stanwell Park, he said, admiring the magnificent view down to the beach and across the sparkling blue of the Tasman Sea.

'Much nicer than Coalcliff,' Sarah said, noting the sealed roads lined with classy beach houses set in well-planned gardens that ran down the slope to the beach. Once she realised that Grandpa Pedersen and Lucy were determined to buy a beach house, she had joined them to make sure they bought the sort of place she was prepared to spend time in.

'But it was Coalcliff I fell in love with.' Lucy said as she looked at the fine homes with big windows and wide open decks.

'Don't be silly Lucy. It's still a little beachside village with a couple of hundred houses, but it's much better laid out. Look, it's got two creeks running down from the hills where Coalcliff has only one. That means fresh water and more native plants and birds for you to look at.'

They drove around the streets seeking "For Sale" signs until they came to a house high on the southern side. It was older than Sarah would have liked, but it was tidy and faced north so it would get sun all day.

Feeling like burglars, they followed Sarah through the little gate to a path that ran alongside the driveway leading to a double garage. They crept around the house, peering through gaps in the drapes on the side windows. It was very 1970s with cathedral ceilings, exposed beams, good-sized rooms and glass doors sliding open onto a large bleached wood deck.

'It's well maintained,' Grandpa Pedersen said as he assessed the new guttering and well-oiled woodwork.

The wooden deck on the beachside of the house faced out across the sea to the horizon. The land under the deck sloped down and was roughly mown until it merged with hardy costal scrub that fell more steeply down to the sandy beach below. The scrub was dense but a dirt path, worn smooth over many years of bare feet padding over it, gave the property direct access to the beach.

Lucy was looking south towards Coalcliff when she saw another path snaking its way around the edge of a rugged headland jutting out into the sea. 'Look, this path around the cliff could go to Coalcliff,' she said hurrying towards it.

'Be careful,' Grandpa Pedersen called as he hurried to the start of the path. It was narrow and he could just make out surfers sitting beyond the waves, waiting for the big one that would send them skimming to shore. 'It's a long vertical drop,' he called nervously. 'One slip and you'll be smashed on those rocks. Lucy, don't go any further until we know more about it.'

'I'm okay!' Lucy called triumphantly as she reappeared. 'I can see Coalcliff from around that bend. It's narrow but reasonably well worn.'

'You could live at Stanwell and walk to Coalcliff.' Sarah said, with a hint of sarcasm. She did not like the look of the cliff path and would not be walking around it.

Grandpa Pederson was relieved when Lucy was safely off the path. 'You'll need to fence it off from the house. If anyone goes on that path and slips, there's nothing to stop them falling all the way to the rocks.'

'We can send people we don't like around it.' Sarah gave a short laugh. 'We'll call it our fatal path.'

L U C Y

The hands on the little clock beside the bed seem to be moving faster than normal. The big hand has just reached the number eleven. By the time it reaches twelve, Sarah will have crossed Victoria Road and be on the last leg to the hospital gates.

A chill runs through me. I know her visit is going to end the peace I've known in here.

I think back to the ten weeks we had to wait for settlement on the house at Stanwell Park. That was another time when I knew peace. Sarah had wanted me to stay with her at Birchgrove, but it gave me the creeps to sleep in that house, so I moved in with Dot and Bob and their simple life. Bob drove to work at the shipyards in Balmain early every morning and Dot lost herself in her studio. Every evening we sat on the veranda for a quiet drink then had dinner, watched television or read. When Bob watched sport, Dot and I would go to her studio. I could sit for hours watching her work. She used very fine brushes to produce a twig or a bird of infinite beauty.

She showed me the differences between male, female and juvenile birds of the same species. She taught me how to mix paints to get an exact colour and how to sketch. Sadly, I hadn't inherited Daddy's eye.

Dot did not appear to let other people's problems bother her, but she was surprisingly perceptive. She had removed all the red and orange floaty fabrics from Tich's room as well as all candles from the house. Sometimes I would think of Mummy and Daddy and cry and she would wrap me in her soft body rocking me like I was a little girl again. Every weekend she packed her folding chair and the week's work into boxes Bob had made and went to the Orange Grove Market.

I didn't go with her because, at that time, I avoided going into the city as much as possible. I still hadn't returned to work although I knew I would have to soon. I needed the money but, more importantly, I needed to make myself cope with being among strangers.

When Damon came home, he and Bob went fishing. Fishing was about all they had in common. "'E's a good boy but I don't really understand him,' Bob told me one evening. 'Arty farty like his mother. I'm not sure that's good for a boy.' But Bob would bring home metal and wood scraps from old boats that came into the shipyard, and would sit riveted watching Damon sculpt them into animals or people or shapes that meant nothing to him.

I was living in a bubble during those weeks. I spoke to Sarah by phone most days and eventually went back to casual work for the newspaper. I was reviewing plays and always got excellent seats along with an extra ticket so I could take Sarah or Kylie or Damon, sometimes Mary.

If I took Sarah, she always wanted me to stay overnight and I could never refuse her, but there were demons in that house. They came to me at night. I would lie rigid until morning when I would have a quick breakfast with Sarah and drive back to Coalcliff.

Damon was in his third year at the National Art School then, majoring in sculpture and photography. I would pick him up after classes and we would go for a cheap meal then to a play. People thought he was an actor with his long blond ponytail and gaunt good looks.

'They're trying to work out whether you're famous,' I would say in an exaggerated whisper from behind my program.

'Smile nicely at them, Lucy. I'll need their cheque books when I start exhibiting.'

I would promise to give him good reviews although we both

knew I would never write anything I didn't believe to be true. At intervals we would eavesdrop on the audience and that's when I learnt that very few people made their own judgement about the arts. Most people would quote from a review they had read before coming to the play. We felt like conspirators listening in and thought we were very clever. Those evenings taught me to keep my opinions to myself and to schedule interviews away from the hype of opening nights and media promotions.

Damon was a very special part of my life during those days. He was studying the "lost-wax" method of sculpture at the NAS and desperately wanted me to love it as much as he did. I knew this, so one day to surprise him, I arrived at the NAS on the day they were doing a "pour". The pour, he had told me several times, was very special.

The day started well. He took me on a tour of the old brick buildings that had started life as a jail in the 1820s. As we walked among fellow students, most as tall and thin as he, standing at long benches chipping away at their newly made sculptures or at sanding machines that sent a fine dust over everything, he explained that the lost-wax method had been around for six thousand years.

He explained that early Egyptian and Roman sculptors used the lost-wax method, but it was the Greeks who discovered a way to cast big statues in hollow bronze. 'That's what we do,' Damon told me as we continued around his little fiefdom. 'Each statue takes weeks, months ... years sometimes. We start with a shape, say a face, and mould that in wax. Then we put a heat resistant material around the wax and when that's hardened, we melt out the wax. This leaves a hollow mould in the shape of the face. We then pour the hot molten metal we've chosen for our statue into that hollow mould – that's what we're doing at the foundry today.'

This method reminded me of the garden gnomes I made as a kid using rubber moulds and plaster of Paris.

He led me outside to a narrow alleyway between tall brick buildings which he said was a safe place for the foundry. I remember being amused by students wearing T-shirts saying: 'Once I was lost but now I'm foundry'.

There was a long, narrow sandpit in the alleyway and the students placed their hollow moulds in neat lines in the sand. Damon told me the sand held the hollow moulds steady when the hot molten metal was poured in from the crucible.

It looked medieval with the big iron crucible hanging on massive chains above the unlit furnace.

The students waited in a reverential silence for the foundry boss to arrive. Damon looked like he was waiting for God but when the boss arrived, he didn't look like any God I knew. He was a short stocky man with massive arms and a serious demeanour. He checked the moulds in the sandpit and the piles of scrap metal to be put into the crucible as soon as the fire under it was lit. By the time he was ready to flick the lighter I was as engrossed as the students. The lighter comes down, touches the fuel and a thunderous roar rolls up the walls as a holocaust of flames erupts from the furnace and curls around the crucible.

In that split-second Damon realised his mistake and spun around to wrap his arms around my head but the terror that ripped through me was so great I wrenched myself from his grasp and fled the alleyway. I could hear Damon yelling at me to stop but it wasn't until he caught up with me and dragged me to the ground that I stopped screaming and started to cry. He held me down, crying with me, apologising over and over again.

CHAPTER 41

The weekend after settlement on the beach house at Stanwell Park, Grandpa Pedersen drove the twins and Grandma down to look it over.

'For the past few weeks, this Stanwell house my granddaughters have bought is all I've heard anyone talk about,' Grandma said. 'So I feel it my duty to check it out. Not that my opinion matters now it's all settled.'

Lucy patted her hand. 'Grandma, finding it was a drag and you would have hated it. Now we finally own a house we're so pleased you're here and we need you. You have the best eye for design and we want you to help us choose the furnishings.'

As they walked through the gate Lucy grabbed Sarah's hand and held it tight. 'Can you believe it? Our very own place. Just us.'

'And our guests,' Sarah said, looking at the vacant land beside the house to assess how many cars they could park there. But she kept hold of Lucy's hand as they walked up the path. 'You can be the caretaker. I'll be the provider of entertainment,' she said as she visualised the parties and weekend stayovers she would arrange. She had warmed to the idea of the beach house and the status it would give her among the legal profession.

All that week, Lucy drove back and forth transferring her belongings from Birchgrove to the beach house, as they called it. She hung a series of black and white photographs Kas had given her as a housewarming gift and stood back to admire how well they complemented the lemon leather couches and Italian glass tables Grandma had helped them choose. The last things Lucy brought to the house were the gun safe for their rifles, the small safe in which she locked the ammunition and bolts, Damon's shell which she put beside her bed, and an agitated tail-swishing Yami.

'You'll love it here,' she said as she cuddled her and put butter on her paws which someone told her would stop cats returning to their old home. 'Lots of sunny spots to sleep and wild places to explore.'

Two weeks later Lucy drove Nonna down for an overnight stay. As they walked through the sliding glass doors onto the bleached floorboards of the deck, Nonna looked at the cliffs and the sparkling blue sea and pulled a hanky from her pocket and cried. 'It reminds me of the Mediterranean,' she sobbed, but Lucy knew it really reminded her of her only son who she missed terribly. She put an arm around Nonna's shoulders as tears ran down both their cheeks and the warm sun soothed their memories. When Nonna calmed down, Lucy led her to the new deck furniture they had bought, sat her down and pushed up the umbrella for shade. Then she went inside to make coffee to serve with the cake Nonna had baked.

'I don't miss Sydney at all,' Lucy told Mary when she came to look at the house. 'The waves rolling in have a steady rhythm that I find comforting. The birds wake me early and I walk on the beach or around the cliff path to Dot's. And George came last week to talk me into going back to the rifle club.'

'Aren't you a bit frightened being here alone at night?'

'No,' Lucy said. 'I have Yami, and Sarah comes down more than I expected.' She didn't tell Mary Sarah recently had arrived with a group of friends without warning her or how she had run into the bedroom and sobbed.

'You must phone when you're bringing friends,' she had told Sarah. 'I like to walk around without my wig, with bare arms and I hate other people seeing me like that.'

'It's also my home and I don't expect to have to announce my arrival,' Sarah had snorted. 'Anyway, you should never be unprepared. Jill taught us that.'

The mention of their mother upset Lucy. Sarah hid a little smile then she softened the blow saying she would ring in the future. She had discovered a new pleasure in hurting people she liked, especially Lucy.

Of course, Sarah didn't ring in advance. She just arrived with boxes of delicious food, bottles of wine and lively company. Lucy learnt to listen out for the sound of the garage door going up which gave her just enough time to pull on her wig, long sleeves if needed and a quick dash of lipstick. Sometimes Sarah brought a man she had just met, or a few friends from her university crowd. If it was Pete, he would rush in and spin Lucy around.

'Hi gorgeous. How's my favourite beach bum?'

When Kylie came down a few days later Lucy had told herself she would not mention Sarah bringing Pete, but a few wines weakened her resolve and she let it slip out. 'I'm uncomfortable when she brings Pete,' Lucy said.

'Oh,' Kylie responded looking fixedly into her glass.

'Don't get me wrong,' Lucy jumped in. 'He's one of my favourite people but he should have stayed with you. He just can't say no to her and I know he doesn't love her. They're not even going steady, just casual dating when it suits Sarah mostly.'

'I know, but I'm too quiet for him.' Kylie looked out over the beach, her eyes misting up. 'It hurts to know he prefers to be with her but she's so much fun, he's like a rabbit caught in the lights of an oncoming car. Anyway, I'm here because I want us to be friends forever.'

Kylie sipped her wine quietly, letting her emotions settle down before she spoke again.

'Did you know my boss has offered to sponsor me to do another course in London. Then he wants me to do a stint at the company's zinc mine in Ireland. I need to get away so I'm going to do it.'

'Oh Kylie, that's wonderful, but I'll miss you. You're my best friend.'

'Why don't you come to London? Live with me for while?' Kylie suggested. 'I've got a company flat. It wouldn't cost you anything and you could do freelance work, interviews, that sort of thing.'

'Sarah wouldn't let me go.'

'Let you go? She's you sister, not your keeper! Did you know Pete and I tried to get together again? Lasted about three weeks then she found out and called him up. I'm sorry Lucy, but she's a bitch. She just has to control everyone.'

Kylie's bottom lip quivered and Lucy moved over to hold her hand. 'Why do you think he jumps when she calls when it's really you he loves?'

'He needs the glamour and the excitement. You know what his parents were like. He grew up believing life was all about parties and dressing up, travel and being rich. I love him but I'll never be the person he thinks he wants.'

'Give him time. He'll wake up one day and realise you're the right person for him.'

'It might be too late,' Kylie said forlornly. 'I leave next week.'

CHAPTER 42

Lucy knew it would be months before she saw Kylie again. She was despondent the day she left to drive back to Sydney and was pleased when she heard a knock at the door.

There stood Damon. They had seen each other several times since the foundry visit and he had apologised so many times that she had made him agree to never mention it again.

'What's up?' He put a finger under her chin to tilt her head so he could look into her eyes. He was the only person she would let do that to her.

'Nothing.'

He walked into the kitchen and, taking two beers from the fridge, handed her one and led her onto the deck. They sat side by side watching the horizon waver as the sun set slowly behind them.

'Now tell me. What's upset you?'

'I know I sound pathetic, but Kylie's going to London, now you're going to America. My two best friends are leaving and it's nearly Christmas.'

Damon nodded.

'How long will you be in America?'

'About a year. The fellowship I have is at an institute of sculpture in New Jersey where I'll be learning all the latest techniques. I hope to get some paying work helping at galleries or with some famous artist who might need a willing helper. The school's arranged a share house with other students, so it's all good.' He tilted his head back to take a long swig of his beer.

'Damon, that's everything you've ever wanted. I'm so happy for you ... but I'll miss you terribly.'

He smiled softly as he saw the sadness in her eyes. 'Come on, let's go for a walk on the beach. It's great at this time of day.' At the bottom of the cliff path they kicked off their shoes and left them on a rock. The sand was cooling as evening fell, but the summer air was still warm and soft on their bare skin. They walked, holding hands, letting the waves slop over their feet.

'Only the waves dare make a noise like this late in the day,' Lucy whispered. 'They rule the shores ... gentle on beaches, dangerous on the rocks, threatening in storms, life-giving to reefs and marine creatures.'

'That's very poetic.' Damon stopped as he took off his clothes, letting them drop like rags at his feet. 'It's also the best time to swim. Everyone's gone, the sun's going down, the moon's rising and the dark water makes me feel free ... like I'm levitating.'

The dark was Lucy's friend, but she was nervous in the shadowy water. She stayed close to Damon as they floated; keeping their bodies in the warm layer that lingered just along the surface. After a while Damon let his feet drop and stood beside her, bouncing her body lightly above his hands. She closed her eyes and let herself become soft and pliable, levitating like he had said. She let him bounce her towards the beach, carry her out of the water and onto the beach where he lay her across their pile of clothes.

Slowly, tenderly, he knelt between her legs and licked the salty water from between her legs. This was the first time they had seen each other naked and she lay spreadeagled on the clothes, feeling his tongue leave warm patches on her moist skin. His fingers caressed her with the softness of petals as she let her senses flow until she was rising up, aching for him, calling out his name, pulling him into her.

Little waves flopped down and rolled along the sand, drowning out their cries as the salty water mingled with their juices and his tears.

'Why are you crying?' She asked as they became quiet and she felt his tears drip onto her chest.

'Because you're so beautiful,' he said as he lifted her tenderly so he could put his arms around her and hold her body against his for a few more precious minutes. When he released her they gathered up their clothes and, keeping their bodies close for warmth, returned along the path to the house where he stood Lucy under a hot shower and washed her body with sweetly scented shower gel until there was no trace of salt left on her skin. She succumbed completely, letting any lingering thoughts of his departure be washed away. After he had dried her with a soft towel, he put her into bed and sat there kissing each finger until she was asleep.

'Look after her,' he said to Yami as the cat curled on the bed. 'You're all she has now and she needs you.'

Damon had come to say goodbye but because she had looked so sad, he hadn't the heart to tell her he was leaving the next day to spend a month in Auckland on the way to America. Neither could he bring himself to tell her that he could never give her the full benefits of a man's love that a woman needed. That he would always love her as his best friend but that he had met a man and knew for sure now that he was gay.

LUCY

That whole year after Mummy and Daddy's accident I was tossed about like a leaf on the harbour. I felt as though someone or something else was controlling my thoughts and actions. Buying the beach house was a high point. The visit to the foundry was a low point. Damon was high, then low. I would sit outside on the deck on a calm evening thinking how wonderful our one night of lovemaking was, then his letter arrived telling me he was gay. My sensitive best friend gay. It didn't change the way I felt about him because deep down, somewhere in my soul, I had always known. But like a growing child not wanting to give up her favourite dolls, I hadn't let myself think it through.

I cried a lot.

'Did Sarah visit you at the beach house very often?' Dr Singh is always interested in her actions.

'She would arrive with a group of friends and the house would be full of their noise and laughter and smells. Then they'd leave and the voices in my head would go over everything they had said. I couldn't stop myself reliving every moment, trying to work out whether they liked me or not. I don't know why it mattered, but it did.'

I let my mind drift back over the year. On Christmas Day, Sarah and I went to Grandpa and Grandma's for lunch then Nonna's for dinner. All Nonna and I seemed to do was cry. We tried not to, but it was only a year and we couldn't stop the flow of memories. Dear Nonna had shrunk and was withering away. She loved us, but Daddy was the baby boy she had nurtured and watched grow into a lovely man.

'That first Christmas after the accident was dreadful. I'd jump off the cliff path at Stanwell before I'd live through another one like that,' I told Dr Singh more dramatically than I meant to.

He waited for more, so I obliged by telling him about New Year's Eve. 'Sarah had invitations to lots of parties but said she wanted just us, together. We had drinks with Dot and Bob at Coalcliff then sat out on our deck. It was a warm night. The sea was quiet and a big moon shone a band of silver across the surface like an invitation to follow it to heaven. Sarah became unusually melancholy. She told me how much she missed our parents. That we must never let anyone come between us. She seemed almost frightened of the future. We held hands and I promised I'd always be there for her. I felt once again I was the strong twin and I told her this. Why did I say that?' I ask Dr Singh

He doesn't answer.

'I wasn't the strong one, was I? Grandpa had insisted I return to Dr Kilter because the drugs he prescribed kept me stable. It was hearing Sarah say she loved me more than anyone else, that she needed me, that made me feel strong again and proud to be her twin.'

He nods.

'Dr Kilter didn't know why I had the cat nightmare after Sarah left. What do you think Dr Singh?'

'Tell me about the nightmare,' he says.

'I'm kneeling naked, alone in a red desert when a black cat with suppurating sores and raw patches of skin rises up and rubs against me. I shudder as blood from its scabs and bits of fur flake off against my bare skin. Its green eyes stare unblinking. I feel they are mocking me. Then behind it a hazy wavy shape of a woman emerges. I try to rise but my legs are stuck in the sand. At this point, I wake up and see Yami sitting bolt upright staring at me. I must have made a noise that woke her. Then I grab her and hurl her across the room. She smashes against the far wall, drops to the floor and flees.'

I start to cry and Dr Singh pushes over his box of tissues.

Summer continues with its eternal blue skies, spectacular sunsets and sweet heavy air. Bushes produce a procession of splendid flowers, blossoms become fruits, seeds float in the air and baby birds mimic their parents. All around me nature is bursting with new life, but I can't rid myself of the feeling that my life has stopped. It makes me frightened to go to sleep. I can't drive out the feeling that the diseased cat is always lurking in the shadows.

CHAPTER 43

Summer became autumn, then winter with its cold water and icy winds. Lucy liked sitting on the deck watching the whales cavort off the shore as they made their annual migration from the freezing Antarctic waters to the warmer oceans off the coast of northern Australia. She thought about the times when Mario would take her and Sarah to The Gap, a popular cliff where Sydneysiders went to look out over the Tasman Sea to watch the whales pass. He explained that the mother whales were going north to give birth in the warm waters and that they would stay there until spring when their calves would be fat and strong enough to make the long journey back to the Antarctic. As she sat, comfortable in her warm ski fleece, the beach was deserted and the birds hunched against the chilly winds.

'Winter is a time for recuperation,' Lucy told Dot. 'Yami and I know all the places where the sun warms the house. I take my laptop to work and she sleeps on a cushion beside me.'

In this new-found peace, Lucy's nightmares stopped.

'Has Sarah been down lately?' Dot asked one morning when she drove over for morning tea.

'No, but she's coming this Saturday, on her own believe it or not. I'm going to cook a special dinner and open a good bottle of wine.'

'Oh. Do you know why she's coming?' Dot probed. She knew Sarah well enough to know she didn't do anything without a reason.

'To keep me company I suppose. She's good like that. It's not that I mind being here alone but at times I really do miss Kylie and Damon.'

'Do they write? I certainly hope my Damon does.'

'Yes, emails and a few postcards. Kylie's loving Ireland. Says the people are wonderful and the work is fascinating. It's good she's so happy after all that stuff with Pete.' Dot never judged and this made it easy for Lucy to tell her things she wouldn't tell others.

'Did I tell you I've gone back to shooting?' Lucy continued.

'What? Full-on competitions and all that?'

'Sort of. I'm back at Malabar but I miss quite a few competitions because I can't always get from the club into the city in time to do a theatre review. I've missed a few major tournaments because of work.'

'Are the people you went to Bisley with at this Malabar club?'

'No, that was a university team. My best friend at uni was Tracy and she joined Malabar so we could be together, then she got a job in Melbourne and has gone down there. I hated her going but I put on a big farewell lunch for all the team two Sundays ago. Sarah couldn't come because she had some- thing else on, but everyone else turned up which was fabulous.'

'Is Sarah still shooting?'

'Sometimes. I don't know why because she has so much else on in her life. To please me I think.'

'Hmm,' Dot didn't say any more but Sarah pleasing Lucy without something in it for herself didn't ring true.

Late on Saturday evening, Sarah breezed into the house, dumped bags of food on the bench and her overnight bag in her bedroom.

'I went to a university party the other night and bumped into David and John from the rifle club. They send their love. Did you know Tracy has moved to Melbourne?'

'Yes. Remember I had a farewell lunch a couple of weeks ago.'

'Oh, that's right. I couldn't come.' Sarah shrugged as she wrapped her arms around Lucy. 'The house is lovely and warm. Talking about farewell dinners, well, I've come to talk about another farewell dinner. Pete's leaving.'

'What? Leaving Sydney?'

'Yes. Going overseas. Leaving you and me – like all the males in our lives.'

'Why?' Lucy felt an irrational sense of loss. Just when everything was going so well.

'I ask myself the same thing. Strange isn't it. I thought Pete was your special friend and mine of course, sometimes.' Sarah carried two glasses of wine to the couch. 'Dear Lucy,' she leaned forward to look sympathetically into Lucy's eyes, 'I understand how you must feel, being deserted yet again. It's terrible the way men keep deserting you.'

Lucy thought wearily of all those she had grown to like who had left her – Kylie, Damon, Tracy, now Pete. Michael, Mario and Jill's names hung in the air as she took a deep shuddering breath. Jane had told her she must not let herself wallow in self-pity.

'Tell me about the farewell dinner,' she said, to give herself time to clear her head.

'We'll have it Saturday two weeks from now. Pete has a morning flight to London the following Monday. Anna, Loraine, Bill, Ian and myself are taking three days off lectures to ski at Thredbo. We'll get here late Saturday morning, have the farewell dinner that night, a late brunch on Sunday then drive on to Thredbo. Pete can stay here with you on Sunday night.'

'And I'll drive him over to Coalcliff on Monday morning so Bob can take him to the airport on his way to work. It fits perfectly.'

'You'll be tired after all that partying. Let Pete walk around the cliff path.'

'It'll be too dark that early in the morning and not safe.'

'Pete's done it before.'

'I'm happy to get up for Pete.'

'Would it matter if he slipped LL?' Sarah's emerald eyes glittered as they started hard at Lucy.

Little Lucy, the insulting initials filled her with fear she couldn't pinpoint.

'He dumped Kylie and now he's dumping us. Do we need him anymore?'

Lucy could hardly breathe.

'Think about it.' Sarah stroked Lucy's hand gently, but her voice was devoid of emotion. 'Michael – Damon – Kylie – Tracy – Jill – Mario. Did they ever really care about us? Did they care that we suffered? I live in the city alone, because they all left me and now Pete's going.'

Sarah let her eyes fill with tears that dropped dramatically onto her hands. She did not say that Lucy had also left her to live in Stanwell, but guilt smudged Lucy's thinking as she watched her twin cry.

'Poor Sarah,' Lucy said as she reached over to take up Sarah's damp hands. 'I've only thought about myself and my own pain. You lost all those people too and now Pete! How can help? Tell me what I can do?'

'You can stop him from leaving Sydney.' Sarah said softly as her wet eyes came up to lock into Lucy's eyes. 'You can shoot him when he walks around the cliff path in the morning.' Her voice was so soft that Lucy had to strain to hear the words, but they registered with frightening clarity in her subconscious.

CHAPTER 44

Every day after Sarah left, Lucy stood on the deck to study the cliff path around the headland. Their beach house was on the high side of the bay a bit apart from other houses and the little cluster of shops. The start of the cliff path was across a narrow reserve of open space that was mown occasionally by the council. A few local people used it to walk to Coalcliff, but most considered it too dangerous and preferred the safer option of driving.

Several points of the cliff path were visible from the deck as it snaked around the jagged headland. Lucy presumed animals used it before the council had made it slightly wider and safer for the miners travelling to and from work each day – back when the mine was fully operational.

Lucy assessed the first bend to be no more than two hundred metres from the house. A fullbore resting on one of the cushions from a deckchair or her upturned hand on the deck rail would be accurate at that distance and at 6 am there was not usually any wind. If anyone heard the noise, they would think it was an early blasting at the mine.

Lucy forgot to eat. She sat on the deck watching the cliff path, thinking about what Sarah had said and yet not really thinking about it. Her mind was like a roller coaster that never quite came to a stop. She had not disputed Sarah's suggestion, but she had not agreed with it either. She wanted so much to please Sarah and obviously Pete wasn't ever going back to Kylie. He obviously hadn't even told her he was going to London because Kylie hadn't mentioned it in her recent emails. But shoot him? He wasn't a rabbit. Yami purred around her legs, asking for food and Lucy kicked her away.

The black cat returned to her dreams, more belligerent and slobbering as Lucy grew weaker from the dizzying desert heat. And the wavy female figure moved closer to better watch Lucy struggle to lift her legs out of the sand.

Too frightened to sleep, Lucy prowled the house, sustaining herself with coffee and vodka.

CHAPTER 45

The following week Lucy stumbled inside when the phone rang. She flopped into a chair and watched the phone. After six rings the answer service clicked in. 'Hello, Lucy dear' Mary said. 'Just a quick call. I haven't heard from you for ages so I thought you might come up for dinner one night and stay over, or I could come down to you.'

Yami pushed against Lucy's legs but she ignored her. Slowly she walked into the kitchen with Yami at her feet, purring and spinning in circles with excitement. But it wasn't cat food Lucy took from the cupboard; it was a large knife from the drawer. Moving with sluggish steps she walked outside to sit on an upturned log in the garden. Yami followed, disappointed but forgiving.

Keening and rocking, Lucy picked up Yami and rubbed her soft warm fur against her face. 'I'm sorry, I'm sorry,' she droned as she stretched the cat out on its back over her thighs, gently rubbing its tummy in the way it liked. Yami let her head drop back and purred with pleasure. It was so quick Yami didn't feel the knife enter her throat and jab up into her brain.

Keening more loudly, Lucy gently lifted Yami's head and gazed at it with a flush of maternal love. As her emotions overwhelmed her, she felt a deep sadness flow down through her body like muck draining from a sump. Weariness crushed her as she slumped on the log, blood and tears mingling as they flowed over her arms and knees. Yami's little body lay limp across her thighs, still warm from the life that had just left it.

The sun burned into Lucy's back as Yami's blood ceased to flow. Was it a minute? Was it an hour? Lucy did not know but she placed Yami carefully on the ground and went inside for a soft towel. Very tenderly she wrapped her small furry friend in the towel then lay her back on the ground while she dug a grave. Keening more softly now, she placed the towel containing Yami in the grave, filled it with pale sandy soil and planted three red geraniums she had taken from a pot. Then she watered the geraniums, one by one.

Satisfied that all that could be done was done, Lucy left the garden, threw the knife and her bloodied clothes into the garbage bin and ran a bath. She lay there for a long time, her mind blank. When the water cooled, and the oils formed patchy patterns on the surface, Lucy towelled herself dry then went to bed. Her sleep was deep and heavy, and the black cat did not appear.

Mary arrived the next day to find the front door wide open. She walked into the kitchen with the food she had brought for lunch and saw the bench covered in food stains and unwashed dishes. Mary put down the food and called out as she stepped carefully through the debris of unopened newspapers, mugs with coffee rims turning mouldy, empty vodka bottles and scattered clothes. All the doors were wide open, so Lucy couldn't be far away she thought. She finally found her curled up in bed, naked, her wig a yellow splash on the floor.

When Lucy saw Mary, she sat bolt upright, her eyes glazed with shock. 'I'm thirsty,' she stammered.

By the time Mary returned with a glass of fruit juice, Lucy had dressed. Her wig was in place, although carelessly brushed.

'Sorry about the mess,' Lucy said. 'I've had a bit of flu.'

Mary didn't detect any signs of physical sickness in Lucy, but her concern back in Sydney that something was amiss was confirmed by the mess. She was relieved she had decided to just come down without waiting for Lucy to reply to her phone message.

'It's a sunny day,' Mary said as she handed Lucy the juice.

'Yes, let's go out on the deck,' Lucy said suddenly embarrassed as she looked around the untidy room.

'Have you seen Sarah lately?' Mary asked as they relaxed into deckchairs.

'She was down a few days ago,' Lucy said. 'We're having a farewell party for Pete next weekend.'

'Is that Kylie's Pete?'

'Yes. He's going to London. He might see Kylie over there.'

'Didn't she tell you that she's left London and gone to work with World Vision in Romania for a few weeks?

'Of course she did,' Lucy stuttered and Mary realised Lucy was upset about something so she chose her words carefully.

'I've been expecting to see you after a show, or one of your visits to that psychiatrist, Dr Kilter isn't it?'

'I don't see him anymore. He was invading my mind.'

'I thought you found him a great help.'

'It worked for a while but as Sarah says, I can't spend the rest of my life talking to shrinks and taking drugs.'

Mary knew better than to disagree with anything Sarah said to Lucy. She would call Grandpa Pedersen when she got back to ask what he thought.

CHAPTER 46

On the weekend of the party the two cars arrived in convoy. With much yahooing they lugged in jackets and overnight bags and loaded up the fridge with wine and food. The sea sparkled in the brittle winter sun and the forecast predicted good falls of snow in the mountains. Lucy had cleaned the house and decorated it with gum leaves and wildflowers that gave off a fresh earthy perfume.

'How's my favourite beach bum?' Pete said as he grabbed Lucy in a bear hug and spun her around. If she recoiled from him a little, he didn't notice.

The night stayed clear, so they barbecued prawns and swordfish on the deck and ate at the outdoor table under electric heaters set into the arms of the umbrella. After dinner Lucy sat quietly under the heaters while she smoked a little grass. The others were inside dancing and the music was blaring.

'Duplicitous, isn't he,' Sarah said as she filled Lucy's glass and sat down beside her. 'Look at him in there snuggling up to Anna. And in two days he leaves us both.'

'Yes, but I've been thinking but I don't know ...?'

'Don't think.' Sarah butted in before she could finish. 'He's a selfish bastard and he doesn't deserve to live. Are you ready for Monday morning?'

'It can be done.' Lucy hesitated, 'But do you really mean ....?'

Sarah leaned closer, oozing charm. 'We have to stick together, you and me. You promised me.' She clinked her glass against Lucy's and waited to let her words sink in. 'Have you got everything ready?'

'I've cleaned the rifle and put the bolt and two rounds in

the safe with it. But I don't think I can do it, Sarah I don't ...'
Lucy stood up, too agitated to stay still. How could she
explain to Sarah that she did not want to shoot Pete? She
didn't even like shooting the rabbits but there was a good
reason for doing that. How could she explain this to Sarah
who seemed totally untouched by what they were planning
to do?

'Don't forget what Michael did to you LL,' Sarah goaded.
'And Mario. And Damon, your once very best friend.'

Sarah pulled Lucy down beside her to hold her in her
arms. 'You realise Pete's not happy,' she said rocking
slightly. 'His parents never wanted him; wouldn't know
whether he was alive or dead. Kylie gave up on him and went
overseas. I'm his friend, but he knows I'll never marry him.
I'm putting on this farewell party because I want him to feel
loved. Don't you see? Tonight is as happy as he's ever going
to be. You'll be doing him a favour.'

Lucy watched Pete dancing inside. Her target rifles were
special to her, each custom made with an adjustable cheek
piece and a trigger that perfectly fitted her hand. She had
never asked them to shoot a living target.

The next morning everyone had a hangover. Sarah went
from bed to bed, handing out tall green drinks, which she
said were her special cure. By eleven they had all staggered
up, roused by the smell of eggs and bacon frying in the pan
and ground coffee. Even so, the skiers were so lethargic it
was late in the afternoon before they set out for Thredbo.

Pete and Lucy stood at the gate to wave them off.

'Is everything all right?' he asked as he put a brotherly arm
around her shoulders. 'You've hardly talked to me all
weekend.'

'I'm so sad you're going. Do you have to?'

'I've been doing a lot of thinking lately,' Pete said gravely.
'I'm in the wrong crowd, I'm going nowhere and it's not going
to get any better if I stay around.' He was tempted to tell her
his real reason for going but what if it didn't work out as he

hoped? What if Kylie didn't agree to marry him. The only person he had told was Sarah and she had promised to keep it a secret. He knew people thought Sarah was fickle, but she was always honest with him. 'We can go out together and do wonderful things together, but that's all I will ever give you – a special friendship,' she had said one morning after a wild party and a night of sex.

Kylie had sent Pete an email two months earlier to tell him she was leaving London to work in Romania. It was just a casual "keeping in touch" email but it had started him thinking so he had phoned her. It was a genuine conversation, both delighted to be speaking to each other, although he could tell Kylie was unsure of his real reason for calling. That's when it hit him. When he saw what a fool he was. It had always been Kylie he loved and as he listened to her soft voice, he knew he had to go to her. They came to an agreement that he would fly to London then Bucharest but that they would not tell anyone. He had broken that rule when he told Sarah, but he suspected Kylie would be more faithful to her word and would not have told Lucy.

'Will you come back?' Lucy closed her eyes, praying he would say yes. If he said he was coming back, then she could tell Sarah he really was just going for a short break from Sydney.

'That depends on how things go over there,' he said. With his arm still around her shoulders, they returned to the warmth inside.

'I've bought a shoot-'em-up video, which I'm going to give to Bob as a thank you for taking me to the airport tomorrow morning. Want to watch it with me?'

'Sorry, but I feel dreadful. Usually a good breakfast clears a hangover, but it hasn't worked today.'

'You go to bed,' Pete said giving her a big hug. 'I'm a bit hyper so I'll watch the video then crash. And I'll set my alarm and just take off so you don't have to get up. Sarah's given me a torch so I can see my way around the cliff path.'

He watched Lucy walk sluggishly to her room. Had he not been so excited about seeing Kylie in Bucharest he might have wondered more about Lucy's lethargy.

Before letting herself go to sleep, Lucy set two alarms for 5 am. Everything was ready, but she wanted to be awake for at least half an hour beforehand to clear her head. She put the key to the gun safe on the table beside her bed and fell into a deep sleep.

LUCY

'Tell me what happened when the alarms went off the morning Pete walked around the cliff to Coalcliff.' Dr Singh says lightly as though we're having a normal chat.

I knew this question would come one day. There is a terrible pressure in my head as I try to answer him honestly. 'I turned them off quickly so Pete wouldn't hear. He was in the kitchen, getting something from the fridge. I didn't leave my room. I knew I mustn't let him see me. I remember putting warm clothes over my pyjamas – my big warm ski fleece – then I waited until he stepped outside and I heard the door close. Then I ran to the gun safe, unlocked it and ran out onto the deck. I had to do it quickly. It worried me that he was wearing a backpack because there could be something in it that would deflect the bullet.

'The force of it threw him spinning into the air.'

'You stood there and watched him spin?' Dr Singh asks.

'He dropped like a stone,' I say.

'So, he spun around then dropped like a stone?'

My forehead is tight and my hands are shaking. I wish Dr Singh would ask about something else.

'Take a few steady breaths and go on when you're ready,' he says quietly.

'Like a stone. I thought about going to look over the cliff to see if he was on the rocks – or in the sea – but I didn't. I cleaned the rifle and put the shell and rags in the rubbish. I remember putting the second round back into the small safe and the key on its hook. I'm careful about doing everything correctly because I don't want to lose my licence.'

'Was Sarah there that morning?'

'No.'

'Did you talk to her about it?'

'I told her everything when she got back from skiing. She was gentle with me and kept repeating everything I said over and over.'

'Did you tell her about the backpack and Pete dropping like a stone or did you say he was spinning?'

'She wanted to hear every detail. She made me repeat it again and again. She said it would help me to talk it through; that talking is cleansing.'

Dr Singh writes quickly then looks up. 'You have a remarkably clear memory of that morning. Can you also remember how you were feeling ... sad, excited, frightened?'

'No. I think I must have gone straight back to bed because I didn't wake up until the next afternoon.'

'And what did you feel on waking?'

'Lost. Sarah was away skiing, Pete had gone. Yami was missing. I recall being very thirsty and needing to go to the loo. But really I just wanted to sleep.

'Then Grandma and Grandpa arrived. They didn't ring, just drove down and walked in. When I told Sarah, she was furious. Said it was rude of them not to ring first. But that's what family does, isn't it? Grandma wasn't pleased by the state of house and fussed about, putting dishes in the dishwasher and puffing up the cushions.'

'What did you talk about with your grandparents?'

'The party. They wanted to know where Yami was. I told them Sarah thought she had been stolen but I thought she might have fallen over the cliff. Grandpa didn't believe this. He said cats are very sure-footed and that Sarah was probably right. He wanted to ask around the neighbourhood, but I wouldn't let him.'

'Why hadn't you asked around the neighbourhood?'

'I don't know. I seemed to know Yami was gone and would never come back. Then Grandpa asked why I had cancelled *my appointments with Dr Kilter. That's when I realised Mary must have rung them and told them about the mess I was in on her last visit, so they had come down to check on me.'*

'Did they insist you go back to Dr Kilter or was that your decision?'

'Grandpa said if I didn't, I would have to return to Sydney and live with them. They couldn't make me of course, but I didn't want to upset them, and I sort of hoped Dr Kilter could explain the nightmares. I was having a new one about water entering my body.'

'Did you tell Dr Kilter you believed you had shot Pete?'

Sometimes Dr Singh acts as though I'm making up things and this annoys me. 'It's not something I "believed". I did shoot him. But in answer to your question, no, I didn't tell Dr Kilter.'

'Did you have a reason for not telling him?'

'It's obvious isn't it? I didn't want to go to jail or be put into a mental asylum. Sarah told me not to. She's studying law and knows about these things. I just told him I felt a bit sad sometimes and he put me on a medication that worked really well. I felt calm again and was able to go back to writing reviews; I even considered starting painting classes with Dot.'

'Is that when you met Jeff?'

The room swirls and goes dark.

CHAPTER 47

Dot was well known among ornithological groups for her willingness to provide photos of her bird paintings for newsletters and exhibitions. She also gave occasional talks on fine-brush painting at the Wollongong University which was no more than half an hour south along the coast from Coalcliff and she lent a few ceramics to one of the professors for his annual lecture on nature photography. He was a keen birdwatcher and admired her work. 'I want you to study this artist's work closely,' he would tell the students. 'Study how she paints the whole bird, so you can see every variation in its colour. The subtle differences she reveals between the sexes, the breeds, the lie of the feathers, even the scale of their feet. This is what you must train yourselves to recognise when identifying different species so you can capture it in your photographs.'

Dot always attended the lecture because the students were enthusiastic, and she enjoyed talking to them. Jeff was one of the students and after a lecture he approached her to ask if he could drive up to Coalcliff one day to see more of her paintings. He seemed a nice keen young man so she readily agreed.

He arrived on a Tuesday afternoon when Lucy was there, and she couldn't stop looking at him. He was very meticulous as he picked his way carefully around the studio, examining the sketches that hung on the walls and were stacked on shelves and in corners. He was of average height with the strong build of a country boy used to physical work. He took in everything with unfeigned curiosity and admiration.

'They're beaut aren't they,' he said looking across to Lucy. She noticed his hazel eyes had gold flecks that matched his hair.

'Your birds are amazing,' he said to Dot. 'I've got to learn to do this with my camera. Catch all those little details.'

Jeff stayed all afternoon chatting to them both. When Dot told him Lucy lived at the next bay, he offered to drive her home in his red MGB. It had a few rips in the driver's seat and a soft top that he folded back. 'I always wanted a sports car but this is all I could afford,' he said as he held the door open. Lucy dropped into the low seat.

'It's my fun car. When I finish uni I'll work mostly in the Outback, so it'll be a 4WD again.'

Lucy enjoyed the feeling of sitting so low and yelled at him above the wind. 'Your car likes this winding road.'

'You in a hurry? Want to go further?'

She nodded as he settled back with a wide grin. They skimmed around the cliff faces and roared down into the bays. The air flicked Lucy's hair about and made her eyelashes flutter. She wished the drive would never end but all too soon they were back at Stanwell Park where she directed him to the beach house.

'Want to come in for a coffee, or something stronger?'

'I've got a lecture in an hour, so better go.' He seemed to hesitate. 'Maybe I could come out tomorrow evening and walk on the beach. You be home?'

'All day,' she said as she climbed out. Her legs were wobbling from the low angle of the seat, or was it, she asked herself, the excitement he aroused in her? She watched him turn the car and roar away. As the sound disappeared over the rise she walked inside, planning the future.

I'll take him down the beach path to walk on the sand then I'll invite him to stay for dinner. He's obviously a country guy, so I'll have a big steak to barbecue and a good red wine, or maybe beer. I'll get both she decided. And I won't tell Sarah. I'll have to keep him away from her because she'll want him.

Lucy felt her shoulders slump as she thought of Sarah. What if Sarah takes him?

'Stop thinking like that,' she said aloud, punching her fist into her other hand.

The next day Jeff arrived at four and they walked down the beach path for a swim. The sea was quiet and he swam strongly while Lucy sat beside his clothes. He didn't ask why she didn't swim, nor did he mention the obvious scars on her face. She watched him wade out of the water, his tanned body glistening except for the clump of fairish hairs in the middle of his chest. After he rubbed himself vigorously with a towel and heaved on a loose T-shirt, they walked towards the southern headland.

'This is a great rock platform,' he said as they picked their way over slabs of flat rock. 'Look at the colour of these anemones and molluscs. Do you know what made this crazy paving look?'

'Maybe an earthquake? It would probably leave cracks like that which could fill with sand and hardened over time. Like the way proud flesh puffs up in a cut.'

His laugh was lusty and appreciative. 'An interesting theory. In fact, it's sandstone, which doesn't bend easily so any movement, such as your earthquake, would cause the cracks. Then, water carrying iron oxides from the soil gets into the cracks and with the continual wetting and drying, it expands and swells to form these little hard ridges – just like your proud flesh.'

Jeff pointed to the fishermen spaced along the edge of the platform as they walked on. 'They look like a row of telephone poles down a country road,' he chuckled, pleased with his clever simile. 'What do they catch?'

'Bream, tailor, striped mackerel, sometimes salmon in the gutters. But they're dirty people. They leave beer bottles and plastic bags and chewed chicken bones all over the place. This platform never goes under water so the junk just stays there. Dot, Damon and I clean it up occasionally. Or at least Dot and I do now Damon's overseas.'

Jeff hadn't met Damon, but he had listened carefully when

Lucy and Dot had talked about him on that first day. 'Did you and Damon go out ... like date?'

'Sort of yes and sort of no. He's been a close friend since primary school. We email now he's in America.'

'Were you upset when he went away?'

'I suppose so. It leaves a big gap when a good friend goes away.'

Jeff took her hand to give it a little squeeze. He came often after that and chatted easily about his past. 'Dad's an environmental scientist, Mum's a biologist. I'm an only child and we've lived all over the world in tents and deserts, like gypsies.'

'Where are they now?'

'Working north of Perth at Shark Bay. They were in Perth when I was born but you'll find them working anywhere up and down the west coast. WA is my favourite place in the world.'

He was so easy to talk to that Lucy found herself telling him about her family, skiing, the horror of New Year's Day, her accident and the long painful treatment. When she spoke of the fire he listened without comment until she had finished, then he took her hand and said very gently, 'Poor you. I've never had a bad accident but tomorrow I could lose a leg. You're doing good, facing up to it and getting on with your life.'

'Jeff's an Outback sort of guy.' Lucy told Mary when she could no longer resist the need to tell someone about him. 'He doesn't see my scars, just takes people for what they are. He loves animals and nature and the wilderness.' Lucy stopped with an embarrassed giggle. 'I'm rambling, but Mary, he's so gorgeous I could eat him. That's my problem. What should I do about ... you know?' She didn't need to say exposing her body. Mary understood.

'From what you've told me about him, I'd say he'll make the decision when he's good and ready.'

Jeff and Lucy were walking on the beach after a swim when he suddenly pointed. 'Look,' he said, his voice tight with excitement.

High in the sky two big birds with dark-brown backs and white chests rose up until they were mere specks in the open sky then they plunged. Just before they hit the water, they swung up again. It was a dramatic and skilful performance.

'I've seen them here before,' Lucy said. 'They have a brown line around their necks. Are they albatross?'

'No, osprey. That's their courting ritual. It's unusual to see them this far south and mating this late.'

'Are they endangered?'

'No, but we humans have eliminated them from Tasmania, Victoria and, I thought, this southern part of New South Wales. They're protected everywhere now. That courtship ritual means this pair has a nest near here and it would be great to find it.' Jeff was following their every swoop and rise. 'They'd be perfect for the project I'm working on about the effects of human occupation on the size of coastal chicks.'

'That pair are always here.'

'That figures. Australian osprey don't migrate the way the Northern Hemisphere species does. They just repair the same nest every year. My bet is this pair has a nest in that headland near your house.' He pointed as he talked. 'We could walk around that path. See the one going around that cliff? I'm sure from the way they're acting that'll be where it is.'

Something dark and dank crawled across Lucy's mind. Even though she had used the cliff path to Coalcliff many times when she first moved into the house, she had not used it since the ski party. Every time she went towards it to walk over to Coalcliff, she was overcome with such a sense of foreboding that she returned to the house for the car. She gave her head a little shake to clear it. 'What would the nest look like?'

'Big. Bulky. Made of sticks and driftwood. Probably lined with seaweed or grass. It could be anywhere along that cliff face. Or lower down just above the high-water line.'

By the time they returned to the house, it was too dark to walk along the cliff path. 'Let's explore it another day.' Jeff said as he lifted her chin and kissed her long and passionately. 'Right now, I plan to explore the most beautiful woman in the world.'

That was when he put his hands on her shoulders to push her gently but firmly into the bedroom.

Lucy rang Mary as soon as he drove away the next morning. 'You were right. He did decide.'

'I'm so happy for you. I knew he would. The love you wait for is always the best, that's what my mother used to say. By the way, Kylie phoned last night to confess that she and Pete have been corresponding. He was supposed to fly to Bucharest after that party you had. They were going to travel around Europe together but at the last minute he was offered a six-week job as a driver/guide on some safari tour in Africa.

'Kylie thinks he's doing this job to earn a bit of extra spending cash. She's on cloud nine so isn't that perfect, my two girls both happy.'

'Did you say Pete phoned her last night?' Lucy could hardly get the words out.

'No Kylie phoned me. I think she said Pete sent her an email. That's what you all do nowadays, isn't it?'

Lucy felt the warmth from Jeff's lovemaking drain away as she held the phone rigid against her ear. There was something she needed to remember. Something she needed to tell Mary.

She put down the phone carefully. Sat down on the couch carefully. Folded her hands on her lap and looked at the floor. What was it she needed to remember to tell Mary?

CHAPTER 48

Two weeks after the night Jeff took Lucy to bed, Sarah phoned. 'I haven't seen you for ages. How's the new boyfriend going?'

'Great.' Lucy said, wondering how Sarah knew about Jeff.

'Just ringing to let you know I'm bringing a group down next weekend for the hang-gliding comps. Probably six of us. Don't worry about food, we'll bring it. Will Jeff be there?'

'Maybe.' Jeff had no lectures that weekend and they had already agreed to spend it on the beach watching the competitions. Panic gripped Lucy as she put down the phone. How did Sarah know about Jeff?

Why did I lie to her? she asked herself. It was only a little lie, but it troubled her. She stared at the phone as she let her mind drift back. There was that time when Sarah played up to both John and Andrew at Bisley. The night with John in the library on their twentieth birthday. The way she'd taken Pete from Kylie. So many times Lucy had watched Sarah glide into a room, fix her eyes on the person she planned to charm and go straight to them with her arms outstretched in greeting. The person chosen would recognise themselves as the chosen one and stand a little taller, especially guys.

Lucy looked across the quiet room. Sometimes she felt so desperately in need of someone to talk to, or cuddle. She wished Yami hadn't disappeared. She rang Mary.

'It's natural to feel insecure when you want someone so much,' Mary said, even though she realised Lucy was really worrying about Sarah. 'You're frightened of losing him, but he sounds sincere. Just be yourself.'

Afterwards, Mary wondered if she should have put more

emphasis on the need to trust Jeff. She hadn't met him but from everything Lucy had told her he sounded to be well-grounded and not likely to be swept away by Sarah's charm. The problem, Mary thought, is that Lucy's confidence is so fragile, the smallest provocation will make her give up.

On the weekend of the hang-gliding competition, Lucy waited nervously for Jeff to arrive. As soon as he roared up in his MGB, she raced outside and flung herself into his big warm embrace. His closeness filled her with such confidence, she chatted away, telling him Sarah was coming for the weekend with a few friends.

'About time I met her,' he gave Lucy a big squeeze. 'I'll bet she's a doll like you.'

'She's much more beautiful than me,' Lucy said, feeling suddenly apprehensive. 'She's perfect.'

Jeff stopped abruptly to look at her. 'Nobody's perfect. Mum taught me that. Everyone's a mixture of good and bad, beautiful and not so beautiful. You might think the osprey is graceful. You might admire the way it catches fish for its chicks, but it looks pretty damn ugly if you're the fish and it's zooming down on you.' He chuckled, pleased with this thought.

Lucy felt her heart swell with love as she watched him search the sky for the osprey.

They were sitting at the table on the deck with a bottle of chardonnay in an ice bucket and nibbles on several plates when Sarah and her crowd arrived. Sarah slid stylishly out of her gleaming new red Mercedes convertible and, dumping her leather overnight bag in the lounge, walked out onto the deck. Her hair fell like satin over a soft denim shirt and her cream leather pants moulded to her buttocks and legs.

'You must be Jeff,' she said, eyes smiling and arms outstretched in greeting. Two weeks earlier Lucy had become secretive, so she had gone to the Orange Grove Market for a little chat with Dot, who had unwittingly told her all she needed to know.

He appraised her for a split second then leaped up to give her a big hug. 'And you're obviously Lucy's twin.'

Lucy greeted the others. She knew Anna and Bill who Sarah told her had become a couple during the ski weekend, but she hadn't met Hamish before. 'Hamish is a partner at his father's law firm which I'm joining next year when I finish uni,' Sarah explained as she introduced him. 'It's the best criminal law firm in the country.'

Jeff held out his hand. 'G'day mate.'

After everyone settled in, they gathered on the deck to watch the sunset. Jeff followed the osprey through his binoculars, fascinating them all with an explanation of what the birds were doing as they glided back and forth over the water, then dropped feet first to emerge with a fish squirming in their talons, sprays of silver droplets flashing in the air.

'The male is good to his partner,' Jeff told them. 'If he makes a catch he'll often give it to her. He helps build the nest and when she's sitting on it, he works like a drover's dog to feed her and the chicks.'

'So, you're into birds.' Hamish said in a patronising tone.

'Grew up roaming the bush, watching wildlife,' Jeff replied with a sideways glance at Hamish.

'Jeff's parents worked on Project Eden, one of the most ambitious conservation projects in the world,' Sarah said rising from her seat for better effect. 'It was established by the West Australian government to restore native wildlife to the Peron Peninsula. To create a predator-free environment, they built an animal-proof fence then teams worked to eliminate all the introduced species – sheep, cats, goats, foxes, etcetera.'

'Most people only know that area for the touristy bits like Shark Bay and the dolphins at Monkey Mia,' Jeff said impressed.

'We have a group of avid conservations at uni,' Sarah replied smiling, 'and I follow its projects from time to time.'

This was a lie. Sarah had never known any conservationists, she had simply done a little investigative work on Jeff's parents. 'Peron is very forward thinking,' she added.

'Sure is. Mum and Dad also work on other projects, but Peron is special. Eradicating the cats has been the biggest hurdle.'

'Because they're too cunning to show themselves and too smart to take bait' Sarah finished off for him.

Lucy watched in dismay as Sarah took Jeff's arm to guide him inside where they could talk more privately. She could not believe Sarah knew so much about him. She knew Mary would not have said anything because she was hoping Lucy would find happiness with him.

Did Sarah have spies like her mother had at Liam's New York office? She's being horrible Lucy thought as she sat rigidly sipping her drink, trying desperately to not watch them.

The next morning, they all filed down the beach path carrying rugs, umbrellas and picnic baskets bulging with food and wine. It was a fine clear day and the beach was filling up fast as they picked their way between spectators to find a space for eight. Sarah sat beside Jeff to help him open the wine and hand around the glasses. Hamish, with his cotton shirt and hat firmly in place, sat a little apart, seemly disinterested.

The others lolled back on the rugs to watch the passing parade and the hang-gliders floating through the air like autumn leaves. Leaflets being handed out told them that in the late 1800s Lawrence Hargrave had made the world's first successful unpowered flight off the cliffs over Stanwell Park beach. Although his glider had crashed into the sand dunes that then covered the beach, his box kite design was deemed a success and later on the Wright brothers used it for their successful powered flight. There was a long list of the countries that were represented in the competitions.

During lunch Anna wiggled closer to Lucy. 'Don't worry

about Sarah,' she said softly. 'She can't help herself. She always has to flirt, but Jeff's not her type and she's definitely not his. Believe me.'

'But look at him listening to her,' Lucy said.

'He's just being polite.'

'He was impressed by her knowing so much about his parents and that peninsula place in WA.'

'Why wouldn't he be?' Anna said rolling her eyes. 'None of us have ever heard of it.'

'So how did Sarah know about it?' Lucy asked.

'And what are you two beauties gossiping about?' Jeff flopped down beside Lucy as he handed her a slice of bacon and egg pie. Anna winked at Lucy and moved away.

Jeff was attentive all day but nothing he did could calm the chaos in her head. All she could see was Sarah smiling up at him with her green eyes translucent in the sunlight. Lucy was too caught up in her own thoughts to notice that his hazel eyes watched Sarah with the same polite interest they watched everyone else who spoke to him. She was too anxious to perceive that although Sarah reached over to touch his arm often, Jeff never touched her.

The hang-gliding was fascinating but after it finished, and they were all drifting back to the house, she wished she had the evening alone with Jeff. She smiled for group photographs, served up the Thai curry she had made for dinner, and thanked them politely when they all raved about how it was the best they'd ever tasted. After a day in the sun with copious amounts of food and wine, they all collapsed on the couches after dinner and very soon were making their apologies to Lucy as they headed for their bedrooms.

As the silence settled, Lucy wandered out onto the deck and sat gazing out to sea.

'What's up, pet?' She felt Jeff's arms go around her and longed to lean back against his chest and pour out her jumbled thoughts. But the words wouldn't come. Instead she stiffened and mumbled that she wasn't tired. 'Come on, you've hardly spoken to me all day. Have I done something wrong?'

'Don't be silly,' she snapped, fighting the urge to reach up and wrap her arms around him. 'You go to bed. I want to sit here for a bit.' She felt his arms drop then listened wretchedly to him walk inside.

Her head told her she should be angry with Sarah, not him. He may not have understood everything, but he would have tried.

LUCY

Dr Singh and I have been working through my life since I came here – and Jeff is near the end. It was inevitable of course but talking about him felt unclean.

'From what I'm hearing your relationship with Jeff was going along very nicely until the weekend of the hang-gliding,' he says. 'That's when you first felt you had lost him. But he rang quite soon after that weekend, so why did you think you had lost him to Sarah?'

By now I know how Dr Singh's mind works. He brings up a subject that gets me to say things out loud that I barely admit to myself in silence. However, I appreciate that our sessions are good for me, so even though I'd sooner not, I make myself cooperate.

'Because Sarah hogged all his attention that weekend. Jeff had gone quietly to bed that night acting as though nothing had happened, but it had in my mind. I waited until I could tell by his breathing that he was asleep, then I crawled into bed behind him and lay facing him but not touching him. The next morning I didn't go to the beach for the finals – said I had a headache and stayed in bed. I know it sounds childish, but I couldn't pull myself out of my melancholy to be nice to him.'

'What about that girl at the beach, Anna, who said Jeff wasn't Sarah's type? Did you think about that?'

'All I could see was Sarah and Jeff together, laughing and sharing.'

'Did Jeff try to talk to you before he left on Sunday?'

'Yes, but I didn't let him. No one since Michael had made

me forget my scars and believe someone could love me. Not since Daddy died had a man held me so tenderly. I had this insane notion that they had both dumped me and I wasn't about to let another guy do that.'

'He rang a few days later and you agreed to meet him. What happened then?'

'He came on Friday night. I could tell he was nervous. He took me in his arms and kissed me carefully – it was like a question. One wrong move from me and he was going to leave. But as I felt his arms go around me and his scent spread through my head, I simply broke down and couldn't stop crying.'

'Did you explain to him why you were so upset?'

'No.'

I wonder now how different things might have been if I had opened up. But I didn't know how to. He kissed me again and again until we were in the bedroom, devouring each other with the frenzy of hungry animals.

'I cried and he comforted me.'

'Do you recall what you did the next day?' Dr Singh asked.

'Jeff wanted to walk around the cliff path to look for the osprey's nest. I forced myself to go but I became nervous as we approached it. He thought I was frightened of the height and the crash of the waves down below, so he held my hand as we walked. But it wasn't the height or the waves. It was something I didn't understand and couldn't talk about.'

'Have you tried to recall what it was you couldn't understand?'

'Yes, but I still don't know.'

I sense Dr Singh wants something more from me.

'Jeff didn't stop to look for the nest. He just held my hand tight and glanced about quickly until we were off the cliff and walking into Coalcliff. He was funny about Coalcliff, called it "yuppie heaven". He once told me that when city executives retire they buy a weatherboard house near a beach, put in sliding glass doors so they can sit outside and still watch* telly, and noise-proof the roof so they aren't kept awake when it rains. He was mischievous and was always making me laugh.'

Dr Singh asks if I thought Jeff was serious or teasing me.

'Serious! He said he'd probably be an old yuppie one day and buy a house near the sea. Then he took my hands in his and said very sweetly: 'Do you like that idea, pet?'

'Did you feel he was including you in his old yuppie's house by the sea.'

'I know he was.'

'So why did you agree to the events that followed?'

'Because at that very moment Sarah pulled up in her car looking stunning.'

CHAPTER 49

'Didn't see you at the house so guessed you must be here at Coalcliff. Want a lift back?'

Lucy's heart sank. 'I thought you had a party in Sydney tonight.'

'I did, but it was with Hamish and his crowd is so boring. I bought some goodies from the gourmet deli and thought, what could be nicer than to spend an evening down here, just the three of us. Jeff, you better hop in the front because you've got long legs.'

Lucy squashed into the back seat where she sulked watching Sarah chatter and smile across at Jeff. Sarah's hair was loose and glossy. She wore a sporty golf shirt tucked into narrow cord jeans and a thick leather belt with an R M Williams buckle; a carefully planned country-girl freshness that would appeal to Jeff.

'We can look for the osprey's nest this evening,' Sarah said. 'They soar above it when they're courting so we should be able to pinpoint where it is.'

'Right on,' Jeff nodded. 'Lucy and I have decided it's somewhere along that steep cliff path on the way to Coalcliff. We've just walked along it but didn't find the nest.'

'French bubbles first, then I'll get a torch and walk along the path with you. I've got good eyes for finding things.'

'Jeff prefers beer,' Lucy mumbled resentfully from the back seat.

'I brought a case of VB, your favourite.' Sarah said, giving Jeff a teasing pat on the knee.

Lucy felt her face flush. How did Sarah know Jeff preferred VB? When did they discuss that? And now she was chatting on about the shy albatross, the only one of the species that nested in Australia. How the hell did she know that? Lucy knew her thoughts were sliding from sulky to angry and desperately tried to control herself.

'Possibly talking about seabirds last weekend stirred her interest,' Jeff said that night when they were curled up in bed. 'People do that, you know. I've seen volunteers who work with Mum and Dad for a week on a conservation project go away total converts. They join wildlife groups, lobby the government for more protection, more funds ... Mum and Dad love them.'

'But Sarah's a city girl.' Lucy scoffed. 'She's not damn well interested in birds.'

'I know. I can see that she's showing off, but she's a doer and if she got on our side, she'd be the sort to go out to lobby big companies and governments for money. And she'd be good at it. Our wildlife needs people with her abilities.'

The following Thursday, Mary rang to say she was just leaving Birchgrove and bringing lunch. Lucy looked around in a panic. After Jeff and Sarah had left on the Sunday, she was emotionally drained. It would take Mary a bit over an hour to get here so she had time to clean up the mess. She ran around shoving things out of sight – the weekend linen into the washing machine and the garbage out the back.

By the time Mary arrived the house was tidy, but Lucy's wig was tangled and there were stains on her white shirt. Mary also noticed her eyes were puffy as though she had been crying, or not sleeping well.

They drove to the beach because the track running down from the house was a bit slippery for Mary. Oleanders, hibiscus, banksias and wild convolvulus in full bloom covered the cove in splashes of brilliant colour. All the birds except the scavenging seagulls were sheltering in the shade of trees and the waves were hushed by the neap tide.

'This is so pleasant,' Mary sighed as she settled down on

the rug they had spread under a tree. 'Now tell me what's happening with this man of yours.'

'He's gone off me.'

As Mary listened, she wished Mario was here to give advice. He understood Lucy's mood swings and the anger that followed better than she did. 'Nothing you've told me indicates he has changed his feelings for you. He insisted you go with them when Sarah wanted to walk around the cliff path. He wouldn't go for a swim with her when you had a headache and didn't want to swim. From what I'm hearing, you're seeing things that aren't there. You have to trust him a bit more.'

'I do trust him, but I also understand if he prefers Sarah. She doesn't have scars and is more interested in the things he's interested in. She knows so much about seabirds and asks him all the questions he just loves answering.'

'Now Lucy, we both know that's not true. Sarah is most definitely not interested in birds.' Mary felt herself getting cross. 'When she wants to win someone over, she learns everything she can about them so she can impress them. She's always done that. This bird thing is no exception.'

'So why does she want to impress Jeff when he's mine?' Lucy said peevishly.

Mary knew the answer but didn't want to say it. Just before she went to London Kylie had told her about Sarah inviting Pete to ski with her in Aspen. Even though it was a long time ago, Kylie had cried bitterly as she told Mary how it had caused the breakup between her and Pete. She said she'd lost a boyfriend as well as a girlfriend she had loved and trusted.

Mary watched the seagulls squawking at each other and thought of the way Sarah pursued people then dropped them without a second thought. She did it even as a little girl. Mario used to say it was because she was ambitious like her mother, but Jill was never malicious. Jill's ambition drove her to push people too hard sometimes, but she never schemed to hurt anyone. Sarah didn't have Jill's basic decency nor her fierce loyalty.

Sadly, Mary thought, Sarah does seem to be making a play for Jeff.

CHAPTER 50

Lucy felt a bit better after Mary left, but later that evening Sarah rang from Wollongong. She was at the apartment building where Jeff lived.

'Is Jeff with you?' Sarah asked impatiently.

'No. Why?'

'Well I'm outside his apartment and I want to give him some research papers on seabirds from Japan which he'll find interesting. Do you know if he keeps a spare key hidden somewhere?'

'Why?'

'Because I'm outside and I don't enjoy hanging around student buildings. If I could let myself in, I could wait for him inside.'

Lucy had only visited Jeff's apartment twice, but he had shown her the pot plant at the end of the hall under which he hid a spare key. 'You can use it whenever you like.' He had winked at her with a wicked grin. 'Come down and surprise me. I'd love to come home from a hard day's study to find my pet curled up on the couch waiting for me.'

Lucy was shaking so much after the call that she let herself slide down the wall to sit on the floor. She visualised his old-fashioned couches, unmatched armchairs, shelves and corners piled high with books, the hanging cage with two pretty little finches excited by his return home, his messy bedroom, the bed unmade!

'Stop this,' she told herself. Mary had said she must show more trust in him. It was Sarah making the moves, not Jeff.

But Lucy's mind would not leave it alone. She imagined him walking in the door mouthing squeaky noises at the finches and dumping his bags on the table. He would be surprised to see Sarah, but politeness would make him offer her a drink. Sarah would bring out the research papers and they would study them, heads close, shoulders touching. He would not want her to drive back to Sydney without something to eat so he would pull two steaks out of the freezer and open a bottle of wine.

'No!' she screamed at the silent house.

She felt the walls closing in on her. 'No.' She beat the floor with her fists. 'Please God, no.' She slid down and rolled over onto her stomach as great sobs wrenched at her innards.

With baleful eyes the house watched her. A cool wind drifted in off the sea and slid over her skin like a portent of lonely nights.

The evening became night. Finally, shivering and puffy-eyed, she lifted herself from the floor and poured a large vodka, then another and another. They fortified her as she stalked the house visualising the finches being covered with a black cloth for the night. Jeff's unmade bed.

At midnight, she rang Sarah at Birchgrove. No reply. She rang Sarah's mobile and the message service answered. With hands shaking so much she could hardly press the buttons she dialled Jeff's landline but slammed the receiver down at the first shrill ring.

Lonely and depleted, she slumped on the couch and let herself fade away. As she sunk deeper into an alcohol-induced sleep the black cat appeared and rubbed its flaking sores against her bare skin. She wanted to move away but her legs were still stuck in the sand. Then she saw her rifle on a branch above her. If she could reach it, she could shoot the cat. But each time her fingertips nearly reached it the rifle moved a tiny bit further along the branch. Then she saw the wavy woman's figure and a pale hand with red fingernails wrapped around the barrel of the rifle. She wanted to scream with frustration because she knew her, she knew her ... but the name wouldn't come.

Early next morning Jeff rang to say his mother had been bitten by a snake. 'She's okay. Dad knew how to treat her but it's a deadly species, so he's rushed her to Carnarvon for the antivenin. She's pretty crook so I'm going over for a few days.' When Lucy didn't respond he asked if anything was wrong.

'Yes ... I mean no.' She shook herself trying to clear the fog from her head and concentrate on what he was saying. 'I hope your mother's all right. How long will you be gone?' Her voice sounded false, as though it belonged to someone else.

'Probably a week. The flight goes through Perth, so I may stay there a couple of days on the way back to catch up with the old crowd. I'll miss you, pet.'

She very much wanted to ask about Sarah but didn't want to hear the answer. Had she stayed? Was she still there, standing beside him as he spoke?

When Lucy didn't say anything, he spoke again. 'Got to go now. My plane leaves in two hours. Luckily I've got a lift to the airport. I'll ring as soon as I get back.'

'Yes. Lucky. I hope your Mum's all right.'

'Mum's a tough old nut. It would take more than a snake to bump her off the twig.' The phone clicked and he was gone.

'Trust him, trust him,' she whispered to herself as she put the phone down. 'Anna and Mary both said you should have more trust in him.' But she couldn't still her mind of the wild thoughts racing through it. Was Sarah the person giving him the lift? Who else could be there so conveniently driving to Sydney?

When the phone rang later that day, she grabbed it hoping it would be Jeff so she could tell him she would miss him. She wanted to ask if she could send flowers to his mother. But it was Sarah.

'Did you hear about Jeff's Mum? Bitten by a snake. He was so upset last night he wanted me to go with him to keep him company. I couldn't of course because I've just started this new job. Did he ring to tell you?'

'Yes.'

'Did he tell you how he got to the airport?'

'Said a friend took him.'

'It was the only thing I could do.' Sarah's lie was quick. 'Made me a bit late for work but I was going right past the airport.'

Sarah put the phone down with a sardonic smile. 'That will give Lucy something to worry about,' she thought. She was annoyed with Jeff. He had politely invited her in but had not offered her a drink when she gave him the research papers. Then his father had phoned with the news about the snakebite and he'd asked her to leave because he had people to ring, arrangements to make.

After putting the phone down, Lucy walked out to the patch of geraniums in the garden. She often came here to sit quietly when she was upset, but this time seeing the shovel she had left leaning against a tree she grabbed it and began to dig. Stalks, leaves and red petals scattered like drops of blood over the sandy soil as Lucy's digging became more frenetic. She was sweating profusely by the time the shovel squashed into the towel that held Yami's remains.

On the verge of hysteria, she clawed at the gritty soil with her bare hands as it shredded the skin along her fingers and chipped her nails until they bled.

Her hands shook violently as she gently opened the once-pink towel to expose Yami's remains – the bare skull, the empty eye sockets. For almost an hour she kneeled there not moving, barely breathing. As the sun sank towards the horizon, she closed the towel around the bones, placed it back in the hole, scraped the soil back and replaced the geraniums. For a long time, she patted down the soil and tried to repair the tattered geranium petals. Then she went inside to wash her hands, soaping them over and over until they were soft and wrinkled.

The phone rang many times over the next few days, but she didn't answer it. She didn't eat. She didn't wash. She had fits of fury and extended times of lethargy.

When Sarah arrived unannounced, she found Lucy covered in filth and the house looking as though a mad animal had raged through. Tenderly she stripped off Lucy's clothes, then her own, and taking Lucy's hand led her into the shower. After they were both clean, she ran a hot bath, poured in soothing oils and helped Lucy into it. 'I'll come to help you out when it's time to get dressed for dinner,' she said softly.

Moving quickly Sarah ripped the soiled sheets off Lucy's bed and remade it with fresh ones. She put empty bottles into the recycle bin and the rubbish into rubbish bags that she tied tightly to contain the stench. Into the boot of her car she piled the cushions Lucy had shredded. She would take them back to Sydney to dispose of them. She filled the dishwasher and set it going. By the time she helped Lucy into clean clothes, the pizza she had put into the oven filled the room with a warm cheesy smell.

Sarah watched Lucy eat and was content. This is how it would be. Lucy by her side, she in control. It was the same at her new job. She had accepted a short-term contract with a law firm that had chosen her because she was in the top five in her graduation year. Charles, her boss, was increasingly recognising her intelligence and skill at dealing with difficult clients and she knew he would offer her a permanent position when the time came. She also knew he would be annoyed when she left him to join Hamish's father's company. He would no doubt make her a better offer, but she would move on. She was always going to work for Hamish's father, he was the best in the country. She just wanted to be inside another company first to learn the internal workings of a law firm and observe those who had made it to the top. She would console Charles with lavish gratitude and thanks for how well he had taught her. Her power over people was maturing and she increasingly scorned them for their weaknesses.

Now she must focus on Jeff! Jeff! She had watched Lucy's confidence grow when she was with him. She knew that as her twin, she should feel pleased for her, but she didn't know how to. She only knew control or destroy. She had tried to win over Jeff, but he was a country hick and a fool. She would get Lucy another cat, but she would not let her keep Jeff.

After they had finished the pizza Sarah sat forward. Putting her elbows on the table, she looked deep into Lucy's troubled soul.

'We must deal with this man,' she said gently. 'You're fragile dear twin and he's playing with your emotions. Can you believe he wanted me to go across to Western Australia with him to meet his parents? He's a cheating bastard. He can't hurt me because I'm strong, but he can hurt you and I'm not going to let him.' She moved around to a chair beside Lucy to take her into her arms. 'You and me together, always. We don't need men like Jeff.'

Lucy sobbed. 'Everyone said I could trust him.'

'What do they know. Remember our code: FWTW, *From Womb to Worms – born together, live together, leave together.* That's our pledge to each other forever.'

She took Lucy's limp hand and pressed their thumbs together as they had done when they had shared their blood. Her green eyes were devoid of emotion as they watched their fingers.

'But I want to be loved,' Lucy said, clinging desperately to the last shreds of her desire for Jeff. 'I want someone to love.'

Sarah listened with callous indifference as the emerging woman in Lucy faded and the child who would be submissive to her will returned.

'You are loved Lucy. Loved very deeply by me ... your twin. Remember how we always played together, slept in the same room, even in the same bed when we were allowed. What a duo we were,' she chuckled lightly. 'I would be so lonely if you ever left me.'

Lucy's thoughts leaped about wildly; in a quandary between the now with Jeff and the past with Sarah. Sarah who had always been beside her – always loved her – always been there with help when she needed it most.

'I wish that snake had bitten him,' she sobbed vehemently. 'He wants to tear us apart ... doesn't he?'

'That's right, Lucy. He wants to tear us apart, but we won't let him. You can stop him. Stop him now before it is too late.'

Sarah smoothly pushed on. 'We'll get rid of him – just as we did Pete.'

Lucy's body went rigid with shock.

'No,' she wailed. 'I'll tell him not to come around anymore. I can do that.'

'Maybe you can dear Lucy, but he will still come after me.'

'You can tell him too.' Lucy clawed at Sarah's knees. 'Please Sarah. Please, not Jeff.'

'There is no other way.' Sarah took Lucy's hands and lifted her gently from the chair to lead her inside.

CHAPTER 51

Jeff returned ten days later and phoned Lucy immediately, his voice deep and cheerful. 'Hi pet, I'm back. Mum's made a good recovery and they're leaving Carnarvon to drive up into the Kimberley.'

'Why the Kimberley?'

'They're going to a remote area where Dad's wanted to go for years to do some special research. There'll be less pressure there which will make it easier for Mum,' he gave a light laugh 'although knowing her she'll be in boots and all, writing madly and taking photos. It's so remote the only contact is by radio. It's wonderful country and I can't wait to take you there one day.'

Lucy's mind was so fixed on what she had to say that she didn't hear the last sentence. Like a child repeating painstakingly rehearsed lines she said, 'I've got good news, too. I found the osprey's nest and there are two chicks in it.'

'Really. Where?'

'Near the first bend of the cliff path as you suspected, tucked in under it, which is why we didn't see it before. I had to lie on my stomach to look over the edge.'

'Did you say there are two chicks in it?'

'Yes. They're a mottled brown.' She was talking quickly now, her eyes shut as she tried to repeat the words as Sarah had taught her. 'You should come and take photos before they fly away.'

He laughed. 'They don't leave the nest that quickly, but I can hardly believe there are chicks already. Those birds were still courting when I left. They incubate their eggs for nearly forty days. Are you sure they weren't eggs? They're also a mottled brown?'

Lucy hesitated; he wasn't supposed to say that. 'I thought they were chicks. I was too frightened to lean out too far.'

'It's possible to mistake them because the chicks tend to lie flat in the nest. Either way I want to photograph them, but more importantly I want to see you. I've missed you pet. Can I come up on Saturday?'

'Yes, that would be wonderful.'

'Great, and I'm chuffed you went out there for me. I've brought you a special wine from Margaret River, which we'll open to celebrate.'

As Lucy replaced the receiver, Sarah handed her a coffee.

'Well done. Drink this then we'll go to Malabar for a practice shoot, then home to Birchgrove until Friday. I'll help you buy food for a special dinner.'

Sarah had worked at Stanwell Park for the past two weeks so she would be there, beside Lucy, when Jeff phoned. It had gone exactly as she had planned.

Sarah and Lucy went to Malabar, but Lucy couldn't stay the night in the house at Birchgrove. She felt Mario watching her and frowning, and Jill hovering like a warning presence. She would have liked to go through the gap in the fence to talk to Mary, but she was out for the day. For the sake of old memories Lucy did check the gap but new shoots had grown across it and when she pushed them gently, she could feel their resistance. It was like a closed door but was she locked in, or locked out?

She fled back to Stanwell Park.

'You had no right to sneak out of the house like that,' Sarah threatened on the phone that night. 'I get home with two delicious pork chops for our dinner and you've gone.'

'I'm sorry.' Guilt pounded Lucy like a hailstorm.

'Don't cry.' Sarah replied, her need to admonish Lucy fulfilled. She softened her voice. 'The chops will keep until Friday. I'll leave work early and come down Friday afternoon so we can finalise our plan.'

As Lucy replaced the receiver she glanced around the

deathly quiet beach house. If she strained, she could hear the faint drum of the waves and the final twitters of birds settling in for the night. She shivered. Feeling the need to be outside with those familiar noises she walked across the lounge to go out onto the deck, but as she reached out to slide open the doors, her arms froze, refusing to touch the doors. She looked at her arms as a child looks at an egg it has accidentally dropped and broken. She tried to reach out again, but still she could not touch the doors that would let her go outside. Puzzled, but accepting that they knew what they were doing, she walked back across the lounge to the back room where her rifles were locked in the gun case. The key was in her bedside drawer but she did not take it out. She just stood silently acknowledging her friends in there, gleaming, waiting to feel her hands on them.

'I'm sorry,' she mumbled softly.

Jeff arrived with a roar and leapt out of the car as soon as it stopped. His fair hair, which had grown longer during the trip away, flapping about below his cap. The sky was grey and a cold wind stung his cheeks as he grabbed the wine from the back seat and bounded up the steps to give Lucy a great big bear hug.

'Did you miss me?'

When she saw him, Lucy went rigid, but his enthusiasm dissolved her doubts and she threw her arms around him and led him laughing down the hall into the bedroom. Not until they both lay back exhausted did her mission return to her and she shuddered.

'I hope that was a shiver of pleasure,' he said, pulling her close into his chest. 'I missed you all the time I was away.'

She didn't reply as she tried to quell the jumble in her head. Sarah had told her she must be natural and not weaken. 'You can go to bed with him but remember he tried to get me into bed too, so don't believe anything he says.'

Jeff, mistaking her silence for agreement, drifted into a

contented sleep. When she was sure he was asleep, she extracted herself from his arms to go to the kitchen to prepare dinner. Sarah had said he would have had plenty of fish while with his parents, so she should cook a rare roast beef with crispy roast vegetables and a deep apple pie with lashings of cream.

LUCY

I must calm down before Sarah walks in, must not think about Jeff. She will be at the car park, looking for a free space, three, maybe four minutes away.

But even as I try to clear my mind, I'm dragged back to that session where Dr Singh persisted in asking about Jeff.

I remember I told him I hadn't been sleeping well. 'I keep having this nightmare about a bird I was trying to photograph, but it kept swooping me. Then it opened its huge beak and I was inside its throat with flaps of bleeding flesh slapping against me. I was naked and couldn't protect the camera, so I hugged it to my body. Blood oozed through my fingers and I knew if I let it reach the camera it would be ruined.'

'Did you think it was Jeff's camera?'

I can't answer because I can't remember.

'What about the camera?' Dr Singh persists. 'Did it look like Jeff's camera?'

'It had Nikon written on it. He used a Nikon.'

'Can you remember whether Sarah came down that weekend?'

I knew where his questions were going.

'She came Friday afternoon. I remember she was angry with me. She hit me across the face and made me clean up the house, said I was living like a pig and Jeff would leave me if he saw that side of me. She made me go to bed early so I would be clean and bright when he arrived on Saturday afternoon.'

'What did you and Sarah talk about on Friday night.?'

'Men and how deceitful they are.'

'Did you talk about Jeff?'

'A bit.'

'What did Sarah say about Jeff?'

I refuse to answer because I have already told him how Jeff had tried to get Sarah into bed, how he had asked her to go with him to visit his sick mother. Sarah didn't keep secrets from me; she told me about all his phone calls pestering her to go out with him.

'Did you ever ask Jeff if he had made those phone calls to Sarah?' Dr Singh asks.

'Why would I do that? He would just lie. Sarah said he had a good reason to lie because he wanted both of us.'

'Did you ever think it could be Sarah who had a reason to lie? You had a nice boyfriend and she didn't.'

I scoff at Dr Singh's naïvety. 'She has guys queuing up. She didn't need Jeff and anyway he wasn't her type. Everyone said so.'

'Was she there when you woke up on Saturday morning?'

'Yes, but she left quite early.'

'Were you still taking your antidepressants at this time?'

'I don't think so.'

'Did you and Sarah drink any alcohol?'

'Sarah arrived with a bottle of vodka and some wine. She was always so thoughtful.'

'Did she drink with you?'

'Maybe a glass of wine. She seldom drinks alcohol and never takes pills or medicines. She's very health conscious, which is why she didn't want me taking the pills Dr Kilter prescribed. She said doctors create addicts to boost their income.'

'What I'm hearing is that Sarah left Saturday morning and Jeff arrived later in the afternoon. What did you and Jeff talk about?'

This I don't remember, I've tried. Was I nice to him? Did he touch me? What did I say? Speaking about Jeff has brought back such a flood of emotions that I start to cry. Dr Singh passes over his box of tissues and stays quiet for a bit.

'Now Lucy, think back to that Saturday afternoon,' Dr Singh says. 'Jeff arrives in his red MGB. You're all clean and tidy waiting for him. It's dull and windy so he decides to leave photographing the nest until the next morning. He gives you a big hug then hands you a bottle of Margaret River wine onto which he has tied a red ribbon and a note thanking you for finding the nest. You walk inside, probably arms around each other. Do you go to bed immediately to make love, or does he open the wine and you clink glasses?'

I want to help but no matter how hard I try, how many times I revisit that scene, I can't remember anything. It's as though there's a hole in my head and that night has dropped out the bottom. I remember Sarah leaving on Saturday morning but nothing after that.

'Why can't I remember anything at all about that night?' I ask Dr Singh.

'It's possible you were in a fugue state, which means it's too painful to remember. Your mind won't let you.'

'Because of what I did?'

'Or what you think you did. The fugue could be because of what you did, what you think you did, or what you and Sarah had discussed doing.'

'But we know Jeff is missing so I must have done it – mustn't I?'

'I don't know what you did. What I do know is that he was there on Saturday night, which is why you rang Mary the next day.'

CHAPTER 52

The phone rang in Mary's house late that Sunday afternoon.

'Help me. Please, help me.' The voice was faint and girlish.

At first Mary thought it was a crank call. She was about to hang up when it spoke again. 'Mary, help me.'

'Lucy?'

'Help me. Please help me.'

Mary coaxed and questioned, a cold dread settling over on her. She could hear Lucy breathing which kept her going. Finally, after what seemed like an age, Lucy spoke again.

'He's dead. Smashed on the rocks.'

'Dead? Smashed? Who? Speak to me Lucy.'

'Gone.'

'Lucy are you hurt?' Mary asked as she ran around the house throwing a change of clothes, food and medicines into a bag. 'Is Sarah there?"

'No, gone.'

'Lucy dear, please carry the phone into your bedroom and lie down on your bed.' Mary listened to Lucy's scuffles at the other end of the line. When she was as sure as she could be that Lucy was lying down, she continued. 'Please stay there with the phone beside you and rest. I'm leaving now so will be with you in about an hour. I'll keep ringing as I drive so please don't leave the phone.'

'The ospreys are flying over their nest.'

'That's lovely, dear. Now just rest. I'll be there very soon.'

Mary shrugged into a jacket, zipped up the bag and ran to her car. As she backed out the driveway, she looked across at the Borgetti's house and hesitated. Should she rush in to tell Sarah? An inner voice told her not to. Lucy's desperate cry had been to her, not Sarah. As she negotiated her way out of Birchgrove, through Balmain then the southern suburbs she rang Dot but there was no reply. Dot would be at the market and she supposed Bob was fishing.

Once out of the city Mary drove fast. She knew she had to get to Lucy before it was too late. Too late for what, she wondered, as storm clouds gathered and the sky darkened.

Stanwell Park resembled a ghost town, with all doors and windows closed against the approaching storm. Mary found Lucy's door unlocked so she walked straight in and through to the bedroom. At first she thought Lucy was asleep but then she opened her eyes and Mary saw the depths of despair. She dumped her bags and sat down on the bed.

'What's happened?'

'It's over now. He's gone.'

'Who's gone?'

'It's better now. Sarah knows.'

Mary felt the skin along her spine crawl as she looked into Lucy's vacant eyes. 'You said on the phone someone is dead. Who is dead Lucy?'

Lucy sat up with a jolt, her eyes wildly bright. 'Mary! What are you doing here? Why are we in the bedroom?' She pulled Mary into the lounge. 'Sit down while I wash my face then I'll make coffee.'

Stunned by Lucy's rapid change, Mary did as she was told and sat looking around at the clean and tidy room. The radio was playing softly.

If it weren't for Lucy's initial appearance followed by her sudden mood change, Mary might have believed the phone call was in her imagination. But those words ... 'he is dead' hung heavy in her mind.

When Lucy returned to the lounge she had changed into clean jeans and a rollneck jumper. Mary watched her closely. Apart from her movements seeming sluggish she was acting normally. Lucy filled the coffee grinder; watched it spin as it ground the beans and a delicious aroma permeated the room. She didn't speak again until Lucy set plates and coffee before her. 'Where did you get that lemon tart?'

'Sarah brought it down on Friday night. Have some, it's delicious?'

'I thought Jeff was coming this weekend?'

'Jeff?' Lucy looked around as though expecting to see him.

'You told me he was back from WA and was coming over on Saturday to photograph the osprey chicks.'

'No. Sarah came.'

'Didn't Jeff come yesterday ... Saturday?' Mary watched as Lucy looked towards the door as though expecting an answer. 'You told me during the week he was coming to take photos.'

'I don't think so.'

Mary couldn't get Lucy to talk about Jeff so she let the conversation drift onto other matters. After a while, Lucy leaned into the couch and fell asleep. Mary wondered if Lucy's tendency to be tired and unfocused, then almost immediately brittle and agitated, bordered on a mental illness. She racked her memory, but her nursing hadn't included anything about mental issues.

When Lucy woke she begged Mary to stay the night. 'I'm frightened of storms.'

Mary had no difficulty encouraging Lucy to go to bed early. Then she was free to wander about the house looking for clues although she had no idea what a clue would look like. Everything seemed to be in place, and it wasn't until she went in to check that Lucy was asleep that she saw a camera bag poking out from under the bed.

Feeling like a thief, she took it out to the lounge. It was a normal black Nikon camera bag with a few bits and pieces in it – a cleaning rag, a blower, a brush, spare batteries, a polarising lens, but no camera and no name tag. She sat there replaying over and over in her mind the phone call from Lucy. Then, not knowing why, she took the bag into the spare bedroom and standing on a stool pushed it to the back of the wardrobe shelf where it was hidden behind old clothes.

The next morning, when Mary put out the garbage a wine bottle with a red ribbon caught her attention. Hanging from the ribbon was a gift card with the words "For my pet" scrawled on it. There was no signature, but she knew who had brought it to the house. And she knew it was for Lucy, not Sarah.

CHAPTER 53

Before Mary left the house on Monday, she peeped into the address book Lucy kept beside the phone and copied Jeff's phone number and address in Wollongong. She would ring him when she got home to see if he could throw any light on Lucy's strange phone call.

She decided Jeff had most likely stayed with Lucy on Saturday night, that they had drunk the wine, gone to bed, had a huge argument on Sunday morning and he had stormed out. She speculated that Jeff had taken the camera out of the bag to photograph the birds but was so angry he just leapt into his car and drove off leaving the bag behind.

This didn't sound like the easygoing Jeff she had been hearing about, but she didn't know him well enough to judge him any other way.

It was Wednesday before she got around to making the phone call to Jeff and was surprised when an automated voice told her that the number she was calling had been disconnected. On impulse, she leapt into her car and drove to Jeff's address in Wollongong, but when she got there two hours later she stood looking at the block of flats feeling silly. What if it was just a lovers' tiff and he thought she was an interfering old woman?

Lucy was relatively inexperienced about men. She may have read more into the relationship than was ever there. Or Jeff may have decided to opt out before he got in any deeper. What if it wasn't his camera bag she had so impulsively hidden?

All these thoughts floated around her head as she sat in her car watching people come and go from the building. From their age and casual dress, she guessed they were students from the university Jeff went to. What would Mum do? she asked herself. In Ireland people look out for each other but Australians are different. Racked with indecision she started up the car and headed back to Sydney.

But her doubts wouldn't rest. The highway home took her past the turnoff to Stanwell Park and when she reached it, she decided to pop in on Lucy for a quick chat. 'It can't do any harm and it's not much out of my way,' she told herself.

As she entered the beach house, the shock of what she saw hit her with sickening force. Lucy was lying in the same jeans and white top on the couch where she had left her on Monday morning. Her wig was lopsided as though she had been tearing at it and the skin on her face was the colour of dirty linen.

Lucy contemplated Mary with an expression of ancient weariness.

'Lucy dear, what's happened?' Mary rushed over and wrapped her arms around the limp body. 'Did you have an argument with Jeff? A lovers' tiff or something?'

With an effort Lucy pushed Mary away to sneer 'He's fish food'. Then she fell back again, as lifeless as a rag doll.

The vacant look in Lucy's eyes frightened Mary. She was relieved when the phone rang, giving her an excuse to do something positive. The call was from an editor wanting to know why Lucy hadn't sent in her review from the play she went to two nights ago.

'Tell her I didn't go,' Lucy mumbled 'I'm sick.'

Confused and more than a little frightened Mary sat beside Lucy. What should she do? If only Mario were here. Even James would have the right answers. Then unexpectedly Lucy spoke, so softly that Mary had to lean over to hear.

'Please help me. I'm frightened.'

'Would you like to come back to my place?'

'Yes.' Lucy was submissive as Mary helped her to shower and pack a bag. She didn't speak as they drove to Sydney. At Mary's house she solemnly went upstairs to the bedroom where she usually slept, and Mary bought up tea and toast on a silver tray.

'I don't know where Sarah is but as soon as I see her arrive home, I'll call her in,' Mary said as she put a rug over Lucy's knees and watched her nibbling the toast.

'No!' Lucy howled, tossing about so violently Mary had to grab the tray before it fell to the floor.

'Okay, I won't. I won't. What about Grandpa Pedersen, would you like me to get him over?'

'No!' Lucy barked as she flung off the rug Mary had put over her knees, then, just as suddenly, she froze and sat still staring at the floor.

Mary was now utterly terrified. 'What about Dr Kilter? Do you want to speak to him?'

Lucy's body lost its tension. She dragged her eyes around to look at Mary as though seeing her for the first time.

'Yes, please. I'd like to speak to Dr Kilter.'

CHAPTER 54

When Mary rang Dr Kilter's office, she was told he had left his practice and had referred all his patients to Dr Singh.

'Oh dear. Lucy, my young friend, has been seeing Dr Kilter since she was in kids' hospital for burns years ago,' she told the doctor's secretary. 'She will be upset. She has a lot of faith in him, we all do. I don't think she knows this Dr Singh.'

But there was no other option, so Mary agreed to speak to Dr Singh. His soft deep voice on the other end of the phone helped settle her nerves as she explained the situation with Lucy.

'Mrs Clarke, I understand your concern. I'm busy right now, however as it's an emergency and you don't feel confident about bringing Lucy here, I could call into your place this evening. Would that suit you?'

When Mary led Dr Singh into the bedroom, Lucy was looking out the window. He quickly took in a tall slim woman wearing black and white check, straight-legged pants and a white cotton top with a raised collar and elbow-length sleeves. To cover her scars, he thought as she turned to face him. He looked into her brown eyes lined with dark lashes, seeing suspicion and fear.

'I know you are a long-term patient of Dr Kilter, but he has gone overseas. I have taken over his practice. Before we start, please let me assure you I've read your file very thoroughly and am well able to discuss anything you want to talk about.'

Lucy looked at the doctor's dark skin, sensual lips and his ill-fitting suit. Everything she saw was unfamiliar, but his resonant voice and the chocolate-brown eyes regarding her with sincerity triggered a memory of other brown eyes that had looked at her like that.

'Why don't we both sit down?' Dr Singh said as he moved to a chair beside the bed and indicated to Lucy that she sit on the bed.

Mary watched Lucy obey Dr Singh like a child. When they were both seated she left, closing the door quietly behind her.

Mary watched the wall clock as she sat reading her book, so she knew at least an hour had passed when she heard Dr Singh coming downstairs. She offered him a cup of tea which he accepted and sugared heavily.

'I would like to speak to her family at some time but for the moment she has put her complete confidence in you. She has asked me to not speak to anyone else and as she is of age that this is acceptable.'

'What's wrong with her?'

'She's no longer sure how life works or how safe she is. She feels intense fear and helplessness, a common consequence of the extreme trauma she has suffered. It would have helped if she'd had more counselling after her parents' death. I see from Dr Kilter's records that this happened rather erratically with visits being cancelled at short notice and medication not taken as prescribed. This is a shame, because she was still coming to terms with her own development. At the age she was when she suffered her burns, she should have been gradually separating from her family and making her own way in the wider social world. Her grief over her parents' death has added to her lingering traumatic reaction from the fire. It's possible she hasn't fully completed either process.'

'She moved to the south coast to get away from the city after her parents' accident,' Mary understood what he was saying.

'Yes, and although she says she likes living alone, I feel she may be in terror of actually being left alone. Several of her closest friends have left Sydney so she has become dependent, in fact I would say extremely dependent, on her twin sister Sarah. I need to speak more with Lucy to better understand of how this is affecting her.'

'Did she mention Jeff?'

'No. But she is terrified of seeing her twin sister again. She seems to think she has done something very bad and that Sarah will be angry with her. I need more time before I will understand the significance of this.'

Mary looked at Dr Singh, wondering if she should tell him what Lucy had said over the phone. 'Could she have done something very bad, even criminal, and not know it?'

'A traumatised person can do very intense things without any clear memory of such action or, alternatively, they can remember every detail but without emotion.'

'She has a lot of nightmares,' Mary said. 'One about a horribly diseased cat and another about falling into water. She says the water pours into her through every hole it can find.'

'It's too early to say what that means,' Dr Singh replied. 'It's not unusual for burns patients to dream about water. We think it could be a re-enactment of the fire in a disguised form with the water enveloping her and penetrating her in place of the flames.'

'Oh!' Mary gave a nervous titter of relief. Her mind had run riot after Lucy said Jeff was fish food. She'd imagined them arguing and Jeff storming off around the cliff and falling in or, even worse, Lucy pushing him, which would explain why she was so distressed. She decided she would visit Jeff the next day. Maybe he would be over the argument and agree to visit Lucy. As she planned what she would say to him, she turned to see Lucy coming down the stairs with her bag in her hand.

Dr Singh stood. 'I'm a visiting medical officer at the Rozelle psychiatric hospital in the next suburb. Lucy has agreed to become a voluntary patient. She will feel safe there and I will be able to give her the treatment she needs.'

Lucy moved sluggishly into Mary's embrace and whispered, 'I'm sorry.' Then she turned to follow Dr Singh out of the house.

CHAPTER 55

Mary drove to Wollongong the next day and climbed the stairs to level two, apartment four. She had just reached the landing when the door opened and a girl in her late teens walked out.

'Can I help?' she asked, seeing the confusion in this older woman standing on the landing.

'I'm not sure.' The last thing Mary had expected was to see an attractive girl coming out of Jeff's flat. 'I was looking for someone.'

The girl smiled brightly. 'I can probably help. I've been in this building about two years and know pretty much everyone.'

Embarrassed, Mary realised she didn't even know Jeff's surname or what he looked like. 'I'm um … looking for a boy from Perth called Jeff who a friend wants me to contact.'

'Oh Jeff?' The young girl beamed, pleased she could help. 'He's gone. This was his apartment and I've taken it over. A snake bit his mother about a month ago and she had an unexpected relapse. I think she died,' the girl hesitated. 'He just took off.'

'Was his mother a biologist working in Western Australia?' It was all Mary could remember from what Lucy had told her.

'Yes. He must have panicked because he cancelled his phone, stored his furniture and was gone.' The girl looked at Mary who looked as though she might faint. 'Would you like to come inside and sit down?'

'No, I'm all right,' Mary said, struggling to gather her thoughts. 'But would you mind terribly if I asked a personal question. I'm sorry but it would help my friend immensely.'

The girl nodded. She looked so friendly that Mary went on. 'Were you, I mean are you ... Jeff's girlfriend?'

The girl gave a short laugh of amusement. 'Oh no. I've been in a crowded apartment downstairs for over a year. When this one came vacant last week, the landlord gave it to me. Jeff has a girl up the coast somewhere. Doesn't say much about her but we all think he's pretty keen on her. If she's your friend then she's very lucky. He's a great guy.'

CHAPTER 56

Sarah had missed the lights at Victoria Road so arrived at the hospital a bit later than she had planned; however, she was now in the car park and looking for a free space. What did Singh really understand about Lucy, she thought sourly. Did he know she liked sports cars? Did he know she kept a clump of her cat's fur in a locket that she wore around her neck? Did he know she sucked her thumb in bed at night?

He had continually refused her permission to visit Lucy, but she was doing it now. Yes, her mission was about to be accomplished. Very soon Dr Singh wouldn't matter anymore.

But before getting out of the car she sat a moment and thought back to the only meeting she had ever had with Dr Singh. It was a few months after Lucy had gone into this hospital. He had been refusing to let her see Lucy, saying she needed time alone to come to terms with all that had happened. Sarah had accepted this for a while, but as the days became weeks, she finally insisted on a meeting with him. She had dressed with care – denim skirt short enough to show off her long tanned legs, and a cream silk top with a low scooping neckline. She had brushed her long blond hair so it would fall silkily over her shoulders and then tucked the sides back behind her ears. Her aim was to look fresh and trustworthy, but a perceptive observer would detect her sophistication and intelligence. She had determined that she would show that Indian psychiatrist she had every right to visit her twin.

Sarah was confident of her ability to manipulate people, but that meeting had not gone well. Dr Singh was taller than she had expected and not weedy as she had presumed him to be. In fact, he was handsome in a dark and disturbingly sexy way. He was also thoroughly professional and so in tune with himself and his capabilities that she had to change her tactics. Coming on heavy as the twin sister was not going to work. This man needed to be handled with diplomacy.

That meeting had taken place in his tidy office and although he was polite, and quite obviously enjoyed looking at her, he remained annoyingly unaffected by her attempts to win him over.

'It is important for Lucy to do things at her own speed,' he had said with a slow smile and neutral voice. 'It would be unwise to force her into situations in which she may feel uncomfortable.'

'I am hardly a situation,' she had retorted, as a warning that she would not be patronised. She allowed time for this to sink in then lowered her voice. 'Dr Singh I'm sure you see me as merely Lucy's sister, but it goes far deeper than that. We are twins and until she came in here we were never apart for long. As you will have discovered, she is plagued by fears and mysterious worries. I'm sure she has told you that I have always been at her side when she needed someone to support her. This was especially after our parents died. You could say I'm her muse, her nurse, her best friend, the person who held her when she was frightened in the night. But there are other things you will never know about us. Things we have experienced that she will never talk about, not even to you Dr Singh. This is why she needs me, and why I'm here to see her.'

'I understand you are very close. But maybe you do not realise that it has been her decision not to see you – not mine.'

Sarah had not expected this. It was all she could do to not show her surprise. She was trying to fathom how to respond when he continued talking, as though he had not just dropped such a bombshell.

'But don't let that worry you, Miss Borgetti. It is not unusual for people who have been traumatised to distance themselves from everyone and everything they know well. They are unable to cope with anything. They need to curl up for a while in a very safe place where they don't have to make any decisions or think about how to act. Reminders of the trauma can be overwhelming and Lucy needs time out from past memories and people.'

'But others have visited.' She regretted saying this as soon as it came out. It sounded weak.

'She asked to see those people and I permitted the visits because I felt her reasons for wanting them were correct.'

Sarah watched him closely, absorbing this new information. She was incensed because Mary had told her that she, Nonna and Damon had all visited. She recognised in Dr Singh strong moral boundaries that it would be unwise to cross. She might have to have him removed or arrange to have someone more malleable put in charge of Lucy.

'I know you are probably wondering if I have influenced Lucy's decision so let me assure you this is not so. No matter what has gone on between you, it is very clear to me that you have been at Lucy's side all her life. However, whether you have failed her in reality or in imagination, your presence in her life has been constant. She needs that constant in her life. She will want to see you again I can assure you of that and I will encourage it. What I can't tell you is when this will happen, nor how that meeting will go. That will be largely up to you.'

'What do you mean, up to me?'

'Lucy will be looking for something from you. She needs someone to hang her trust on. While she's in here she surrenders her trust to the nurses and to me. When she leaves, she will need to give that trust to someone outside this hospital.'

'Are you saying she doesn't trust me?'

'Let's just say she is unsure about what she feels.'

'What has she told you?' Sarah could see he knew more than he was admitting, but she held her anger in check, keeping up eye contact and letting her shoulders relax as she took a breath to speak again. But he beat her to it.

'As a fellow professional, you know I cannot divulge what my patient has told me. You must understand that everything I do is for the benefit of my patient, your sister. She's here of her own free will. I advise her, but she is free to make her own decisions. However, I must warn you that any more shocks could slow her recovery.'

Sarah felt the air between them prickle. He did not trust her, and she realised with some irony that he knew she knew this.

She appreciated that he would maintain this cordial doctor-relative relationship indefinitely so there was nothing more she could gain by staying here. She gave him her most charming smile and leaned over the desk to shake his hand. 'Thank you for your time Dr Singh. I appreciate your honesty and look forward to seeing Lucy soon.'

As Sarah pulled out of the car park, she saw his silhouette at the window and with disdain drove the Mercedes sedately along the crunchy driveway.

'Be warned, Dr Singh. I will be back and next time I will take Lucy home with me.'

Now she was here to fulfil that pledge!

After that meeting, she had taken a short posting to Auckland in New Zealand reasoning that it was only a three-hour flight away should she need to get home if Lucy asked for her. But Lucy didn't. It was only after Sarah returned to Sydney that she put this new plan into action.

This plan involved an oath they had made as children. When they were about five, Lucy had started to speak in a strange language, a jumble of meaningless words that surprisingly Sarah understood. It had confused and irritated their parents who were told it was called cryptophasia and was quite common with twins, even fraternal twins. The stage passed but, later, when Lucy was going through an emotional time at school, they had initiated a written code. In high drama from a movie they had seen, they cut their thumbs with a sharp knife and pressed them together, letting their blood mingle as they swore allegiance to the secret code FWTW *From Womb to Worms – born together, live together, leave together.*

For Sarah the code was inconsequential. For Lucy it was her bond, her promise, a code that would bind her loyalty for the rest of her life.

Knowing this, Sarah had written the note Lucy now had in her hospital room and on the outside of the envelope she had printed in thick black ink FWTW.

Sarah knew Lucy well enough to know she would feel honour-bound to open the envelope and respond to her call for help.

LUCY

I recognise the car immediately. Sarah has the hood down, so her lemon top and golden ponytail blend elegantly against the pale leather upholstery. Even from this distance I can see her red fingernails, evenly spaced like drops of blood along the top of her head as she smooths down her hair. It's not too late. Dr Singh says I am not ready to meet her. That I need more time. That I am not yet able to control my emotional need for her. I know he is in his study watching her arrive, that he would be more than pleased to stop this meeting.

I can buzz and tell him to meet her in reception to say I've changed my mind.

But a hot wave of love flows from me as I watch her steer the car around the car park. Even from this distance I long to hold her in my arms and giggle as we used to. I can't see her green eyes behind the sunglasses but I know how they will be serious as she contemplates which space to take. I watch the tanned hands that have held me when I've been down, bathed me when I've been careless, and fed me when I've been too sick to feed myself.

A shiver runs through me and I hug my arms. Maybe I should have asked Mary to be here. Dr Singh had suggested it, but I wanted to do this on my own. Now it's happening, I am not so sure. Even before she is out of her car, I feel Sarah's will enter the room and I sit down to steady my shaking.

I drag myself into the bathroom to check lipstick, hair, clothes. Dr Singh has emphasised that I must talk to him after I know Sarah's "secret". He is very worried about this "secret" and has warned me against making any decisions without speaking to him first.

She will be entering the hospital. Asking directions. I sit again. Rise. Pace the room. Look out the window. My stomach flutters and I think I might be sick. I hear George telling me that good shooting is all about controlling the mind. I force a smile and tell myself I am happy to be seeing her again. She's my twin who in a moment I will hold in my arms.

My bottom lip starts to quiver. I stop pacing and put Damon's shell to my ear.

Then there's a short sharp knock and the door opens.

CHAPTER 57

Sarah quickly took in the room – simple furniture, window overlooking the grounds, a door to the bathroom, Lucy standing with Damon's seashell against her ear. She watched the shock leap into Lucy's eyes with quiet satisfaction. She closed the door slowly, deliberately, and lifted her sunglasses to let Lucy see the malevolence in her eyes.

Lucy froze and the colour drained from her face.

'No!' The word burst out as if she'd been punched in the lungs. 'Please God, don't let it be you.' The shell crashed to the floor and bounced several times as her hands clutched at her face. 'Why?'

'Because I wanted to hurt you.' The words came out slowly as Sarah savoured her triumph. Lucy's reaction justified her artfully prepared performance.

Lucy couldn't take her eyes off the tracksuit Sarah had put on over her clothes just before she entered the room. Comprehension stopped her breathing. She stared in disbelief as the memories flooded back ... *I am eleven. We have just arrived home from skiing at Thredbo and eaten dinner in front of the fire. Daddy is asleep under the paper. Mummy has fallen asleep reading her book. Yama is curled in front of the fire with her ... and Sarah ... Sarah is leaning over the fireplace wearing – a blue tracksuit.*

'You're the blue presence I saw in the room. It was you! The fire. The logs. You pushed the logs onto me.'

Each sentence came out with the force of separate gunshots – bang, bang, bang. 'But why?'

'Because. You – Are – Not – My – Real – Sister.' Sarah left ominous gaps between each word.

'But we're twins. Born the same day, from the same mother and same father. It's on our birth certificates.'

'Same mother, yes.' Sarah replied as she walked across the room and stood gazing out the window. 'Pretty garden.' Her voice was steady, but her mind was aflame with a hatred that had been fermenting for years. It was here at last, her day of revenge.

She turned back from the window to stare at Lucy. 'But not the same father.'

'My secret LL, my secret that you and that puffed-up Indian doctor have been panting to hear about, was revealed on a freezing Saturday night at Thredbo. You remember we skied all day with Liam, then we met in the hotel dining room for dinner. What you won't remember is that between main course and dessert, I went to the toilet. That is when I learned what an imposter our mother was.

'When I was walking back through the lounge, I saw Dwight talking to Jill and he looked furious, so I ducked down behind the drapes to listen.' Sarah leaned forward and looked at Lucy with such venom that Lucy felt the hairs rise on her arms. 'Every word was imprinted on my brain forever. And now, dear stepsister, I will repeat it for you.'

Sarah started with Dwight, imitating his deep voice:

'So, this is why you wanted to speak to me privately. To tell me this rubbish.'

Jill replied in that cold voice she used with us when we were little and wanted no argument. 'I had my suspicions medically confirmed. Remember eleven years ago at the company conference in Hawaii when we slept together.'

'How could I forget! We got so carried away we fell off the bed.'

'This is not a joke. Shortly after I got home I realised I was pregnant. I became worried about who the father was. So, I had a DNA test.'

'And it says I'm the father of your twins!'

'I could hear the dirty smirk in Dwight's voice when he said this, LL. But Jill had done her homework.'

'No,' she said. 'You both are.'

'So you and I conceived one ... and you and Mario the other?'

'Quite so my dear Dwight – Lucy and Sarah are superfecundation twins.'

As she repeated this conversation, which was imprinted on her mind forever, Sarah's mind strayed back to that evening. It still made her angry, but she quickly regained control. With cold intent she watched Lucy struggle to understand the implications of what she had just heard, knowing that somehow her world was about to fall to pieces.

'Do you know what superfecundation means?' Sarah asked. 'Of course, you don't. Jill explained it to Dwight that night, but I looked it up to be sure. It's when a woman conceives twice in the same menstrual cycle. It can be with different men. It's rare but it happens and is usually only discovered when there is a paternity investigation.

'Our mother, the talented Jill Borgetti, HAD Dwight in Hawaii.' Sarah lifted her eyes to the ceiling and let them roam around the room before returning to look hard at Lucy. 'I refuse to say they "made love" because that's too pure for what they did. She fucked Dwight – my father ... then flew home and fucked Mario – your father.

'Shortly after all this fun and fucking she discovered she was pregnant. Then, after we were born, she began to worry about who our biological father was, so she took a strand of Mario's hair with the root attached and, at the next company, meeting she nicked Dwight's toothbrush from the bathroom. The DNA test showed we were twins – but with different fathers.'

'Lies!' Lucy screamed, even as an inner voice warned her to be careful. She knew Sarah could lie without batting an eye, but deep in her being she knew Sarah was telling the truth.

'Dwight was shit scared,' Sarah continued. 'He knew Jill too well to think she was making up a story. He grovelled, he begged and ended up pleading with her. He said she mustn't tell anyone because he was going out with a rich man's daughter and the family was very religious, and he was about to ask her to marry him. If she found out he had an illegitimate child in Australia she might not agree. He offered to pay for my upkeep, schooling, anything. Jill just had to name it, so long as she promised to keep his paternity quiet.

'Did my being his daughter awaken any feelings of paternal love in him? No.

'Did she plead my case? No.

'Did she ask that he acknowledge me as his daughter suggesting they would keep it quiet within the family? No.' Sarah watched Lucy closely. 'What she did do was to use me as a pawn. She simply said that as long as he stayed out of the Asia/Pacific region, their secret – my secret – would stay hidden forever.'

Sarah's eyes were empty. She didn't care about Jill who was dead. Dwight's time would come one day. For now, she was just enjoying her power over Lucy as she watched her struggling to come to terms with what she had just heard. Silence hung in the air for a long time before Lucy spoke.

'But why hurt me? I wasn't to blame.'

'You, fucking miss perfect, were conceived in love and wedlock. I'm the bastard. The convenient bargaining tool.'

'But it should have been Mummy you wanted to hurt.'

Sarah laughed. Even at eleven she had been too smart for that. As she crouched behind the drapes that night listening to Jill play her cards, Sarah instinctively knew she would never have a better teacher than her mother. By watching Jill, Sarah would learn how to play the game, how to win at any cost, how to deal the aces.

By rejecting his parenthood, Dwight showed her that a winner never lets sentiment get in the way of a potential rich and powerful marriage. Sarah knew then that she would watch and learn from these two and one day she would show Dwight he had made a critical mistake in rejecting her.

'People like you and Mario are putty to be moulded to the needs of people like us. I am the product of champions. You two are lumps of bakers' dough.'

Lucy looked away from Sarah and drew in a long, slow breath. 'Did you mean to kill me when you pushed the logs from the fire?'

'Probably not but I did want to make you less perfect. It was interesting the way those logs kept rolling onto you, then the fire took over and everything went out of control. You looked like a firecracker running across the room. It was spectacular to watch. And you can't complain. Look at all the sympathy and the attention you got from then on. You should thank me. Because of the fire you took up shooting and became famous, among shooters that is,' she added to belittle the praise she had just given. 'And Mario loved you more than ever with your sad-sack face and the wrinkled patch where your tit should be.'

Lucy dropped onto the bed and held her head in her hands as she thought back to the agony of the flames, the hospital baths, the painful exercises and her longing to be normal. Surely Sarah didn't mean what she had just said. Sarah who had everything – beauty, intelligence and success in everything she took on. It didn't make sense, but as she sat there Lucy began to see it from Sarah's perspective. She lived in the family home knowing Mario was not her father, that her real father would not acknowledge her as his daughter. She lived with a lying mother who was prepared to let her daughter live that lie too.

Lucy finally said very quietly: 'But we're still twins, aren't we?'

'Of course, we are, that's why I'm here today. You're my very own very precious twin and I want you to come home with me, so you and I can live together. We'll be a family again.' Sarah moved across to sit beside Lucy in no doubt now she would be taking her home. 'And guess what? I've bought you a pretty little kitten. She's waiting at home for you right now.'

Sarah's words floated over Lucy with the warmth of a soft blanket. Home, kitten, family. They made Lucy's throat tighten and her eyes sting. More than anything in this world, she longed to know the comfort of family again, to be with people she'd known all her life, people who knew everything about her and still loved her.

Sarah was promising that this would happen. Even though she was shocked by what Sarah had revealed about the fire, she desperately wanted what Sarah promised. Lucy stood up and packed her bag.

Sarah didn't want to stop at Dr Singh's office, but Lucy felt guilty and went in while Sarah stood resolutely outside. Dr Singh rose from behind his tidy desk and came around. 'So, you're going,' he said looking at the bag in her hand.

Fighting off feelings of guilt Lucy nodded. 'I appreciate everything you've done for me, Dr Singh. I don't want you to think I'm ungrateful but I'm stronger now and Sarah needs me. I'm going back to Birchgrove to be a proper sister. I owe it to her for all she's been through.'

He heard the unspoken doubts. He could not stop her going, but he could not let her go without trying to convince her to stay.

'We had an agreement that you would not make a rash decision, that we would talk about what you should do after you learned Sarah's secret. We agreed that once we both knew the secret; we would be in a better position to discuss what was best for you.'

'I know, but it wasn't what I'd expected.' Lucy hesitated, wanting to tell him, to hear his wise counsel, but Sarah would regard this as disloyalty. 'It's more personal,' she said as she looked nervously towards the door beyond which Sarah stood. 'I understand why Sarah has acted the way she has and why she's so complex. When we were very young, before the fire, I was the strong one who looked after her. I must be that person again. I'm all she has, you know. Through all of my problems she never once left me.'

'Protective or possessive? Lucy, we have discussed this many times and agreed you are strong enough now and you don't need her to watch over you. We agreed you can look after yourself. I cannot stop you going, but if you must go, I would recommend you stay with Mary for a while, or Damon. Sarah could visit you.'

'Damon would never allow Sarah in his house,' Lucy replied looking nervously towards the door. 'Anyway, it's too late. I've promised I'll go home with her.'

At that moment the door swung open and Sarah looked directly at Dr Singh, savouring his anger. 'I want to be in time for you to give Nefertiti her dinner and for us to sit on the veranda before it gets too cold and dark.' She had removed the blue tracksuit and looked fresh and athletic in her short denim skirt.

Dr Singh accepted that Sarah had finally got what she wanted, but he couldn't help but worry about Lucy's future, possibly even her life.

'I professionally advise against this move, Lucy, but I realise you have made up your mind, so I wish you all the best. I will be here expecting you for our Wednesday morning meetings. And feel free to call me at any time of the day or night if you need to talk.'

He nodded to Sarah as they left the room. As soon as the door closed, he hurried back to his desk where Lucy's file lay. Starting at the beginning he meticulously worked his way through every page of his and Dr Kilter's notes.

He tracked Sarah's life through Lucy's retelling of the fire, school, skiing in Aspen, the rifle club, university, Bisley, the loss of their parents, buying Stanwell Park, family and boyfriends. Every time Lucy experienced misfortune or an unhappy period in her life, Sarah had been there. He noted how Sarah manipulated the people or the event in such a subtle way it was easy to overlook her direct or indirect involvement.

He didn't believe Lucy had shot Pete or Jeff, but they

hadn't contacted her since she had been at Rozelle Hospital and that concerned him. Someone would have told them she was here; it seems out of character that they hadn't visited or even tried to contact her. From what he had been told, neither were the sort to just go disappear, especially Jeff who so often said he loved her.

Was it possible they were dead?

Dr Singh read his notes again, looking for clues. Was it possible Sarah had shot them and convinced Lucy she had done it? He wished he knew more about Sarah. From what Lucy has told him, she was highly intelligent but possibly mentally barren. She knew what she wanted and demanded satisfaction.

Such a person could easily manipulate an insecure person like Lucy. Lucy had told him Sarah always brought alcohol to the beach house, even though she didn't drink much herself. And it was Sarah who made Lucy stop taking the drugs Dr Kilter prescribed. Then she gave her other drugs to overcome sleepless nights.

Dr Singh concluded that Lucy's memories of her time at Stanwell Park were unreliable. He clicked his pen on the desk as he made a note in the file.

But, he pondered, why would Sarah shoot Pete and Jeff? There is no obvious reason. She might have resented how much Lucy and Jeff loved each other and wanted him out of the way, but that was not enough reason to shoot him. Sarah could easily have found another way to get him off the scene. And Pete? He and Lucy were never anything more than good friends and Kylie was overseas. If Dr Singh had known Pete had confided to Sarah that he was going to Budapest to ask Kylie to marry him, he might have thought very differently.

Dr Singh put his head in his hands. What was he missing? With a sigh he picked up a pen and neatly added Lucy's departure to his notes. He looked at what he had written then added: *If Lucy remains pliable to Sarah's needs it may work out. However, if she rebels and tries to assert her independence, Sarah may do her harm.*

Below this, he wrote *Is Sarah a psychopath?* and purposefully placed a dot under the question mark.

Several weeks later when Mary phoned, Dr Singh knew Lucy was in serious trouble.

CHAPTER 58

'I don't want to bother you unnecessarily,' Mary said in her soft Irish lilt, 'but I haven't seen Lucy for about three weeks. She usually pops over for a coffee or I see her pottering outside ... could be away of course. I was just wondering if you're still seeing her.'

'We had made a regular Wednesday appointment, but she only came twice. You realise, of course, that it is her choice to come or not. I have no jurisdiction over her.' Dr Singh twiddled his pen thinking. 'Have you spoken to Damon?'

'He hasn't seen her for a while either and he's a bit surprised because they'd been seeing quite a lot of each other. He said she was a bit strange on the phone last time he spoke to her.'

'Strange? In what way?'

'Vague. Evasive. We discussed it and thought maybe you'd changed her medication, which is sort of why I'm ringing. Sorry to bother you but she didn't seem happy, not taking care of herself. Sloppy clothes, no make-up, you know the sort of thing. Like she's reverted to how she was at the beach house before she went with you to the hospital.'

'Have you asked her how she feels?'

'She's evasive ... mumbled a lot.'

Dr Singh thought about his file. 'Have you spoken to Sarah lately?'

'I see her go to work every day. Please doctor, I don't want you to think I'm prying but Kylie called me from Budapest and said she's worried about Lucy being in the house alone with Sarah. She asked me to keep an eye out over the fence, sort of thing. I know she doesn't like Sarah, but some strange things have happened, haven't they? There was

Lucy's breakdown and the way Jeff just dumped her overnight. It doesn't make sense, does it?'

'Kylie thinks Sarah had something to do with Jeff leaving Lucy. Also, she hasn't heard again from Pete since he arrived in London and that worries her.'

'Have you gone over to talk to Lucy while Sarah's at work?'

'A couple of times. I knocked quite loudly but no one answered. Everything looked normal, although I couldn't see upstairs. If Lucy's home with the kitten, they're very quiet. I only saw it outside once. Haven't seen it again.'

Dr Singh sensed Mary was bordering on panic. Lucy's case had been a disturbing case for him, and interesting. He knew Lucy had left the hospital before she was emotionally strong enough to cope with someone as manipulative as Sarah. Although it was not his usual practice to visit clients at home, this was an uncommon case and there was the possibility of murder, remote maybe, but not impossible. He checked his diary. 'I have appointments all day but could call in this evening if you like?'

Mary felt weak with relief. She and Damon were sure something was terribly wrong and with Lucy's grandparents overseas, they didn't know who else to turn to.

Dr Singh arrived just before Sarah was due home from work, so Mary took him into a side room that overlooked the Borgetti's house. They watched Sarah open the garage doors automatically from inside her car, drive in then close them behind her. Despite being dusk there were no lights on in the house to indicate Lucy was there.

'The drapes along this side of the house have been closed lately,' Mary whispered, 'and they're so thick I can't see how many people are moving about inside.'

Mary outlined what she and Damon had observed of Lucy's actions since she had come home and the pattern disturbed Dr Singh. The downstairs lights went on as Sarah moved through the house.

'What's that room,' he asked as an upstairs light went on.

'It's a spare bedroom. When they were little, the girls used it as a playroom. It's got floor-to-ceiling glass doors that open onto a small balcony. Mario installed security bars around the balcony because he was worried they might go onto it and fall off.'

As he concentrated on the house, Dr Singh's instincts told him something was wrong. On the two Wednesday meetings Lucy had attended after leaving the hospital she had been calm and looking good. She had settled back into the family home without any difficulties and was captivated by the kitten Sarah gave her. Sarah had chosen a grey tabby kitten, so Lucy would not be reminded of her Burmese cats, Yama and Yami. Lucy said Nefertiti was gorgeous and suited her name perfectly. She had chatted freely. 'I've caught up with Damon who is living in Sydney with his boyfriend, Bobby. They've bought a little terrace house in Newtown which they've decorated together. It's just divine. He's getting a few commissions for sculptures, a good one from a big mining company, and teaching some nights. Oh, and I have my old job back writing theatre reviews.'

Then, without explanation, she stopped coming. He had phoned her a few times but put the phone down when the answer machine cut in.

Dr Singh walked out onto the veranda. The silence next door was sinister. Two young women in a house together should be playing music, watching television or sitting out on the veranda. 'Do they ever have friends over?'

'Not that I've noticed.'

'There isn't anything I can legally do,' he said quietly, 'but maybe together we can keep an eye on Lucy. Would you mind making a few phone calls to Dot and the editor she's been working for? Keep it casual. Ask if they've seen her or know where she is and jot down what they say. There may be a clue there. I'd be interested to hear what they have to say. Also keep an eye out for the kitten. It should be running about outside so listen for Lucy calling it in for meals.'

Mary heard the concern in Dr Singh's voice and struggled to stop her bottom lip from quivering. 'You think she's having another breakdown, don't you?'

'Possibly.' He didn't want to say more and frighten Mary.

CHAPTER 59

Nefertiti clawed at the carpet under the door until a few tufts came loose. Then she tore at them with her teeth until they came away and angrily flicked them over her head. The pile behind her grew steadily as the bare patch alongside the door spread. When she became bored with her futile attempts to escape the room she stalked around, brushing against everything that was by now so familiar: the solid wooden legs of the bed; the padded armchair where she sharpened her claws and left long threads hanging like ringlets; the wheels of the trolley that held a small television set; the tray of kitty litter; and, most interesting of all, the ceramic potty under the bed with its variety of pungent smells.

Nefertiti pushed her head under the drapes to look out at the trees. Her bright young eyes followed a flitting bird. When the sun was out she basked in its rays but on a dull day like today she preferred the bed so she turned and walked across the room to leap lightly onto it. With delicate steps she moved along the tumble of sheets and blankets until she found a hand, limp and still. She pushed her nose into it, sometimes it would scratch her under the chin. Not today.

With a soft purr, she stepped over the hand and up to the face of her only companion. She sniffed around the loose mouth, twitching away each time a soft breath from the nostrils puffed into her face. The lips didn't whisper her name, so she settled under the smooth chin and purring quietly, went to sleep.

On arriving home from work Sarah changed out of her work clothes into loose pants and a soft V-necked black velvet top, laid out the food for dinner and poured two vodkas, one stronger than the other. She entered the dark room at eight o'clock.

'Wake up,' she said as she lifted Lucy's limp body into a sitting position to lean it against the pillows she had piled up against the bedhead.

'What's the time?' Lucy slurred as she looked over at the small alarm clock on the bedside table. 'Oh no! I've slept all day again. Why am I doing this?'

She struggled up and took the vodka with a weak smile. 'Have you been at work?'

'Yes, and I've two trout downstairs ready to cook. Why don't you have a shower and come down as soon as you're ready. I've put clean jeans and a jumper for you over the chair.'

'Come down?' Lucy mumbled. 'What? Downstairs?'

'Of course.'

Warily Lucy watched Sarah slip her hands under the blankets to unlock the chain that bound her ankle to the bed. Lucy wondered if she had the energy to make it down the stairs. She had been chained to the bed for days and her legs felt a bit wobbly but the thought of leaving the room filled her with pleasure.

'Am I better?'

'Not yet. I'm still worried you might try to harm yourself but it's time for a change.'

'He's downstairs, isn't he?' Lucy's eyes filled with hope then went dull again when Sarah shook her head. 'Tell me. Please, tell me he's phoned.'

As Lucy spoke, Sarah dropped into the armchair, put her head into her hands and cried. 'You only ever think of Jeff. You don't love me. No one does,' she sobbed.

Panicked by her twin's tears, Lucy scrambled unsteadily from the bed and stumbled over to kneel on the carpet at Sarah's feet. 'Please don't cry. I love you very much, I truly do.'

Sarah's hands were wet with her tears as she patted Lucy's cheeks and looked deep into her eyes. 'Say it again. I need to hear you say it,' she sniffled, gulping for air.

'I love you more than Damon, more than Mary, more than Kylie, more than Dr Singh.'

'Again, so I can believe what you say.'

Lucy chanted the words Sarah had taught her to say until she too was crying. But Lucy's tears were real. The fear she felt was real. There were many things she didn't understand, but the fear she felt when Sarah cried was very real. Even as a little girl Sarah had seldom cried, so to see her crying now filled Lucy with dread. Sarah never lost control. Only Lucy did. That was why Sarah had chained her to the bed, so she wouldn't harm herself or Nefertiti when she was in one of her black moods.

'Remember what you did to Yami,' Sarah had said the first time she put on the chain. 'You stuck a kitchen knife into her neck and killed her.'

Lucy wasn't sure she remembered doing that but lately she had been so tired she wasn't sure about anything. 'I'll shower then come straight down.' She patted Sarah's hand and brightened her voice to please her sister. 'We can have dinner together; it will be like old times.'

Lucy was finding she couldn't cope with the tension that had built between them since she'd come home. She sighed with relief when Sarah wiped her tears and gave her hand a gentle squeeze.

'Thank you.' Sarah sat quietly, her eyes downcast so Lucy couldn't see the gloat of conquest in them. She had expected Lucy to be more pliant after she came home from the hospital, but Dr Singh had done his job well. He had instilled a confidence in her own thoughts and judgements. This had been helped by her close friendship with Damon and his lover, and Mary with her coffee and chats. Also, Lucy had less need of Sarah now she had her job back and was re-establishing herself with the theatre crowd. Most of this Sarah could accept, but it all soured the night Lucy suggested that she – Sarah – should make an appointment to see Dr Singh.

'You only have to talk to him,' Lucy had said earnestly. 'I can see you're still angry with Dwight and Mummy and talking about it will help you, it really will. Dr Singh won't pressure you and he won't make you take drugs if you don't want to. He just listens. I know he'd like to talk to you.'

'I'm sure he would,' Sarah had sneered, her body flaring hot with fury.

That had been the turning point. Lucy's innocent suggestion that she, Sarah, go to see Dr Singh was the end of their sisterhood. There was a flaw in Sarah's personality that meant she could only love if she could possess and control. If she couldn't possess and control, she would have to destroy.

Sarah had anticipated it might come to this and made her preparations. She had visited her doctor and complained of insomnia, caused by the stress of her twin's illness. The unsuspecting doctor had been prescribing a strong sleeping pill for nearly two years and Sarah had been storing them away. Then two weeks after Lucy came home from hospital Sarah convinced her to stop going to the Wednesday meetings with Dr Singh. To further strengthen her control over Lucy, she had taken over the administration of her prescription drugs 'So you don't get muddled and take the wrong ones,' she had said. And because she wanted to please, Lucy had acquiesced.

The day Lucy suggested Sarah see Dr Singh was the day Sarah stopped the prescription drugs. Without her medication and on a menu of sleeping pills and vodka, Lucy slipped into a state of confusion and indecision. She would watch the phone ringing, unable to make the decision to reach out and pick it up.

The caller would hear the answer phone cut in and end the call.

Sarah steadily increased her control. 'You've been doing too much since you came out of hospital and it's making you tired,' she said one day. 'I want you to stay home to be quiet with Nefertiti and me for a while.' She handed Lucy the phone and said gently, 'Give your editor, Damon and the others a call and tell them you're very tired and need a little time on your own to chill out.'

She then convinced Lucy that she might harm herself or Nefertiti if she got into one of her black moods and got her to accept 'A little chain connecting your ankle to the bed, as they do in some hospitals.'

Eight weeks after Lucy came home from hospital, Sarah saw Dr Singh's car outside Mary's house. It was impossible to miss the name of the hospital printed in small neat letters on the door.

'Devious bitch,' she had muttered and put her plan into fast forward.

CHAPTER 60

As Dr Singh had suggested, Mary phoned Lucy's friends, keeping it light and chatty. One by one they said they had received a call from Lucy saying she was terribly tired and felt she had been doing too much since she came out of hospital. She asked each of them to leave her alone so she could chill out for a while, and to understand if she didn't ring or answer the phone.

Dot told Mary she had called in one Saturday after the market and Sarah had said Lucy was asleep upstairs and she felt it best not to disturb her.

'I'm never sure of Sarah,' Dot had said. 'But she was pleasant and concerned. She said Lucy was having difficulty adjusting. She thought it might be a touch of agoraphobia and that Lucy needed some quiet time in the security of her old home. I was impressed by her concern,' Dot had said. 'Sarah assured me she would get Lucy to call me as soon as she felt better.'

After speaking to everyone, Mary decided she would let herself into the house while Sarah was at work. Mario had given her a key all those years ago, 'In case of another emergency' he had said. She found the key tucked away in a box of odds and ends and was wiping the dust off it when the phone rang.

'Would you like to come over and join us on the veranda? It's a perfect evening for a drink and I'm about to pop a bottle of Moët to celebrate Lucy's big win.' Sarah's voice was bright and inviting.

Mary could only stammer a startled thank you.

It was, as Sarah had said, a very pleasant late winter evening. A glowing outdoor heater beside the table took the chill out of the air and Lucy was casually dressed in jeans and a jumper. She was pale, but her greeting was enthusiastic.

'Oh Mary, thank you for coming over,' she said leaping up to give Mary a big hug. 'You look wonderful. Sorry I haven't been over more, but I've been so tired. You wouldn't believe how much I've been sleeping.'

'I was getting a bit worried,' Mary said, feeling Lucy's frail body under the loose jumper.

'I've been up and about but not going out.'

Mary tried to absorb as much as she could to tell Dr Singh. After the initial hugs and greetings Lucy had sat down heavily. There was no sparkle in her eyes.

'She needed her own space for a while,' Sarah said, smiling as she handed over a flute of champagne with tiny beads rising in a steady stream to the surface. 'I've been encouraging her to rest. She was too full-on after she came out of hospital and her body had started to shut down.'

Mary looked at Lucy who was looking into her wine as though undecided whether to drink it or put it down. 'Are you sure you're all right?'

'She gets overtired,' Sarah said, realising too late that she should have cut down on the sleeping pills before inviting Mary over. She had not given her any today, but yesterday's dose was still in her system. Realising it would be better if she did most of the talking, she indicated for Mary to sit beside her. 'Lucy's got some exciting news to tell you but I'm going to break it … do you mind, Lucy?'

Mary watched Sarah look at Lucy and Lucy nod distractedly then her head dropped as though she had fallen asleep. It might be exciting to Sarah, but Lucy couldn't care less Mary thought.

'She's got a commission to write a book on a tribe of Aboriginal peoples living in East Kimberley at the top of Western Australia,' Sarah said with hushed enthusiasm. 'A geologist working up there discovered this tribe that has had very little contact with white Australians, so its customs and lifestyle are virtually intact. Coincidentally his brother publishes beautifully presented coffee-table books called *Our Unknown World*, so they approached the tribe and the elders agreed so have a writer live with them to write their story. The books are about remote areas and indigenous peoples around the world. The publisher knew Mario and reads Lucy's reviews so believes she has the empathy to write an honest and compelling story.'

'Where?' Mary tried to mask her surprise and disbelief.

'In the northernmost tip of the Kimberley just above Wyndham, which has a good airport. It's about as remote as you can get. Crocodiles and the largest known population of the rare Gouldian finch in Australia.' Sarah turned with a big smile to Lucy who was resting her chin unsteadily on her hand.

'It's the opportunity of a lifetime.' Sarah added quickly.

'But are you strong enough for all that heat and rough living?' Mary directed her question at Lucy. She wanted to hear Lucy say something.

'Sarah will come for the first week and it's June so the coolest month of the year,' Lucy said, lifting her head from her hand with an ineffective show of enthusiasm. 'She'll help me settle in. Being out there with nature will be good for me. Maybe the Aboriginal peoples will understand my malaise, might even be able to help me overcome it.'

Mary felt uncomfortably sure Lucy's words were rehearsed.

'I'll show you the letter,' Sarah said over her shoulder as she hurried into the lounge. Returning, she unfolded a two-page letter on company letterhead which she had bribed a friend in the publisher's office to provide. Triumphantly she smoothed it out in front of Mary, then refilled their glasses. 'It explains everything.'

The letter, addressed to Lucy, was signed by a woman with the title of Editor, Non-Fiction. Mary's eyes raced down the pages.

'The idea of the book was received favourably at our meeting on Monday,' it said. 'The consensus is that we will cover your travel and living costs for as long as you feel necessary, but no longer than six months. You will take photographs and provide these for the exclusive use of the publisher. Your contract is attached, please sign and return to this office.' The final sentence read: 'I am excited by this project and look forward to working with you.'

It was such an unexpected turn of events that Mary couldn't think what to say. She couldn't remember Lucy ever showing interest in writing a coffee-table book and the only Aboriginal peoples she was aware Lucy had met were singers and dancers in the shows she reviewed. She knew the family had never roughed it in the wilderness, and looking at Lucy now Mary doubted she was well enough to cope with the heat or be so far from friends and medical help.

Mary wished she had more time to think but she could feel Sarah watching her, so she gathered her thoughts and said, 'This all sounds wonderful, but would this sort of book sell very well?'

'There's a growing interest in aboriginal cultures worldwide, so much so that two years from now is The Year of Indigenous Cultures,' Sarah replied, the lie popping into her head easily. 'The publisher plans to release it in time for that. The countryside in the Kimberley is stunning, so the book will have dramatic photos as well as an astonishing story of how the tribe has survived there for thousands of years.'

After Mary left, Sarah carried the glasses inside and ordered Lucy upstairs to her room. She waited until Mary's lights went off before she went upstairs. Lucy had fallen across the bed but sat up groggily when she felt her wig being pulled off.

'Get up,' Sarah said. 'What do you mean falling asleep at the table?' She leaned close to Lucy, holding a burning candle in front of her face. 'Look at this. Flames. Red, orange, hot burning flames. I've done it before and I'll do it again. Do you understand?'

'Yes,' Lucy whispered, recoiling.

'Yes, what?'

'Yes, Sarah dear. I'm so sorry. I promise I won't fall asleep again.'

'You certainly won't. I give you safety, a nice bed, a loving kitten, good food. I let you live here because I'm a good person. If you hadn't been born, I could have grown up in New York instead of this shithole of a city.'

With her confidence a little bolstered by seeing Mary, and with a remnant of the strength Dr Singh had instilled in her, Lucy gave a tentative smile and suggested, 'We could sell up. Get a nice apartment together in New York.'

'And what? Walk into Dwight's office and say "Hello Daddy".'

'Not quite like that. But you could tell him you know he's your biological father and that you would like to have some time together. He will love you. I know he will because you're so beautiful. Once he sees you again, he'll want you to be his daughter.' Lucy didn't see the shoe coming until it smashed into her cheek. She felt a blinding pain before she lost consciousness.

Sarah never stayed angry for long. She was humming by the time she closed Lucy's bedroom door. What a great idea the publisher's letter had been. Mary had swallowed it hook, line and sinker. What a pathetic soul she was; she would be on the phone to Dr Singh first thing tomorrow. For a fleeting moment Sarah was sorry she couldn't be there to hear their conversation. He would be cautious because he was not absolutely sure what he was up against, but he wouldn't risk his career by acting too hastily. That would give her the time she needed to do what she now knew had to be done.

It was time to move on, alone.

CHAPTER 61

I should have shot you too, Sarah decided as she straightened Lucy on the bed and clipped the chain around her ankle. How easy getting rid of the others had been. The Sunday morning after Pete's farewell party she had put four sleeping pills into each of the green hangover drinks she handed out to everyone except Pete and herself. After eating the big brunch she had cooked she and the skiers set off to drive to the Thredbo ski fields. It wasn't long before the sleeping pills took effect and they were all too tired to keep driving. Sarah had not taken any pills, but she feigned tiredness and suggested they stop at the first motel they came to, so they could sleep off their hangovers and be fresh and ready for an early start the next morning. They all willingly agreed.

Once they were asleep, she had driven back to the motel at Stanwell Park that she had booked the week before. She stayed hidden there until it was time to creep into the house on Monday morning before Pete and Lucy's alarms went off. She quietly turned off Lucy's two alarms and shot Pete as he walked around the cliff path to Coalcliff, checked to make sure he fell all the way to the sea, then disguised her voice over the phone to tell Bob she was an old friend who had turned up to take Pete to the airport.

Immediately after the call to Bob, Sarah had driven back to the motel where the skiers were still asleep. On the way she made a quick stop to buy freshly baked croissants, which gave her an excuse for being out in the car if anyone had woken before she got back.

She had drugged Lucy so heavily she slept through it all.

Two days later her contact in London would send an email from a busy backpackers' café to Kylie in Bucharest. It would say: 'Hi Gorgeous, I landed in London yesterday and met a guy who I'd worked for in Africa a couple of years ago. He offered me another six-week guiding contract in Africa and I had to take it – great money and it ties in with your World Vision contract finishing. Sorry I won't see you next week, but when we catch up we'll both be free and can spend as long as we like travelling around Europe. I love you and can't wait to have you in my arms. xxxx Pete'.

Jeff had been even easier. As planned, Lucy had fed him a big roast dinner with red wine, then they'd gone to bed and fucked themselves stupid. Sarah had instructed Lucy not to take her night-time pills (which were really the sleeping pills) until after she and Jeff had made love and he had gone to sleep.

'You don't want to dull the pleasure of him, do you?' she had said.

It didn't matter to her whether Lucy got pleasure from Jeff or not, but it was necessary that she take the sleeping pills late at night for her plan to work.

Sarah had rented a motel room near the beach house and had driven down in a rented car – all under a false name. She had slept in the motel on Saturday night and set the alarm to go off before daylight so she could walk to the beach house in the dark and be there before Jeff woke on Sunday morning.

Sarah knew he would wake early because he wanted to photograph his precious osprey chicks, or were they eggs? Who cared? By the time he was walking across the clearing to the cliff path she had the rifle resting across her upturned hand on the balcony rail and lined up. There was just enough light to see his tall frame striding out. She had a moment of alarm when Lucy woke to what she thought was the sound of rifle shot, but she was so groggy she was easily placated. Sarah eased her down onto the pillow and Lucy immediately sank back into her drugged sleep – she didn't remember waking.

All Sarah had to do then was return to the motel and cancel Jeff's phone with the details he had given her when she had lured him into a joking conversation about modern phones and convoluted passwords. She then drove to his flat in Wollongong in his MGB, opened the door with the key under the pot plant, and let the removalist in to take Jeff's furniture into storage. She had, of course, provided a false name to the removal company. Once the furniture was gone, she had locked the flat and driven the MGB to the train station where it was picked up by the same underworld figure who had provided her with two false passports.

She took the train back to Stanwell Park, drove the rental car back to Sydney, took a taxi from the rental car depot and was home in Birchgrove in time to cook Sunday dinner. As she sat on the veranda sipping a chilled chardonnay and looking out over the harbour, she knew the satisfaction of having removed two problem people from her life.

CHAPTER 62

Ever since the night Mary had read the letter offering Lucy a job in the Kimberley, she had watched the comings and goings next door. She saw Sarah moving about and going to and from work, but she never saw Lucy or Nefertiti. She was beginning to wonder whether she was being silly when the next Saturday after that evening, she saw Sarah backing her car out of the garage and realised Lucy was in the passenger seat.

Sarah backed out on the road and kept backing until she was in front of Mary's house.

'Mary,' Sarah called out, giving little toots on the horn. 'Come and say goodbye to Lucy.'

Uncertainly Mary walked up to the car and bent down to talk to Lucy through the passenger window. Lucy was smiling but her eyes were lifeless and her face pinched and thin.

'Are you all right?' Mary asked quietly.

'I've had the flu but I'm fine now.' Lucy croaked. 'I'm going to the Kimberley to research the book we told you about.'

Mary looked at the single bag on the back seat. 'Just one bag? That doesn't seem enough for two people. I thought Sarah was going with you for the first week?'

'My bag's in the boot,' Sarah answered quickly.

'When will you be back?'

'Not sure.'

Mary watched Lucy gaze around as though unsure of her surroundings.

'Maybe I won't come back ... if I like it. Sarah thinks it will do me good to be away from Sydney and all its memories.'

Mary's mind raced. She thought of what Dr Singh had said

about psychopaths; of the vast deserts and deep gorges in the north where a person could disappear without a trace. She had to keep Lucy talking while she desperately worked out what to do.

'We have to go now,' Sarah said. 'Got a plane to catch.' She waved a cheery goodbye, pushed the button that closed Lucy's window and drove away.

Mary watched in horror as Lucy's gaze slid lazily away and she let her head slump back against the headrest. She rang Dr Singh immediately, but he was out so she left a message.

Later that day she was wandering around the house feeling she should do something when she saw the key Mario had given her, still on the bench where she had put it when she received that phone call from Sarah. He would want me to, she thought as she walked around the end of the fence and across onto the Borgetti's veranda. He always said I should trust my instincts.

But when she got to the door she couldn't make herself go in. She could not invade its privacy. She walked back around the fence and returned to her own kitchen where she felt so despondent, she wanted to cry. Later in the day when the phone rang, she leaped out of her chair and grabbed it. 'Lucy?'

'No, it's Damon. I was wondering if you could tell me what happened to the house at Stanwell Park? I thought Sarah sold it?'

'No, she rented it ... to a family I think she said.'

'Well that's strange because Mum was over there this afternoon visiting a friend when she saw Sarah's car drive into the garage and the door close on it. She couldn't see who was in it, but that red Mercedes of Sarah's is pretty distinctive. Later on Mum knocked but no one answered. Does that seem strange to you?'

'Yes, very strange. Sarah left this morning with Lucy in the car and told me they were going to the airport to catch a plane to the Kimberley, Wyndham I think they fly to.' She told Damon about the book Lucy had been commissioned to write and how Sarah was going to spend the first week with her to help her settle in.

'Really? She doesn't know anything about Aboriginal tribes, or photography.' Damon was incredulous. 'It's a fantastic coup to get a commission like that, strange she never mentioned it to me. She would have been so excited she would have told me for sure.'

'Damon, I feel something's dreadfully wrong. She was all dopey like she was before she had her earlier breakdown. I have a key to their house and was going to go in there today to have a look around ...' Mary couldn't go on, tears welled as the words stuck in her throat.

'Wait there,' he said. 'I'll come right over.'

When he arrived they let themselves in, speaking softly with nervousness and guilt. They went into the garage first, the gaping space where Sarah's car normally stood making their voices echo.

'Look at this.' Damon said as he stood in front of the gun safe. The door swung open to expose a void – the guns were gone.

'Oh my God. Sarah's taken the rifles to the Kimberley.'

'Or to the beach house.' Damon was uncomfortable with the strangeness of it all. 'Lucy told me they brought them back here when Sarah sold the beach house, or rented it, or whatever she did with it. Come on let's go into the house.'

Upstairs they found the bedroom with the chain that had held Lucy, still attached to the leg of the bed. The bed was unmade and the room smelled of stale linen and urine.

'Blood?' Mary pointed a nervous finger at dark stains on the pillow.

'Christ. Look at this!' Damon had lifted a towel that had been thrown over the portable cat's cage and was looking down at Nefertiti slumped on the bottom.

'Is she dead?' Every nerve in Mary's body was on edge. She thought she might throw up.

'As near as. Starved I'd say.' Damon lifted the wasted kitten and held its limp body against his face. 'It's still warm so we might be able to save it.' They left the room and hurried over to Mary's house where she found an eye-dropper to dribble cool water into the kitten's slack mouth.

'You keep doing that. I'm going back see what else I can find.' Damon hurried outside. His heart was thumping but he had to keep going. He was sure Lucy was in terrible danger.

CHAPTER 63

Mary was sitting in Dr Singh's office. She and Damon had agreed she needed to talk to him urgently.

'The letter was right there in front of me,' she said. 'On letterhead and signed by the editor.'

Dr Singh nodded. 'I'm guessing Sarah saw me at your house the other night. It's too much of a coincidence. The perfect excuse for Lucy to be out of touch for at least six months.'

'I memorised the name at the bottom of the letter and wrote it down as soon as I got home. Do you want me to ring her?'

'No. Sarah's smart. She'll have covered that track.'

Mary felt little hairs stand up on her arms. 'Sarah wanted Lucy at home to care for her and now she's letting her go off into the wilderness. What am I not understanding?'

Dr Singh weighed up how much to tell Mary. In many ways she was naïve, but she had spirit and good instincts. He had to trust her because Lucy needed her help. 'Damon has a gut feeling about Sarah that he's formed over the years. My approach is more academic, formed from an accumulation of behavioural patterns that Lucy has described in her conversations with me. I haven't spoken in any depth with Sarah, so it's conjecture at this stage and I don't want you to be alarmed, but I believe Sarah could be a psychopath.'

Mary stared at him in disbelief. 'A psychopath ... you mean ... like a serial killer?'

'Although the common perception of psychopaths is that they are killers, this is not necessarily so. Many psychopaths live in our society and never commit a crime. If they come from a good background and education, they often have excellent social skills and live behind a façade of normalcy with their dark side never revealed. However, if they are caught out, friends and family tell amazing stories of a lifetime of on-and-off emotional abuse, promiscuity, deceit and generally offensive behaviour. Lucy senses something is not quite right, but as Sarah is her twin and she loves her she will let herself be destroyed before she will admit it. Good people like Lucy can't believe that someone they're so close to can be seriously evil.'

Mary thought back before she spoke carefully. 'Everyone used to say Sarah was like her mother, but she wasn't you know. Jill wanted to get her own way, but she was also generous. Sarah doesn't have that. At the party Jill and Mario threw to celebrate Lucy's win at Bisley, Sarah was acting as though she was the star which we all accepted because that was her way. The next day Kylie told me the team hated Sarah and had not even wanted her in the team photos.'

'They must have seen something of her dark side at Bisley,' Dr Singh added. 'Lucy has had many small dramas that independently don't mean much, but they add up to a lifetime spent in a state of agitation and insecurity. I believe Sarah is responsible for much of this.'

Mary looked at Dr Singh. 'I've always believed Lucy didn't really get over the fire.'

'We can't discount the trauma of the fire totally,' Dr Singh replied, but his mind was thinking back over his talks with Lucy. She had good family support, counselling, friends her own age, financial security. A person with that level of support should have overcome the trauma of the fire over time. She was popular at university and the rifle club. She should have coped better unless someone or something was purposely keeping her unstable. Even after she moved to the beach house and had work that she enjoyed, she had continued to slide into a state of unreality.

'If only Jeff hadn't left her.' Mary's voice interrupted his thoughts. 'He was such a nice man.'

Surprised, Dr Singh looked across at Mary and realised she didn't know that Lucy believed she had shot Pete and Jeff as they walked around the cliff path. Mary knew that Pete had gone missing because his father had listed him as a missing person. Sarah and her ski friends were the last to see him and they all confirmed that he had a shocking hangover at the beach house on Sunday morning, but so did they all. They confirmed he had brunch with them before they left to drive to their lodge at Thredbo and they believed he flew to London the next day. Lucy was judged an unreliable witness because she was on medication and hopelessly vague about the whole weekend.

The police had contacted Kylie who confirmed she had received an email from Pete from about a safari job in Africa. The email was traced to a busy backpackers' café in London.

Bob told them he didn't take Pete to the airport because a friend had turned up at Lucy's house that morning to drive him. The police checked and confirmed that Pete had a ticket to London, but he didn't get on the plane. They did not find any trace of his bags or his computer. Thinking he may have decided to walk around the cliff path to Coalcliff and fallen over, the police sent divers down, but they found nothing. Eventually Pete's file was added to those of the hundreds of people who go missing every year.

As for Jeff, not even Mary or the grandparents had met him or knew anything about his parents. They all assumed he was back with his family and had simply decided to cut off all contact with Lucy. Dr Singh had contacted the Wollongong University and Jeff's tutor had confirmed he had stopped coming to classes suddenly and without explanation. The tutor had sounded annoyed.

The lack of contact from Pete and Jeff worried Dr Singh. Lucy claimed to have shot them, but he didn't believe this. She didn't have the motivation or the personality traits for such a violent act. But Sarah? Could she shoot someone in cold blood? He had discussed her with a colleague who agreed Sarah showed some psychopathic traits, but had agreed Dr Singh would need to talk to her in depth before they could assess whether she was capable of murder.

With a little shake of his head he dragged his thoughts back to Mary. 'I won't confuse you with too much detail,' he said, 'but I should tell you a little of what we understand about psychopaths. First, I must emphasise it is clinically accepted that psychopaths are not mentally ill. They know what they are doing. They choose to act regardless of whether what they do is criminal, hurtful or cruel. A significant aspect of the psychopathic disorder is that they feel no remorse. They have no conscience and no sympathy for any pain they cause others. For example, a psychopath in prison for killing his mother said over and over that he had done her a good turn because she was worried about the family finances, and now she didn't have to worry anymore.'

Dr Singh hesitated. He didn't want to frighten Mary, but he was concerned for Lucy. 'Psychopaths can be violent and have no inhibitions about destroying others, mentally or physically. They lie with ease and will glibly carry on if caught out.'

As Mary digested this, she recalled the distress on Mario's face when he had told her about finding Sarah trying to flush Yama down the toilet. She calmly said she was washing the cat even though we both knew that wasn't true, he had said.

'Are you telling me that Sarah might hurt Lucy?'

'Maybe she just wants to humiliate Lucy for a while. Maybe she has discovered that she enjoys inflicting pain on those she loves. Maybe she has tired of Lucy but doesn't want anyone else to have her. Psychopaths don't need a reason for what they do.'

A sense of dread overwhelmed Mary, leaving her breathless. Maybe she had always known something was wrong with Sarah. Maybe Jill and Mario had too. Mary left Dr Singh's rooms with an agreement that she would watch the house and report anything unusual.

CHAPTER 64

Lucy was asleep when Sarah drove past the airport turnoff and on to the beach house, which was neither sold nor rented. She pulled into the garage and locked the door before waking Lucy to lead her inside.

Lucy stood in the lounge looking out over the deck to the sea beyond. The late winter air was crisp and whitecaps flashed in the sunlight like gulls chasing fish. 'Why are we here?' she asked.

'Jeff wants to meet you tomorrow night at the osprey's nest,' Sarah said, leading her out onto the deck.

An involuntary tremor ran through Lucy as her eyes drifted over to the cliff path that snaked around the headland.

'He phoned to say he got back to Wollongong this morning. That's why I changed our plans and brought you here. It's a surprise I've arranged for you.'

'Jeff's back?' Lucy turned to look at Sarah, frowning as she struggled to take in this surprising information. 'But it's winter. The birds will be gone.'

'He said the eggs hatched and the chicks are still there. Said they're almost grown now and getting ready to fly away.' Sarah directed Lucy onto a chair then went inside to pour a vodka for Lucy and a mineral water for herself.

Lucy slumped. There was something she needed to remember. Something very important.

'Isn't it wonderful that he's back?' Sarah said as she handed Lucy the vodka and sat down beside her. 'I was thrilled for you when he phoned. He wanted to speak to you, but you were asleep. I didn't want to wake you, so I promised him I'd bring you down here as a surprise.'

'But he's gone.' Lucy's tongue rolled around the words. 'He flew away ... or fell.'

'No, he didn't. You've been sick for a long time. That's what your imagination is telling you. He went to visit his parents when a snake bit his mother. Remember that. Well she's better now and he's back and can't wait to see you and the chicks. He told me he's in love with you and can't wait to hold you again. You're so lucky to have such a loving man.' Sarah said as she leaned forward to guide the vodka to Lucy's lips.

Nature was on Sarah's side. A storm had been forecast for the following night. This would make the cliff path dark and difficult to see Lucy, but lightning was also forecast and this would give flashes of light. Sarah was impatient now to get Lucy out of the way. She had found a real estate agent who, for a substantial fee, had marketed the Birchgrove house overseas and found a buyer who agreed to a private treaty, with no publicity. Forging Lucy's signature had been easy. Sarah suspected the overseas buyer was laundering money because he agreed to register the sale price for a certain amount in Australia and put the rest in cash in an overseas bank account, which she had opened under what was to become her new name.

Everything was ready. She had her airline ticket to New York, suitcases packed, two false passports and money from the Birchgrove house in an American bank. To cover her location during the week she was supposed to be with Lucy in the Kimberley she had booked a motel near the airport. She would hide there until it was time to go back to Birchgrove to tell Mary convincing lies about the meeting with the Aboriginal peoples and how happy Lucy was. She had even bought a small dot painting by an Aboriginal artist as a gift to Mary from Lucy. It came from a souvenir shop downtown, but Mary wouldn't know that.

Sarah knew Mary was suspicious that something was up, but she was a simple Irish girl and wouldn't know what to do even if she did work it out. By the time she and that Indian psychiatrist decided to investigate, it wouldn't matter because she would be long gone.

Lucy had drunk her vodka and was struggling to stay awake on the deckchair. 'Why are we here? We told Mary we were going up to the Aboriginal peoples somewhere?'

'I told you LL. Because Jeff is coming tomorrow night.'

'Why is he coming at night. He can't see the chicks in the dark.' Her head hurt and her eyes wouldn't focus properly.

'Come on,' Sarah said helping Lucy out of the chair to guide her inside. 'You need your sleep to be pretty for him.'

Lucy crawled into bed and lay holding the photo of Jeff that Sarah had put on her pillow. She forced her eyes to focus on his strong face and kind hazel eyes. She wanted to run her fingers through his hair and hear him whisper sweet words, but she was having difficulty staying awake. 'My darling,' she sighed, holding the photo to her lips. If only she weren't so tired.

When Sarah came in with her bedtime pills Lucy roused herself and, making a great effort, pushed them away.

'I'm not taking any more of Dr Singh's medication,' she said, her lips tight. 'I think they are making me tired. I must be thinking clearly for Jeff tomorrow night.'

'You're right. No heavy medication, just this one little sleeping pill so you get a good sleep tonight. You don't want bags under your eyes tomorrow when you meet him.'

Sarah held out the pill and a glass of water and smiled conspiratorially. 'After tonight you won't need to take them ever again,' she gave a half-smile at her choice of words. 'Down the hatch.'

'I'm frightened Sarah. There's something I need to remember,' Lucy whimpered as she leaned back on the pillows and let her mind slide into the black void that had become her life.

Sarah hummed to herself as she cleaned the rifle later that night. Lucy's miserable life is almost over, she thought. It's best for her. She has nothing to live for anyway and I need to be free.

She was not so pleased when she saw Damon drive up the next morning. He knew the place so well, he just walked up the side steps onto the deck and through the open doors into the lounge.

'Hi,' he said, as though it was a normal Sunday morning and he was expected. He forced himself to be calm, but his heart was thumping and his hands were damp with trepidation. Although he had come suspecting Sarah and Lucy might be there, once he knew they were, he was less sure of himself. He wished he had called in at Coalcliff to bring his father along for support.

'Where's Lucy?' he asked, with a pretence of normalcy that did not fool Sarah.

'Still in bed,' she replied, playing along with his casual demeanour. 'Go in. She's probably awake by now.'

Damon walked uncertainly through the lounge and along the hall to Lucy's bedroom.

As soon as he was out of sight, Sarah hurried into the garage where she grabbed a large hammer they used to break up rocks in the garden. Its short handle was easy to manoeuvre. She stopped at the door to Lucy's bedroom for a second to take in the situation. In his shock at seeing Lucy pale and apparently unconscious, Damon had rushed to her side and was leaning over the bed trying to wake her.

Sarah took two quick barefooted steps forward and brought the hammer crashing down onto his head.

The thud spread through his brain like mud as he crumbled unconscious across Lucy.

'What's that?' Lucy sat up eyes wide. She was too slow to catch sight of Damon's body as it slid off the bed and onto the floor.

'I just dropped a vase. Go back to sleep.' Sarah waited until Lucy had drifted off again before she dragged Damon's body out of the room and down the hall into the garage.

'What a pathetic creature you are,' she said as she tied his hands and legs with a piece of rope and pushed his limp body under a pile of old car covers in the corner.

Gay is a misnomer, she thought as she wiped the blood off the hammer.

'You can follow Lucy over the cliff tonight.'

She kicked the covers over a foot that was sticking out and locked the garage door.

CHAPTER 65

Mary woke very early on Monday morning. Damon had told her he was going to the beach house and had promised to ring to let her know what he found. She had not heard from him and this worried her.

She left James sleeping to go downstairs. The night before she had given him a sketchy outline of what Dr Singh had said about Sarah, but he liked Sarah and had very little time for psychiatrists. He had just given her a condescending look and said that everyone was different and not to make mountains out of molehills. 'Start talking to psychiatrists and the like and they'll have you believing Kylie travels because she hates her parents and I joined the navy because I'm homosexual.'

She made a cup of tea and walked out onto the veranda. The rising sun was a ghostly glow on the horizon as it tried to penetrate the fog that hung over the harbour. She jumped when a ship sounded its foghorn. She wondered whether James was right and she was becoming over-dramatic. But Damon was so reliable and had said he would ring after he had checked out the beach house on Sunday.

By midday she could stand it no longer. She phoned Dr Singh and bought him up to date.

'Have you tried to phone Damon?'

'Several times but his mobile is just taking messages. His boyfriend said he didn't come home last night and Dot said he didn't go there.'

'It does seem strange,' he agreed. 'The few times I've met Damon he's seemed a reliable sort.'

'Do you think I should go to the beach house to see if he's there?'

'If it would ease your mind but I don't think you should go alone. Do you have someone who could go with you?'

'My husband's home. He might.'

James thought Dr Singh and Mary were stirring each other into a silly frenzy, but he had two weeks shore leave and a drive down to the south coast would be nice. He hadn't been there for years and he'd never visited the girls' beach house. They took the scenic route through the Royal National Park after lunch as a storm rolled across the sea towards the shore.

'They'll sleep rough tonight,' James said, giving Mary a wry grin.

By the time they reached the beach house, the storm had rolled across the beach and enveloped Stanwell Park in a thick sea mist.

'That's Damon's car,' Mary said, pointing. James parked behind it and walked up to test a door. It was unlocked.

'That's their house with a light on,' she whispered.

'Where would the light be?'

'One of the bedrooms, I think.'

As they huddled undecided, a loud noise cracked and echoed through the sea mist.

'That's a gunshot,' James said, shocked. Although he hadn't been here before, he knew from Mary's description that there was a large deck at the back of the house that faced out over the Tasman Sea and had a side view across a narrow reserve to a headland with a path that led to Coalcliff. Shaken by the sound, he raced around the side of the house, trying frantically to recall everything Dr Singh had told Mary about Sarah's state of mind. He didn't stop until he reached wooden steps which he guessed led up onto the deck.

He crouched for a moment to gather his wits then crept up the steps until he could just see onto the deck. In the faint light filtering from inside the house, he saw the outline of a woman in jeans and a dark jacket with a rifle resting loosely in the crook of her arm. He knew as soon as Sarah turned towards him that he had badly misjudged Mary and the situation.

'Who's there?' Sarah's voice was unnervingly calm.

'James,' he replied, staying below the level of the deck, his mind racing. 'I was in the area and just thought I'd drop in for a drink with you and Lucy.' Even to his own ears the words sounded false.

'Lucy's not here. She's gone to live with the Aborigines.'

'Mary thought she'd come down here with you.'

'No. I dropped her off at the airport. You can come up. I won't bite you.'

'I thought I heard a gunshot?' he said as he mounted the steps signalling to Mary to stay out of sight.

'You did,' Sarah replied evenly. 'Rabbits eat our vegetables. I just shot one. I'm not loaded so you're quite safe.'

He knew he had not fooled Sarah, but she would be wondering if he were alone or if there was a row of police lined up in the darkness behind him. She was terrifyingly calm. He could feel sweat dribbling down his back as he strained to see her face. She seemed ethereal in the cold air. Years of experience in the navy told him she wouldn't lift the rifle until she was sure. He was playing a deadly game and had no doubt she would shoot him if she thought they were alone. He cursed himself for not believing Mary and for so recklessly getting them into this situation.

'I saw Damon's car outside?' he said stalling for time.

'He also thought Lucy was here. Strange, isn't it, that you both thought that.' Sarah shifted slightly, squinting into the dark void behind him. 'When I told him she wasn't here, he went down to the beach.' Her voice slid through the air like a poisoned thread. 'But enough of that, come inside for a drink.'

He was closer now so he could see she was smiling. She had the rifle pointing down. Her free hand was open, palm up, waving him in through open doors into what he presumed was the lounge. She was in total control of her emotions and very dangerous.

How long could he play along?

Steeling himself to stay calm, he started to walk past her and into the house when a terrifying scream pierced the dark.

Sarah moved so quickly he didn't see her arms come up. All he felt was an intense pain as the rifle butt crashed into his face, sending him sprawling across the deck. He felt his nose break and blood spurt, blinding him and filling his mouth with sticky warmth. Dazed by the pain, he crawled frantically towards the steps, guessing the direction and expecting at any moment to feel a bullet explode into his body. When it didn't come, he realised she still didn't know who else was out there and she wasn't going to expose her position until she did.

Seizing this slim advantage, he practically fell down the steps in his haste to get out of her line of fire.

He knew the scream had come from Mary, but Sarah didn't. He raised his head to let the first raindrops cool the burning in his eyes and wash away the blood so he could see a little better. In a flash of lightning he established that the land sloped steeply and the deck above him extended out on steel poles from the house. There was a dark cavity where house and land met that could be a hiding place. He staggered along under the deck towards where he thought the scream had come from.

Mary saw him in the same flash of lightning and called softly. 'Over here. I've found Lucy.'

Bending low he left the safety of the space underneath the deck to cross the clearing and squat beside her. 'Is she alive?'

'I thought she wasn't. But she moaned when I touched her, and I got such a fright I screamed. I'm sorry.'

'Is she badly hurt?'

'She's bleeding ... here.' Mary directed his hand to a sticky puddle of blood. Lucy moaned as he touched it.

'Will Sarah come after us?' Mary whispered.

'She might.' He knew the enemy always had two choices – stay and fight or panic and run. 'Or she may choose to run.' If Sarah ran, they were safe. If she decided to reload and come after them, they didn't stand a chance out here in the open. Although his eyes would soon close over, he could still pick out land features in the bursts of lightning that lit up the clearing every few seconds. He could hear the sea crashing below them so guessed they were close to the edge of the cliff.

He felt around Lucy's upper arm where the bullet had passed through the soft flesh. Working by feel, he rapidly wrapped the arm firmly with the scarf Mary had been holding against it to stem the flow of blood.

'That's as much as I can do for now,' he whispered, stroking Lucy's forehead to calm her. Turning to Mary, he asked 'Are there any bushes nearby where we could hide Lucy? I can't see very well.'

Mary knew the council kept the strip of reserve land leading to the cliff path cleared of bushes, but beyond the clearing was uncared-for bush. Staying low, they dragged Lucy to this area and hid her as best they could.

James knew he had only seconds to get them both away from Lucy and safely hidden before the next flash of lightning. Sarah had the advantage at this distance but if he could get close, he would be stronger. He knew she would have realised by now that there were no police with him. She may even have guessed that the scream came from Mary. Why hadn't she used her advantage and come out on the deck to finish them off? Her silence made his skin crawl.

He put an arm over Mary's shoulders. He could feel her body shaking and marvelled that she wasn't crying. Putting his lips close to her ear he spoke softly. 'We must move away from Lucy to hide. Is there anywhere other than here?'

Mary was hunched under his arm, thinking frantically. 'There's only under the house.'

'Then you must take my hand and run for the space under the deck. I can hardly see.'

Her hand felt small in his, but she ran low and fast. Miraculously, they reached the deck and crawled along the dirt to the cavity he had seen under the house. It was such a dark shallow space that even Mary couldn't see very well. Gasping for air, James pushed her further up until she was well hidden, then he sat in front of her facing out. The cold dirt seeped into his buttocks and water dripped onto his head.

'Where do you think she is?' Mary whispered.

'Shhh.'

No sooner had she spoken than they heard a scraping noise above their heads and strained to make out what it was. Reaching out, James pushed Mary further into the cavity and moved away. He didn't want Mary near him if Sarah came down the steps and started shooting, and he didn't want to be in such a cramped position if he needed to defend himself. His vision was still blurred, but he found one of the poles holding up the deck and positioned himself against it to make his silhouette less easy to define.

Then he heard the scraping sound again. It wasn't like someone walking across the deck. It was more the sound of a large door opening. His ears were ready to burst with the strain when he realised it was the sound of an automatic garage door sliding open. He froze, rigid with disbelief as the sound stopped and a car engine gunned into action. He stayed there listening as a car backed out of the garage and sped off.

'She's fled.' He called, overcome with relief. 'Mary, where are you? We're safe.' His eyes strained to see into the darkness under the house as he listened to Mary groping along the ground. Then she was out of the cavity and in his arms.

They clung to each other, too choked up to speak.

CHAPTER 66

The poor light had affected Sarah's judgement and the bullet had entered the top of Lucy's arm tearing through the soft flesh, the force of it knocking her down. Had she been a few steps closer to the cliff, the impact at such close range would have sent her over the edge.

'Jeff wasn't there, was he?' Lucy said, her eyes desperate.

'No, dear,' Mary replied as they lay her gently on the bed and pulled warm blankets over her.

'I think I always knew he wasn't ... but I wanted to believe,' Lucy slurred as she struggled to stay conscious.

'Rest now. We'll talk about it later.'

Lucy looked from Mary to James then let her eyes close and allowed herself to drift away.

The police found Damon unconscious under the car covers in the garage. With treatment from the paramedics he regained consciousness but was confused and complaining of a violent headache. After two days in hospital, his doctor said he could go home. He needed to rest but the blow had not inflicted any long-term damage.

CHAPTER 67

Benny flopped into the office chair and swivelled it to face his brother at the next desk. 'You should see the chick who's rented the Franklin Street loft. Legs up to here.'

'I did you dumbass. I passed her on to you, remember?'

'Too busy! When will you get a life? There aren't many chicks as good looking as that one begging for a fuck from guys like us,' Benny said as he stood and jerked his hips.

'Sit down and shut up.'

Laughing, Benny sat. Their father had financed his older brother into the real estate business on the condition he employed Benny until he decided what he wanted to do with his life. Benny rather enjoyed his role as the irresponsible younger sibling.

'She's from Australia you know. Wonder how she knew about Tribeca?'

'She looks rich. Loaded families always know their way around.'

'Maybe she wants to be a model or a writer. I'll pay her a visit to tell her about Dad's chain of magazines and how I can get her a job.'

'You know the rules.'

'I'd just be offering a helping hand to an Aussie chick all alone in the Big Apple.'

'With her looks, she won't be alone for long.'

'She gave me the come-on,' Benny said, remembering the deep brown eyes, laughing and teasing. 'She took it for two years and is sitting there panting, waiting for my call.'

After Benny had left her at the loft, Sarah popped out the brown contact lenses and shook out her black hair. She would need a better disguise, but a quick change of hair and eye colour, along with extra heavy make-up had matched her false passport and got her through immigration.

She wandered through the loft with satisfaction. It was in an original 1860s Italianate building with white walls, seventeen-foot ceilings, Carrera marble floors and large windows through which she could see the New York towers welcoming in the twenty-first century. A famous artist owned the loft. He had added a mezzanine level for the master bedroom with his-and-her bathrooms and a mini-gym with an exercise bike strategically placed to look out over the city while pedalling. She scrutinised the huge Salvador Dali print on one wall. This place was pure New York chic and the artist was away for two years.

After landing in New York, Sarah had been checking the phone book in her hotel room for a D Marshall when she came across Dwight Marshall listed as a real-estate broker in Tribeca. She had almost laughed out loud when the elegant young man from behind the desk had stood up, put out his hand and introduced himself as Dwight Junior. They had discussed rental accommodation in the area, then he had apologised for having another appointment and passed her on to his younger brother, Benny. She didn't argue. Benny was the spitting image of the man in the photo she had put into her wallet before leaving Sydney.

Sarah walked over to a lamp hanging from the ceiling on a thread of silver chain to study the photo she kept in a hidden niche in her wallet. She had found the photo among Jill's personal papers when they were clearing out her desk after the car accident. It was dated two years after the AGM in Hawaii where Dwight and her mother had fucked. The faces of Dwight and his new bride smiled brightly at her. Her stepmother, Mrs Marshall, was slim and very elegant.

As Sarah put the photo back into her wallet she kissed the air. Two sons. Perfect. She knew now how she would ruin her biological father.

She speculated it would take Benny less than three days

to call her. The serious older son, Dwight Junior, would be more of a challenge.

L U C Y

I'm back as a voluntary patient with Dr Singh. I have the same room overlooking the garden, but it looks better because I have photos on the dresser: a large one of Mummy and Daddy looking tanned and happy in Arnhem Land; smaller ones of Kylie, Mary, Damon, Nefertiti, my grandparents and dear Nonna, who passed away last year. Also a snap of Sarah and me at eleven years old skiing at Threbo.

I'm at peace.

Dr Singh is pleased I've put out the photos. He says it shows I'm accepting the past and coming to terms with the people who have been with me all my life.

Mary and Damon refuse to look at the photo of Sarah when they visit. I understand because they don't know of the secret that has festered inside her since she was eleven. I've thought about telling them, but I don't think it would change their opinion of her. Anyway, its Mummy's secret as much as Sarah's and, of course, mine now.

I'm also accepting my body with its scars, and now my shoulder has healed am able to joke about having another scar. Once I feel in control again, I'll go to a specialist and arrange for the plastic surgery Mummy always wanted me to have.

It was a shock to hear that the house at Birchgrove had been sold, but I couldn't have lived there anyway. When I leave here, I'm going to live with Grandpa and Grandma for a while. I hear Grandma is in a frenzy over all the hairs Nefertiti moults on her furniture. But Grandpa loves her so much, he lets her onto his favourite chair and, when Grandma isn't looking, he collects her hairs to bring to me. I put them in a little jar with a lid so they don't fly away. I give Nefertiti a little pat before I go to bed every night and promise that I will be with her soon.

I watch the mail every day for a letter from her. I know she will eventually contact me, but I don't know how I will react. She's still my twin. I can't cast off the memories of curling up in bed every night, loving each other when we were little. Some days I just want to hold her against me and love her and put my hand on her heart to feel it beating. Other days I want to hear she has been caught and locked up forever.

ACKNOWLEDGEMENTS

I am grateful to so many people who gave freely of their knowledge and time to help me write this book.

To the professionals who were vital to the accuracy of my story in matters medical, psychological and guns. Many had not met me before our interview, and I thank them for their time and their generosity in sharing their knowledge. The hospital staff at the Concord Hospital and especially those in the Burns ward at the then recently opened New Children's Hospital at Westmead who showed me around and answered my endless questions over several visits. To my friend Flip Waters for her keen eye and professional guidance. I could not have written about rifle shooting without the help and enthusiasm of several shooters: Euan Leckie, James Corbett and especially Alyson who at 18 years of age was already being hailed as a talent to watch in Australia and later went on to compete at Bisley in England.

To my writers group Lesley, Pattie, Jean and the late Pauline who were there at the beginning. To Susanne and Elle from my readers group who read the 'nearly' final draft and gave me insights that opened my eyes to the way readers would interpret my words and led to changes that improved the clarity of my story. And to the professional editors who tidied up everything else and put commas in the correct places. Thank you all.

Finally but certainly not last, my husband Lex who was always encouraging and fed and watered me on those days when I simply could not drag myself away from my emerging characters.

ABOUT THE AUTHOR

Shirley Laplanche, born in New Zealand, is a passionate traveller, environmentalist and lover of life. After travelling the world for several years she landed in Australia to become an editor at *The Australian* newspaper and a contributing writer for *The Bulletin* and the *Australian Tourist Commission* (now *Tourism Australia*). The urge to travel again triggered a move to a successful freelance writing career specialising in travel, skiing, golf and a book on ecotourism.

Stepping Lightly on Australia – A Traveller's Guide to Ecotourism was published by HarperCollins in Australasia and Globe Pequot in the USA.

This novel *The Fatal Path* shows a darker side of this versatile writer who currently lives in Sydney, Australia.

CPSIA information can be obtained
at www.ICGtesting.com
Printed in the USA
LVHW020333010921
696555LV00001B/25